CHARMS & WITCHDEMEANORS
A WICKED WITCHES OF THE MIDWEST MYSTERY BOOK EIGHT

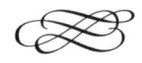

AMANDA M. LEE

WINCHESTERSHAW PUBLICATIONS

Copyright © 2016 by Amanda Lee

All rights reserved.

No part of this book may be reproduced in any form or by any electronic or mechanical means, including information storage and retrieval systems, without written permission from the author, except for the use of brief quotations in a book review.

❀ Created with Vellum

PROLOGUE

SIX YEARS AGO

Tillie Winchester's enemies were numerous and varied.

Yes, they looked like harmless elderly people, but beneath their friendly facades Tillie knew they were evil. She wasn't even willing to give them the benefit of the doubt and call them "misunderstood." No, the people who frequented Hemlock Cove's senior center were – without a doubt – Senator Palpatine, Sauron and Lord Voldemort evil.

They were dastardly in their manipulations, hoping to take her down with false accusations, vigorous finger-pointing and dirty looks.

Tillie had no doubt she was a force of goodness standing in the way of Hemlock Cove's destruction. She was the Han Solo of the town (because Luke Skywalker was far too whiny, and she would never wear doughnuts on the side of her head and call it a fashion choice). She had to defeat evil.

"What happened?"

Terry Davenport, Hemlock Cove's police chief, looked weary as he regarded the mayhem surrounding him. It was a Friday and he'd already been looking forward to his weekend when the call about the senior center's card tournament turning into a possible poisoning came across his radio.

"Tillie lost at euchre and poisoned the coffee," Margaret Little volunteered. "She claims we cheated, but she's just a terrible loser and everyone knows it. She wanted to win the tournament and lost, and this is how she paid us back."

Terry shifted his tired eyes to Tillie. "Is that true?"

"Of course it's not true," Tillie sputtered. "I'm an excellent euchre player. I could go on a professional circuit and everything."

"Not that," Terry said, shaking his head. "Is the other part true? Did you poison everyone because you lost?"

Tillie was affronted. "I don't poison people."

"She's a witch," Maude Galbraith interjected as a paramedic knelt next to her and checked her vitals. She was one of the "afflicted" who began violently vomiting after downing a cup of coffee. She also happened to be one of the tournament winners. "Everyone in town knows she's a witch. She poisoned us because she's a poor loser."

"That's not true," Tillie protested. "I didn't poison them. I'm a great loser. Do you want to know how I know?"

Terry didn't care in the slightest. "Let's get back to the problem at hand," he prodded. "I think … ."

Tillie cut him off. "I know because I've lost so few times I remember each instance with absolute clarity," she said. "I was gracious in defeat, just as I am magnanimous in victory."

Terry snorted, and it took him a second to realize it wasn't merely in his head but also out there for public consumption. "Okay," he said. "I understand that you're a great loser … ."

"Gracious loser," Tillie corrected.

"Gracious loser," Terry said, fighting the urge to roll his eyes. "Why does everyone think you poisoned the coffee?"

"Because they're asshats," Tillie replied, blasé. "There can be no other explanation. They're jealous and they made themselves sick with envy."

"Yes, that must be it," Margaret deadpanned. "It couldn't have anything to do with the fact that you got all red in the face and promised retribution when you didn't win the tournament. Then people saw you pouting by the coffee pot for a good twenty minutes. Then everyone who drank the coffee got sick – I mean they actually puked on the floor in front of people and some ran to the bathroom holding their bottoms because of other ... um ... issues. That's all a coincidence, right?"

Terry looked pained. "Thank you for the colorful ... retelling ... of today's events, Mrs. Little," he said. "Just because Tillie stood next to the coffee pot doesn't mean she poisoned everyone."

"You know as well as I do that she's a mean and vindictive snake," Margaret said. "She actually bought every tire in town last year when I had a flat just so I couldn't attend the fair in Traverse City and win the pie contest."

"That is a lie," Tillie hissed, extending a finger. "You wouldn't have won that competition anyway because Winnie and Marnie entered their pies. You didn't have a chance. If someone did do that – and I'm not saying anyone did – they did you a favor."

"Whatever," Margaret said, crossing her arms over her chest.

"She peed on my rosebush when we had that flower contest a few years back because she wanted her roses to win," Agatha Milton said, leaning back as a paramedic checked her blood pressure. She was one of the afflicted, too. "She actually peed on them to kill them."

Terry was horrified as he shifted his gaze to Tillie. "Did you really do that?"

"I didn't pee on anything," Tillie replied. "I was walking past Agatha's house and I accidentally tripped while carrying a jug of doe urine. It wasn't my fault. If anything, I should've sued because I could've broken a hip when I stumbled on her uneven walkway."

Terry was flabbergasted. "Why would you have doe urine?"

"I'm an excellent hunter," Tillie answered, not missing a beat. "You need doe urine when you hunt. That's why they sell it at those outdoor stores."

"You were hunting deer in the spring?" Terry challenged. "You know that's out of season so it's against the law, right?"

Tillie was unfazed. "I spend the spring lulling the deer into a sense

3

of calm so they're not afraid of me," she explained. "If they see me out there with the doe urine, they get used to me. That makes hunting them in the summer easier."

"It's illegal to hunt deer in the summer," Terry pointed out.

"Fine. I hunt them whenever it's legal."

"Uh-huh."

"Just out of curiosity's sake, when is that?" Tillie asked. "Is that a winter thing?"

"It's a November thing," Terry replied, shaking his head. "That's not the point of the conversation. These people say you poisoned them because you lost at cards. Please tell me that's not true."

Terry was shrewd. Tillie had to give him that. He knew she was innocent and being persecuted, but he was trying to lull her enemies into thinking he was on their side so they would slip up and make a mistake.

"I have no reason to poison these people," Tillie argued, winking so Terry would know she was in on his plan. "I don't care about losing a card tournament."

"She hopped up and down and called us all cheaters and said she was going to turn us into toads," Maude said.

"I would never threaten to turn anyone into toads," Tillie countered. "That's just … beneath me. My ideas are much less … cliché."

Terry lifted a challenging eyebrow in Maude's direction. "Did she really say that?"

"I might have made up the toad part," Maude conceded. "She said the rest, though. She screamed and hollered about making us pay and teaching us a lesson."

"She did do that," Margaret agreed. "You know she's a terrible loser, so I'm not sure why you're fighting this. We want her banned from the center."

"Banned? We want her arrested," Agatha snapped. "We could've died. Heck, we still might die because we have no idea what she poisoned us with."

Terry glanced at the closest paramedic. "Is there any way of knowing what they ingested?"

CHARMS & WITCHDEMEANORS

"We'll run tests at the hospital, but I can't say right now," the paramedic replied. "It honestly could be something as simple as a laxative overdose."

Terry fought the mad urge to laugh thanks to the visual. "I see."

"It also could be something more serious," the paramedic added. "We simply don't know yet."

Terry nodded. "Okay, well, until we know what's going on, everyone needs to just chill and take a breather from one another," he said. "That means no euchre tournaments until we get to the bottom of this."

"Wait a second." Margaret narrowed her eyes. "Are you saying you're going to let this ... evil beast ... walk free while we're suffering?"

"You're not suffering," Tillie pointed out. "You didn't even drink the coffee."

"Ha! You just admitted you poisoned the coffee," Margaret crowed, extending a finger. "I heard it. Who else heard it?"

Agatha and Maude raised their hands.

"I did not admit it," Tillie shot back. "I just said you didn't drink the coffee. Try cleaning your ears once in a while so you're not deaf and dumb at the same time. It's a terrible combination – especially on you."

"You said you poisoned it," Margaret argued. "Chief Terry, you heard her say she poisoned it, right?"

Terry looked as if the last thing he wanted to do was get in the middle of a senior center group freakout. "I did not hear her say that," he said. "I did hear myself say that we'll have to wait for the test results before moving forward. This might have been something as simple as bad creamer."

"Humph." Margaret planted her hands on her hips as she regarded her cronies. "That's not good enough for me."

"I don't know what to tell you," Terry said, tugging on his fraying patience. "I have no proof, and I can't arrest someone without any proof. That's the way the law works. You should know that."

"I'm not talking about you," Margaret said. "I don't care what you

5

do. We all know you're going to take Tillie's side, even if a deadly poison is found in the coffee. You always take her side."

"Yeah, it's because you've got a thing for her nieces," Agatha said, making a disgusted face. "You like all three of them. It's ... perverted."

"Oh, stuff it, Agatha," Tillie argued. "The only thing perverted is your mind. I don't have to sit here and take this. I'm out of here." Tillie strode toward the door that led to the parking lot.

"I might have more questions when the tests come back," Terry called to her back.

Tillie didn't bother turning around. "You know where to find me."

"Until you're cleared – and I mean by the board here and not Chief Terry, mind you – you're banned from the senior center," Margaret said, her upbeat voice causing Tillie's shoulder's to stiffen as she grabbed the door handle. "I'm the president of the board, so my decision is final. You can file an appeal, but it will take weeks before we get to it."

Terry's eyes widened at how evil the woman sounded as she threatened Tillie. "Do you really think that's necessary?"

"I think it's done," Margaret replied. "You're banned, Tillie. I hope you're proud of what you've done, because you won't be magnanimous in victory or defeat here for the foreseeable future."

Instead of crying – or begging Margaret to change her mind – Tillie sent her a one-finger salute as she pushed open the door. "You have to do what you have to do," she said, taking the high road as she marched out the door.

"Well, that went better than I expected," Terry said, shaking his head. "I thought she would yell and scream."

"She flipped me off," Margaret argued. "Isn't there a law on the books about that being illegal?"

"Not last time I checked," Terry replied dryly. "Besides, if that's the worst thing she did, I think you should consider yourself lucky. Things could've gone a heck of a lot worse."

"Wait for it," Maude said.

Terry shouldn't have been surprised when the door opened again and Tillie's head popped back into view. He knew her well enough to know she would never let this go, and yet he still had hope right until her eyes flashed evil and she wrinkled her nose.

"You're all on my list!" Tillie bellowed. "Live in fear!"

ONE

PRESENT DAY

"Don't do that."

"Don't tell me what to do."

"Okay ... please, don't do that."

I smirked as I watched my cousins banter, relaxing on the couch in their magic store called Hypnotic and laughing as they conducted inventory. Thistle and Clove could be a reality show – but a funny one – and the ratings would be through the roof.

Thistle, her short-cropped hair a bright lavender this month, planted her hands on her narrow hips. "Why do you always have to act as if you're my boss?"

Clove brushed a strand of her long dark hair away from her face and adopted a petulant look. "Why do you always have to act as if you're somehow better than everyone else?"

"It's one crystal ball, Clove," Thistle snapped, gesturing toward the shelf. "Why can't it be on this shelf instead of the one you picked?"

"Because ... that's not its home," Clove replied. She's something of a control freak and when her plans get messed up she can't seem to stop herself from fussing – even if it's over something absolutely ridiculous. She grabbed the crystal ball and moved it one shelf over. "It wants to live here until it finds a proper home."

"Did it tell you that?" Thistle challenged.

"It did," Clove confirmed. "It also told me you're being loud and it wants you to shut up."

Thistle flicked Clove's ear, earning an outraged shriek that was overly dramatic – even by Clove's standards – and then turned her attention to me. "Bay, what do you think? Which shelf does the crystal ball want to live on until some kind person comes in to offer it a forever home?"

There was no way I was going to answer. I knew my cousins well enough to realize that whoever I sided with, the other would pay me back. That's what happens when you share a roof with people for the better part of your life.

"I think the crystal ball doesn't want me to get involved," I replied. "What's that?" I cupped my ear and pretended to listen to a soft voice. "Oh, the crystal ball also thinks you two are being big babies and should just let it go."

Clove had the good sense to giggle. Thistle was another story.

"I'll make you eat dirt if you don't take my side," Thistle threatened.

Frankly, I didn't think the crystal ball looked good on either shelf. It was kitschy, and I much preferred Thistle's homemade candles and Clove's ornate herb displays. "I don't know," I said, rolling my eyes. "I can't figure out why it even matters. Shove it on a shelf and be done with it."

"You make me want to punch you in the face sometimes," Thistle muttered, although I couldn't help but notice she left the crystal ball where Clove wanted it and returned to her inventory checklist. "I'm going to have Aunt Tillie curse you for not taking my side … and it's going to be a good one."

I frowned. No one wants to admit they live in fear of a senior citizen with itchy witch fingers, but I do. We all do. We can't help ourselves.

My name is Bay Winchester and I'm a witch. Apparently I'm a cowardly witch today. My entire family – Clove and Thistle included

– are witches, too. We come from a long line of practitioners, although Aunt Tillie is definitely the scariest.

"Do you want to know what I think?" I asked, opting to change the subject.

"Nope," Thistle replied, not missing a beat. "I think if you're not going to be on my side you should get out and go to your own place of business. That is my decree for the day. Be gone, traitor."

My entire family is dramatic. I can't explain it. I think it's in our genes, along with a propensity to be busybodies and the ability to screech at the top of our lungs when our feelings are hurt.

"I'm here for lunch," I reminded her. "You insisted I had to eat here because you two were too busy to leave."

"Well, I changed my mind," Thistle said. "That's a woman's prerogative. That's what Aunt Tillie says, anyway."

Since Thistle and Aunt Tillie preferred hating each other rather than joining together, I couldn't help but be a little suspicious. "Since when do you listen to anything Aunt Tillie says?"

"Since she's been nice for three consecutive days. I think it means the world is coming to an end, but I'm enjoying it."

I snickered. "She has been pretty quiet," I mused, searching my memory for an instance when she acted out of line. "She's kind of been keeping to herself."

"That's probably because she's plotting something," Clove said. Those were bold words coming from her, and I couldn't help but notice she glanced over her shoulder to make sure Aunt Tillie hadn't sneaked into the shop. "The last time she behaved this long we found out she'd been cursing all of the women in that sewing club to use the wrong thread."

"Ah, yes, the great quilting catastrophe of 2014," I said, smirking at the memory. "They shouldn't have kicked her out of the group if they didn't want repercussions. That was really on them."

"The woman can't even sew," Thistle argued. "She only wanted to be a part of the club because she sold them wine. Those were some ugly quilts that year, though. Sheesh."

"Oh, I don't know. I kind of liked the one that had red and pink hearts all over it. It was like Valentine's Day threw up." Clove preferred looking on the bright side of things.

"Those weren't hearts," Thistle shot back.

Clove was confused. "What were they?"

"I believe someone was singing a song about apple bottoms because of all the wine Aunt Tillie gave them," Thistle replied.

"Oh, well, that's less pretty."

We fell into amiable silence, and while I knew it wasn't the last time we would hang out like this, part of me felt a little sad because once Clove moved out of the guesthouse we shared, things would be markedly different. She was the first to leave the nest, so to speak. Because we shared the guesthouse on our mothers' property and lived on top of one another, it was frustrating, maddening and annoying every single day. It was also comfortable and familiar, and I never fare well with change.

"When are you officially moving in with Sam?" I asked, shifting my eyes to Clove.

Sam Cornell owned the Dandridge, a local lighthouse, and after months of dating and helping him refurbish the place, Clove was taking their relationship to the next level. She was excited, which was kind of cute. Thistle pretended to be excited, but I could tell she was really upset – though she didn't want to admit it.

"We haven't picked a set day yet," Clove replied. "I'm moving my bed out there because it's so much nicer than his, and I have several loads remaining at our place. I think he wants it to be soon, though. Maybe really soon."

I expected the answer, but it was still sobering. "Well, we should plan a fun chocolate martini night before you go," I suggested. "It will be the last one with us as a group."

Clove balked. While she was happy to be moving in with Sam, she was frustrated to think the group dynamic wouldn't be the same. She would still be one of us, of course, but it wouldn't be the same. "It won't be our last martini night," she said. "It's not as if I'm leaving the family."

"It's close enough," Thistle challenged. "Now you're going to be all the way across town. When we have martini nights you'll have to drink one and then leave so you're not drunk when you drive. You won't wake up with a raging hangover to find upset mothers watching you. You're out of that particular loop."

"That sounded bitter," I said.

"I'm not bitter."

"You sound it."

"Oh, shut your mouth," Thistle muttered. "I'm not bitter. I'm happy for Clove."

"It's okay if you're bitter," Clove said. "I know you're going to miss me. You can even cry a little if you feel the need."

"Ha!" Thistle bellowed so loudly it caused me to jolt.

"Ha what?" I asked.

"I'm going to see her five days a week here, so I won't miss her," Thistle said. "You guys are making a big deal out of this move when it's a normal part of life and very little will change."

"You just said you were upset Clove wouldn't wake up with a hangover at the guesthouse again," I reminded her.

"I didn't say I was upset," Thistle argued. "I said it's going to be different. Different isn't bad. I'm looking forward to it. It will give us more room to spread out. That guesthouse is too small for six people, and when Sam spends the night, that's how many people live under that roof."

"Bay, you're going to miss me, right?" Clove was in desperate need of emotional encouragement. Fear often held her back, and I knew she was looking forward to this move. Her biggest fear was being forgotten, though. That was impossible, but she couldn't see it.

"I'm definitely going to miss you," I said.

Clove shot a triumphant look in Thistle's direction. "See!"

Thistle made a comical face. "Whatever."

"You always take my side in fights with Thistle," I added. "Now we won't have a deciding vote. It'll be a fight to the death when we argue."

"Yes, I'm looking forward to it," Thistle said, her eyes gleaming. "We both know you can't take me."

"You're going to miss me for other reasons, too, right?" Clove appropriated a whiny tone. "You're going to miss me because you love me. I know it."

"I love you," I said, nodding. "I'm going to miss you most because of the arguments, though. I'm sorry if that hurts your feelings, but I'm worried about myself and what will happen when Thistle starts acting like Aunt Tillie Junior."

Clove didn't want to laugh, but she couldn't help herself. "Yeah. I feel a little sorry for you on that front."

"You should feel a lot sorry for me," I said. "On days when Landon is here it will be okay because he has a badge. When he's not around, well, look out world. I knew the fact that Thistle was most like Aunt Tillie would come back to bite me eventually."

My FBI agent boyfriend Landon Michaels spent as many nights as possible with me in Hemlock Cove, a small tourist town in northern Lower Michigan. His office was in Traverse City, though, so at least three nights a week he had to stay in his small apartment near Grand Traverse Bay. That's where he was now, in fact. I wasn't due to see him until the following evening – and I only felt like crying a little bit. What? He's hot. Sue me.

"I am nothing like Aunt Tillie," Thistle snapped. "Take that back."

"You're exactly like her ... except, well, you dress better," I said. "That said, I can see you wearing a combat helmet and yoga pants with the word 'juicy' on your rear end eventually."

Thistle shifted her murderous eyes to Clove. "Tell her I'm not like Aunt Tillie."

"So we've reached the lying portion of today's festivities? Is that what you're telling me?" Clove deadpanned.

"You're both dead to me," Thistle grumbled, rolling her neck until it cracked. "I just ... I get absolutely no respect in this family. I'm sick of it."

"I believe Aunt Tillie said that last week during dinner when Mom told her that sequins were banned from the dinner table so her new coat had to go," I said.

"I will make you eat dirt," Thistle warned, evoking a popular family threat. "It's hot as Hades out there, but I'm willing to work up a sweat to shut your mouth. If I do it with dirt, it will be all the better."

"I can't hear you over all of Aunt Tillie's inane chatter," I shot back, smirking as Clove's eyes widened. I had no doubt the first few weeks without Clove as a buffer in the guesthouse were going to be interesting – and by "interesting" I mean all-out war.

"I'm going to cook a mud pie with worms in it," Thistle said. "Just you wait."

"Whatever," I said, lifting myself to a higher position and glancing at the street. Two women, both of whom I recognized as advertisers in The Whistler, the weekly newspaper I edited, stood outside the door excitedly gesturing to one another. "What do you think that's about?"

Thistle suspiciously followed my gaze, as if I was trying to distract her long enough to make her forget I had been irritating her. "I don't know," she said. "They do look worked up, don't they?"

"Isn't that Beth Farmer and Toni Johnson?" Clove asked.

I nodded as I pushed myself to a standing position. If something big was happening – even if it was only big by Hemlock Cove's pitiful standards – I should probably check on it. So far my cover story for this week's edition focused on the new fence in front of the diner's outdoor seating area. I was desperate for something else – anything really – to bump the fence story inside.

"I'm going to see what's going on," I said. "Don't kill each other while I'm gone, and decide where we're getting lunch. I'm starving."

When no one answered, I turned to see if they'd heard me or were purposely ignoring me. I found both of them trailing me to the door. I shouldn't have been surprised. Winchester women love gossip. It's second only to drinking when it comes to family activities enjoyed by the lot of us.

I pushed open the door, fixing a pleasant smile on my face as I regarded the women. I wasn't particularly fond of either of them, although I didn't openly dislike them. We didn't run in the same circles, so we didn't spend a lot of time trading life secrets. Okay, you got me. They're a little too prim and proper, and they bug me. I prefer my friends bawdy instead of boring.

"What's going on?" I asked. "You guys look excited."

"Haven't you heard the news?" Beth asked, her blond bob gleaming in the sunlight.

I shook my head. "What news?"

"Patty Grimes is dead."

I stilled. "Patty Grimes?" I was pretty sure that was the woman who lived a relatively isolated life on the north side of town.

"Isn't that the old lady up on Winchester Road who talks to her cats?" Thistle asked, making a face.

"She's a very nice woman," Beth shot back. "A lot of people talk to their animals."

"Yeah, but she once told me the cats talked back to her and one of them told her the flowers were alive and planning a mutiny," Thistle replied, unruffled.

"She was elderly," Beth said. "Many people lose certain … faculties … when they're elderly. You should know. I believe you have an elderly aunt who does much worse things."

"I would argue, but it would be useless," Thistle said, taking me by surprise with her capitulation. "What happened to Patty? Did she die in her sleep?"

"She was murdered," Toni said, her tone ominous. "She was poisoned, and I heard the police already have a suspect in custody. Her body was found a few hours ago and they moved quickly, so they must have open-and-shut evidence."

I couldn't help but be dubious. It wasn't often I missed a story this huge. "She was murdered? How do you know that?"

"Skip Taylor heard the paramedics say they smelled something around her mouth and her skin was blue under her fingernails," Toni replied, puffing out her chest. "That means she was murdered. Skip saw it on television, and I believe him."

"Did she just explain something?" Thistle asked, annoyed.

"Changing skin pigment is a sign of poisoning," I offered. "Landon told me when we were watching one of those mystery shows on television one night."

"So you learned it from television, too? That must mean it's true." Thistle said, wrinkling her nose and forcing me to ignore her.

"Could it be true?" Clove asked. "I mean ... who would harm a little old lady like that?"

"I just told you they made an arrest and they're bringing the person in," Beth said.

"But ... who?" I asked.

Beth pointed toward the police station across the road and down a block. Hemlock Cove's Police Chief Terry Davenport pulled in to his usual spot, and I watched as he exited the driver's seat and moved to the back of the cruiser so he could open the door.

The person he ushered out – all four feet and eleven inches of her – took my breath away.

"No way," Clove intoned, her eyes widening to anime proportions. "It can't be."

"Who is it?" Beth asked. "I can't see through Thistle's very loud hair."

"Oh, stuff your mouth like you do your bra, Beth," Thistle said. She hadn't caught sight of the person in the car either and stood on the tips of her toes as she tried to get a glimpse of Hemlock Cove's latest murderer. "Who is it?"

"Aunt Tillie."

"Oh, well, I guess that explains why she's been on her best behavior," Thistle said. "Whoops."

TWO

"This is … unfreaking believable," Thistle said, her eyes locking with mine. "I … there are no words."

"This can't be right," Clove protested. "Aunt Tillie would never kill anyone."

Beth narrowed her green eyes. "Haven't several people gone missing after attacking your family? Word on the street is that Aunt Tillie killed all of them, and you buried the bodies on your property during one of your naked dancing rituals."

Technically, she wasn't wrong. Not about the bodies, mind you, and the naked dancing is a long story. In each case in which Aunt Tillie eradicated a threat there was no body to bury. Now probably isn't the time to bring that up. "Yes, that sounds just like us," I deadpanned. "In our spare time we bury bodies while my FBI boyfriend eats popcorn and watches."

"Hey, I'm not casting aspersions on you," Beth said, raising her hands in a placating manner. "I'm just saying that's the word on the street."

"Hemlock Cove has exactly one street, Beth," Thistle snapped. "Who are all these people talking on it?"

"There's no need to get snippy, Thistle."

"Oh, I beg to differ," Thistle said, clenching her fists as she worked overtime to control her temper. "I think there's definitely a reason to get snippy."

"Knock it off, Thistle," I ordered, grabbing the back of her neck and tugging her toward the street. "We have to check this out. We don't have time for you to ... smack Beth's stupid head around."

"Hey!" Beth was affronted. "I resent being talked about like that. It's not my fault your family is full of weirdos."

"Beth, if we were burying bodies on our property, do you really think messing with us would be the brightest course of action?" I asked, causing her to take a step back. "Come on, Thistle," I ordered, grappling with my wiry cousin as she muttered about a chick fight on Main Street. "We have to check on Aunt Tillie."

"I'll lock up the shop and follow you over," Clove said. "I ... do you think I should call our mothers?"

The question was enough to knock some sense into Thistle, and she immediately stopped struggling against me.

"Absolutely not," Thistle said. "If we call out there and tell them Aunt Tillie has been arrested for murder they'll completely freak out. They're making pie tonight. They cannot freak out on pie night. I've been looking forward to Marnie's strawberry-rhubarb pie for days."

"Yes, because that's the most important thing here," I said, rolling my eyes. "They probably already know she's been arrested. It's as if she wanders around town. Chief Terry had to pick her up somewhere. Where do you think that was?"

"Hell?" Beth offered.

"I will rip your fake blond hair out with my teeth if you don't go away," Thistle threatened, causing Beth's cheeks to flush with color. "If you think Aunt Tillie is terrifying, you should see me!"

Beth and Toni exchanged a look before scurrying down the sidewalk in the direction of the ice cream shop. I knew the gossip there would be terrible, but I couldn't worry about that given Aunt Tillie's predicament.

I risked a glance across the street and found Chief Terry struggling with Aunt Tillie. My elderly great-aunt was putting up quite the fight.

Every time Chief Terry tried to grab her arm or usher her toward the building she slapped his hand back – and hard. Because he'd known our family since before I was born, I understood how difficult this was for him.

"We have to help Chief Terry," I said. "She looks to be in a mood."

"When isn't she in a mood?" Thistle asked. "Oh, and I'm not helping Chief Terry throw her in a jail cell. Can you imagine the curses that will be flying if we help him? I like my hips the size they are, thank you very much."

I scowled. "I'm not saying we help put her in a jail cell," I clarified. "I'm saying we help him figure this out so he doesn't lock her up. We don't even know what's going on yet. He might only want to question her."

"About a murder," Thistle supplied. "He wouldn't have brought her in if he didn't have evidence. He's too afraid of our mothers."

"And of never having a home-cooked meal again," Clove added.

"He took her in for a reason," Thistle said. "That means he has to be pretty darned sure."

I hate it when she's right. Crud. "Well, we can't make a plan of action until we talk to Chief Terry," I said. "Clove, lock the store and meet us over there. No matter what you do, though, don't call our mothers.

"If they know, they'll be down here shortly and things will … get ugly," I continued. "If they don't, perhaps we can nip this in the bud before the massive Winchester meltdown burns us all."

"Oh, I love it that you still seem like a naïve kid sometimes," Thistle said. "You're so … cute."

"I hate you," I muttered, slapping her hand away as she tried to pet the top of my head. "Come on. We have to deal with Aunt Tillie."

Thistle and I took a slow approach, giving Aunt Tillie a wide berth as we approached. Chief Terry looked almost relieved to see us, although that relief turned to regret when he realized how this looked.

"I'm sorry I had to take her in, but I have some questions for her and she refused to answer them," Chief Terry said, holding his hand out and pressing it to Aunt Tillie's forehead to keep her from punching him. He was a tall man, and even though Aunt Tillie is big on personality, she's short on stature. She couldn't quite manage to get her hands on Chief Terry.

"I will smite you if you don't stop that," Aunt Tillie hissed, trying to find a way around Chief Terry's massive reach.

"She's a little worked up," Chief Terry said.

"I see that," I said, tentatively reaching a hand out and pressing it to Aunt Tillie's shoulder. "Aunt Tillie, um, can you calm down for just one second?"

"Can you shut up for just one second?" Aunt Tillie shot back. "Can't you see I'm in the middle of maiming law enforcement?"

She was definitely in the middle of something. I just couldn't figure out what.

"Aunt Tillie, if you stop fighting Chief Terry we can get to the bottom of this and hopefully take you home," Thistle said. "Although, to be fair, I'm kind of curious about what would happen if he locks you up, so I'm genuinely on the fence about what I want you to do. I'm going to play the good girl card, but if you want to be bad, I say go with your gut instinct."

"I will kill you," I said, reaching over and viciously pinching her arm. "Don't say things like that to her."

"Yes, please don't say things like that to her," Chief Terry intoned, his weariness evident. "Tillie, if you would please stop doing that, we could go inside and talk about this like rational adults."

"I'm not rational!" Aunt Tillie kept swinging her arms as Chief Terry held her in place. He could stop her physical antics without a problem. I worried she'd pull a witchy one out of her bag of tricks, though, and then we'd all be in a world of hurt.

"Can you say that again?" Thistle asked, and when I glanced over my shoulder I found her taping Aunt Tillie with her phone. "Try to look at the camera when you do it, too. That will make the YouTube experience so much better."

"I will break that phone if you don't put it away," I threatened, lowering my voice to an ominous level. "Now is the time to help the situation, not inflame it."

"I'm good with the way things are going," Thistle replied, cackling as Aunt Tillie fought to kick her stubby leg out in the direction of Chief Terry's knee. "This is good stuff. Hey, Aunt Tillie, scream about how you're not rational again."

"Knock it off," Clove said, grabbing the phone from Thistle as she joined us. "I locked the store. What's going on? Is she under arrest?"

Actually, that was a pretty good question. "Is she?"

"She's not under arrest," Chief Terry answered.

That made me feel better.

"Yet," he added.

Crud on crackers! Seriously, could this get any worse?

Aunt Tillie suddenly stopped fighting, dropping her arms to her sides and standing quietly. It was as if all the fight fled her body at the same moment. For lack of anything better to do, Chief Terry kept his hand on her forehead. I think he was as surprised as I was.

"What is she doing?" Clove asked, leaning forward.

"Don't let her go," Thistle warned. "In horror movies, this is where the supposed-to-be-dead killer always comes back to kill one more idiot. Given the odds, that will be you, Clove."

"I hate you sometimes," Clove muttered, crossing her arms over her chest.

"We need to get her inside," I said, frowning when I realized half the town was on the street watching the spectacle. "This is going to get out of hand if we're not careful."

"Don't kid yourself," Thistle said. "It's already out of hand."

"Tillie, if I let you go, do you promise to come inside and answer a few questions?" Chief Terry asked.

"I would rather eat worms and curse your thing to fall off and use it as bait next time I go fishing," Aunt Tillie replied, not missing a beat. She may have looked defeated, but her mind was clearly busy.

"Well, that's delightful," Chief Terry said, shifting his groin to a minimum safe distance.

"I've got this," I said, pushing his hand away. "Aunt Tillie, we need you to come inside. Things will be much better when you're in there. I promise."

"Yeah, just think, you can swear up a storm in there and no one will be the wiser," Thistle offered.

"Fine," Aunt Tillie snapped, resigned. "I want you to know, though, you're on my list."

I knew better than to show fear in the face of the enemy, but I couldn't help but gulp. "Duly noted."

"Come inside," Chief Terry said, gesturing toward the front door. "We do not want to do this in front of an audience."

We formed a line, Thistle and I following behind Aunt Tillie to make sure she didn't make a break for it. When we got to Chief Terry's office, he gestured toward the chairs across from his desk.

"You should sit," he said.

"I don't want to sit," Aunt Tillie said. "I want to go home."

"Just ... calm down," I ordered, reaching out to pat her arm and then thinking better of it. "What exactly is going on?"

"Patty Grimes is dead," Chief Terry replied.

"We heard that from the gossip groupies in front of Hypnotic," Thistle said, making a face. "We heard she was poisoned and you had a suspect in custody. Then we saw you pull up to the station with Aunt Tillie in the car."

"Aunt Tillie wouldn't kill anyone," Clove said.

Chief Terry arched a challenging eyebrow. "I saw her unleash a wind monster to kill a man about a year ago. Then there's that whole thing about bringing a storm down to kill a man at Hollow Creek. He's still missing, by the way."

"He was a murderer, and no one cares that he's missing," Thistle countered. "I would love it if you went in front of a judge and told him about the wind monster, though. That would go over well."

"You've always had a smart mouth, Thistle," Chief Terry said. "I don't appreciate it today."

"And I don't appreciate being arrested for something I didn't do," Aunt Tillie sniffed.

23

"You're technically not under arrest," Chief Terry clarified. "You're being officially questioned in a murder investigation."

None of this was adding up. "Let's start from the beginning," I suggested. "When did Patty Grimes die?"

"We're not sure yet, but it looks like she expired during the night," Chief Terry answered. "We'll have to wait for an official time of death from the coroner. The paramedics at the scene noticed some ... problems ... with her body."

"The blue tint to the skin under her fingernails and the odor around her mouth," I supplied. "Yeah, we heard that, too. Those could be signs of poisoning, but until the autopsy is complete, you don't have a cause of death."

"How did you hear about the skin and odor?" Chief Terry asked, irritated.

"This town is thick with gossips," Thistle replied. "It always has been and that's never going to change. Everyone already knows."

"Well, it's true we haven't declared it a murder yet, but it certainly looks like a murder," Chief Terry said. "I'm trying to get my ducks in a row before the coroner declares it a murder – and I fully believe he's going to do that. One of those ducks is Tillie."

"Quack." Aunt Tillie made a hateful face as she mimed flapping wings and waddling in a tight circle.

I ignored her. "But why would Aunt Tillie poison Patty Grimes? She has no motive."

"She might not have a motive, but I was already looking into Tillie's whereabouts yesterday because she was sighted at the senior center," Chief Terry explained. "She's not supposed to be there. She's been banned. News of Patty's death aggravated an existing situation."

"Why were you at the senior center, Aunt Tillie?"

"Quack."

I pressed my lips together and reined in my agitation. "Aunt Tillie, why were you at the senior center?"

"Quack."

I exchanged an annoyed look with Thistle. "Is it duck-hunting season?"

Thistle shrugged. "I have no idea. I just ... stop doing that duck thing, Aunt Tillie. We're trying to talk to you."

"Quack."

When Aunt Tillie wants to ruffle feathers – pun intended – she's the champion. I was legitimately torn between saving her and letting Chief Terry lock her up. Instead, I pinched the bridge of my nose to calm myself.

"Okay, even if she was sighted at the senior center, what does that have to do with Patty Grimes?" I asked, changing tactics. "Why were you investigating her for going to the senior center?"

"Because Margaret Little called four times to complain about Tillie being there," Chief Terry answered. "She says Tillie put something in the coffee and she wanted it investigated. She refused to let it go. You know how she is."

Aunt Tillie changed her routine, mimicking a clucking hen as she continued her charade.

"Exactly," Chief Terry said, not missing a beat. "Margaret claims Tillie was sighted by the coffee machine, and there are multiple witnesses who say she put something in the coffee. I was looking for her to check the accusations."

Oh, no. I wasn't home during the notorious senior center poisoning a few years back, but I'd heard all about it. "But ... I still don't understand what that has to do with Patty Grimes."

"She drank an entire mug of coffee before anyone could warn her, and then she dropped dead during the night," Chief Terry said. "I wanted to talk to Tillie last night – that's why I stopped out at the inn – but she dodged me when I wanted to question her. I was too afraid to follow her out to the greenhouse, so I let it go. That was probably a mistake."

Aunt Tillie directed her chicken sounds in Chief Terry's direction, causing me to bite the inside of my cheek to keep from laughing. It wasn't a funny situation, yet there was something so surreal about her reaction I couldn't swallow my chuckle.

"What do they think Patty Grimes was poisoned with?" Thistle asked. "Just because Aunt Tillie was at the senior center doesn't mean she poisoned anyone. That's a huge leap, and Aunt Tillie has no reason to kill Patty."

"I've told you everything I know," Chief Terry said. "I just want to nail down information from Tillie before we get the autopsy results. It would be nice to rule her out before I have to start ruling people in."

"But ... ." This was preposterous. "Why would she poison anyone? She has absolutely no motive."

"Some psychopaths don't need a motive."

I snapped my head in the direction of the open door, frowning when I saw a strange man standing in the archway watching us. He was dressed in an expensive suit, a gun and badge on his hip, yet his expression was so ridiculous I could've sworn I was on a hidden camera show.

"Who are you?" Thistle asked, wrinkling her nose.

"That's a very good question," Chief Terry said. "This is a private matter, sir. If you wait in the lobby, I'll be with you shortly."

The man grabbed the badge from his belt and held it up. "I'm with the FBI. I'm here to solve a murder."

"How do you even know there is a murder?" I challenged.

"We got a call in the Traverse City office," the man answered. "They sent me here to solve it."

This guy couldn't be for real, could he? This had to be some sort of joke. "Who authorized you to come here?" I pressed.

I recognized Landon's familiar figure as he stepped into the office behind the stranger. His expression was grim. "That would be me."

THREE

"Landon?"

I didn't know what to do. I felt caught and out of place, which was exactly how he looked.

"Hey, Bay." Landon generally greeted me with a flirty wink, a warm embrace or smoldering kiss. He seemed out of his element. "I'm sorry about ... all of this." He gestured to the stranger.

"Why are you apologizing to her?" the man asked, confused.

"Because she's my girlfriend and you're being a ... moron," Landon replied, his dark hair brushing against his shoulders as he shook his head. "Just ... chill out."

The man looked affronted, but the way he took a step back made me believe Landon was his superior. That was probably a good thing, but since I didn't understand anything going on right now, I couldn't be sure. I opened my mouth to ask who Landon's "friend" was, but Chief Terry beat me to it.

"What's going on, Landon?" Chief Terry asked. "Why are you even here?"

"That's kind of a long story," Landon hedged, his apologetic eyes locking with mine. I could tell he had something to say but didn't feel comfortable doing it given his present companion. "We got a call from

Margaret Little. She claimed Tillie Winchester murdered someone named Patty Grimes and the police were trying to cover it up. My boss wanted to make sure this didn't get out of hand – and given my relationship with the suspect – he decided to send help."

"That would be me," the man boasted, puffing out his chest.

"This is Noah Glenn," Landon said, his eyes flashing with irritation. "He's ... new."

"Does that mean he's special?" Thistle asked. "Like ... I don't know ... does he ride the short FBI bus?"

Landon pressed his lips together, and I got the feeling he was trying not to laugh as Noah scowled.

"That means I've been in the area only six months," Noah replied. "I'm new to the area."

"You look like a walking penis in a toupee," Aunt Tillie said, looking him up and down. "How long have you been out of diapers?"

Noah's mouth dropped open. "I ... ."

"He is a new addition to the FBI family," Landon said, choosing his words carefully. "He's been on active duty for six months."

"Seven months," Noah corrected.

"Yeah, because seven months sounds so much better than six months, doesn't it, Skippy?" Aunt Tillie rolled her eyes until they landed on Chief Terry. "Am I done here?"

"We haven't even started," Chief Terry argued. "Sit down."

"You sit down," Aunt Tillie shot back.

"I am sitting down." Chief Terry was clawing at a shredding curtain of decorum.

"Well, keep doing it," Aunt Tillie said, her tone blasé. "I'm ready to go home. Can we go home? I don't trust any of you to drive me, so I need the keys to someone's car."

"If you're not careful, you're going to walk," Thistle said, glancing at me. "This is going to get out of control really fast. You realize that, right?"

I figured that out before Landon brought Noah and his ark of buffoonery to the party. I could only deal with one problem at a time, though. "I still don't understand why you're here," I pressed. "I know you said Mrs. Little called you, but why would you come on her word alone?"

"We didn't have a choice because of the accusations being bandied about," Landon answered, shooting me a small smile. "My boss is worried this will somehow come back to bite Chief Terry, and he's been a valuable member of the law enforcement family in this area, so ... here we are."

He wasn't telling me the whole story, but I realize questioning him in front of Noah was a terrible idea.

"That's all well and good – and I'm so thankful you're watching out for me – but that doesn't change the fact that we don't technically have a murder yet," Chief Terry said, his voice practically dripping with sarcasm. "We have a dead body that shows the signs of a possible poisoning, but we don't have confirmation of a murder."

"I know that," Landon said. "My unit chief is worried about Mrs. Little making a fuss. She called yesterday spouting nonsense about some threat she wouldn't describe. She called again this morning saying the threat had turned into a murder, and that was harder to ignore. He wants to make sure we don't get to an uncomfortable place when it's too late to do anything about it. He's trying to be ... proactive."

"I couldn't possibly care less what Margaret Little thinks," Chief Terry said.

"You tell him," Aunt Tillie interjected, bobbing her head. "She's evil. Everyone knows it."

"I know you're evil when you want to be, so you might want to snap your trap shut," Chief Terry finally flared. "We've had Patty Grimes' body for exactly four hours. Emergency personnel were on the scene two hours before that. We've barely begun the investigation."

"And yet you've already arrested a suspect," Noah pointed out. "How do you explain that?"

"I haven't arrested anyone," Chief Terry clarified. "I was looking for Ms. Winchester because I needed to question her on another matter. It just so happens that this other matter overlaps Patty Grimes' death. It's a ... coincidence."

"What other matter?" Landon was understandably suspicious.

"Don't worry about it," Aunt Tillie replied. "It doesn't concern you. There's no reason for the FBI to get involved. In fact, I think that should be the new rule whenever it comes to the fuzz futzing with my life. The FBI is not allowed."

"Don't start doing that," Landon chided, wagging a finger in her face. "I'm here to help you."

"Which is why I'm the lead on this case," Noah said, smiling. "Given Agent Michaels' relationship with the family, our boss thought it best I handle the case. It's my first shot at being the point man, and I'm really looking forward to it."

I narrowed my eyes. "You mean you're looking for a conviction to start out on the right foot and you're willing to railroad my great-aunt to do it," I countered. "We're not going to let you do that."

"I'm on the fence," Thistle said, crossing her arms over her chest. "I think it might be funny if she goes to prison."

"You're on my list," Aunt Tillie hissed, causing Thistle to balk. "In fact, you're the top five spots."

"Of course, we really need Aunt Tillie at home," Thistle said, recovering quickly. "Our lives would be incomplete without her."

"That's true," Clove said. "I love her as if she was my own mother."

"Thank you, suck-up," Aunt Tillie said. "Save the act for when you're called to testify in my defense. Can you still work up tears at the drop of a hat? That might come in handy."

"Don't even think of doing that," Chief Terry said. "I hate that. You're a wonderful adult, Clove, but that crying thing you did to get your own way as a kid was just ... unbelievably upsetting."

"I didn't cry to get my own way," Clove protested. "I was genuinely sensitive."

"I'm going to make you cry by putting my foot in your behind if you don't focus on me," Aunt Tillie said. "I am innocent. I'm being railroaded. 'The Man' is out to get me ... like he always is."

"Don't look at me that way," Landon said, leveling his gaze at Aunt Tillie. "I am not out to get you."

"That's my job," Noah said, shifting uncomfortably when Landon shot him an incredulous look. "I mean that ... um ... I'm here to find out the truth."

"I'm still confused," I said. "Patty Grimes died this morning and Margaret Little was on the phone with the FBI long before Aunt Tillie was taken in for questioning. How did she even know that Patty's death might be ruled a murder?"

"That's a good question," Chief Terry said. "I'm going to have a talk with her this afternoon so we can figure that out."

"I don't think that will be necessary," Noah said. "I'm taking over as lead investigator on this case."

"Over my dead body," Aunt Tillie snapped.

"And I will be using her dead body as a hammer if you even try," Chief Terry added. "This is my case. You don't have jurisdiction here."

"But ... you've invited the FBI in before," Noah said.

"Yes. Invited. That's the operative word," Chief Terry said. "I'm not inviting you in. I don't know that this is a murder. Right now it's just a bunch of old people ... er, I mean lovely senior citizens ... casting stones at one another."

"And I'm going to find a boulder to squash them all by the time I'm done," Aunt Tillie said, rubbing her hands together as her mind wandered to revenge fantasies.

"Noah, you have to understand that this town is small and all the people here know each other," Landon said. "They have old fights and grievances. We don't know what we're dealing with yet."

"But I was assigned this case," Noah argued. "Also, you're supposed to address me as Agent Glenn when we're in public. You know people don't respect me if I don't look authoritative."

I was pretty sure most people didn't respect him because he looked like a child pretending to be a man, but I kept that myself. "I hate to sound like a broken record, but there's still no motive for Aunt Tillie to kill Patty Grimes. If Margaret Little knew Aunt Tillie would be a suspect, that's because she called Chief Terry so many times yesterday it bordered on harassment to point him in her direction. There has to be a reason for that."

"And why would she do that?" Landon asked.

I'd told him about the senior center poisoning, but apparently he needed a refresher. "Because Aunt Tillie was at the senior center when she shouldn't have been," Thistle replied. "She's been banned."

"Because?"

"There was an ... incident ... several years ago," I said, rubbing the back of my neck. "Aunt Tillie thought some people were cheating at cards ... ."

"They were cheating!" Aunt Tillie's voice was becoming increasingly shrill.

"People were cheating at cards and then some of them got sick," I said. "Aunt Tillie was blamed, but no one was technically poisoned."

"What did technically happen?" Noah asked.

"Technically?" Chief Terry was pretty close to letting his irritation come out to play. "Technically we tested the coffee and found no identifiable foreign substances. That didn't stop Margaret Little from banishing Tillie. They've always had a ... tempestuous ... relationship."

"That's because she's evil," Aunt Tillie said. "As a fighter of evil, I must smite her."

"Stop saying things like that," I said, lowering my voice. "You're not helping your case."

"There is no case," Aunt Tillie said. "I'm innocent. In fact, I want a lawyer. Someone get me Johnnie Cochran!"

"I'm pretty sure he's dead," Clove said.

"Well, that figures," Aunt Tillie muttered. "Who else got O.J. off?"

"You might not want to say things like that in front of him," Thistle said, jerking her head in Noah's direction. "He'll think you're trying to get away with murder."

"I don't care what he thinks," Aunt Tillie said. "He's the least of my worries. He's ... a child."

"I can legally drink and carry a gun," Noah argued. "What child can do that?"

Aunt Tillie gestured toward Thistle, Clove and me. "They snuck into my wine as teenagers and I taught them how to shoot. How hard is it?"

"I don't think that's helping you," Landon said, pinching the bridge of his nose. "I just ... come on!"

"Are you admitting to serving minors alcohol?" Noah asked, not missing a beat. "That's against the law."

"Someone make him stop talking to me," Aunt Tillie said. "I can't even look at him."

"Okay, this is getting out of hand," Chief Terry said. "We don't technically have a murder. I'm not asking for assistance, so there's no need for you to be here, Agent Glenn. As for the rest of it, I can't do anything until I talk with Tillie."

"I plead the fifth," Aunt Tillie said, crossing her arms over her chest and staring at a spot on the wall above Chief Terry's head.

"That's something you do in court," Clove said, shrinking when I shot her a dirty look. "What? I saw it on television."

"Aunt Tillie, just tell them what you were doing at the senior center yesterday," I instructed. "Everything will be fine when you tell them you didn't poison anyone."

"I don't have to tell you people diddlysquat," Aunt Tillie said. "In fact ... I'm done talking."

"I'll believe that when I see it," Landon said.

"Quack."

Landon's face shifted from annoyed to confused. "I'm sorry ... what?"

"Quack."

Landon directed his attention toward me. "Why is she doing that?"

"She's a duck," I replied, weary.

"But ... why?"

"Chief Terry mentioned something about getting his ducks in a row and Aunt Tillie being one of them and then she started quacking," I explained. "She's a duck."

"It's better than her being a chicken," Thistle added. "She was a chicken for a little bit, too."

"Is this some elaborate ruse to lay the groundwork for an insanity defense?" Noah asked. "If so, I can tell you it's not going to work on me."

"Quack."

"I may cry soon," I said. "I just ... ."

Landon took a step in my direction, his intention to give me a hug evident, but he stopped himself when Noah fixed him with a quizzical look. Now I hated the little ferret even more.

"I think we should call our mothers," Clove said. "They'll know what to do."

"Speaking of that, I can't believe they're not here," Thistle said. "Chief Terry took Aunt Tillie into town in his cruiser. They had to see it. Why aren't they all over this situation?"

"First, no one is calling your mothers," Chief Terry said. "They'll kill me. It's strawberry-rhubarb pie night. I don't want to die.

"Second, they don't know I brought Tillie into town," he continued. "They were not ... present ... when I approached her."

Uh-oh. That didn't sound good. "Where did you approach her?"

"It wasn't in the shower or anything, was it?" Thistle asked. "I will never get that picture out of my head."

"Oh, now I'm going to have nightmares," Clove complained, slapping her hand over her eyes. "Why did you have to say that, Thistle? This is worse than the time you made me watch *Hostel*."

"It wasn't in the shower!" Chief Terry bellowed, slamming his hands on his desk. "What is wrong with you?"

When I was younger, Chief Terry's temper displays always upset me. Now, not only was I used to them, I also enjoyed them. "Was she shaving her legs, too?"

"That's it, Bay," Chief Terry warned. "I'm at my limit."

"Batten the hatches," Thistle said.

"I wasn't in the shower, you perverts," Aunt Tillie said. "He just happened to catch me ... doing business ... at the end of the driveway."

Well, that couldn't be good.

"Doing business?" Landon challenged.

"I was selling my wares," Aunt Tillie replied. Because her "wares" included illegally made wine and the occasional dime bag of medicinal pot, that was a potential land mine in a sea of absurdity.

"I don't know what that means," Noah said. "Is she a prostitute?"

"Yes, Noah. She's an eighty-one-year-old prostitute in Hemlock Cove," Thistle deadpanned. "She's rich!"

Sarcasm was obviously wasted on Landon's new partner. "That's against the law," Noah said. "You should probably refer to me in a more professional manner, too. It's Agent Glenn."

"I'm going to call you Agent Genital Wart," Aunt Tillie said, causing Thistle to snicker and Landon to drop his head. "So, Agent Genital Wart, if you have no further questions … ."

"I haven't asked you any questions yet," Noah said. "Don't call me that, by the way. That's not my name."

"And you're not going to ask her any questions," Chief Terry said. "This is my case. If I need the FBI's help, I'll ask. As of now, I don't. This isn't even a murder investigation yet."

"Well, I'm going to have to converse with my boss," Noah said. "He's not going to like this."

"No one likes this," Landon said.

"I think I should be in charge," Noah offered. "I'm the only one without a personal connection to this case."

"No one is listening to you," Aunt Tillie said, grabbing my arm. "Give me your keys. I want to go home."

"You're not driving my car," I shot back. "I'll drive you home, but you can't drive my car."

"I'll make you smell like bacon for a month if you don't give me those keys," Aunt Tillie warned, referring to a favorite curse she liked to lob when the mood struck.

"Don't give her your keys, Bay," Landon said, perking up. "Take a stand."

"I'll make her smell like rotten eggs if you're not careful," Aunt Tillie threatened.

"I don't understand," Noah said. "Does this have something to do with her wares?"

"Yes," Thistle said, nodding gravely. "She gets all decked out in her hooker garb and fries eggs by the side of the road waiting for unsuspecting motorists to pass by and fall into her evil clutches."

"You don't need to understand," Landon said, scorching Thistle with a dour look. "In fact ... ."

He didn't get a chance to finish his sentence because the sound of angry voices filled the lobby, causing me to cringe when I recognized them.

"Where is my aunt? I want her right now!"

"Well, Mom might not have known when you picked her up, but she certainly knows now," I said, offering Chief Terry a rueful smile. "You're in big trouble, mister."

"I'm guessing strawberry-rhubarb pie is off your menu forever," Thistle added.

"I hate my life," Chief Terry said, dropping his head into his hands.

FOUR

"Aunt Tillie!" Mom, my aunts Marnie and Twila close on her heels, barreled into Chief Terry's office without knocking. I've read a lot of fantasy novels over the years, and right now Winnie Winchester looked more like the dragon about to decimate the townspeople than the mother I'd grown up with. She was truly terrifying.

"You," Mom hissed, narrowing her eyes in Chief Terry's direction. "Did you arrest my aunt?"

"Without even telling us," Marnie added, her hands landing on her hips. Most of us resemble our mothers, but Clove and Marnie could practically be twins – if they didn't have that pesky twenty-year age difference.. They were both diminutive – like Aunt Tillie – but stacked on top. It was a frightening combination when anger collided with heaving bosoms.

"I didn't arrest her," Chief Terry protested. "I brought her down to the station to answer questions."

"Why didn't you tell us?" Mom challenged. "You were out at the inn. You could've stopped inside to tell us what was going on. Instead you put her in your car and drove off with her. We wouldn't have even known if one of the guests didn't tell us."

"Who is watching the guests?" Thistle asked. "If you're all here ... ?"

"Is that really important right now, Thistle?" Mom's nostrils flared and I was almost convinced I could see fire licking the edges of her skin.

"Belinda is watching the inn," Twila supplied. "She's just as worried about Aunt Tillie as we are, and Annie, well, she's a mess. She keeps screaming about 'The Man' taking Aunt Tillie."

"Well, that's just great," Landon said, rolling his eyes. "I knew this would happen."

"Chill out, drama queen," Aunt Tillie said. "You didn't take me into custody. Chief Terry is 'The Man' today, not you."

Belinda was a recent transplant to Hemlock Cove. After an accident rendered her unable to work for a few weeks, my mother and aunts took her in and gave her a room on the top floor. She now works for them – and has multiple extra sets of eyes to watch her precocious daughter Annie – while she gets on her feet.

"Who is this 'man' everyone keeps referring to?" Noah asked. "Is he one of these ... crazy people ... too?"

"Who are you?" Mom asked, swiveling quickly and fixing Noah with a look that would've shriveled the courage of most mortal men. Unfortunately for everyone, Noah wasn't mortal. Well, he might be mortal, but he certainly wasn't smart.

"I'm Agent Noah Glenn," Noah finally choked out. "I'll be investigating your great-aunt's culpability in a murder."

"Who was murdered?" Twila asked.

"Technically no one yet," Chief Terry answered. "Patty Grimes was found dead in her home this morning. I was already looking to talk to Tillie because Margaret Little informed me she was at the senior center yesterday and was sighted near the coffee machine. Patty Grimes just happened to be at the senior center – and drinking coffee – yesterday."

"What did you do?" Marnie asked, turning on Aunt Tillie.

"I'm back to wanting a lawyer," Aunt Tillie said. "Who got off that chick who killed her kid in Florida? You know the one who partied while the kid was dead? If he got her off, I should be a breeze because I'm innocent."

"Shut up," I said, shaking my head. "You're making matters so much worse."

"Oh, I don't think they can get much worse," Thistle said.

"Why would Aunt Tillie kill Patty Grimes?" Twila asked, tilting her flame-red hair to the side. She thought she looked like Lucille Ball, but she often reminded me of Ronald McDonald. "Is this because Patty has been dating Kenneth?"

A "whoosh" went through the room as everyone exhaled at once.

"Kenneth Langstrom?" Chief Terry asked, narrowing his eyes.

Twila nodded, seemingly oblivious. "I was at the grocery store the other day, and Donna Fitzpatrick told me that Kenneth and Patty were dating."

"Who is Kenneth Langstrom?" Noah asked, pulling a notebook from his back pocket and clicking a pen. "Is he a possible suspect?"

"He's … ." Landon broke off, unsure how to answer.

"He's Aunt Tillie's ex-boyfriend," Thistle supplied, groaning when I smacked her arm to quiet her. "What? It's not like it's a secret."

"He was not my boyfriend," Aunt Tillie argued. "He was … my gentleman caller. There's a difference."

"Okay, Blanche," I said, annoyed. "That doesn't change the fact that if Patty was seeing Kenneth we now have a motive. You … idiot."

"You're now on the top of my list," Aunt Tillie warned.

"Just think bacon," Landon said, nodding appreciatively.

"I don't care if she did have motive," Mom said. "Aunt Tillie is not a murderer. You just said you didn't technically have a murder yet, Terry. How can you arrest my … feeble and elderly … aunt?"

"Oh, well, look out," Aunt Tillie grumbled. "I'm back to liking Thistle and Bay, and now Winnie is my mortal enemy."

"Shush," Mom ordered. "She's not capable of doing what you're accusing her of, Terry."

"I beg to differ," Noah said, flipping to the front page of his notebook. "When Margaret Little called, she said Tillie Winchester was a suspect in no less than seven murders. Mrs. Little said Ms. Winchester got off in each case. She thinks she might be a serial killer."

"Seriously, who is this guy?" Mom asked, turning to Landon. "Did you bring him here?"

"I didn't have a choice," Landon replied, his cheeks flushing. "My boss is aware of my relationship with your family."

"I believe he called Landon a 'whipped puppy for love' with the Winchester girl," Noah helpfully offered, winking in my direction and causing me to cringe. That was creepy, right?

"Thank you, Noah," Landon gritted out. "Anyway, my boss believes I can't be objective because I'm close with you. He insisted I bring Noah along ... and let him lead our part of the investigation."

"You have no part in this investigation unless I say you have a part," Chief Terry said.

"And while I would normally agree with you, I think you should invite us in," Landon said, his tone even. "We both know why."

"I don't know why," Mom challenged. "Why don't you tell me why?"

Landon shifted uncomfortably and I took pity on him. He didn't want to state the obvious, so I did it for him.

"Because if Mrs. Little goes to the state police or a local politician with her story, they could make a big stink about this," I said. "If another agency is involved from the start, Chief Terry will be able to sidestep those issues. He won't be accused of bias and he won't be under state or political scrutiny."

"Then why can't Landon do it?" I had to give it to my mother. She was stubborn when she wanted to be. Unfortunately, she was also oblivious when she was angry.

"Because Landon's loyalty will be called into question," I replied. "People could say he covered up information because of his relationship with me. It would put his job at risk."

"Well, then why doesn't he just break up with you until this case is solved?" Mom suggested. "You can survive a little time apart."

I balked. "What?"

"That's not going to happen," Landon said, ignoring Noah's

pointed stare as he rested his hand on my shoulder. "I'm not risking our relationship. Agent Glenn being here – and being involved in the investigation – can only help Aunt Tillie."

"I'm pretty sure I don't see how that can possibly be true," Mom argued.

"We need an outside person to prove Aunt Tillie is innocent," I said. "That's why we're stuck with Agent Glenn."

"Yes, but Agent Genital Wart couldn't find his own tool with a magnifying glass and a set of tweezers," Aunt Tillie snapped. "How am I supposed to trust him?"

"I don't see where you have a choice." Landon was grim. "If you don't let him in on the investigation, we could all lose."

I FOUND Landon in The Overlook's library several hours later. He had a whiskey in one hand and his forehead in the other.

"Hey."

Landon jerked his head up, a warm smile playing at the corner of his lips. "Hey, sweetie. Close that door and come in here. I've been waiting for you to show up."

I did as instructed and joined him on the couch, sighing when he pulled me in for a tight hug. "I'm sorry I had to be away for so long, but talking my mother into letting Agent Glenn stay here was ... difficult."

"I can imagine," Landon said, pressing a kiss to my cheek before pulling back. "I've wanted to hug you all day. Actually, I've wanted to hug you for several days. I just thought it would be under different circumstances."

"Me, too," I said, resting my head against his shoulder. "Agent Glenn is checking into his room right now, by the way. Twila is helping him."

"Well, if anyone deserves Twila's special brand of torture, it's him." Landon sipped his whiskey and shifted closer.

We sat in comfortable silence for a moment, but my mind was too busy to let it last. "How bad do you think this will get?"

"I just don't know," Landon answered, opting for honesty. "We may luck out and find Patty Grimes died of natural causes. A blue tint under the fingernails could mean heart or circulation problems."

"And the scent around her mouth?"

"Maybe she had bad breath."

I knew he was going for levity, but it was hard to muster a smile. "I'm worried."

"I know you are," Landon said. "I'm doing the best I can. We have other issues, though, and they're witchy in nature. With Noah around …."

"We could be in big trouble if he sees us engaged in something magical," I finished. "I get it."

"Do you?" Landon brushed my hair from my face with his free hand. "He cannot see you guys doing something unexplainable. Magic will make him lose his head. He's a … by-the-book … kind of guy."

"Is that code for tool?"

Landon snorted. "Pretty much," he said. "He's not a bad guy. He's just full of himself. He can't see past his first big case, and that will be bad for us if discovers the truth."

"What do you think he'll do?"

"I don't know," Landon answered. "I know I can't live without you, though, so let's not give him the opportunity to find out. Can you talk to the rest of your family and make sure they understand the consequences?"

I nodded. "I can try. Aunt Tillie is going to be a bear, though."

"She's always a bear. Try your best."

"I didn't know about Kenneth and Patty," I said after a moment. "I didn't think Aunt Tillie had a motive. Now that she does – no matter how weak – I can't help but feel someone is setting her up."

"Don't get ahead of yourself," Landon cautioned. "We don't have a murder yet. Even if we do, Aunt Tillie's ties to Kenneth were tenuous at best. She cut him loose."

"Actually, it was more like he got sick of her being mean to him and just stopped coming around," I countered. "He wanted to get back with her after their big fight, but she was annoyed and said horrible things to him. I think she thought he would keep begging, though."

"Well, we can't dwell on that," Landon said. "We're in a weird place right now. Aunt Tillie isn't under arrest. Even if Patty Grimes was murdered, we don't have enough evidence for an arrest. That's good for us."

"She also didn't deny being at the senior center yesterday," I reminded him. "That means she was there. That's bad for us."

"I love you, Bay, but you're kind of a defeatist sometimes," Landon said. "As of right now, we're in an okay position. Chief Terry – however grudgingly – agreed to let Noah investigate with him. I'll also be there, although not in a supervisory position."

"Aren't you Noah's boss?"

"Technically, yes. I can't get too involved in this, though. I have to sit back and let him do his thing. It could come back to bite us if I don't."

I leaned forward and hugged him again, taking solace in his warmth. "I know you'll help us however you can. Don't risk your job, though. That's too important to you."

"You're more important, Bay," Landon said, rubbing the back of my neck. "I don't want to lose my job, but I won't lose you. We'll have to play it by ear."

I swallowed the lump in my throat. His kind words warmed me. "I love you."

"Of course you do. I'm a catch."

This time the joke landed and I couldn't help but laugh. Landon planted a lingering kiss on me, which didn't linger nearly long enough because that's when Noah decided to join us.

"There you are," Noah said, pushing open the library door. "I've been looking for you everywhere."

"I wasn't hiding," Landon said dryly. "You couldn't have looked very hard."

"This place is huge," Noah said, settling on the couch next to me and forcing me to edge closer to Landon. "Why did they name it The

Overlook? Didn't they know that was the name of the hotel in *The Shining*?"

"No," I replied. It was a normal question, but for some reason the way Noah asked it set my teeth on edge.

"This place is huge ... and beautiful," Noah continued, seemingly oblivious to Landon's darkening mood. "Did you know there's a little girl running around here, and when she saw me she yelled about 'The Man' and raced into the kitchen?"

"That would be Annie," I replied. "She's very fond of Aunt Tillie. Ignore her."

"I followed her into the kitchen because I was worried she was in trouble. The women there were not happy to see me."

Uh-oh. "Don't ever do that," I said, wagging a finger for emphasis. "Everyone knows the kitchen is off limits. My mother already hates you. Do you want her to chop you up and serve you in a soup?"

"What are they hiding in there?" Noah asked, ignoring the "soup" comment.

"Nothing," Landon answered. "They cook in there. They don't do anything else. That room is just off limits. Stay out of the kitchen. There's plenty of space for you to spread out. While you're at it, though, stay out of the greenhouse, too. That's also off limits."

I hadn't even thought of that. Aunt Tillie had been warned about keeping her pot in the greenhouse. She had a small field on the property, but it was magically cloaked so law enforcement couldn't find it. Now would not be the time for her to break that rule and leave illegal plants out for anyone to stumble upon.

"Um ... speaking of that ... ."

Landon glanced at me. "What?"

"I need to run a quick errand with Thistle and Clove," I said, hoping Landon would realize what I was really doing and keep Noah busy while I checked for contraband.

"I'll come with you." Landon was handsome and intelligent, but I wanted to strangle him for being slow on the uptake.

"You should entertain Noah," I countered.

"But ... ." Landon knit his eyebrows. It took him longer than it should have to realize what I meant. "Oh, right. I'll come down to the guesthouse to get you for dinner after you're done with your ... errands."

"That would be great," I said, relieved.

"Which room are you in, Landon?" Noah asked. "I didn't see you check in. I'm on the second floor."

"I didn't get a room," Landon said. "I'll be sleeping in the guesthouse."

"Isn't that a conflict of interest?"

Agent Stick-up-the-butt was starting to wear on me. "Why would that be a conflict of interest?"

"You're ... one of them."

"Yes, but Bay isn't a murder suspect, and I'm sleeping at the guesthouse with her," Landon said. "There's no reason to charge a room on the bureau's dime when I don't need one."

"I'll check with the boss to make sure that's okay," Noah said, pulling his phone from his pocket.

"You do that," Landon muttered, shifting his blue eyes to me. "Run your errand now. I'm not sure how long I can hang out with him."

"I'm on it."

FIVE

"What are we doing?" Clove asked, scurrying behind me as I led her and Thistle toward the greenhouse. "We're not supposed to go in there."

"We have to go in there," I argued. "Agent Glenn is staying on the property and he's curious. He's bound to find his way down here, and if Aunt Tillie has anything illegal he'll arrest her. We have to scour the greenhouse for pot."

"But ... Aunt Tillie said there would be dire repercussions if she caught us in here," Clove whined. "I'm going to be moving in with my boyfriend soon. I don't want dire repercussions. I want to wear cute pants."

Thistle snorted. "I think you mean you want to wear sexy lingerie."

Clove's cheeks colored. "You have a dirty mind."

"Yes, and I saw you perusing the Victoria's Secret website last week, so don't bother denying it," Thistle said. "Bay is right, though. We have enough on our plate right now. We can't risk Agent Gasbag stumbling across pot on top of everything else."

"But ... ugh." Clove was resigned. "Fine. If my pants don't fit tomorrow, though, I'm going to make you eat dirt until they fit again."

"Bring it on," Thistle said, watching as I opened the door and then following me inside. "Okay, let's split up and go up and down the rows."

"Look close," I instructed, opting for the row closest to the wall. "I wouldn't put it past her to plant a pot seed along with a geranium to disguise it."

"I don't even remember what pot looks like," Clove complained, taking the middle row. "It has thorns, right?"

"Those are roses," Thistle replied. "Good grief. You used to steal from her pot field as much as I did when we were teenagers. How can you not know what pot looks like?"

"Because I was always stoned when we did it," Clove replied. "That's the only time you could talk me into it. I was too afraid otherwise."

"I forgot about that," Thistle said, tilting a clay pot forward and studying the plant. "It looks like she's gearing up for another herb garden."

"Are they real herbs or witch herbs?" I asked.

Thistle shrugged. "Both. Does it matter?"

Did it? "It could if it turns out Patty Grimes was really poisoned," I said. "Look for anything that could kill someone."

"How am I supposed to know what that is?" Thistle complained. "I can barely recognize the kitchen herbs. There's a reason Clove has to handle all of the herbs in our store. They all look the same to me."

"And yet you know what pot looks like," Clove said. "I think there's a lesson in that."

"There is," Thistle agreed. "You're a kvetch."

Clove scowled, wrinkling her ski-slope nose. "I hate it when you call me that."

"Oh, admit it," I interjected, hoping to diffuse the tension. "You're going to miss this. When you're living out at the Dandridge you won't have to be on pot patrol. That sounds ... relaxing."

"It does sound relaxing," Clove agreed. "It's just ... I don't think I should leave when all of this is going on. I talked to Sam and he cleared his schedule and wants to move the rest of my stuff tomorrow. He's really anxious for me to move in with him."

Tomorrow? I knew it was coming, but … . "Clove, you're moving across town," I reminded her. "You're not leaving the country." Part of me didn't want her to go. The other part knew it was the best thing for her. Thistle and I both had overbearing personalities – Thistle much more than me, mind you – and Clove was often lost in the maelstrom because she wasn't as loud. "You'll be able to keep up on everything even if you do move tomorrow."

Clove didn't look convinced. "But … what if you need someone to help you search for pot?"

"You don't know what pot looks like," Thistle pointed out.

"What if you need someone to steal from Aunt Tillie's wine stash again?" Clove pressed.

"Then we'll call you and you can drive over and help us," I said, turning my full attention to my worried cousin. Something was going on here, and it wasn't just the upheaval in Aunt Tillie's world. "Clove, have you changed your mind about moving?"

"No, of course not," Clove protested. "It's just … I know you're going to laugh at me, but it feels like I won't be part of the family."

"That's ridiculous," Thistle scoffed.

"Is it?" Clove challenged. "I already feel like an outsider sometimes because you guys don't like Sam."

"That's not true," I said. "I like Sam. We had issues at first … and I'm never going to like the way he came to town and hid his true intentions … but he loves you. You're good together."

"He also saved Bay's life," Thistle said, referring to an incident when Sam got shot in the foot trying to save me from a crazy former classmate.

"That, too," I said, bobbing my head. "You're always going to be a part of the family. We can't all live together forever, though."

"Yeah, Bay is almost thirty," Thistle said. "It's getting a little pathetic for her to have a roommate."

I scorched Thistle with a dark look. "Thanks."

"You're welcome." Thistle beamed. "Do you want to know what I think, Clove?"

"Not really," Clove said, returning to her plant search.

"I'm going to tell you anyway," Thistle said. "I think you're so excited about moving in with Sam that you're letting your nerves get the better of you now that it's really going to happen."

"I think she's right," I added, narrowing my eyes as I stared closer at a plant. Crap. "Thistle, come over here, please."

"What is it?" Thistle asked, hurrying in my direction.

"I can't be one hundred percent sure, but ... is that what I think it is?" I pointed toward a small sprout.

"Yup," Thistle said, shaking her head. "Son of a ... she's hiding pot in with the other plants. We have to search every single pot."

"That'll take forever," Clove whined. "I have to pack."

"We'll help you pack after dinner," I offered. "We can even break out the chocolate martinis while we do it. It will make the work feel like fun instead of ... work."

"That was almost poetic," Thistle teased.

"What are we going to do with the pot when we collect it all?" Clove asked, worried. "We have to get rid of it somewhere no one can find it."

"That means we're going to have to burn it," I said. "I don't see another option. We'll take it up to the ritual site and toss it in the fire pit."

"Or ... we could smoke it," Thistle suggested.

"We can't do that," I protested. "Agent Glenn will notice if we're high."

"Then he'll arrest us and I'll never get to move in with Sam," Clove said.

"Fine. We'll burn it," Thistle said, although she didn't look happy at the prospect. "It seems like such a waste, though."

"Right now we have to worry about collecting it," I said. "We'll fret about wasting it later."

"IS THAT ALL OF IT?" I studied the clump of plants in Thistle's hand. "That doesn't look like very much."

"I know," Thistle said. "For all the work we had to do to get it, you'd think it would be a big pile of pot. Dried, this wouldn't even be a dime bag."

"You know way too much about drugs," I said, grabbing the plants from her and tossing them on the fire. "I blame Aunt Tillie."

"Oh, man! I blame you," Thistle shot back. "Why did you do that? I was trying to figure out a way to make you let me keep it."

"I know. That's why I did it."

"You suck," Thistle muttered, crossing her arms over her chest.

"We're sure we got it all, right?" Clove asked. "I'd hate to think we did all of that searching and missed something."

"We inspected each pot three times," I said. "We got it all."

"Then let's go up to the inn," Thistle said, her eyes wistful as she watched the fresh plants wilt in the small fire. "I'm starving. I have the munchies and we didn't even get to smoke it."

I flicked her ear. "We can't leave an open fire burning. It could jump to the trees and burn the inn down."

Thistle snorted. "Now you sound like Clove," she said. "Worry, worry, worry. Whine, whine, whine."

"Hey!" an affronted Clove shouted. "I hope you know that now I can't wait to move away from you."

I knew Clove well enough to realize she would regret those words. It happened sooner than I expected, though.

"That's not true, though," Clove said. "I'm going to miss you guys. Now who will I watch Saturday morning cartoons with?"

"You don't watch those with us," Thistle said.

"No, but Landon and Marcus liked them. Sam is more of a *Meet the Press* guy."

My heart went out to my cousin. "Clove, it's really going to be okay," I said. "You're going to have a great time. Just think, now you can decorate the Dandridge."

"I know that," Clove said. "I just … who is going to watch Lifetime movies with me and make fun of all the pathetic women?"

"We can still do that," I pointed out. "We can set up regular girls' nights. We're still cousins. Heck, we're still sisters. And, you know, if things don't work out and you want to come back you'll always have a room with us."

Clove was bolstered by the offer. "Thank you."

"You can't have your room back, though," Thistle said. "I'm turning your room into a crafts room. If you come back, you'll have to sleep on the couch."

Clove's mouth dropped open. "What?"

"That's not what's going to happen," I snapped, batting some of the smoke away from my face.

"Thank you," Clove said, exhaling heavily. "I was worried there for a second."

"We're turning your room into an office," I said. "I need somewhere to keep my computer, and I thought we could put a couch in there and turn it into a little library or den."

"But .... ." Clove's eyes were glassy. "You are the worst people I know."

"It's going to be a crafts room," Thistle argued. "I already measured it for a pottery wheel."

"No way," I shot back. "You can put a pottery wheel in the basement of the inn now that Aunt Tillie's wine business is in the greenhouse. By the way, I stowed all that wine in the back of my car to be on the safe side. Remind me to tell Aunt Tillie so she doesn't go on the warpath when looking for it."

"Yeah, that would suck," Thistle said, staring blankly into the fire for a moment before shaking her head. "What was I saying?"

"You were saying you were going to put the pottery wheel in the inn's basement and let me turn Clove's room into an office," I said.

"I'm pretty sure I said nothing of the sort," Thistle challenged. "You don't need an office. You have an actual office at the newspaper."

"Yes, but I want one at home, too."

"No."

"Yes."

"No!"

"Yes!"

"I think you're both being really insensitive," Clove sniffed. "That's been my room for ... like ... forever. You can't turn it into something else. It's not fair."

"Do you want us to turn it into a shrine to you?" Thistle asked. "That's not happening. Space is at a premium in that guesthouse with Landon and Marcus practically living there."

"That's why I need an office to get away from it all," I added.

"That's why I need a crafts room!"

"Office!"

"Crafts room!"

"You two deserve each other," Clove said, rubbing her stomach and frowning as it gurgled. "Is anyone else hungry?"

"I'm starving," I said, studying the fire. "It's almost completely burned. Five more minutes should do it."

"Good," Clove said. "I want that strawberry-rhubarb pie. I'm going to eat five slices."

"That's going to make fitting into your cute jeans tomorrow difficult," Thistle pointed out. "And that's before Aunt Tillie curses the dickens out of us for burning her pot. I ... did you hear that?"

I tilted my head to the side. "What?"

"I heard someone," Thistle said, scanning the bushes by her feet. "I ... what was I saying?"

She was acting weird. Well, actually, she was acting weirder than usual. "Stop being paranoid," I ordered. "There's nothing in those bushes."

"There could be something in those bushes," Thistle shot back. "You don't know. You can't see in these bushes. For all you know there could be a ... you know ... thing in there. What was I saying again?"

"Hey, here you guys are. I've been looking for you."

I jerked my head in Landon's direction as he joined us by the fire. "Where did you come from?"

"You weren't in the bushes, were you?" Thistle asked. "I told you something was in the bushes. It was him. He was spying on us."

"Stop being paranoid," I instructed. "He's too big to hide in those tiny bushes. He's big ... and strong ... and pretty to look at." I rubbed my hand over Landon's washboard abs. "What were we talking about?"

"I don't think you guys should turn my room into an office or a crafts room," Clove said. "I think you should leave it as it is."

"And I think you're dreaming," Thistle said. "Wait ... did you hear that?"

"What's going on?" Landon asked, grabbing my hand when I refused to stop petting him and forcing my gaze to him. "Why are you guys acting so weird? Did Aunt Tillie curse you because you went through her greenhouse?"

"You're so pretty," I said, smiling.

"You're pretty, too," Landon said, refusing to return the smile. "You're acting strange, though."

"Aunt Tillie didn't catch us," Clove said. "Bay put the wine in the trunk of her car, and we ripped out all the pot and burned it."

Landon stilled. "You burned it?"

"Not in a fun way like I wanted," Thistle said. "Bay threw it in the fire ... like a ... what was I saying?"

"Oh, good grief," Landon muttered, grabbing my chin and staring into my eyes. "You're stoned."

"No, we're not," I argued. "We destroyed the pot. Thistle wanted to smoke it, but I said no. I'm a good girl."

"Yes, you're a very good girl," Landon said, his frustration evident. "You're still stoned, sweetie. You stood too close to the fire when you burned the pot."

"But ... no."

"Oh, well, this is just ... ." Landon released my face and tugged a restless hand through his hair. "How will I explain this at dinner?"

"Maybe no one will notice," Clove said. "You probably only noticed because you're trained to see these things."

"And so is Agent Goober," Thistle said. "He's going to arrest us. We can share a cell with Aunt Tillie. That might be fun."

"Not if you go down to the guesthouse," Landon said. "I'll tell everyone you had something to do, and you can order pizza. That way no one will notice."

"Uh-uh," Thistle said, shaking her head. "It's strawberry-rhubarb pie night. I'm not missing that."

"I'm not either," Clove said. "I don't care if I fit in my pants or not tomorrow. I'm eating pie."

"I'll bring the pie down to you guys," Landon suggested. "That's just as good, isn't it?"

"They made kebabs and fattoush for dinner," I said. "I need my fattoush."

"Bay ... ." Landon's temper bubbled toward the surface.

"Fattoush." I sounded the word out and then gave Landon's rear end a gentle squeeze. "It sounds like tush."

"Oh, why couldn't you have done this when I didn't have a nitwit looking over my shoulder?" Landon complained. "This would've been fun if he wasn't around."

"Fattoush," I repeated.

"What were we talking about?" Thistle asked.

"This dinner is going to bite the big one," Landon muttered. "I just ... ugh."

SIX

"This looks delicious," Noah said, rubbing his hands together as he surveyed the dinner feast. "Do you guys always cook like this?"

"We like keeping our guests happy," Mom said, beaming at the only two guests staying at the inn, a younger couple seated at the far end of the table. More were due to arrive Friday for the weekend, which would only make things more uncomfortable. "You're not a guest, though, so I don't care whether you're happy."

I snorted, Mom's anger somehow striking my funny bone. "No one cares whether he's happy."

"Bay, eat your kebab," Landon ordered, slapping a steak skewer on my plate.

"Yum." I reached for the kebab, frowning as I tried to use my fork to force the meat to dislodge. "It's stuck."

"Here." Landon grabbed the skewer and easily manipulated the steak and vegetables onto my plate. "Do you want me to cut your steak for you?"

"I'm good."

Mom shot me an odd look. "What's going on?"

"Nothing is going on," I said. "I'm ... good."

"We're all good," Thistle agreed, reaching for a chicken kebab and handing it to her boyfriend Marcus. "Get my chicken off please."

"Okay." Marcus' handsome face twisted as he studied his girlfriend. "I ... ."

"Let it go," Landon ordered, sending Marcus a firm headshake. "I just ... let it go."

"Okay." Marcus is easygoing, but he was obviously confused. Landon's demeanor told him pressing the issue was a rotten idea, though. "So, how was everyone's day?"

"I got hauled in and questioned about a murder," Aunt Tillie replied, causing the young couple to widen their eyes. "If anyone's interested, I didn't do it."

"Of course you didn't," Mom said, patting Aunt Tillie's hand. "Only one person in this room is dumb enough to think you did it."

"I'm actually on the fence," Thistle said, earning an elbow in the ribs from Clove. "Oomph. That hurt."

"It was supposed to," Clove said, staring at her plate. "Where is the pie? I want pie."

"Dessert comes at the end of the meal," Marnie chided, knitting her eyebrows as she studied her daughter. "You look ... different."

"It's probably the heat," Landon offered. "It got up to ninety today and it's supposed to be just as bad tomorrow. She needs to drink more water."

"Yes, I'm really thirsty," Clove said, reaching for her glass of water. "Really thirsty." She didn't drink the water, though. Instead she stared at it for a moment before returning the glass to the table.

I chewed on a piece of steak that was much too large for my mouth as I watched Clove's antics. "She's so obvious."

"Don't talk with your mouth full," Mom snapped. "Seriously, what is going on?"

"I told you, the heat got to them," Landon said. "Can't you let it go?"

"I just ... they're acting odd," Mom said.

"I like them this way," Aunt Tillie said, sipping her wine. "They're fun."

"Yes, they're lovely," Landon deadpanned. "I tried to get them to stay at the guesthouse and rehydrate, but they refused because of the strawberry-rhubarb pie. This had better be the best pie I've ever tasted."

An absolutely filthy thought wafted through my mind. "Um ... ."

"Let it go, Bay," Landon said.

"Okay." I went back to chewing my steak.

"So, tell me about Hemlock Cove," Noah said. "I heard it used to be called Walkerville. Is that true?"

"No, that's just a lie we tell the tourists because we like to have fun at their expense," Thistle said. "Where is my kebab?"

"It's on your plate," Marcus said.

"Oh, right," Thistle said, smiling happily. I honestly didn't know she had that many teeth. She usually doesn't smile that broadly. Her grins are more evil than ecstatic. "What was I saying again?"

"Nothing," Landon said. "Hemlock Cove did use to be referred to as Walkerville. They rebranded the town a few years ago to appeal to tourists."

"And they picked a paranormal theme, right?" Noah asked, seemingly oblivious to the mental mayhem occurring around him. "Does that mean you guys are witches?"

"Some of us more than others," Aunt Tillie replied.

"I'm not a witch," Clove said. "I'm a good girl. In fact ... I'm thirsty." She grabbed her water and downed half the glass, gasping as she finished.

"You were saying," Noah prodded.

"I said I was thirsty," Clove said, making a face. "Did you forget that already?"

Landon groaned as he stabbed his fork into his steak. "I'm going to kill all three of you when I get you back to the guesthouse," he muttered under his breath.

"You're still pretty," I whispered.

He didn't want to smile. He fought the temptation with everything he had. He couldn't stop the corners of his lips from turning up, though. "Thank you, Bay. Eat your dinner."

"I want to go back to the murder thing," Marcus said. "Why would someone suspect you of murdering Patty Grimes? That's who we're talking about, right? People were gossiping about it down at the stables. I thought for sure she died in her sleep or something. She was old."

"She wasn't that old," Aunt Tillie shot back, annoyed. "She was only two years older than me. Am I old?"

Marcus swallowed hard. "Of course not." He was used to being Aunt Tillie's favorite since he helped with her gardening needs. Yes, including the pot garden. "You're young and ... spry."

"Good word," Thistle said. "You should be a professional ... you know ... word guy."

"Uh-huh." The way Marcus slanted his gaze in Thistle's direction made me realize he was on to our current predicament. "I need you to eat your dinner, Thistle. Then we're going to go for a walk in the cooler night air to clear your head of this ... heat stroke thing."

"That's a great idea," Landon said. "Everyone needs a walk."

"Oh, I would love to walk around the property," Noah enthused. "I'll go with you."

"I'm sorry, who are you?" Marcus asked.

"No, I'm sorry," Landon said. "I forgot everyone didn't know him. Marcus, this is Noah Glenn. He's in town investigating Patty Grimes' death."

"Oh, I see." Marcus looked as if exactly the opposite were true. "Why is he staying here if Aunt Tillie is the prime suspect?"

"Because Bay whined and her mother capitulated," Aunt Tillie said. "If I had my way we'd kick him out and let the wolves eat him."

"Wolves?" Noah's eyes widened. "Are there really wolves in this area?"

"Yes, and they have big teeth," Thistle said, mock growling.

"Eat your chicken, Thistle," Marcus said, locking eyes with Landon. "Maybe we should take them home now."

"I tried that," Landon said. "They want their pie."

"I don't," I said. "I don't like rhubarb. I only wanted my fattoush. Fattoush. Fattoush." I had no idea why the word fascinated me so.

"Oh, sweetie, I may have to gag you," Landon said, shaking his head.

"Fattoush."

"Can we get back to Patty Grimes?" Marcus asked.

"I really wish we wouldn't," Mom said. "It's distasteful dinner conversation."

"I have news," Clove announced, snapping her head up. "I'm officially moving out tomorrow. We're going to finish packing my things tonight. Bay says we can drink chocolate martinis and everything."

"That sounds like a fabulous idea," Landon said. "Let's add huge buckets of alcohol to this equation. That can't possibly go wrong."

"Don't be like that," I chided. "This is Clove's last night home. It's … sad."

"It's not sad, Bay," Landon argued. "It's a good thing. Clove will be happy and we won't be tripping over people in the guesthouse."

"I'm going to turn her room into an office," I said.

"It's going to be a crafts room," Thistle snapped. "Stop fighting me on that. I will beat you if you don't give me what I want."

"Oh, this is lovely," Marnie said, shaking her head. "My daughter is leaving, and these two are going to fight to the death over her room. It's like they're teenagers again."

"In more ways than one," Mom said, her expression dark. I had a feeling she knew what was going on, too.

"I like the idea of an office better than a crafts room," Landon said. "That will allow me to work in private when I'm here."

"Well, I don't really care what you like," Thistle said. "I want a pottery wheel."

"I told you to put a pottery wheel in the basement here," I argued. "It's too big for that room. It's going to be an office."

"Crafts room."

"Office."

"It's not going to be either," Aunt Tillie said, shaking her head. "It's going to be my room."

"No way. It's … wait … what?" I felt unnaturally slow. She didn't just say what I think she said, did she?

"Yeah, what?" Landon challenged. "You have a room. It's here."

"Not as long as Agent Get-a-load-of-me is under this roof," Aunt Tillie shot back. "He's trying to lock me up for something I didn't do. I don't feel safe staying here."

"Well, you can't stay with us," Thistle said. "That house isn't big enough for five of us."

"Technically Clove is still there and it's big enough for five of you now," Aunt Tillie pointed out. "I'm smaller than Clove. It will be fine. It will be great, in fact. I'm a fun girl."

"Your body is smaller than Clove's," I said. "Your mind is bigger than everyone else's put together, though."

Aunt Tillie preened. "Thank you, Bay. I think that's the nicest thing you ever said to me."

"Your ego is twice as big as your brain, though," I added.

"And both your ego and brain are evil," Thistle said. "You can't live with us. We'll have to kill you if you try."

"You and what army, fresh mouth?" Aunt Tillie has a tendency to dig in her heels, and she was doing precisely that now. Even my fog-filled brain could sense the danger.

"There's absolutely no way that's going to happen," Thistle said. "We'll kill each other – or ourselves when you get out of control and start demanding things."

"You'll live." Aunt Tillie looked a little too pleased with herself as she reached for her wine. "I think this is a great idea."

"I think this is the worst idea ever," Thistle complained. "I totally lost my appetite. I don't even want pie."

"Oh, you're eating the pie," Landon said. "If I have to force it down your throat, you're eating it. The stupid pie is the reason we came to dinner … and now you have a new roommate. I hope the pie tastes like dirt."

"Thank you, Landon," Marnie said, scorching him with an evil look. "Are you insinuating the pie is going to be bad?"

"I'm insinuating that living with Aunt Tillie is going to be … a special treat," Landon clarified.

"I'll bet you're looking forward to it, aren't you?" Aunt Tillie asked, winking at Landon. "Make sure you check who is in the shower before climbing in. You're in for a big surprise if you get me instead of Bay."

I snorted at the visual. "Oh, good goddess."

"This isn't going to be funny when the heatstroke wears off, Bay," Landon said. "You're going to be a screeching mess when that happens."

I knew he was serious, but I couldn't help getting lost in his eyes. "Have I told you how pretty you are?"

"I just ... you're killing me, woman," Landon said. "I love you, but ... I don't think I can live with Aunt Tillie."

"Then you should move up to the inn," Mom suggested. "That way you can watch your friend and make sure he doesn't get into trouble, and the girls can take care of Aunt Tillie. I think that's a marvelous idea."

"I think you've gotten heatstroke with the other three if you think that's going to happen," Landon argued. "I'm not being separated from Bay."

"You'll be a five-minute walk away," Mom said. "That's not being separated. That's ... adding a little adventure to your relationship."

"Yeah, I'm on to you," Landon said, waving his fork. "That's not going to happen. I hate spending three nights away from her every week as it is."

"It's sad really," Noah said. "He stares at that photo on his desk and you can just tell he's missing her. It's so ... pathetic."

"No one asked you," Landon snapped. "You don't even have a girlfriend."

"That's because I'm all about the job."

"Then you're always going to be unhappy," Landon said. "Don't turn your nose up at my life. I happen to like it."

Noah had the grace to look abashed. "I didn't mean anything by it."

"Just ... shut up," Landon said, shaking his head. "This night couldn't possibly get any worse. Eat your dinner, Bay. You have ten minutes and then I'm forcing you outside for a walk. Period. Don't bother arguing."

"Okay," I said, shoving another oversized piece of steak into my mouth.

"I wouldn't be so sure about the night not getting worse," Thistle said, inclining her chin toward the door. "Something tells me Mr. Happy over there is about to prove you wrong. In fact ... wait, what was I saying?"

I turned to see Chief Terry standing in the doorframe. Thistle was right about him looking dour.

"Oh, geez," Landon whined. "Now what?"

"I got the autopsy results on Patty Grimes," Chief Terry replied. "This is now officially a murder investigation. She was poisoned with something called hemlock. It's an herb."

"It's a witch herb," Noah said, taking on an air of authority. "That means someone who thinks she's a witch killed her."

"Or someone trying to frame a witch," Landon said, turning his conflicted eyes to me. "I guess I was wrong about things getting worse after all, huh?"

"You're really pretty."

SEVEN

"*I* feel better." Landon leaned against a tree, his arms crossed, and stared me down. He didn't look happy.

I decided to try a different tactic. "I'm sorry?"

Landon was unmoved.

I had no idea what to say to him, so I flashed him my most adorable "you love me and can't stay angry for long" look.

"What are you sorry about?" Landon asked, his tone even and remote. "Are you sorry for getting stoned not five minutes after I told you we had to be on our best behavior because Noah was here? Or are you sorry about Aunt Tillie threatening to move in with us for the foreseeable future?"

I wasn't sorry about the Aunt Tillie thing. Don't get me wrong, I felt really sorry for myself because of that. I still didn't think I'd done anything wrong. "What do you want me to feel sorry about?"

Landon let loose with an exasperated sigh. Dinner had only gotten worse – yes, it was possible – after Chief Terry arrived. Mom plied him with pie and smiles, but I could tell his announcement worried her. Heck, it worried me.

"We didn't mean for it to happen," I offered. "It was an accident. It's not as though we planned it. We were trying to do the right thing. When we found the pot in the greenhouse all I could think was we had to get rid of it. I guess I should've given the destruction method more thought."

"No, you did the right thing," Landon said, pushing himself away from the tree and dropping down on the ground next to me. We picked an isolated spot between the inn and guesthouse during our walk so we could be alone. "I'm not angry about what happened. Don't get me wrong, I'm not happy about it, but any other night I would've laughed and enjoyed it."

"You're worried about Noah, aren't you?"

Landon collected my hand and held it between his. "I'm worried about you."

I stilled, surprised. "What's going to happen to me?"

"Sweetie, I love you and it's put me in the position where I'm desperate to protect you," he said. "Noah isn't a bad guy. He's just gung-ho and desperate to make a name for himself. I was like that at one point, too."

"And now?"

"Now I'm happy spending Friday nights having dinner with your family and then drinking with the gang," Landon said. "Priorities change. My problem is that I'm extremely worried about Noah staying here."

"Then why did you want him to stay here?" I prodded. "We could've put him up in another inn. Heck, we could've put him in the Dragonfly."

The Dragonfly, a competing inn, was owned by my father and uncles. They'd left town when we were children, returning only recently to re-forge neglected bonds. They would've let us put Noah up at their inn. I was sure of it.

"I want him close enough to watch," Landon replied. "I want to know what he knows. I want to see what he sees."

"I've put you in a terrible position, haven't I?"

"You haven't done anything but stand too close to a fire when you were burning pot," Landon answered. "I'm sure that's an important lesson learned."

"Yeah," I said, trying to cleave my tongue from the roof of my mouth. "I have cottonmouth."

Landon snorted. "You're so cute I can't stand it sometimes," he said, laughing as he reached over to haul me onto his lap before sobering. "I need to ask you something, and I want you to think about it before you answer."

"You want to know whether I think Aunt Tillie is capable of killing someone, don't you?"

"I know she's capable of killing someone," Landon replied. "I've seen her do it – even though I didn't understand how she was doing it at the time. I want to know whether she's capable of killing Patty Grimes."

"No."

"You didn't think about that very long."

"No."

"Tell me why," Landon said, rubbing his cheek against mine. "I don't believe she is either, but you know her better than I do. Tell me."

"Aunt Tillie talks a good game, but deep down she has a good heart," I explained. "The times she's unleashed her magic and done real damage – every time – was to protect us. She had no reason to kill Patty Grimes."

"What about Kenneth?"

"I think she liked the attention Kenneth lavished on her, but Uncle Calvin was the love of her life and she never cared for any other man," I said. "She didn't care about Kenneth enough to kill Patty. Heck, if she wanted Kenneth, she probably could've taken him back at any time. You saw how he was with her."

"He was smitten," Landon said. "Just like I'm smitten with you."

"Cute."

"I try," Landon said. "I think if she really wanted to fight with someone she wouldn't kill them through underhanded means. She would go straight at them and make them suffer. Killing an enemy isn't what gets her off."

"No," I agreed. "She likes playing with them too much. She's a fan of the game."

"Exactly," Landon said. "That leads me to believe someone is framing her."

"Maybe," I said. "Or maybe someone else had a grudge against Patty and they're using Aunt Tillie as an easy scapegoat and timed Patty's death so it would be easy to point the finger at Aunt Tillie."

"That's the same as framing her."

"Only kind of."

"You really drive me crazy," Landon said, tightening his arms around my waist. "As much as I would love to stay out here and drive you crazy, I think we need to get back to the guesthouse. Don't you have packing to do with Clove?"

"Oh, yeah. I almost forgot."

"Are you sad to see her go?" His eyes were serious when I locked gazes with him. "It would be natural if that's what you're feeling."

"I'm feeling … torn," I said. "She wants to go but she's terrified we're going to forget her."

"Well, I'm pretty sure that's impossible."

"I knew we wouldn't live together forever, but … ."

"You're going to miss her," Landon finished.

"I'm also … jealous."

Landon shifted me so he could study my face. "Why?"

"She's being an adult and moving forward," I replied, opting for honesty. "Thistle and I are staying behind. I know that won't be for long either because Marcus and Thistle are going to move in together, so where does that leave me?"

"I'm hoping it leaves you with me."

"Yes, but … you live in Traverse City," I pointed out. "I'm not sure I'm ready to move out of Hemlock Cove … not that you've asked me to."

"I've considered asking you, but I don't want you moving to Traverse City," Landon said, taking me by surprise.

"Oh." My voice sounded weak and small, and I hated myself for it.

"Not because of whatever you're thinking," Landon said. "I like Traverse City. It's a nice town. I don't see it as my future, though."

"What do you see as your future?" Did that sound girlie and needy?

"You," Landon answered. "You need to be here, though. This is your home. I want it to be my home, too. I have to figure out some things first, though."

"Like?"

"Like technically I'm supposed to live in Traverse City so I can be close to the office," Landon said. "I get around that as often as possible, but it's still a requirement."

"I guess I didn't think of that."

"Things are okay right now, aren't they?" Landon asked. "We have a little more time before we have to make any big decisions. We'll figure it out."

"But you want to figure it out, right?"

Landon's handsome face split with a wide grin. "Yes. I want to figure it all out."

"Good."

"I thought you might like that," Landon said. "We can't dwell on that right now, though. We have more pressing things to worry about."

"Like Aunt Tillie."

"And getting through your last night with Clove as a roommate," Landon said, giving me a soft kiss and then pushing me to my feet. "Come on, stoner. Let's go get one of those tasks behind us, shall we?"

I linked my fingers with his and let him lead me toward the guesthouse. For the first time since Clove's moving became a reality, I realized everyone was moving forward. It wasn't only her.

"Do you think my mother is going to say something about the pot when she gets me alone?"

"Definitely," Landon said. "Live in fear."

"That's the way I roll in this family."

"**OH, LOOK** AT THIS," Clove said, extending a framed photograph. "I forgot this was in my drawer."

I sat on the floor in front of Landon, carefully wrapping some of Clove's breakables while he and Marcus watched a baseball game. The photo showed Thistle, Clove and me as teenagers. We were dressed in short cutoffs and tank tops, mugging for the camera.

"Let me see that," Landon said, grabbing the photograph. "You look cute. I would've been all over you in high school."

"No, you wouldn't have been," I countered. "You would've thought what everyone else thought."

"And what's that?"

"That I was the weird girl who always talked to herself and was going to end up in an asylum or something."

"I don't think that's true," Landon said, handing the photograph back to me. "I think I would've loved you even then."

"I think you're drunk," Thistle said from her spot on the floor in front of Marcus where she diligently paired socks. "I don't understand how we always lose socks. You have two orphans. This place isn't big enough to lose socks."

"I maintain there's a sock monster in every home," Marcus said. "He's invisible ... and hungry."

"I think you're drunk, too," Thistle said, grabbing her martini from the coffee table.

"I think we're all drunk," I said, sighing as Landon massaged my shoulders. "We probably should stop now so we're not hungover tomorrow. I don't think Agent Glenn is going to be pleasant when we're hungover."

"Agent Glenn wouldn't be pleasant if he were hungover," Thistle said, closing the box in front of her. "Is that it? Is that everything?"

"Everything but the stuff I'll need to get ready tomorrow morning," Clove said, glancing around. "It's ... done."

Perhaps it was the alcohol – and I knew I would blame the martinis when I thought about this night in the future – but tears pricked my eyes. "It's not done," I said. "It's just ... different."

"Okay, there will be none of that," Landon said, tightening his grip on my shoulders. "Don't cry. I don't like it."

"I'm not crying," I said, working overtime to collect myself. "I'm happy for Clove."

"Yeah. She gets to decorate a lighthouse and live in it," Thistle said. "How many people get to say that?"

"You'll come and visit in a few days when everything is moved in, right?" Clove asked. I couldn't help but notice how watery her eyes were. "I'll cook dinner for everyone. We'll make a night of it."

"That sounds good," Landon said. "You guys are right on the water, and you have that bonfire pit close to the shore. It will be fun."

"And you'll be nice to Sam, right?" Clove pressed.

"I'm always nice to Sam," Landon protested.

Everyone raised dubious eyebrows.

"Fine. I haven't always been nice to Sam," Landon conceded. "You have to understand, though, from my point of view he was a threat. I realize now he wasn't – and I will be forever thankful that he went out of his way to protect Bay – but he worried me when he first showed up."

"I think that's because you thought he was going to hit on Bay," Thistle said. "He had better taste than that."

Clove giggled. "Thanks for that."

"I'm surprised Sam isn't here," Landon said. "I would've thought he would spend your last night here with you."

"He was going to, but then he decided to give me the night alone with Bay and Thistle," Clove said. "I think he was worried we would fight ... or cry."

"I'm worried about it, too," Landon said. "You're all very close to the edge. I can feel it."

"You're not going to see tears until tomorrow," Thistle said.

"Oh, that's so sweet." Clove pressed her hand to the spot above her heart. "I'm going to cry, too."

"I'm going to cry because I just know Aunt Tillie will try to move in to my crafts room," Thistle said.

"Office," I automatically corrected.

"There's a big pile of dirt in the garden outside," Thistle threatened. "I'll make you eat it."

"You're too drunk to make me do anything," I countered, leaning back so I could snuggle closer to Landon. "You don't think she's really going to try to force her way in here, do you?"

"No way," Thistle said. "She was only saying that to irritate us. She can't anyway, because Clove is taking her bed."

"I forgot about that," I said, brightening. "There's no way she'll sleep on the floor."

"She doesn't want to live here," Clove said. "She's only upset about being suspected of murder. I can't say I blame her. Did you see her face when Chief Terry announced Patty had been poisoned?"

"No," I replied, my interest piqued. "I was staring at Chief Terry. What did Aunt Tillie do?"

"She looked ... sad," Clove replied. "I think she felt sorry for Patty. Hemlock poisoning isn't a pleasant way to go."

"I don't think any poisoning is a pleasant way to go," Landon pointed out.

"Who do you think did it?" Marcus asked. "It wasn't Aunt Tillie. I know she didn't do it."

"I don't believe it was her, but until we start investigating I have absolutely nowhere to focus my attention," Landon said.

"Poisoning is generally a female thing," I said. "Men use guns or knives because it's phallic."

"That's profound, sweetie," Landon said. "Have you ever noticed you're prone to deep thoughts when you're drunk?"

"That wasn't a deep thought."

"It was close enough," Landon said. "You're right about the poisoning, though. Most women don't like to get their hands dirty, so they kill from a distance."

"I'll bet it was Mrs. Little," Thistle said, slightly slurring her words. "She's the one so desperate to pin it on Aunt Tillie. We all know she's not a nice woman."

"Peddling porcelain unicorns is evil," I agreed, referring to the kitschy shop Mrs. Little owned and operated. "Maybe I should go in and talk to her tomorrow."

"Don't get involved," Landon warned. "Let the professionals handle it this time."

"I'm a professional."

"Right now you're a professional drunk and stoner," Landon said, leaning forward so he could grab my waist and hoisted me up. "That's why you're going to bed before you can have another drink and make matters worse."

"That's probably what we all should do," Marcus said.

I glanced at Clove, my heart rolling. This wasn't goodbye – it never would be – but it was as close as we would ever get. "Goodnight."

"I'll see you in the morning," Clove said, forcing a bright smile. "It's going to be a big day."

"It's going to be a great life," I said. "You've earned it. Now, get some sleep so you'll look cute in your special moving outfit."

EIGHT

My hangover was minimal the next day – and by that I mean three aspirin killed it in less than an hour.

Sam arrived right at eight, the grin on his face so wide as he greeted Clove I couldn't help but like him a little more than I previously did. Despite what Clove thought, I did like and trust him. I kind of wanted to smack him for stealing my cousin, mind you, but Clove was so giddy and happy I also wanted to hug him.

"I think that's everything," Sam said once Landon and Marcus helped him take apart Clove's bed and move it to his truck. "Well, everything but my girl."

Clove smiled shyly as she took his hand. "Yup."

"If you need help putting that bed together, I can come out and do it this afternoon," Marcus offered. "I'll be in town most of the day, so give me a call if you need anything."

"Thanks, but I think we have it covered," Sam said. "I appreciate the offer, though."

"I would offer to help, but I don't want to," Landon said, rubbing my back as we sat in the armchair at the edge of the living room. "I'm lazy when it comes to manual labor."

Sam smiled. "That's okay. I heard you have your hands full as it is."

"Yeah, I'm not looking forward to that," Landon said. "It's going to be a long couple of days. Speaking of that, we should get in the shower, Bay. We need to go up to the inn for breakfast. I'm worried Noah will have gone missing during the night thanks to your mother ... or Aunt Tillie."

I nodded, my eyes trained on Clove. "You should come up to the inn for breakfast," I suggested. I wasn't quite ready for her to leave the property yet. "I know you have a big day of moving and everything, but ... it's the last regular breakfast you'll have here."

Sam frowned. "We'll be here for breakfast at least once a week. I promise."

"I know," I said. "It's just ... last night's meal was a mess because of the pot. She should come for one more big meal."

"But ... ." Sam glanced at Clove, conflicted. "You know what? I don't think either of us is going to feel like cooking today because we have so much work ahead of us. Breakfast at the inn sounds great."

Clove beamed. "Really?" She sounded relieved.

"Really," Sam said, nodding as he slung an arm over her shoulders. "I hope they have pancakes. I'm in the mood for pancakes."

"I'm in the mood for a shower," I said. "We should be ready in a half hour."

"I'll vacuum my bedroom ... I mean the new office or crafts room ... so it's nice and clean for when you guys stop fighting and start decorating," Clove offered.

"You don't have to do that," I said. "We're not going to stop fighting for weeks."

"That's the truth," Thistle muttered, rubbing her forehead. Of everyone present for the packing party the previous evening, she had the worst hangover. "That's going to make moving my pottery wheel in that much sweeter when I claim victory."

"Dream on," I said, struggling to a standing position. "We won't be long. I ... ."

The front door popped open, cutting off the rest of my response. It wasn't important anyway, especially given the sight standing in the doorway. Aunt Tillie, clad in heart-shaped sunglasses with multicolored lenses, camouflage pants, purple Dr. Martens boots and an odd-looking kimono top, smiled brightly when she saw us. She had a suitcase in her hand. "Hello, roomies."

Uh-oh. "I'm sorry ... what?"

"No, no, no!" Thistle hopped to her feet. "What do you think you're doing here?"

"I'm moving in," Aunt Tillie announced, unperturbed by our less-than-enthusiastic reception. "I told you last night I was going to."

"Yes, but ... we thought you were joking," I said, glancing at Landon for help. "Do something."

"I saw this coming, pothead," Landon said, pursing his lips. "I can't fix this for you. You have to fix it yourself."

"But ... ." This couldn't be happening.

"Hello, Clove," Aunt Tillie said, leaving me flustered and stewing on the other side of the room. "Are you excited about your big day? You look excited."

"I'm fairly excited," Clove said, her face unreadable as her gaze bounced around the room. "We're going to have breakfast at the inn before we go. It's going to be a long day and we want a big meal."

"That's a great idea," Aunt Tillie said, her enthusiasm on full display. "Did you clean all of your stuff out of your old room? I'm going to need to spread out. I do yoga every morning and sometimes it gets ... vigorous."

"Uh-huh."

Aunt Tillie graced each individual in the room with a smile before bouncing into Clove's room. Once she was out of sight, I took the opportunity to turn on Landon. "Do something!"

"What do you want me to do?" Landon asked. "I told you last night that this would happen. It's here, and now you have to deal with it."

"But ... this will ruin everything."

"Like what?" Landon challenged. "What do you think she's going to do to you?"

"I think she's going to make it so it's impossible for us to sleep together under this roof," I replied.

Landon wasn't convinced. "Define sleep."

"She means have sex, you moron," Thistle said, cuffing the back of Landon's head and causing him to scowl. "Do you have any idea how uncomfortable it'll be for us to do anything ... romantic ... when Aunt Tillie is here?"

"She also snores so loud you're going to think a tornado is touching down," I added.

"So do you when you're really tired," Landon shot back.

"I can't believe you're for this," Thistle said. "Generally Aunt Tillie drives you crazy. You know she's going to monitor every single little thing we do, right? How is that going to work out for you?"

"Yeah, I don't think this is going to work out for any of us, and I happen to love Aunt Tillie," Marcus said.

"That's because you're her favorite and you won't share the wealth," Thistle snapped. "This can't happen. We have to stop it."

"We're not going to stop it," Landon argued, taking me by surprise.

"We're not?"

"Bay, we talked about this yesterday," Landon said. "I'm worried. I'm so worried my stomach hurts. Noah is up at that inn. I didn't want him on this property, but I thought it was more dangerous letting him wander around on his own.

"My big concern was him sharing a roof with Aunt Tillie because I thought she might lose control and set something on fire ... or throw pot at him when he wasn't looking ... or curse his hair to fall out," he continued. "This doesn't solve that problem, but it does make it easier to deal with."

"How?" Thistle challenged.

"Noah will be with me during the day," Landon answered. "I'll be able to control the information coming his way – or at least minimize the damage it could cause. I have no intention of being separated from you at night, Bay, but I was worried about what would happen if I was separated from Noah and he ticked Aunt Tillie off. Now she's here, so the odds of that happening are slimmer. This isn't perfect. It's not going to be perfect again until we get Noah out of here. This is the easiest solution, though."

"You might not say that when she tries to put a wedge between you and Bay," Thistle argued.

"No one can put a wedge between Bay and me," Landon replied. "It can't happen. Aunt Tillie will be a pain. She's always a pain. The most important thing is keeping her out of jail, though. The second most important thing is keeping this family's magical abilities under wraps."

"I get what you're saying, but this is going to be a nightmare," Thistle said. "Just for the record, I called it first."

"We all called it," I said. "Landon is right, though. We have to do our best to keep Aunt Tillie away from Agent Glenn."

"Fine," Thistle said, holding up her hands and conceding defeat, "but if this goes horribly wrong, I'm moving in with Marcus and leaving you guys to deal with Aunt Tillie."

"Fine," Landon said. "You need to try to get along with her, though. Don't needlessly push her buttons."

"Oh, come on!" Thistle was annoyed. "She needlessly pushes my buttons. Are you going to stop her from doing that?"

"No. I often find that funny."

"I didn't think so," Thistle grumbled, crossing her arms over her chest. "This sucks."

"Welcome to adulthood," Landon said. "It's not the ideal situation, but we have to deal with it. That's freaking life, Thistle."

"Oh, I'm kind of sad; I'm going to miss this," Clove said, smiling fondly at Sam. "Of course, I'm really glad I don't have to live here while this is going down. It's going to be utter chaos."

"Yes, timing is everything, isn't it?" Sam said, grinning. "We'll make sure to stop by for frequent visits so we don't miss too much of the action."

Clove clapped her hands, her newfound giddiness making my stomach turn. "Yay!"

"I think this will be okay," I said, forcing a bright smile. "It probably won't be as bad as we think."

"You're such a moron sometimes," Thistle muttered. "This is going to blow up in all of our faces. Just you wait."

As if on cue, Aunt Tillie poked her head into the living room. "Did you know there's no bed in here?"

"Clove is taking hers to the Dandridge," I supplied.

"I guess that means Marcus and Landon have to carry my bed down from The Overlook," Aunt Tillie said. "That will be fine. You guys can get it after breakfast."

"I'm looking forward to it," Landon gritted out, locking gazes with me before lowering his voice. "You're lucky I love you. A lesser man would run screaming from this house right now."

"Do you still want your shower?"

Landon tilted his head to the side, considering. "You'd better be feeling acrobatic. I have a feeling I'm going to have a lot of excess energy to work off over the next few days. You'd better get in shape."

"That's quite the pillow talk," I said dryly.

"And just think ... she hasn't even been here five minutes."

That was a sobering thought.

"SO, TODAY is the big day, huh?"

Marnie took us all by surprise a half hour later when she moved to hug Clove before she sat at the dining room table. The couple from the previous night opted against staying for breakfast before they checked out – not that I blame them, mind you – so it was just the family, boyfriends and the ever-annoying Noah Glenn.

"I'm still going to see you all of the time, Mom," Clove said, awkwardly patting Marnie's shoulder. "I'll be here just as much as I was before."

"We both know that's not true, but I'm happy you're happy," Marnie said, offering Sam a heartfelt smile. "You'd better treat her well."

"I plan to," Sam said in earnest. "You can come out whenever you want and visit."

"I would rephrase that if I were you," Thistle said, plopping down in her chair. "The last thing you want is one of our mothers having free reign over your domain."

"You're always a joy in the morning, Thistle," Mom said, shaking her head. "Tell me, how do you like your new roommate?"

As if smelling a trap, Thistle narrowed her eyes. "I know you're somehow behind this, and just for the record, you're now my least favorite family member. Congratulations."

"Oh, the love goes right to my head," Mom deadpanned, fanning her face to ward off fake tears. "It makes an aunt so proud."

Thistle was unmoved by the sarcasm. "You're a pain. You know that, right?"

"You had to inherit it from somewhere," Mom said, settling in her regular seat before turning her attention to me. "Aren't you going to complain about your new roommate? I expected wailing ... or whining ... or that really annoying combination of both you do when you're determined to get your way."

She was baiting me. "I'm fine with it," I said, stabbing two pancakes from the plate in the center of the table with my fork. "We're going to miss Clove, so having Aunt Tillie there will be a nice ... distraction."

Thistle snorted. "I thought you were going to say destruction."

"That, too," I said. "It will be fine. I'm happy to have Aunt Tillie so close."

Mom narrowed her eyes, suspicious. "What are you up to? You're not up to the same thing you were up to last night, are you?"

"That was an accident," Landon said, casting a pointed look in Noah's direction. "The heatstroke came about because they were working so hard to clean out the greenhouse. It wasn't wise doing it in this heat, but I've had a chat with them and they won't do it like that again. Let it go."

Mom scratched the side of her nose as she realized what Landon was trying to say – without really saying it, of course. "Oh." She turned on Aunt Tillie. "We're going to have a talk when this is all over."

"I can't wait," Aunt Tillie said. "Our talks are often the highlight of my day."

"Whatever," Mom said, handing Landon the platter of bacon. "I made that for you."

"And here I thought you didn't love me," Landon said, happily accepting his pork prize.

"I don't blame you for any of this ... or bringing him into our lives," Mom said, glaring at Noah. "I know you're doing your best."

"I am doing my best," Landon agreed. "We all need to do our best to get through this. Speaking of that, Noah, you need to eat quickly so we can get moving. We have a lot to do today."

"What are we doing?" Noah asked, his face blank.

"You're in charge of the investigation," Landon said, his patience clearly working overtime. "What do you think we should do?"

"I think we should ... examine the evidence."

I risked a glance at Thistle and immediately wished I hadn't because we both couldn't swallow our giggles when the hilarity of his answer washed over us.

"What's so funny?" Noah asked.

"They're laughing because your answer was a roundabout ticket to nowhere," Landon supplied. "We're going to start out at Patty Grimes' house and go through all her mail and correspondence. After lunch, we'll figure out our next move."

"Are you going to be in town for lunch today?" I asked.

"I ... ."

Noah cleared his throat, cutting Landon off. "It probably wouldn't be wise to have lunch with the chief suspect's niece while we're investigating."

"Thank you, Noah," Landon said, his tone positively dripping with sarcasm. "I so love it when you spout rules, regulations and general suggestions regarding my behavior."

"I guess that answers that question."

"I think you're on your own for lunch," Landon said. "I wish I could keep you with me today, but I'm sure you understand that's against the rules."

"Like ten of them," Noah added.

I fought the urge to sigh – and then fling a pancake at Noah. "It's okay," I said. "I have work of my own to do."

"Not on this, right?" Landon pressed.

"I ... of course not."

Landon didn't believe me. I didn't blame him. He leaned close so only I could hear him. "Be very careful."

I smiled. "I will. Try not to kill Noah when he irritates you."

"I can't make that promise," Landon said, reaching for more bacon. "At least I have the thing I love most in this world to bolster me for a few minutes before I start what I'm sure will be an absolutely terrible day."

"Is that the bacon or me?"

Landon shrugged. "If you'd start wearing bacon, that would be the easiest choice ever."

"I love you, but sometimes you make it really hard."

Landon smirked. "Don't worry. I would choose you over the bacon nine out of ten times."

That was sweet ... and kind of insulting. "What times would you choose the bacon?"

"I'll get back to you after we spend the night in the guesthouse with Aunt Tillie."

Unfortunately, yeah, I could see that.

NINE

Landon had told me to stay out of the investigation. In reality I knew he didn't expect me to do it. He wanted me to be careful and fly under the radar, but we both knew I couldn't let this go without following up on my own.

I figured Landon and Noah would spend the morning at Patty's house, which probably meant they would hit the senior center after lunch. I opted for the reverse order and headed straight for the senior center.

I'd been in the building, located on the opposite side of the town square from The Whistler's office, several times. It was usually because I was writing an article about a function. That happened on really slow news weeks. No one batted an eyelash when I walked inside today.

"Hey, Bay."

I smiled when I saw Kenneth sitting at a table with Arthur Hutton, a retired construction worker. They had coffee in front of them and cards in their hands, but they didn't look as if they were focusing on a game. "Hi, Kenneth. How are you?"

"I've been better."

I grabbed one of the empty chairs from a nearby table and used it to settle between Kenneth and Arthur. "I heard what happened," I said, patting his shoulder. "The rumor is you were dating Patty. Is that true?"

"He's dating everyone," Arthur cackled, shooting me a saucy wink. "I am, too."

"That's nice ... I guess," I hedged.

"He's making it sound worse than it is," Kenneth said. "I did have coffee with Patty a few times, but I've also been having coffee with Myrtle ... and Fay ... and Viola ... and Margaret ... and Edna ... and Dorothy ... and ... ."

"I get the picture, Kenneth," I said, working overtime to hide my distaste. "I see you're no longer a one-woman guy."

"I would still be a one-woman guy if your aunt hadn't broken my heart," Kenneth said, his expression pained. "She crushed me."

Arthur didn't look impressed with Kenneth's attitude. "You're lucky she didn't crush your nuts in a vise, man," he said. "I told you from the beginning that going after Tillie Winchester was a terrible idea. She's got the mark of the demon. No offense, Bay."

"None taken." Okay, I took some offense. I didn't let Arthur see it, though. "Just for curiosity's sake, what is the mark of the demon?"

Arthur rolled his eyes. "Don't you read the Bible?"

"I'm familiar with it," I clarified. "We take a more holistic approach in our house. That being said, I don't remember any passages about the mark of the demon."

"What passages do you remember?" Arthur challenged.

He was just messing with me now. There could be no other explanation. "I remember the part about stealing ... and murder ... and something about turning water into wine. Aunt Tillie made that her life's ambition. Oh, and I remember the part about always being prepared."

"That's the Boy Scout motto," Kenneth pointed out.

"Oh, right," I said. Crap. "I just know it wants you to be good. Am I wrong?"

Arthur sighed. "It's a good thing you're pretty, girl. You're not very quick on the uptake, are you?"

"Hey!"

"Your aunt is the Devil in human form," Arthur said. "You know that mole she has on her lip? That's the mark of the demon."

"That's a beauty mark," I argued.

"Does it make your aunt beautiful?"

I'd never given it much thought. I'd seen photographs of Aunt Tillie back in the day and even though she was short, she was quite striking. "I do think she's beautiful. She has her own sense of style."

"Does she ever," Kenneth intoned, taking on a wistful expression. "How is she? I heard she's a suspect in the murder because of me."

I studied him a moment. Did that make him happy? If so, he didn't look it. "I wouldn't call her a suspect," I said. "She's more a person of interest."

"Isn't that the same thing?" Arthur asked.

"Not really," I said. I'd never spent much time talking to Arthur after returning to Hemlock Cove after my stint as a reporter in Detroit, and now I knew why. He was kind of an ass. "That is what I'm here to talk to you about, though."

"I figured," Kenneth said. "What do you want to know?"

"Did you see Aunt Tillie here the day before yesterday?"

"I was playing euchre with three of my ladies," Kenneth answered. "I didn't see her, but everyone mentioned she was here after the fact. I can't help you on that front."

I couldn't stop myself from asking the next question. "Why do you have multiple ladies?"

"Look around," Kenneth prodded, inclining his chin and urging me to scan the room. "What do you see?"

"A lot of coffee and cards."

"Look closer."

"I ... oh." It escaped my notice upon entry, but now I understood what Kenneth was getting at. "You and Arthur are the only men here."

"Hey, maybe she's smarter than she looks," Arthur said, making a horrifying throat-clearing sound. He sounded as if he was about to cough up a demon.

"Are you the only men ever here?"

"Yup," Kenneth said. "There are thirty women and two men on most days, and dances make it like fifty women and two men."

"Because women outlive men?" I was genuinely curious.

Kenneth shrugged. "I think you're being too clinical," he said. "It's more like women enjoy hanging out in groups and they don't mind admitting they're going to a senior center. Men generally don't do that."

"Yeah. They prefer golfing," Arthur said.

"Why are you here?"

"For the action," Arthur replied, causing my stomach to twist when he made a vulgar gesture with his hands.

"I like hanging out with women," Kenneth explained. "Because I'm one of the only men who comes here, I'm very popular. It's nice for the ego."

I always liked Kenneth. I never understood why he liked Aunt Tillie, but I found him to be pleasant and congenial. I knew he wouldn't rock Aunt Tillie's world ... or cause her to fall in love with him ... but I thought he was good for her in a roundabout way. "And Aunt Tillie was bad for your ego," I surmised.

"I like Tillie because she's fiery and says whatever comes to her mind," Kenneth said. "She doesn't pretend to be something she's not ... like these women. She didn't care about me, though. At a certain point I got the picture and let her go."

"I don't think it's that she didn't care about you, Kenneth," I countered. "I just ... she's set in her ways. She doesn't like change."

"Well, I don't have a lot of time left," Kenneth said. "I can't spend it trying to change her ways, no matter how funny and beautiful I find her."

He was sweet. I had to give him that. "What about Patty? Had she been sick? Was she acting strange? Did she have any enemies?"

"She didn't have any enemies that I know about," Kenneth said. "She wasn't acting sick or anything either. She was a nice woman who played a mean hand of bridge. She didn't really join in with the other women here, though, and I don't think she liked most of them. I get that, though, because I don't like most of them either."

"I honestly didn't know her well," I admitted. "I saw her around town a few times, but I really never talked to her. Did she have family in the area?"

"She had a nephew, but I believe he lives down state."

"No siblings? An ex-husband?"

"The only things I know about Patty are what she told me, and it wasn't much," Kenneth said. "She didn't gossip much. That's all the other women here do. Look at them over there. That's what they're doing now, in fact."

I followed his gaze, internally cringing when I locked gazes with Mrs. Little. I had an unfortunate relationship with the woman. Up until a few months earlier she tolerated me and thought I was nothing more than Aunt Tillie's pesky niece. When a long-held secret between the two women surfaced, though, and the truth about Mrs. Little's infidelity and her late husband's murderous ways came out, she turned her back on me because I lambasted her for keeping the secret at Aunt Tillie's expense. We hadn't spoken since.

"This doesn't look good," Arthur said, shaking his head as Mrs. Little got to her feet and headed in my direction. She wasn't alone. Three of her cohorts – Myrtle Jensen, Fay Reynolds and Viola Hendricks – were right behind her, and they looked to be champing at the bit for a showdown. "You should probably run now, girl."

"They don't frighten me," I countered, and I mostly meant it. "I grew up with Aunt Tillie. She's a lot scarier than these women."

"Don't say I didn't warn you," Arthur said, shuffling the cards and keenly watching as Mrs. Little stopped next to me.

"Bay."

"Mrs. Little," I replied, forcing a smile. "It's good to see you. How are you today?"

"I'm fine," Mrs. Little replied, her tone cool. "Do you want to tell me what you're doing here?"

"I'm here to speak to Kenneth," I replied. "Do you want to tell me what you're doing here?" Something about her mannerisms turned me off. She always fancied herself above everyone else in the community, but after I learned she knew her husband was a murderer and let others suffer to protect him long after his death, I lost all respect for her.

"This is the senior center," Fay supplied.

"I read the sign on the door before I came in," I said.

"That means only senior citizens can hang out here," Viola said.

"Actually, this is a public building paid for with municipal funds and anyone can come in here," I said. "I know you ladies like to pretend you have a little fiefdom – and you think there's power associated with the board you enacted – but you really don't have power over anything."

"Perhaps we should call Chief Terry and ask him whether he thinks that's the case." Mrs. Little was haughty.

"I think that's a great idea," I said, nodding to encourage her. "Chief Terry is aware of the laws. He'll probably even have the patience to explain them to you."

Mrs. Little wrinkled her nose, her eyes flashing with annoyance. "You shouldn't be here, Bay. After what your aunt did ... ."

"Allegedly did," I corrected. "As far as I can tell, you're the one who thinks she's guilty and is going out of her way to point fingers. I think we both know that pointing fingers is a two-way street."

Mrs. Little stilled, her face unreadable. "What are you saying?"

"I'm simply saying that there's a lot of gossip in this town," I said, realizing I was stooping to a level I wasn't entirely comfortable with. Very few people in town knew the truth about Mrs. Little's husband. I was more than happy to change that should it become necessary. "You seem to like to spread it about my aunt. Perhaps I should spread it about you and see who comes out on top."

"That won't be necessary, Bay," Mrs. Little said hurriedly.

I couldn't help being a little smug. "I didn't think it would."

"What do you want to know?" Mrs. Little asked, putting on an air of irritation. I could tell she was nervous, and I enjoyed having power over her. I guess there's a little bit of Aunt Tillie in me after all.

"I want to know exactly what you saw the day before yesterday," I replied. "I want the truth, too. Embellishments are unnecessary and will only cause me to open my big mouth."

CHARMS & WITCHDEMEANORS

"What is she talking about, Margaret?" Fay asked, confused.

"It's nothing." Mrs. Little was resigned to her fate. "For the record, I'm the one who saw Tillie. She didn't come into the room. She hid by the coffee machine in that alcove by the door for a few minutes – I would say it was five at most – and then she left. I didn't think anything of it until Patty died, so if you think I'm working against your aunt, I'm not."

That was a lie and I knew it. "You called Chief Terry about Aunt Tillie being here before Patty's body was found," I pointed out. "We're talking a good twelve hours before. He was out looking for her at dinner the night before. Part of your story doesn't make sense."

Mrs. Little scowled. "I don't know what you want me to say."

"How about the truth," I suggested. "What possible reason would Aunt Tillie have for wanting to hurt Patty? From what I've witnessed over the years, the two of them barely knew one another."

"She did it because she was jealous of Patty's relationship with Kenneth," Mrs. Little said.

"As far as I can tell every woman in this place can claim a relationship with Kenneth," I countered, offering him a wan smile so he knew I wasn't angry about the development. "Why would Aunt Tillie single out Patty if she was jealous and wanted to secure Kenneth's affection for herself?"

"Maybe because she's crazy," Mrs. Little said.

"I'll be sure to tell her you said that." The veiled threat was out of my mouth before I could think better of it.

Mrs. Little blanched but remained silent.

"I don't think it was because of Kenneth," Myrtle said. She wore her completely white hair short. "I heard Tillie and Patty had an old grudge that went back thirty years or so. It had something to do with a piece of property adjacent to the one your family owns."

That was the first I'd heard about this. "I didn't know Patty owned property out by us."

"She never went out there because it was useless," Myrtle said, shaking her head. "Thirty years ago she sold it to a land developer and

87

now it's that empty parcel between you guys and the Mackenzie farm."

I racked my brain to picture the property she referred to. "Isn't that filled with a mucky bog?"

"Pretty much," Myrtle said. "That was only found when they tried to develop condos out there. That's what Tillie was upset about. She didn't want condos and she fought them tooth and nail. She lost at the zoning board level, but when the developers went out there they found the land couldn't be built on. They'd been out there the day before and it was fine, but when they went back to survey it after the zoning board win it was covered in water. It was all very mysterious."

That didn't sound at all mysterious to me. In fact, that sounded just like Aunt Tillie. That was a far cry from murder, though. "What happened after that?"

"The sale was negated because the buyer said Patty hid the water issues," Myrtle replied. "Apparently they hated each other after that."

"That's all well and good," I said. "That was thirty years ago, though. Why would Aunt Tillie kill her over it now?"

"Why does your aunt do anything?"

That was a fair question.

"She didn't kill her over the land," Fay argued, shaking her bottle-blond head. She fancied herself a fashion plate – those low-waisted teenager jeans never looked so out of place – and she was annoyed with her friend's story. "She killed her because she needed a secret place to perform one of her rituals."

I could see where this one was going long before it got there. "Why would Aunt Tillie kill Patty to use her house for a ritual when we have acres of land for her to use if she wanted to conduct a ritual?"

"Because this was a dark ritual," Fay whispered.

"Okay, I'll bite," I said. "What kind of dark ritual?"

"Tillie is close to dying," Fay explained. "She's old."

"So are you."

Fay ignored me. "I hear Tillie has to sacrifice a virgin to stay alive every year. Then she bathes in the blood. That's why she's still so active at her age."

I ran my tongue over my teeth as I decided how to answer. It was a ludicrous assertion, but Fay's head didn't spend a lot of time in reality. "Have you heard of any virgins being sacrificed?"

"She keeps it a secret," Fay said.

"Yes, but have you heard of any girls going missing?" I pressed.

"I ... she hides that," Fay said.

"Okay. I'm done with that story." I turned my attention to Viola. "What about you? Do you have any reason to think Aunt Tillie killed Patty?"

Viola shook her head, her gray hair – it was almost blue really – glinting under the harsh lighting.

"Great," I said, pushing myself up from the table. "It's been a real pleasure, ladies, but I must be going."

"Oh, well, there might be one reason," Viola offered, causing me to snap my head in her direction.

"And what's that?"

"She probably did it for the hidden money."

TEN

"What hidden money?"

Viola's face was blank. "You know ... the hidden money."

"I don't know about any hidden money," I pressed. "What do you know about hidden money?"

"I ... hmm." Viola lowered her eyes and stared at her feet.

I shifted my attention to Myrtle because I knew Faye was probably a lost cause and Mrs. Little was more likely to lie than help. "Do you know about any hidden money?"

"I completely forgot about that," Myrtle said, rubbing the back of her neck. "Until Viola brought it up I seriously forgot all about that story."

I was about at my wit's end. "What story?"

"It's not really a story," Myrtle clarified. "It's a rumor. Let me see if I remember how it goes." She tapped her chin and closed her eyes as I tugged on my limited patience and tried to refrain from blowing up. I knew that wouldn't get me anywhere. "Okay. I think I've got it."

"Great," I said, anticipation coursing through me. Now we were getting somewhere.

"Whoops. I think I lost it." Myrtle looked flustered.

"Good grief," Viola intoned, shaking her head. "I think you've lost more than the story, Myrtle. The problem is, there's not really a story. There's just a rumor."

"What's the rumor?" I asked.

"For years people have said Patty hid money on her property because she didn't trust banks," Viola supplied. "Her daddy was a bank robber. Everyone knows that."

I had no idea her father was a bank robber, but now wasn't the time to press that issue when I knew I could ask Chief Terry about it later.

"He went to prison when Patty was a teenager," Viola said, embracing the story. "He died in prison. They offered to release him close to the end if he told them where he hid the money, but he never did. People always believed he told Patty, though."

I was missing something. "So Patty's father robbed a bank and hid the money," I said. "Do we have any evidence Patty knew where the money was?"

"Just that she was going to lose her house about ten years ago and someone asked her if she was worried and she said that if it came down to it she had the means to save the house," Viola answered. "Everyone always assumed it was because she knew where the money was."

"What about the house? Did the bank move to foreclose?"

Viola shook her head. "No."

"Did Patty pay off the mortgage?"

"I don't know."

I mulled the story over. "That still doesn't give Aunt Tillie a motive," I said. "How can we be sure Aunt Tillie knew about the money?"

"Because she was heard saying she was going to curse a hundred gophers to dig through Patty's yard to find the money," Mrs. Little supplied, her expression smug. "Have you ever heard anything that ridiculous?"

Unfortunately, I had. Aunt Tillie always wanted to create an army of animals to do her bidding whenever she got riled up. The worst was when a local woman wanted to close the bar between Hemlock Cove and a neighboring town to cut down on all the rampant fornication. Those were her words, not mine. Personally, I don't care about rampant fornication. Well, unless I have to see it. I don't want to see it. Anyway, Aunt Tillie decided to curse a hundred rabbits to show up in the woman's yard and ... um ... do what rabbits do. We talked her out of that.

The best was when she wanted to curse a hundred dogs to chase my childhood nemesis Lila Stevens after a particularly brutal bullying incident. Aunt Tillie wanted them to hump her leg. In the end, she could muster the power to curse only two of them, but the outcome was hilarious – and the talk of the town for two straight weeks. Lila never did get that stain out of her favorite jeans.

"This was obviously before Aunt Tillie was banned from the senior center," I said.

"Tillie and Patty never liked one another, not even back then," Mrs. Little said. "Now you have multiple motives for your aunt to have killed Patty. What do you have to say to that?"

Unfortunately, I had absolutely nothing good to say.

I WAITED until I saw Landon and Noah walk into the deli in downtown Hemlock Cove at lunchtime before driving out to Patty's house. I felt guilty for the duplicity, but I didn't know what else to do. There was something important I hadn't tried yet, and I obviously couldn't do it in front of Noah.

Being a Winchester witch is a double-edged sword. There are many good things that come about from it, including an abundance of tasty food and love. There are also a few bad things, and one of those is my ability to see and talk to ghosts.

When I was a kid people thought I was strange and walked around talking to myself. That got really bad when I was a teenager, and it was one of the reasons I was so desperate to move away from town when I graduated from college.

It took distance and maturity to realize that I didn't care what people thought. Okay, I still care a little. In truth, though, the only thing I really care about is being true to myself. If Patty Grimes' death was traumatic, there was a chance her ghost remained behind. If it did, I could talk to her and find out who killed her. I couldn't use her statement as proof, but I could pick a direction and discover other evidence to clear Aunt Tillie.

I opted not to park in front of the house, instead pulling into a small clearing off the side of the road. It was farther up from Patty's driveway, so hopefully Landon wouldn't see my car if he returned early. My plan was to get in and out.

Another thing you should know about the Winchesters is that our plans never go smoothly.

I hurried up the driveway, knowing I had only a limited time to search for Patty's spirit should Landon and Noah return. I considered texting Landon to ask, but I didn't want a record of that conversation on his phone so I let it go. I was lost in my head, the gossip from the senior center filling me with myriad ideas, so I was almost to the front porch before I realized I wasn't alone.

There she was. I recognized her even before she turned around. Aunt Tillie's eyes flashed when she saw me, and I realized her hand was on the door handle and she was muttering a spell to unlock it.

"What are you doing?" I asked, rushing forward. "Are you crazy? Your handprint will be on the door handle."

"They already dusted for fingerprints, nimrod," Aunt Tillie replied, furrowing her brow. "What are you doing here?"

"I'm looking for Patty's ghost."

"That's what I'm doing here, too," Aunt Tillie replied. "Now ... shut up for a second."

I opened my mouth to argue, what I'm sure would've been a reasonable request to stop on the tip of my tongue, but it was already too late because the door popped open. Aunt Tillie looked pleased with herself.

"It's like riding a bike," she said.

"Sometimes I think you're addled," I said, shaking my head. "You can't get caught out here, Aunt Tillie. If someone sees you, how will you explain it?"

"How will you explain being out here?" Aunt Tillie challenged.

I'd already given this some thought. "I'm going to say I was looking for Landon."

"Uh-huh." Aunt Tillie didn't look convinced. "Where is your car?"

"It's ... hidden by some trees up the road," I said.

"And how will you explain that?"

Crap. I hate it when she's right. "How did you even get out here? Where is your car?"

"I walked."

I narrowed my eyes. I didn't believe that for a second. "It's ten miles."

"I'm in excellent shape," Aunt Tillie said. "I could be the world's oldest Olympian."

"You could be the world's greatest liar is what you could be," I said, rolling my neck until it cracked. "Well, come on." I shooed her with my hands. "We don't have a lot of time and we can't waste it arguing."

"I knew you would see my side of things," Aunt Tillie said, grinning as she walked inside the house. "I think we're going to make excellent roommates."

She was unbelievable sometimes. I scanned the small living room, frowning when I realized how rundown it was. I understood Patty not being able to keep up on the cleaning at her age, but if the rumors of hidden money were true, why didn't she hire a maid?

"Be careful not to move anything because Landon and Noah might notice," I ordered, moving toward the kitchen. "We can't risk putting Landon on the spot in case he discovers us."

"Oh, cry me a river," Aunt Tillie said. "Landon won't turn on us. He's loyal."

"I'm not worried about Landon," I said. "If he had his way, I would've come out here with him and there would be no reason to hide. I'm worried about his partner."

"Oh, yeah, Agent Gives-me-a-migraine," Aunt Tillie said. "He's a real piece of work, isn't he?"

"It's funny. I was thinking the same thing about you."

"You're in a mood," Aunt Tillie said, opening the drawer of a desk and looking inside. "What crawled up your butt and died?"

"You!"

"I'm pretty sure I've been otherwise engaged this morning," Aunt Tillie said, unruffled. "Where have you been?"

"I went to the senior center," I answered. "I ran into Kenneth."

"And how is he?"

I watched Aunt Tillie a moment, hoping for signs of ... something. I'm not sure what I wanted her to say, or how I wanted her to react, but some recognition or reaction would've been warranted. I got absolutely nothing. "He's upset about Patty's death. He's also pining for you but says you were mean to him and he can't wait any longer."

"Well, if you want to earn the good things in life, you have to work for them."

"Yes, but you didn't offer any work in that relationship and look where it got you," I pointed out. "You're the only suspect in a murder, and while I initially thought you didn't have a motive, you seem to have, like, four of them."

Aunt Tillie stilled. "What motive?"

"Well, first there's Kenneth," I said, not missing a beat as I looked through a cupboard while keeping one eye on Aunt Tillie through the open doorway between rooms. We were close enough to easily hear one another. "You say you don't care who he dates but I'm not sure that's true. That's neither here nor there, though. Kenneth is apparently wooing every senior citizen at the center, so killing Patty for Kenneth makes no sense."

"You're telling me."

She's so frustrating sometimes I want to choke her into submission. Instead I hopped to one of the other stories. "Then I heard an earful about that mucky parcel of land next to The Overlook property," I said. "I heard that Patty owned it and tried to sell it for condominiums. You apparently hated the idea and when you lost at the zoning board the land magically sprang a leak and it became unbuildable."

"That's a damnable shame, isn't it?" Aunt Tillie actually looked upset by the development, but I knew better.

"Then there's the theory that you wanted this house to sacrifice virgins to stay alive."

Aunt Tillie snickered. "Please tell me you don't believe that."

"I don't. That doesn't mean a wild story can't do damage right now. Agent Glenn looks to be ready to believe just about anything where you're concerned."

"That's because he's a moron," Aunt Tillie said. "Did you hear anything else at the senior center?"

"Just one story," I said, turning fully so I could watch Aunt Tillie closely when I delivered my gossipy tidbit. "I heard Patty was rumored to have hidden money from a long ago bank robbery, and you supposedly knew about it."

"Hmm. I can't recall that."

She was lying. I could feel it. "I heard you were going to curse a rabble of mutant gophers to dig for it."

"The people in this town have outrageous imaginations."

"Aunt Tillie!" I exploded. I couldn't help myself.

Aunt Tillie jerked her head in my direction and scowled. "There's no reason to scream, Bay. I can hear you."

I wasn't sure that was true. "Is there money buried out here?"

"If there was, it's long gone," Aunt Tillie replied, wrinkling her nose. "I can promise you that the story you heard is not the entire story. There is no money out here. It was gone … long ago."

That didn't make me feel better. I decided to put all of my cards on the table. "You didn't kill Patty, did you?"

"Of course not!" This time when Aunt Tillie appeared affronted, I believed her. "How can you possibly think that about me?"

"I don't," I replied. "It's just … you're all over the place. You're covering your tracks. You pretend you're not worried, and yet you're out here searching for evidence to clear yourself. Something is going on that you're not telling me. I want to know what it is."

"The world doesn't revolve around you, Bay," Aunt Tillie said. "I'm sorry, but this is … none of your business."

"At least tell me what you were doing at the senior center the other day," I pressed, refusing to give up. "Were you there to see Kenneth?"

"Hardly."

"Were you there to mess with someone else?"

"Not really."

Her curt answers were about to push me over the edge. "Were you there to poison the coffee?"

"No."

"I just ... I don't know what to do with you," I complained, turning back to my task and jumping when I saw Patty's ghostly visage staring at me from the middle of the kitchen island. "Holy crap on a cracker!"

"What's wrong?" Aunt Tillie asked, scurrying into the room and pulling up short when her eyes landed on Patty. "There you are, you bitch!"

I froze, dumbfounded. Aunt Tillie wasn't known for her tact, but that was one of the worst greetings directed toward a dead person I'd ever heard. "Aunt Tillie! You can't talk to her like that. She's probably traumatized and frightened."

"You," Patty hissed, narrowing her eyes when she caught sight of Aunt Tillie. "What are you doing in my house?"

"I'm looking for you," Aunt Tillie answered. "I need answers. What happened to you?"

"Why do you even care?" Patty asked. "We both know why you're really here."

"I don't know why she's really here," I offered. "I would love to hear your side of it, though."

Patty ignored me. "Get out of my house, Tillie!"

"Make me, Patty!"

I hadn't seen Aunt Tillie this riled up since she found out the nearest McDonald's wasn't bringing back the McRib as a Christmas treat. "Aunt Tillie ... ."

"Shut up, Bay," Aunt Tillie snapped. "You're not a part of this. In fact ... get out."

"You get out," I argued. "I need to find answers and Patty is my best shot."

"What answers?" Patty asked, her fury evident as her ethereal eyes flashed. "The answer is standing right there."

"Where?"

Patty pointed at Aunt Tillie. "There!"

My heart rolled at the insinuation. "Wait ... are you saying Aunt Tillie killed you?"

"Who else?"

"I don't understand," I said, my anger deflating as my worry ramped up a notch. "Did Aunt Tillie poison you?"

"Get out, Bay," Aunt Tillie screeched. "I don't even know what you're doing here."

"I am kind of curious what both of you are doing here."

I froze when I heard the new voice, my shoulders stiffening as I swiveled to face the front door of the house. My heart sank when I caught sight of Landon's face. He looked frustrated ... and terrified.

Noah, on the other hand, looked as if he'd just discovered the Titanic and it was full of gold and he was the sole claimant.

"I think we need to have a talk," Noah said.

"Well, crud," Aunt Tillie said, frowning. "This is all your fault, Bay. I hope you realize that."

I didn't have the energy to argue. "I'm sure it is."

ELEVEN

"Bay."

Landon looked almost tortured when I locked gazes with him.

"I'm sorry," I offered, the two words feeling exceedingly lame.

"Don't talk to Agent Michaels, Miss Winchester," Noah said. "I'm in charge of this case and I'm just dying to know what you're doing here. Talk to me."

"I'm … um … ." I licked my lips as my mind went blank.

"We were out for a walk and we got lost," Aunt Tillie answered for me, her demeanor calm and collected. "It's very hot and we thought we were going to die of thirst so we knocked on the door. No one answered and the door was open, so we let ourselves in to get a drink."

"Do you really expect me to believe that?" Noah asked.

"I have no idea," Aunt Tillie replied. "I can only tell you the truth. I'm an old lady. The heat affects me something fierce. In fact … oh my. I'm seeing spots." Aunt Tillie pressed her hand to her forehead and made a show of swaying back and forth.

"Ms. Winchester, I'm sure you understand that you and your great-niece breaking into a murder victim's house is suspect," Noah said. "You're going to have to come up with a better explanation than that."

"I had no idea this was a murder victim's home," Aunt Tillie said her eyes going wide. "Who died?"

I wanted a hole to open beneath the floorboards and swallow me.

Noah exchanged a look with Landon. He didn't believe us, yet Aunt Tillie has a way of bending people's minds. They can't reconcile their suspicions with the sweet old lady they see before them. Granted, that talent lasts only until someone spends a few hours with her, but it comes in handy sometimes.

"Patty Grimes died," Noah said. "You know that because you're a person of interest in her death."

"Patty Grimes died here?" Aunt Tillie asked. I wanted to give her an Oscar – and a swift kick in the rear end. "Why did she die here? I thought she died in her home."

"This is her home," Noah said, knitting his eyebrows. "You know that."

"No, this Sally Osterman's house," Aunt Tillie countered. "I came here three days ago and visited Sally. We sat on that very couch and had tea and crumpets."

That was probably laying it on a little too thick.

"Who is Sally Osterman?" Noah asked Landon, earning a shrug. For his part, my boyfriend could do nothing but watch the show with dumbfounded interest. Noah turned to me. "Who is Sally Osterman?"

I made up a lie on the spot. "She was Aunt Tillie's childhood friend," I said, shaking my head. "She died in a tragic accident. She was … hit by a train. Aunt Tillie still … sees her … sometimes." That sounded believable, right?

"She didn't see her here," Noah argued. "This is Patty Grimes' house. I'm sure you had to know that, didn't you?"

"I can't possibly know where everyone in Hemlock Cove resides," I replied. "I honestly wasn't paying attention because we came in through the woods on the other side of the house. Aunt Tillie was having a spell and … well … I was terrified. She needed water."

"This is unbelievable," Patty muttered as I worked overtime to pretend she wasn't in the room with us. "There's no way they'll believe this."

"So you're saying you accidentally happened upon this house and due to the heat walked through an open door – which I know darned well I locked – and were just getting a glass of water when we walked in?" Noah pressed.

I nodded, hoping my expression made me look innocent and harried instead of frustrated and guilty. "It's just one of those strange things. I have no idea what else to say."

Noah rubbed the back of his neck as he turned to Landon. "Can you believe this?"

"I ... don't know," Landon said finally. "Aunt Tillie does look a little worse for wear. Perhaps we should take her to the hospital to have her checked out. You know, to be on the safe side."

"That sounds like a great idea," Aunt Tillie said. "We can take Sally with us."

"There is no Sally," Noah snapped.

"Don't yell at her," I ordered. "Sally is very real to Aunt Tillie. You should be sympathetic to her emotional needs. She's ... elderly." I figured if I was going down I might as well go for broke. Really, what did we have to lose at this point?

"I am elderly," Aunt Tillie agreed. She almost sounded pathetic. "Oh, Sally. Where are you?"

"If I could still throw up, this is where I would do it," Patty said.

"Well, I just ... don't even know what to think about this," Noah said. "What do you think we should do, Landon?"

"I think we should give them a stern warning and send them on their way," Landon said, his face unreadable. "You can't arrest an old lady for trying to stop herself from getting heatstroke."

I could tell the "old lady" comment grated on Aunt Tillie, but to her credit she held it together.

"I'm not going to do that," Noah said, reaching to his belt and removing a set of handcuffs. "I'm arresting both of you for trespassing and taking you to the station."

AMANDA M. LEE

"No, you're not," Landon growled, turning swiftly. "You're not taking them into custody."

"Step aside, Agent Michaels," Noah warned. "I don't want to have to report you. We both know what that could mean for your career."

The words had a chilling effect on me and I immediately stepped forward and held my hands out. "Take us in. You don't have to report him."

"Hey!" Aunt Tillie scorched me with a death glare. "I don't want to go to jail. I can guarantee Sally won't be there."

"Shut up," I hissed. "Do as you're told." If Landon lost his job because of me – even if he only received a reprimand – I would never forgive myself. "Take us in."

"That's not going to happen," Landon countered. "Bay … just … don't do this."

"Agent Michaels, will you please put the cuffs on Miss Winchester?" Noah prodded. "If you don't … ."

He didn't have to finish the sentence. I stepped in front of Landon and held my arms out, fighting off tears as I fixed him with a pleading look. "Do it."

"No."

"You have to."

"I can't," Landon gritted out. "I won't put you in cuffs."

"Then put me in cuffs," Aunt Tillie said, stepping in front of me. "Sally says it's okay. Everything will work out. Have faith."

Landon studied her for a moment. "I can put cuffs on you," he said finally, grabbing his set from his belt. "Don't cut off her circulation," he ordered Noah as the man moved to me and started reading me my rights.

When he was done, Landon and Noah led us out to their vehicle. Landon was careful as he put Aunt Tillie in the back seat of the sedan, and then he crossed to the other side of the vehicle and nudged Noah out of the way with his hip so he could make sure I was settled.

"It's going to be okay," he whispered, pressing a quick kiss to my forehead. "We'll figure it out."

"Don't worry," Aunt Tillie said, the smile tugging at the corners of her mouth reflecting malice. "There's no way Terry will put us in a cell."

"I wouldn't bet on that," Noah said, hopping into the passenger seat. "He won't have a choice."

"We'll see about that," Aunt Tillie said, smug. "You don't know everything, Agent Gag Me."

For once I wished I had a little bit of her faith. I had no idea how we were going to get out of this.

"**ABSOLUTELY** NOT!" Chief Terry roared twenty minutes later, slamming his hands down on his desk. "You get her out of those cuffs right this second!"

Noah was taken aback. "But ... ."

"Now!"

"Thank you," Aunt Tillie said, sighing. "I need to sit down. My poor weary legs."

"Not you," Chief Terry said, making a face. "I was talking about Bay."

I pressed my lips together to keep from laughing at the murderous look on Aunt Tillie's face. The situation was not funny, yet Noah's reaction to Chief Terry was one of the most hysterical things I'd ever seen. Huh. Maybe the heat really was getting to me.

Noah obediently uncuffed my hands and I took the opportunity to rub my sore wrists. Landon ignored Noah's disgusted look and grabbed my arm, frowning when he saw the red marks on my skin.

"I told you not to cut off her circulation," Landon snapped.

"I didn't," Noah protested. "I just ... ."

"Shut up," Chief Terry barked. "No one is talking to you, Agent Glenn. Sit in that chair and shut your mouth."

It was obvious from the way Noah threw himself into one of the chairs that he wasn't pleased with the dressing down. I swear he almost looked as if he was about to cry.

"Bay, tell me what happened," Chief Terry instructed.

Uh-oh. I trusted Chief Terry with my life, but when he heard the

Sally story he would know it was a lie. "Well ... um ... we were out for a walk," I explained. "It was very hot, and Aunt Tillie got confused. She thought she saw an old friend ... ."

"Sally Osterman," Aunt Tillie supplied. "She's dead, but I still see her sometimes."

Chief Terry narrowed his eyes. "Okay."

"We came up to the back side of a house we didn't recognize and went up to the front door," I said. "No one answered when we knocked, and when we tried the handle – which we had to do because I was afraid Aunt Tillie would pass out and die – it opened. We were just looking for a drink of water ... and that's when Landon and Agent Glenn came in."

"Is that not the biggest pile of horse manure you've ever heard?" Noah asked.

"I believe them," Chief Terry said. "Let them go."

"They broke into a crime scene," Noah argued. "You can't let them go."

"I can do whatever I want," Chief Terry shot back. "How do you know they broke in?"

"Because I locked the door myself."

"Uh-huh. Did the door show signs of tampering?" Chief Terry asked.

Landon stuck his tongue in his cheek and the look he shot me was one of triumph. "No, it did not," he answered. "We checked on our way out. We made note that the door was not tampered with, even though Agent Glenn was convinced he locked it upon our departure for lunch."

"So how did they break in, Agent Glenn?" Chief Terry asked, lifting a challenging eyebrow.

"Perhaps they had a key."

"Did you search them?"

"Yes," Noah replied. "I didn't find anything, but ... ."

"So you have no proof," Chief Terry said, cutting him off. "You want to put an elderly woman in jail on one of the hottest days of the year without proof? Is that what you're saying?"

"No," Noah protested. "A suspect broke into the victim's house."

"She's not a suspect, though," Chief Terry countered. "She's a person of interest, and she clearly looks as if she's seen better days. I mean ... look at her."

Aunt Tillie frowned. "Don't push it."

Chief Terry ignored her. "Should this young woman have ignored her great-aunt's medical needs and let her die in the woods? Is that what you're saying, Agent Glenn?"

"Of course not," Noah replied, flustered. "You can't let them go, though."

"Oh, it's already done," Chief Terry said. "I invited you in on Patty Grimes' murder. I did not invite you in on a simple breaking and entering that could cause a media firestorm for elderly abuse. That's still under my purview."

"But ... I need to call my boss." Noah was floundering. He sounded as if he was whining.

"I'll handle that call," Chief Terry said. "Landon, uncuff Tillie. I think Bay should take her to the hospital to get her checked out."

"I think that's a great idea," Landon said, pulling his handcuff key out of his pocket and shuffling over to Aunt Tillie. "They should probably poke her with a few needles to be on the safe side."

"You're ticking me off," Aunt Tillie warned.

"Join the club," Landon shot back.

Once she was free Aunt Tillie moved closer to me. "We need to go ... to the hospital."

As relieved as I was that our arrest was brief – and wouldn't appear on our records – I was still irritated with her. "I think you should thank Chief Terry and Landon for understanding your feeble mind and taking your fragile mental state into account."

"Do you want me to curse you?" Aunt Tillie asked.

"Bacon," Landon coughed into his hand as he stared at the ceiling.

"Thank them," I prodded.

"Fine!" Aunt Tillie turned to face Landon and Chief Terry, and I could tell it took every ounce of strength she had to keep pretending. "I apologize for being feeble ... ."

"And mentally fragile," I added.

"And mentally fragile," Aunt Tillie gritted out. "You're true patrons of this great community of ours. Sally salutes you."

"I'm going to salute Sally later," Landon said, pointing toward the door. "Take her to get checked out, Bay."

I nodded. "I'll do it right now."

Landon grabbed my arm before I could exit the office and lowered his voice so only I could hear. "You and I are going to blow the roof off later, and not in a fun way," he warned. "Prepare yourself for a big fight."

"I … I'm so sorry."

"Go," Landon said, my heart squeezing a bit when he didn't offer me a reassuring kiss or hug.

"I'm really sorry."

Landon was firm. "Go, Bay. Consider yourselves warned … and lucky."

TWELVE

"This is all your fault!"

I held my temper in check until Aunt Tillie and I were safely inside Hypnotic, and then I completely lost it.

"I cannot believe what just happened," I railed. "I just ... you're unbelievable. Here I am trying to help you and how do you repay me?"

Aunt Tillie was blasé as she settled on the couch and turned her attention to a surprised Thistle. "I'm thirsty and I want some iced tea."

"Good for you," Thistle replied, shifting her eyes to me. "What happened?"

I told her about my afternoon, leaving nothing out, including my stop at the senior center. By the time I got to the part about breaking into Patty Grimes' house, Thistle was stunned. When I got to the part about Sally, she couldn't stop herself from breaking out in hysterical laughter.

"This is not funny!" I screeched. "How can you think this is funny?"

"I can't help it," Thistle said, wiping a tear from the corner of her eye. "I just ... how did that story work?"

I shrugged, frustrated. "It worked because Landon and Chief Terry were determined to make it work," I replied. "We could've told them a herd of elephants chased us into the house and they would've found a way to let us out of there."

"I think I was brilliant," Aunt Tillie said. "I was so brilliant, in fact, I deserve some iced tea."

"You know where the Keurig is," Thistle said. "Make it yourself."

"I'm tired. The heat is bothering me."

"Then sit there and suffer," Thistle said. "I'm talking to Bay. She's the one who is upset."

"Needlessly so, if you ask me," Aunt Tillie said, shifting on the couch so she could rest her head on one end and stretch out. "Get me some iced tea."

"Oh, stuff it," Thistle said, fixing me with a sympathetic look. "How did you end things with Landon?"

What did she mean by that? "End things? I ... what ... how ... do you think that's what he's going to do?" My heart dropped.

"No, I think you're panicking about him doing that, though," Thistle said, grabbing my arm and jerking me toward the chair in the center of the room. "Sit down. I'll make you a glass of iced tea. We have that Twinings stuff you like. You need to chill out."

"I'll take some tea," Aunt Tillie said.

"I'm not getting you squat," Thistle said, moving behind the counter. "You're perfectly capable of getting your own tea. While you're doing it, you can explain why you and Patty were screeching at each other like that."

"Ugh! What is it with you two?" Aunt Tillie asked, fanning her face and acting as if she was dying of heat exhaustion despite the air conditioning in the store. "If Clove were here, she'd get me some iced tea."

"Well, Clove has the day off so she can get settled at the Dandridge, so I guess you're fresh out unless you want to go out there," Thistle shot back.

"I can't go out there," Aunt Tillie grumbled. "My car is parked in the woods by Patty's house. You're going to have to give us a ride out there, by the way, because Bay's car is there, too."

"Well, great," Thistle said. "That sounds like a delightful way to spend an afternoon."

"You're my least favorite most of the time," Aunt Tillie said. "You know that, right?"

"I'm having a trophy made up and everything," Thistle said, bringing me a cup of iced tea and patting my shoulder. "Drink that and take a breath, Bay. You're overreacting."

Was I? It didn't feel like I was overreacting. "You didn't see Landon's face."

"I've seen Landon make a lot of faces, and some of them are downright ornery," Thistle said. "There's no reason to freak out. I didn't believe Landon was going to break up with you when I asked the question. I didn't mean 'end things' like you thought I meant it."

"How did you mean it?"

"What was the last thing he said to you?"

"Pretty much that we were going to have a big fight and I should consider myself lucky," I said. "He was so … angry."

"Oh, good grief," Aunt Tillie said, grabbing one of the couch pillows and tossing it in my direction. "Smother yourself with that and shut up."

Thistle deflected the pillow and shot Aunt Tillie a withering look. "You're not helping."

"I'm the one who got us out of that mess," Aunt Tillie countered. "I came up with the great invisible Sally story. Who else could've done that?"

"Chief Terry didn't step in and cut you loose because of the Sally story," Thistle said. "He stepped in because he adores Bay and would never let her spend a night in jail."

"He did that one time he caught us drinking down by the lake when we were teenagers," I reminded her.

"Yeah, and he slept on the bench to make sure we were okay while he taught us a lesson," Thistle said. "I know you can't keep yourself from worrying about Landon, but this isn't a big deal. He's not going to break up with you. He loves you."

"He does love you," Aunt Tillie said, sitting up. "Give me your iced tea."

I ignored her. "He refused to cuff me," I said. "Noah told him to do it and Landon said he couldn't. Then Aunt Tillie stepped forward and ordered him to cuff her."

"Which he gladly did," Aunt Tillie said. "My feelings are hurt by his cold-hearted nature."

"Oh, you're so full of crap you're floating in the sewage tank," Thistle said. "You stepped up because you knew Landon was wrecked over having to cuff Bay. You tried to ease his burden. You're not fooling anybody."

"Don't I deserve some iced tea for my selfless gesture?"

Thistle stared Aunt Tillie down. It was a war of silent glares for a moment, and then Thistle finally gave in. "Fine. I'll make you some iced tea. I want you to know I'm only doing this to shut you up."

"I want a cookie, too."

"Don't push it, old lady," Thistle warned, returning to the counter. "Bay, you can't work yourself into a lather."

"Landon told me to go," I said. "He didn't hug me … or kiss me … he just told me to get out."

"Oh, puh-leez," Aunt Tillie said, making a face that would've been comical under different circumstances. "He practically ran around the car after he put me in the back and he nudged Agent Golly Gee out of the way so he could make sure you were comfortable and he kissed you on the forehead and told you everything was going to be okay. What else do you want?"

"I want to go back in time and not put him in an awful position," I replied.

"Well, I haven't figured out how to travel through time yet," Aunt Tillie said. "Maybe I can carve out a window for that discovery tomorrow."

"He could get in trouble for this if Agent Glenn reports him," I said. "He could lose his job."

"He's not going to lose his job," Aunt Tillie said. "Criminy. How I long for the days of Clove being a kvetch. When you do it, I want to smack you silly. At least she's cute when she whines."

"You're a true joy and a loving person," Thistle deadpanned as she handed Aunt Tillie her glass of iced tea. "Now drink that and shut up." She shoved Aunt Tillie's feet away from the end of the couch so she could sit and focus on me. "Bay, Landon loves you. It's going to be okay."

"He does love you, Bay," Aunt Tillie said, adopting a serious tone. "He's just angry. He'll yell. You'll make up. Your mother will give him a plate of bacon. Everything will be fine."

I wanted to believe her, but my heart hurt too much to give in to the temptation. "What if it's not?"

"Well, I think you're about to find out," Aunt Tillie said, gesturing toward the door. "Here he comes ... and he doesn't look happy."

I jolted when the front door of Hypnotic flew open and the sight of Landon in the doorway – something that would usually fill me with pleasure – sent a chill down my spine. "Hi."

"Hi?" Landon stalked toward the center of the room, his face red. "Is that all you have to say to me?"

"I ... ." I had no idea what to say.

"What were you doing at the house?" Landon asked. "How could you be so stupid as to take Aunt Tillie there?"

"Hey," Aunt Tillie snapped, extending a warning finger. "She didn't take me out there. I went on my own and watched in the woods until you left for lunch. She showed up when I was breaking into the house and tried to stop me. It didn't work."

"Oh," Landon said, marginally relaxing. "I thought you two went out there together."

"No," I said. "I went out looking for Patty's ghost. I was going to text and tell you I was out there, but I didn't want a record on your phone."

"That was probably smart," Landon said. "Why didn't you call me so I could stall Noah?"

"I didn't want them listening to the call."

"Who is them?" Landon asked cocking an eyebrow.

"The FBI."

"Bay, they don't do that," Landon said. "You could've placed a thirty-second call. There would've been nothing out of the ordinary about my girlfriend calling me to give me a quick update on her day."

"I didn't realize that."

"Uh-huh." Landon narrowed his eyes as he regarded Aunt Tillie. "How about you? Why were you out there?"

"I wanted to talk to Patty, too," Aunt Tillie said. "You ruined that by showing up early. Who eats lunch in thirty minutes?"

"People who have a lot of work to get through," Landon replied. "I just ... what were you thinking? I can't believe you told that Sally story. I can't believe Noah almost believed it. I can't believe you got caught."

"I'm sorry," I said, helplessness washing over me. "It wasn't planned. I heard some things at the senior center and I wanted to see whether Patty could confirm them."

"Did she?"

"We didn't get a chance to talk to her," I said. "You guys showed up too quickly. I'm ... sorry."

"You keep saying that, Bay, but I'm pretty sure you don't mean it," Landon said. "Do you have any idea how much trouble you could've caused today?"

"I'm sorry you could get in trouble for what I did," I offered. "I'll call your boss and tell him it was my fault."

"Don't even think about it," Landon said. "Stay away from my boss. Chief Terry already talked to him and smoothed things over. Things are fine on that front."

"How did Agent Gullible handle that?" Aunt Tillie asked. "I'll bet he was furious."

"Pouty is more like it," Landon said. "He's collecting himself across the street right now. I have only a few minutes."

"What are you going to do now?" I asked.

"Now we go back to investigating and doing what we were doing before you got put in cuffs, Bay," Landon snapped. "Do you have any idea how much that gutted me?"

CHARMS & WITCHDEMEANORS

"I ... ."

"Don't say you're sorry again," Landon said. "I can't take it."

"Don't yell at her," Aunt Tillie shouted. "She's already a mess and thinks you're going to break up with her over this. She's upset. She was trying to do a good thing and help me. No one needs your attitude ... or screaming."

Landon opened his mouth to say something, what I'm certain would've been a hateful retort on his lips. Instead he shifted his eyes to me. "I'm really angry, Bay."

I shrank down in my chair. "I know."

"We're not done fighting. Heck, we're nowhere near done fighting."

"I know."

"I need to hear what happened at the senior center and the real story of what went down at Patty's house, but I don't have time because I have to deal with my pitiful partner," Landon said. "I can't stay here and hash this out with you."

My stomach twisted. "I know."

"Bay, look at me," Landon ordered.

I forced my eyes to his, two sets of blue – one furious, one fearful – collided.

"We're going to have another huge fight," Landon said. "Actually, it's going to be a continuation of this fight. I need you to realize that I still love you, though. I need you to understand – and not do that freaking out thing you do when we fight. I'm not leaving. I'm sick of saying it, but it's true."

"I ... ."

"No!" Landon shook his head to cut me off. "Don't freak out. A fight is not a breakup. People fight. That doesn't mean they don't love each other."

"I ... ."

"I'm not finished," Landon said. "Nothing you do is going to stop me from loving you. Nothing you do – no matter how sad and pathetic you look – is going to stop us from fighting either."

I nodded, resigned.

AMANDA M. LEE

"Suck it up, Bay," Landon said. "You screwed up today and you know it. We worked it out, though. We're always going to work it out."

"Okay," I said, pressing the heel of my hand to my forehead.

Landon moved to my side and grabbed my chin, his eyes softening. "It's going to be okay. I really have to go, though."

"Will you be at dinner tonight?"

"Yes."

"I guess I'll see you there," I said, forcing a wan smile for his benefit.

"You will," Landon confirmed. "Now you need to leave and get your cars away from Patty Grimes' house. I know they're out there somewhere. I can only give you twenty minutes, so hurry."

"Okay."

Landon grabbed my face and pressed a quick kiss to my forehead. "We're still going to fight."

"I know."

"Then we're going to make up," Landon said, moving toward the door. "I haven't decided how yet, but somehow it'll involve bacon."

I watched him leave, exhaling heavily as I glanced at Thistle. "I feel a little better now."

Thistle smirked. "He's got something about him that I can't help but like even when he's raving like a lunatic."

"I think he's wound a little tight," Aunt Tillie said.

"Shut up," Thistle said, shaking her head. "We need to get moving so we can get your cars. The last thing we need is to get caught out there a second time."

"That would be bad," I agreed, bobbing my head.

"Oh, chill out," Aunt Tillie said. "We'll just say Sally made us do it. I can't believe we didn't think of an imaginary person to blame all of our misdeeds on before. This is going to be great moving forward."

"You make me tired," I said.

"That's the heatstroke," Aunt Tillie said. "Now ... who wants to get me an ice cream cone before we go?"

THIRTEEN

After returning from picking up our vehicles, I headed for the guesthouse to shower and think. Landon had a right to be angry. I knew that. I couldn't ignore the agitation rolling through me, though.

I spent the afternoon working from home, putting together an article on Patty's death that skirted Aunt Tillie's potential involvement and sending all of this week's items to the page designer. Then, with nothing better to do and an upset stomach, I took what was supposed to be a short nap. I had only twenty minutes to get ready for dinner when I woke, and by the time I scurried to the inn I was frazzled and my makeup was smudged.

Aunt Tillie sat on the couch in the family's living quarters as I entered, her gaze trained on *Jeopardy* as she shouted myriad wrong answers while colorfully referring to the contestants as "idiots" and "morons." Guests weren't allowed to pass beyond the dining room, and the only way to enter the private residence area was through a separate door or the kitchen. She glanced at me when I wandered inside, snorting when she saw my rushed efforts to look presentable.

"You look terrible."

"Thank you, Aunt Tillie," I said dryly. "You look … pleased with yourself." I couldn't help but be agitated with her. I had no idea whether I would've been caught had she not made a scene and distracted me, but I was too annoyed to believe anything else.

"I'm always pleased with myself, Bay," Aunt Tillie said. "That's what happens when you don't worry about what others think and focus only on yourself. You should try it one day. You might find it liberating."

Was she actually giving me a lecture? "Have you told Mom what happened?"

"I didn't see the need," Aunt Tillie said. "I wasn't charged with anything. There's no point in upsetting her."

"You mean you don't want her to yell at you."

"I mean I don't care what anyone says," Aunt Tillie said, smiling at the empty spot on the couch next to her. "Isn't that right, Sally?"

I groaned. "You cannot possibly be considering keeping up the Sally ruse."

"Hey, Agent Cry Me a River is in there and he's going to be watching us," Aunt Tillie said. "I don't really have a choice but to keep it up, do I?"

I opened my mouth to argue and then snapped it shut. She had a point. Darn it! "Do whatever you want," I said, refusing to let go of my petulance. "I'm going to check on everyone and see how they're doing before dinner."

"Oh, you're so full of it," Aunt Tillie muttered. "You're going to spy on Landon to see if he's still ticked off. Then you're going to consider crying because you can't stand it when he's angry with you. Just … suck it up, whine box. He'll get over it."

"I am not going to spy on him." I was totally going to spy on him. The fact that she knew that, though, irritated me beyond belief. "I'm going to spend quality time with my mother."

"And spy through the door to gauge Landon's mood," Aunt Tillie added. "We both know you're going to do it. I have no idea why you deny it. If the look is on purpose, though, good job. You look just pathetic enough for him to give in."

Well, that was just about all that I could take. I should've left things alone, but my immaturity was taking cues from my insecurity and ramping up. "You know you would suck if you ever made it on *Jeopardy*, right?"

"You know you might want to wipe your nose because the snot is actually visible, right?"

I frowned, determined not to let her think she got to me. I stared her down for a moment, willing her to look in my direction. She remained fixated on the television, and I finally gave up and stalked toward the kitchen. I waited until I was close to the door before surreptitiously wiping my nose. Hah! I knew nothing was there.

"I saw that," Aunt Tillie said.

I ignored her and strolled into the kitchen, pasting a bright smile on my face for my mother's benefit. "How is everyone?"

"What happened to you?" Marnie asked, wrinkling her nose. "Are you sick?"

The question didn't bode well for my plan to sucker Landon into forgiving me with my cuteness. "I worked from home this afternoon and I fell asleep."

"Well, you should've looked in a mirror before coming up here," Mom said, her expression thoughtful. "You look pale. Are you sure you're not sick?"

"I'm fine," I said, making a disgusted sound as I batted her hand away when she reached for my forehead to check my temperature, and moved toward the swinging door that separated the kitchen from the dining room. "Has anyone seen Landon? Is he back?"

"He's out there," Mom said. "He has his little friend with him. They've been talking shop in front of the guests. I don't like it. Make him stop."

"How am I supposed to make him stop?"

"Do whatever it is you do that makes his eyes sparkle and has him chasing you out of the house like a madman," Mom replied, not missing a beat. "Don't do it in front of the guests, though. We don't want them thinking we're running a brothel."

"Fine," I said, hoping I didn't sound as huffy to my mother's ears as I did to my own. "Is he in the library?"

"Last time I checked," Mom said. "Go make him happy ... and then lower the boom. I don't want any disturbing chatter at dinner tonight. We have a full inn, so every seat will be taken."

I made a face. "You don't want any disturbing chatter at dinner tonight?"

"This is a family-friendly establishment," Mom sniffed.

"So you basically want the entire family to be quiet?" I pressed. "That's what you're saying, right?"

"Bay, I don't know whether you're sick or what, but I've had just about as much mother-and-daughter bonding as I can take tonight," Mom said, fixing me with an "I gave birth to you and you literally owe me your life" look. "Go play with your boyfriend. Make sure his little friend isn't going to be a pain. That's your mission. Choosing not to accept it is out of the question."

I waited until I was sure Mom's gaze was fixed on her dinner preparations before rolling my eyes and pushing open the door.

"I saw that," Mom called to my back.

Of course she did.

I expected Landon to be in the library, so when I found him and Noah already seated at the dining room table I pulled up short. Landon was in the middle of some heavy discussion, but his eyes jumped to me when he sensed my presence.

"Are you sick?"

I bit the inside of my cheek to keep from lashing out and shook my head, traipsing to my usual spot at the table and hesitantly grabbing the chair. Did he want me to sit someplace else? "I ... ."

"What are you doing?" Landon asked, narrowing his eyes as he looked me up and down. "What's wrong with you?"

"She's probably feeling guilty," Noah said. "That's normal when you're dealing with criminals."

I'm pretty sure he had no idea how stupid he sounded. I wanted to tell him, but now probably wasn't the right time. I forced a smile for the guests at the far end of the table before turning back to Landon. "Do you want me to sit in another chair?"

"Do you want to sit in another chair?" Landon asked, his face unreadable.

That wasn't an answer. Sure, I wasn't expecting him to fall to his knees and beg me to sit next to him, but it would've been nice. "Not particularly."

"Then sit down," Landon prodded.

Well, now the last place I wanted to sit was next to him. I couldn't pick another chair, though, because that would incite endless questions from my mother. I blew out a frustrated sigh as I sat, reaching for the pitcher so I could pour myself a glass of water. I could feel Landon's eyes on me the entire time. When I leaned back I jolted as he pressed his hand to my forehead. "What are you doing?"

"Are you okay?" Landon asked, removing his hand. "You don't feel warm, but you look sick."

That was probably the sweetest thing he'd said to me in hours. How freaky is that? "I worked from home this afternoon and I accidentally fell asleep. I didn't wake up until a few minutes ago."

"Hmm."

"What is that supposed to mean?" Initially I envisioned pouting until Landon forgave me. Now I was too angry to pout.

"I didn't mean anything by it, Bay," Landon said, his voice devoid of the flirty mirth I'd grown to love. "I was simply asking whether you were sick. I believe that's what a good boyfriend does."

"And a good girlfriend doesn't break the law," Noah added.

"No one asked you," I snapped, crossing my arms over my chest.

"Good for you," Aunt Tillie said, sashaying into the dining room with a mischievous smile on her face. "I told you crying over it wouldn't do you any good. Anger is definitely the way to go."

Landon scorched Aunt Tillie with a death glare as she settled in the spot to his left. "Do you have to make this situation worse?"

Aunt Tillie shrugged. "I have no idea. I guess we'll have to wait and see, won't we?"

"Where is your friend?" Noah asked Aunt Tillie. "What was her name again?"

That was a test, and it was a bad one.

"Sally is watching the end credits of *Jeopardy*," Aunt Tillie replied, snagging the bottle of wine in front of her. "She has peculiar interests. Personally I don't care for the credits, but arguing with her is like arguing with ... a brick wall."

"Or nothing," Landon muttered.

Aunt Tillie made an exaggerated face as she filled her glass. "Sally doesn't think you're very funny, Fed."

"You just said she was watching the end credits of *Jeopardy*," Landon pointed out. "How can she know what I said?"

"What did you say?" Noah asked. "I couldn't hear you."

Everyone pretended Noah wasn't at the table.

"Sally just came in and she's peeved," Aunt Tillie supplied. "She's very quick. You have to be on your toes when she's around."

"Who is Sally?" Mom asked, opening the swinging door with her hip and carrying a tray laden with Chinese food to the table. "We have a full house. We can't fit anyone else in."

"She doesn't need a chair," Aunt Tillie said, her smile never slipping. Mom's arrival unnerved her, though. I could tell.

Mom pursed her lips. "I'm confused."

"Oh, why?" Noah asked, his gaze pointed as it landed on Mom. "I would think you would know all about your aunt's imaginary friend."

Mom stilled. "Imaginary friend?"

"She's not imaginary," Aunt Tillie clarified. "She was a dear friend of mine who died when I was a teenager. She merely stops by to visit from time to time."

"Child," I corrected. Hey, if we were sticking with the lie we had to make it look good.

"Anything before eighteen was my childhood," Aunt Tillie shot back.

"You had a friend who died when you were a child?" Mom asked. "That's terrible. Why haven't you ever told us about her?"

"Because ... I didn't want to burden you with my strife," Aunt Tillie said. I had to hand it to her. She could lie with the best of them. Sure, her lies were often out there, but she committed to them.

CHARMS & WITCHDEMEANORS

"Uh-huh." Mom shifted her eyes to me. "Did you know about this supposed ... imaginary friend?"

I didn't get a chance to answer because Noah did it for me.

"Your daughter was out at Patty Grimes' house with your aunt this afternoon," he supplied. "Didn't they tell you? They were taken into custody for breaking and entering. However, because of your aunt's potential heatstroke and this invisible Sally person, Chief Terry refused to press charges."

"Oh." Realization dawned on Mom and her eyes narrowed into a disgusted glare. "I see. I hadn't heard about that."

"You act as if you don't believe Sally exists, though," Noah said. "I'm sure Chief Terry would love to hear your take on the situation."

Mom was angry with me, but she despised Noah. She made up her mind on the spot. "I know all about Sally," she said. "For some reason I thought her name was Sarah, though. When you get to be my age, your memory comes and goes at the worst times."

"You're preaching to the choir, sister," Aunt Tillie said, her wine glass already half empty.

"Are you saying your aunt has an imaginary friend?" Noah asked. "If so, perhaps you should have her checked out by a doctor."

"She's fine," Mom said, sitting primly in her chair and resting her hands on the table in front of her. "Frankly, we're happy she has a friend. She's not popular with the human set, so an imaginary friend is right up her alley. It makes our life ... easier."

"What makes our life easier?" Marnie asked, walking in with another tray of food.

"Aunt Tillie's imaginary friend Sally," Mom said.

"Oh, her." Marnie clearly didn't know what Mom was talking about, but she was smart enough to play along. This family is used to covering our tracks. "I love Aunt Tillie's imaginary friend."

Twila, who was entering from the kitchen with the rest of dinner, wrinkled her nose. "What?"

"You know about Aunt Tillie's imaginary friend," Mom prodded. "She talks to her all the time."

"Oh, right," Twila said. "Sally."

How in the heck did she know that? I slid a furtive look in Aunt Tillie's direction and found her expression had shifted from imperiled confidence to smug triumph.

"Apparently Aunt Tillie's imaginary friend convinced her to go to Patty Grimes' house today," Mom said, her eyes locked onto mine. It's creepy how she doesn't blink when she's angry. "Noah arrested her and Bay, but Chief Terry understood about the Sally problem and let them go."

"Well, that's good," Twila said, smiling at an older couple sitting across the table as she settled. "I've always been a huge fan of Sally, and arresting Bay and Aunt Tillie for something so innocent would be criminal."

"How did she pull this off?" Landon asked, his voice low.

I had no idea. I wasn't thrilled with his attitude, though, so I merely shrugged. "Everyone knows about Sally."

"Bay ... ." Landon pressed his lips together, whatever nasty retort he was about to spew silenced. "I'm not fighting with you in front of guests."

"That's good," Aunt Tillie said. "You should learn some manners."

"And you should learn to behave yourself," Landon shot back.

"That doesn't seem like manners to me," Aunt Tillie chided. "Perhaps you should take a class."

"That's right," Mom said. "Bay, I told you to tell Landon and his little ... buddy ... not to talk about work at the dinner table. Why are they doing it?"

"I didn't get a chance to relay the message," I said, lowering my eyes to stare at my plate.

"Landon is ticked off and being mean to her," Aunt Tillie interjected. "The poor girl didn't have a chance. She's been upset about this situation all day. I mean ... look at her. She's practically made herself sick over this."

I didn't look that bad. Okay, I didn't look great. I certainly didn't look as if I was at death's door, though. "Dinner looks great," I said, dishing the pepper steak onto my plate. "You guys outdid yourselves."

"We always do," Mom said.

"I hope you people realize I don't believe any of this Sally nonsense," Noah said. "I know you're all lying. Lying to a federal agent is grounds for incarceration."

"Did he just call me a liar?" Aunt Tillie was incensed.

"I'm pretty sure he did," I said. "That's what 'I know you're all lying' seems to denote."

"Bay, eat your dinner and don't add to the madness," Mom ordered. "Landon, forgive Bay so she doesn't get sick. We all know you're going to do it."

"Yeah, I'm not going to do that right now," Landon said, reaching for the egg rolls. "We have to talk first."

"About lying to law enforcement?" Noah asked.

"Seriously, no one is talking to you," I snapped, instantly regretting my harsh words when everyone at the far end of the table jerked their heads in my direction.

"Oh, this must be the dinner theater everyone is always talking about," one of the female guests said. "I didn't think they would start it on the first night. I'm so excited."

"We're always performing dinner theater," Twila said. "Sometimes we sing."

"We don't sing," Mom said.

"We definitely don't sing," Marnie agreed.

"I sing sometimes," Twila said, benevolence practically wafting off of her. "I sound like an angel when I do it, too."

Are angels tone deaf? I was going to have to look that up. "Where is Thistle?" I asked, changing the subject. I needed backup, and she was my best shot.

"She called and said she's having dinner with Marcus in town tonight," Twila replied.

Son of a.... "She's coming back, though, right?"

Twila shrugged. "I have no idea. I'm her mother, not her keeper."

"But she promised to help with our new roommate," I said. "Aunt Tillie doesn't even have a bed. I'm going to need Thistle's help."

"I'll sleep in Thistle's bed," Aunt Tillie offered. "Don't worry about that."

That was the least of my worries – well, kind of. "This is just great," I said, reaching for the wine as my stomach flipped. "I think I need a drink."

Mom slapped my hand to still me. "You're sick. You don't get to drink."

"But ... ."

Mom shook her head, firm. "I think you've earned this sickness, Bay," she said. "Perhaps there's a lesson in it for you."

There was a lesson in it all right: My family sucks.

FOURTEEN

"Don't walk away from me," Landon said, stomping down the pathway as we made our way to the guesthouse after dinner. "I want to talk to you."

"Well, I don't want to talk to you." As far as immaturity goes, I could win a gold medal this evening. I'm not oblivious to my faults, but that doesn't mean I can correct them when my emotions are out of control. "I can't even look at you."

"How can you possibly be angry with me?" Landon asked, grabbing my arm and spinning me around. "I'm angry with you."

"Then be angry," I said, hating the burning sensation as tears flooded my eyes. "I can't stop you. I know what I did was stupid and wrong, but I can't go back in time and fix it. So ... be angry."

Landon's expression softened. "Bay, don't cry." He reached up to brush away a tear, but I tilted my head away from him. Somehow his being gentle was worse than his earlier aloofness.

"I'm not crying," I said, jerking my arm from his grasp and impatiently brushing my own tears away. Why did this have to happen now?

"Those look like tears to me," Landon said, his voice much softer than before. "I'm sorry you're upset, but I'm upset, too. That's why I want to talk about it and put it behind us."

"Fine. Let's talk."

Now that he had his opening, Landon looked lost.

"Do you want me to start?" I prodded.

"I'm pretty sure I don't want to hear what you have to say because it's going to upset me," Landon said. "This is a relationship, though, so let me have it."

"You knew I would go to Patty Grimes' house," I said. "You knew I would have to see whether she was out there. I don't see why you're so shocked I did it."

"I'm not shocked," Landon argued. "You're right. I did know. I just ... thought there would be a way for us to do it together."

"We can't as long as Noah is here. I didn't bring him here. That's on you."

"Is that what you're really angry about, Bay?" Landon challenged. "You know why he's here. I can't be impartial where you're concerned. I would die to protect you, and that means I would die to protect your family because they're part of you."

Oh, well, great. Now he was going to be sweet, and all of that righteous indignation I'd been building up over the past hour was going to go to waste. "Landon ... ."

He held up his hand to quiet me. "Let me finish."

I crossed my arms over my chest and offered him a curt nod.

"I love you, Bay," Landon said. "I knew you'd go out there. I didn't think you'd get caught. That's not the real problem, though. The real problem is that I'm off my game because of Noah. I know he's watching my every move and it makes me feel exposed.

"There are worse things than me being exposed, though," he continued. "One of them is you being exposed. Noah knows something is going on. He's not an idiot. Chief Terry and I going overboard to protect you makes him even more suspicious. I wouldn't change that, though.

"You have got to be more careful. I know you couldn't predict Aunt Tillie going out there, but in hindsight we should've realized that's exactly what she would do," he said. "We need to be better about hiding what you are from Noah, because he won't understand."

"I wouldn't change who you are for anything," Landon said, reaching over to cup my chin. "You really are my favorite person on the planet. You still did a dumb thing. We have to come up with a better plan of action so you're not exposed and I don't have to be angry with you, because believe it or not, I hate being angry with you."

I waited for him to continue, but apparently he was done. "Can I talk now?"

Landon nodded.

"I'm afraid. I'm afraid Aunt Tillie is going to be arrested and I'm afraid you're somehow going to lose your job over me," I said. "If that happens, I know you'll make a big show of saying it's fine, but eventually you'll grow to resent me for it and I'll lose you. Don't bother denying it because we both know it's true.

"I don't think for a second Aunt Tillie killed Patty Grimes, but something is going on between the two of them and I have no idea what it is," I continued. "She's hiding something. They were … horrible … to one another. Aunt Tillie is going to get worse before she gets better on this one. I can feel it. That's going to put you in professional danger because you're going to risk everything to keep me safe. It would almost be better if complete strangers were investigating this because we're used to lying to people we don't know and love. I can't lie to you.

"I am so worried about you getting in trouble at work that I feel sick to my stomach," I said. "How are you ever going to look at me again if I cost you everything?"

Landon was silent for a few beats. "Are you done?"

"Yes."

He stepped closer and rested his hands on my shoulders. "I always wanted to be a cop – and then an FBI agent – when I was a kid," he said. "I always fancied myself fighting bad guys and winning the girl. I was all about getting to the top of the professional ladder for a long time. I don't worry about that now, though."

"Because of me?"

"Being an FBI agent is what I do," Landon replied. "It's not who I am. It's a part of who I am, don't get me wrong, but it's not the most important thing in the world to me. That's you. I won the girl, and she turned out to be more important."

"But ... ."

"No." Landon firmly shook his head. "I'm talking now. Being an FBI agent is what I do. Who I am is a work in progress. You're what I love more than anything, though. I don't want you to be afraid. That kills me.

"Aunt Tillie is going to do what she always does," he continued. "She's going to make a huge mountain of trouble for us and then somehow swoop in and fix things in the end. You'll probably have a hand in fixing them, too. I have faith in you.

"I would be more bitter and resentful about losing you than anything else," Landon said. "I would take that out on Noah if it happened. Do you want me to become a murderer?"

I didn't want to laugh, but I couldn't help myself. "No."

"Life isn't ever going to be easy and smooth for us because that's not the type of people we are," Landon said. "We can only take the stuff thrown in our direction one thing at a time and move forward. That's the best we can do."

"What if you lose your job because you're protecting us?"

"What if I lose you because I don't protect you?"

"You'll never lose me," I said. "I ... love you."

"I know you do," Landon said. "I love you, too. You need to stop making yourself sick each time we fight, though. It hurts ... and I should be more cognizant of your feelings. I told you not to worry about this earlier. Chief Terry smoothed everything over."

"That's not the way Noah makes it sound."

"Noah is a blowhard," Landon said. "He's desperate to be powerful but the way he talks saps all of his power, if that makes sense. He'll learn eventually. He's young and dumb. Believe it or not, I was a lot like him when I first started with the bureau."

"I'm not sure I believe that," I said. "You seem like a genius in comparison."

"Oh, and there's my ego boost," Landon said, tugging me in for a hug. "Bay, it's going to be okay. I wasn't angry with you because you did something wrong. I was angry because you could've done it in a smarter manner and not risked yourself. Please, think before you do these things. Do it for me."

"I would've been fine if it wasn't for Aunt Tillie."

"Yes, I think you would've been fine," Landon agreed, kissing my forehead. "We can't control her. We have to deal with her on the terms she sets. She's not going to make things easy. She never does."

"You don't think she did it, do you?"

"No."

"Do you have any other leads?"

"No."

Well, that was disheartening. "Do you want to go to bed and pretend this fight didn't happen? I'm exhausted and my stomach still feels weak."

"That sounds good," Landon said, exhaling heavily. "I officially declare this fight over. Everything will be better now."

"You know Aunt Tillie is going to be there when we get to the guesthouse, right?"

"I said things would be better, Bay, not perfect."

I giggled. "I'm going to kill Thistle for abandoning me like this."

"I'm going to help," Landon said, tilting my chin up and offering me a soft kiss. "I love you. We can get through all of this, but we have to be smarter about our methods. We'll have a strategy meeting with Aunt Tillie in the morning."

"Do you really think that will work?"

Landon shrugged. "I really think I need some rest and time alone with you. We'll deal with Aunt Tillie in the morning."

That was something to look forward to ... or not.

I WOKE with my face pressed against Landon's chest and his arm wrapped around my waist. We were both emotionally exhausted upon returning to the guesthouse after dinner, so we left Aunt Tillie to watch HBO and immediately went to bed.

When I lifted my chin, Landon opened his eyes and smiled. "Did you sleep okay?"

"I slept hard."

"You usually do," Landon said. "I worry when I'm not here because you would sleep right through someone trying to break into the house. Clove is a light sleeper and would wake you before. She's gone now."

Clove was gone now. I didn't like the way he phrased it, but it was true. Part of me already missed her. The other part was too worried about Aunt Tillie to give it the thought Clove deserved.

"I'm sure I'll survive."

"I'm sure you will, too, if I have anything to say about it," Landon said, shifting to his back and staring at the ceiling. "I feel better after so much sleep. Apparently we needed it, because neither one of us moved for nine hours."

I ran my fingers over his chiseled stomach. "I'm hungry."

"You didn't eat dinner last night. You just pushed it around your plate. I'm guessing you didn't get lunch either," Landon said. "You need food or you'll really get sick."

"Instead of just looking sick?"

"You didn't look bad," Landon clarified. "You just ... didn't look yourself."

"And now?"

"I'm a big fan of your hair when it stands on end like this," Landon teased, pressing my bedhead down. "How about we hop in the shower and then get breakfast? I was thinking we could go into town to avoid an uncomfortable meal with your mother and Noah, and then I'll drop you off at work and come back alone. I think the last thing you need is another confrontation with my new partner."

"That sounds good," I said. "He won't be your partner for every case, though, right? I don't ever want to see him again after this."

"I might have to take him on some investigations, but hopefully Hemlock Cove won't have another murder for years."

"Yes, because that's been the pattern of late."

"You're so sarcastic," Landon said, grabbing me around the waist and rolling on top of me. "You do look better. The color is back in your cheeks. I wish you wouldn't make yourself sick over this stuff."

"I didn't make myself sick."

"Close enough."

"I'm fine," I said. "In fact, I feel strong – other than my growling stomach."

Landon kissed the tip of my nose. "Let's get in the shower then. Breakfast awaits."

"That's a beautiful sentiment, but we can't shower together with Aunt Tillie under the same roof."

Landon's smile tipped upside down. "Why not?" Now he sounded like the petulant one.

"Because Aunt Tillie won't like it and I don't want her telling my mother about our ... cleanliness ... habits."

"But ... this bites." Landon rested his head on my chest and bemoaned his cruel fate. "That's my favorite part of the day."

"I thought your favorite part of the day was any meal with bacon?"

"Well, it's my second favorite part of the day," Landon conceded.

"I thought your second favorite part of the day was cuddling in bed with me in the morning?"

Landon lifted his head and wrinkled his nose. "Do you remember everything I ever said to you?"

"Yes."

"That's cute and annoying," he said. "In truth, this is my favorite part of the day. We're alone, and you're warm and snuggly. The outside world can't get us here."

My heart warmed. "That's sweet."

"If you could figure a way to keep bacon in here, though, things would be even better."

"You have a one-track mind."

"And you're the track," Landon said, mock growling as he kissed my neck. "As much as I would like to see where our mutual good moods will take us, I'm going to call a timeout on this and suggest you get in the shower first because you take longer to get ready."

"You're just saying that because the bedhead is a distraction."

"I'm saying that because you refuse to shower together and cut down on our morning tasks," Landon countered. "While you're doing that, I'll check on Aunt Tillie."

"She's probably already up at the inn for breakfast."

"No, I'm not."

I froze when I heard the voice, lifting my head so I could look over Landon's shoulder to find Aunt Tillie staring at us from the open doorway. "What the ... ?"

"What are you doing in here?" Landon barked, rolling off me and forcing himself to a sitting position. "This is our private space."

"This is Bay's private space," Aunt Tillie corrected. "I heard you talking and decided to check in ... roomies."

"Oh, well, that's great," Landon said. "How did you know we weren't doing something private?"

"Because most people don't carry on deep and meaningful discussions when they're doing something private."

"Did you have your ear pressed to the wall?" I asked, mortified. "Aunt Tillie, if you're going to stay here, we have to set some ground rules."

"I wasn't eavesdropping," Aunt Tillie protested. "You guys talk loud."

"We do not," Landon argued. "The ground rules are a good idea. The first one is that you cannot enter this room without knocking. Period."

Aunt Tillie rolled her eyes. "Whatever."

"The second one is that whatever happens in this guesthouse stays in this guesthouse," Landon added. "Think of it like Vegas."

"Is Bay going to strip down to tassels and sequins and do a little dance for you?" Aunt Tillie asked, tightening her housecoat and arching a challenging eyebrow. "If so, I'm going to start carrying a bucket of water around with me."

"Maybe. If she does, though, it's none of your concern."

"I think you just want me to promise not to tell Winnie about your dirty showers," Aunt Tillie said. "For the record, I promise not to tell."

"I don't believe you," I said. "You say that now but once you're feeling annoyed you'll rat me out in a heartbeat. I know you."

"I'm wounded," Aunt Tillie said, clutching the spot above her heart and tilting her head to the side. "What's that, Sally? Yes, they are kind of cute."

"Oh, knock it off," Landon said, frustrated. "And get out. We'll get up when we're ready."

Aunt Tillie tilted her head to the other side. "Oh, Sally, you have such a filthy mind. I think he's a pervert, too, though."

"Get out!"

Aunt Tillie wasn't bothered by Landon's tone. "I'm going to get in the shower while you two canoodle. I'll be ready to go to town with you for breakfast in forty minutes. Don't be late. I have to eat on a schedule or I get constipated."

Landon's mouth dropped open, but Aunt Tillie was already gone. "Did she just invite herself to our cozy breakfast?"

"Welcome to a new world of Winchester living."

"I changed my mind," Landon complained, burying his head in my shoulder so I could rub his back. "I want to spend the day in bed."

"What about your bacon?"

"Screw the bacon. This has officially turned from a romantic morning for two into a nightmare for three. I didn't sign up for this."

"Suck it up, big guy. You said you loved me no matter what. Here is the ... no matter what."

"I blame Thistle for this," Landon grumbled. "If she spent the night, this wouldn't be happening."

I blamed Thistle, too, and we were going to have a big talk about it later in the afternoon. For now, though, Landon and I had exactly five minutes to cuddle before the real world dragged us from our sanctuary.

"Just ... relax," I said, kissing his cheek. "We have five minutes of bliss left. Don't ruin it."

"Oh, sweetie, we have an entire lifetime of bliss," Landon said.

"Unfortunately, it's going to be broken up by the occasional segments of apocalyptic mayhem. Those are the rules in the Winchester world."

"Do you still love me despite that?"

"Always."

FIFTEEN

After an uncomfortable breakfast with Landon and Aunt Tillie – one in which Landon talked incessantly about rules I knew Aunt Tillie would never follow – he left me in town and returned to The Overlook with my great-aunt in tow. I could hear them arguing as they left, and I had a feeling their relationship would only grow more tempestuous because we would be spending so much time together. The edges were already frayed. Now I just had to hope they didn't rip.

Instead of heading straight to the newspaper, I turned toward the unicorn store. I didn't have a lot of leads regarding Patty Grimes' death – or life, for that matter – but I knew exactly who to blame for the Aunt Tillie predicament.

Mrs. Little was behind the counter helping a customer check out. I busied myself studying the unicorns – which kind of freaked me out – until she was done. When it was just the two of us, she continued ignoring me. I was petulant on a bad day, but Mrs. Little could win a prize for her attitude. Well, if they gave out prizes for being a busybody pain in the keister, that is.

"Hello, Mrs. Little."

"Hello, Bay." Her tone was breezy and clipped, and she refused to look in my direction. "Do you need help purchasing a gift? Perhaps a housewarming present for Clove is in order. I hear she moved out to the Dandridge."

"She did move," I confirmed. Clove was something of a princess at times, but even she wouldn't want a unicorn to display. "I've already purchased a gift for her." That was a lie. I didn't think insulting Mrs. Little's livelihood would get me the information I sought, though.

"Then why are you here?" Mrs. Little asked, finally lifting her eyes. "If this is about the threats you made yesterday ... ."

"They weren't threats," I clarified, cutting her off. "It was a promise. I have no interest in spilling your secrets, yet you seem fixated on doing something terrible to Aunt Tillie. I want to know why."

"I have no idea what you're talking about."

"I don't want to play games with you," I said, moving closer to the counter. "Aunt Tillie is family, and I protect my family. I want to know why you called the FBI."

"Because unlike you, Bay, I understand that Tillie is a threat," Mrs. Little replied. "She's not a good person. She's not even a remotely likable person. You girls let her run roughshod over this town, and what I saw at the senior center wasn't acceptable."

"See, I have a problem with that," I challenged. "You can pretend you're doing it for the residents ... or the senior center members ... or the overall good of the town, but we both know that's not true. Aunt Tillie didn't kill Patty Grimes. It's not in her nature. You have to know that."

"I don't labor under the same delusion most of this town does," Mrs. Little said. "Everyone wants to pretend you're normal people acting like witches, but I know better. Now, I don't know the whole truth, but I have an inkling about it, and it's terrifying. There's always been something ... off ... about your family."

"And yet you knew your husband was a murderer and said nothing about it for decades," I shot back. "I would rather be off than mean and hurtful."

"And what about Tillie? She's mean and hurtful at every turn."

"You have issues with Aunt Tillie, and that's fine," I said. "You don't

CHARMS & WITCHDEMEANORS

have to like her. You don't even have to pretend to tolerate her. You do have to stop working against her when she doesn't deserve it, though. That's how things operate in a polite society."

Mrs. Little snorted, the inelegant sound coming from a prim and proper woman taking me by surprise. "You're young, Bay, and despite your many faults – and they are numerous and varied – I think you're probably a good person," she said. "I think your mother and aunts are good people. I think your cousins – well, Clove at least – are good, too. Tillie is another story.

"She has made a name for herself terrorizing whoever disagreed with her for as long as I can remember," she continued. "She poisoned the people at the senior center before. I was there. We all saw it. That's what got her banned."

"I don't believe that."

"Then you're naïve," Mrs. Little shot back. "You want to believe your aunt is a good person, and I understand that, but she's not. She'll hurt people to get what she wants. She hurt Patty. She hurt me. She hurts everyone."

"Now you're speaking about things I'm not privy to because I wasn't around when they happened," I said. "How did she hurt Patty Grimes?"

"Why don't you ask your aunt?"

Because I knew she wouldn't answer honestly. I kept that to myself, though. "I'm asking you."

"I'm not here to do your job for you, Bay," Mrs. Little said. "I try to stay out of other people's business."

That was rich. "You called the FBI office in Traverse City and reported Aunt Tillie as a murderer before most people even knew Patty Grimes was dead," I said. "That doesn't sound like staying out of other people's business. In fact, nobody knew how Patty died until hours after the FBI showed up. You wanted to stir the pot, and you did it. Congratulations."

"I knew that Tillie was at the senior center, and I was suspicious of her activities while she was there," Mrs. Little said. "I also know that

Terry Davenport's relationship with your family would never allow him to arrest Tillie, even though she's guilty."

"So you have no problem putting his job in jeopardy because you hold a grudge against Aunt Tillie?"

"I have no problem keeping the people in this town safe," Mrs. Little clarified. "You're blind to your aunt and who she really is. Terry is blind because of your mother ... and I think a little because of you, too. He's always been fond of you."

"That doesn't make him a bad man."

"I don't think he's a bad man," Mrs. Little said. "I think he's ... weak."

"Well, I happen to know you're a bad woman," I said. "I also know Aunt Tillie isn't capable of what you're suggesting. You know as well as I do that she's not the sneaking around type. If she's angry, you'll know it."

"Perhaps," Mrs. Little said. "Or perhaps you're really here because you believe your aunt is capable of killing someone and you're afraid to admit it and need someone else to blame. I'm not beholden to you, Bay. You can threaten me all you want. I know what's right, and killing someone as defenseless as Patty isn't right."

"And I know what's right, too," I said. "Covering up a murder isn't right. Blaming other people for things they haven't done isn't right. I'm not going to just let this go."

"That's certainly your prerogative."

It was obvious Mrs. Little wouldn't be swayed. "If I were you, I would be worried about what happens when Aunt Tillie is vindicated," I said. "She's going to be out for revenge, and when she comes at you, it won't be with poison. You'll see her coming."

I couldn't be sure, but I was almost positive Mrs. Little gulped.

"If you're not shopping, you should probably go, Bay," she said. "I'm very busy."

"You look it," I said, turning toward the door. "If you mess with one member of our family, you mess with all of us. You should realize that."

"I do realize it, Bay. I just happen to believe that justice is more important than Winchester vengeance. I almost pity you, because when the truth comes out about your aunt you're going to have a broken heart. You have a nice day now."

I WAS AGITATED by the time I got to The Whistler, storming toward my office and ignoring the owner, Brian Kelly, as he tried to call me down the hallway for some insipid meeting. He was always coming up with stupid ways to boost the newspaper's circulation, but none of them ever worked because the population in the area was flat. It didn't grow and it didn't shrink. It merely maintained. I wasn't interested in playing games with Brian today.

I booted my computer, gnawing on a fingernail as I waited until I could get on the Internet. I typed Patty's name in a search engine and came up with a lot of hits, but none of them save a few random briefs regarding her death were about the Patty I was interested in. Apparently Patty Grimes is a popular name. I was so lost in thought I didn't notice Edith, The Whistler's resident ghost, until she practically floated through my desk to get my attention.

"You scared the crap out of me," I hissed, narrowing my eyes. "Make a noise or something next time."

"I did make a noise," Edith replied, unruffled. She was used to my moods. "You didn't hear me. In fact, I made five noises, and you ignored all of them."

"I'm ... searching for something," I said, frustrated as I leaned back in my chair. "Mrs. Little is just ... the worst human being ever."

"You're agitated." Edith enjoyed stating the obvious. "What's eating you?"

I told her about the past few days, leaving nothing out. Edith died at her desk decades ago, and she was familiar many of the players in the current conundrum. Sure, she absolutely hated Aunt Tillie, but there was no way she could suspect her of killing Patty Grimes.

"Oh, it was definitely Tillie."

Of course, I've been known to be wrong a time or two. "How can you say that?" I asked, casting a quick glance at the door to make sure I had shut it. Brian could see me talking to myself through the window if he looked, but as long as he couldn't hear anything I didn't care if he thought I was crazy. When Brian's grandfather died he left the newspaper to his grandson, but there was a stipulation in the will that Brian couldn't fire me or sell the newspaper out from under me. As far as I was concerned, Brian Kelly was helpless – which was exactly how I liked him. "I know you and Aunt Tillie have had your difficulties, but she's not a murderer."

"I think she murdered me," Edith said. "You know she hated me, right? It was her. I'm positive."

I fought the urge to roll my eyes. "She didn't like you because she thought you flirted with Uncle Calvin," I said, referring to my late great-uncle. "She's been honest about that. If she wanted to go after you, though, she wouldn't poison you. She would stab you or something. She's more hands-on when it comes to revenge."

Edith made a face that would've been comical under different circumstances. Unfortunately for her, I was in no mood to laugh.

"I know you love your aunt, Bay, but she's not as nice to everyone as she is to you," Edith said.

That was fairly laughable because Aunt Tillie had cursed me more times than I could count. "I don't live under any illusions where Aunt Tillie is concerned," I said. "However, I know her well enough to realize that she wouldn't poison someone. It's not in her nature, because she thrives off the confrontation as much as she does the victory."

"That's true," Edith hedged. "Still, I never made advances on your uncle. I always felt bad for him because Tillie was such a pill. I was nice to him. That's all."

I thought she was probably remembering things as she wanted to remember them, but there was no reason to call her on it. Uncle Calvin died long before I was born. I needed to focus on the woman who recently died.

"What can you tell me about Aunt Tillie's relationship with Patty Grimes?"

"What do you mean?"

CHARMS & WITCHDEMEANORS

"I mean they acted as if they would rather set fire to one another than carry on a civilized conversation," I replied. "There's obviously some very ... unfortunate ... history between the two of them. I want to know what it is."

"I don't specifically remember any fights between them," Edith said, screwing up her face in concentration. "Oh, wait. It might be about Victor Donahue."

I stilled. That name meant absolutely nothing to me. "Who is Victor Donahue?"

"He went to school with us," Edith replied. "He was kind of the big jock on campus, a real superstar, if you know what I mean."

Since Hemlock Cove – or Walkerville, back in the day – didn't really breed stellar athletes I had trouble picturing anything akin to a "superstar." Still, I was willing to take any lead I could get at this point. "Was he in the same grade as you?"

"He was a year ahead of me," Edith answered. "He was very popular, and very handsome. He looked like Clark Gable."

"Is that a good thing?"

Edith rolled her eyes. "No one was better looking than Clark Gable."

"I guess you haven't seen the guy who plays Thor," I muttered.

Edith didn't respond to the comment because she was distracted by her stroll down memory lane. "He was almost breathtaking to look at," she said. "Everyone had a crush on him, especially Tillie."

"Where was Uncle Calvin for this?"

"He was very shy and didn't approach Tillie until she was a senior," Edith explained. "By then, Calvin had been out of school for three years or so. Tillie was still playing games when Calvin came on the scene. She gave up the games – well, at least some of them – not long after they started courting. Because Calvin was older, he forced Tillie to mature."

"That's kind of ... pervy."

"Those were different times," Edith chided. "That age difference was perfectly acceptable back then. Anyway, I was in the same class as

Tillie, but Patty was a few years ahead of us. She was already working at the diner. That didn't stop her from going after Victor."

"Did she get him?"

Edith shook her head. "No one really got him," she said. "It's hard for me to remember exactly what happened, but I lost track of him soon after graduation. That was after Tillie and Patty got in a fight over him, though. They both had crushes on him. Patty thought she was prettier, so she should have him."

"That's all well and good, but I have a hard time believing a high school fight over a boy who probably left town was enough to cause Aunt Tillie to kill Patty sixty years later. Besides, Aunt Tillie went on to marry Uncle Calvin, and by all reports, they were very happy."

"Maybe something else happened between them," Edith said. "I'm simply telling you what I remember."

Unfortunately, it was all I had to go on. "Thanks. I didn't mean to bite your head off."

"It's okay," Edith said. "I understand you're upset. I hate your aunt, but you love her."

"Sometimes I'm not so sure."

"You love her," Edith said, shaking her head. "She's mean and nasty, but you still wouldn't trade her for anything because she's colorful."

I couldn't argue with that. "I ... ." I lost my train of thought when I glanced out my office window and caught sight of Noah. He was talking to Brian next to the front desk, both of them utilizing big hand gestures as they conversed. They seemed to be enjoying each other's company. "What is he doing here?"

Edith glanced over her shoulder. "Is that the new FBI guy? If so, I think he's better looking than the one you're dating. He doesn't have that long hair."

Well, now I was officially insulted on Landon's behalf. "That guy looks like an ear of corn."

"I think he's handsome."

I sucked in a breath to calm myself. "Well, if he's here it's to question Brian," I said. "I can't control what Brian says, but I can control myself. I'm out of here until I'm sure he's gone."

"I'll watch him for you," Edith said, completely losing interest in our previous conversation and floating toward the door. "If he's up to something, I'll find out what it is."

"Thanks, Edith. That will be a real help," I said dryly.

"Don't mention it."

SIXTEEN

"You're dead to me!"

Thistle didn't even bother hiding her smile when I strode into Hypnotic. Clove, who was happily dusting shelves with a peaceful smile on her face, widened her eyes when I stormed in.

"Oh, don't be that way," Thistle chided. "I'm your favorite roommate. There's no way you can deny it."

"I'm going to make you eat a pile of dirt as soon as I find the time," I shot back. "I'm actually going to schedule it in my day planner so I don't forget."

"What's going on?" Clove asked, confused. "Are you guys already fighting without me?" She almost looked hopeful.

"We're going to be," I said. "I'm going to kill her, and then I'm going to claim the guesthouse as my own private domain."

"Only if you get rid of Aunt Tillie," Thistle said. "How was her first night in the guesthouse?"

"Oh," Clove intoned, realization dawning. "That's why you're in such a good mood today, Thistle. I wondered. You're usually crabby in the morning, but you were downright giddy today."

"That's because she's evil," I said.

CHARMS & WITCHDEMEANORS

"I never denied being evil," Thistle said. "If it makes you feel better, I really did plan on going back to the guesthouse after dinner. Marcus and I were really comfortable watching television, though, and I fell asleep."

"Yeah, if you dry that lie out you could fertilize the lawn," I snapped. "I'm not stupid. Do you have any idea what my last twenty-four hours have been like?"

"I don't," Clove said. "I've missed you terribly, and no one called me. It was hurtful."

"It's been a day, Clove," Thistle said, shaking her head. "Give us time to work up to rampant grief and crying."

"I haven't missed either of you," I charged. "Of course, I spent part of yesterday in police custody, so I had other things on my mind."

Clove's mouth dropped open as Thistle arched an eyebrow. One of my cousins was genuinely worried and the other was amused. Of course, Thistle already knew about part of my day because I stopped in to complain when I was freaking out about Landon. She's going to turn into Aunt Tillie's clone one day. I just know it.

"What happened?" Clove asked.

"Well, I snuck out to Patty Grimes' house to see whether her ghost was there, and when I arrived, guess who I found?"

"Aunt Tillie," Thistle said, smiling broadly. "Of course she would go out there to do the same thing. She wants to pretend she's not bothered by the murder rumors, but she really is."

"Yes, you're so smart," I said, scorching her with a dark look. "You already knew the answer, though, because I stopped in here after it happened. Do you mind if I tell Clove the story, or would you rather revel in your genius?"

"I prefer reveling in my genius."

Clove slapped Thistle's arm and shook her dark head. "Don't be mean," she ordered. "Bay is obviously upset. I want to hear all about your terrible day. I'm a good cousin."

"You only want her to say she misses you," Thistle said. "Admit it."

"A few tears would make me feel better," Clove conceded.

"Maybe later," I muttered. "Do you want to hear about my day or not?"

"I'm already bored with the story because I've heard it," Thistle replied.

I ignored her. "So I go to Patty Grimes' house and Aunt Tillie is breaking in," I said. "We argued. She won. We went inside. Patty Grimes' ghost appeared, and she and Aunt Tillie started spewing insults at one another. Patty said Aunt Tillie killed her, by the way."

"Holy crap," Thistle said, leaning forward. All pretense of disinterest evaporated from her face. "What did Aunt Tillie say? You didn't tell me that part yesterday."

"That's because Aunt Tillie was with me, and I was distracted by my fight with Landon. I was going to tell you, but it slipped my mind … and then I was really comfortable and fell asleep."

Thistle frowned. "I get it. You're ticked. Move on."

"Oh, you had a fight with Landon?" Clove's face flooded with sympathy. "Did you make up?"

"I just want to tell my story," I groused. "Can't I do that without fifty interruptions?"

"You have met me before, right?" Thistle challenged.

I pretended I didn't hear the question. "So Aunt Tillie and Patty are screeching at each other when Noah shows up. He questions us, and Aunt Tillie lies about having an imaginary friend who she thought lived in the house. She said the heat confused her. Noah didn't believe her, and he arrested us."

"Where was Landon?" Clove asked.

"With Noah."

"Landon arrested you?" Clove was beside herself. "We need to curse him right now. Did you break up?"

"No, we didn't break up," I snapped, irritated. "Landon had no choice. He could've lost his job over that. He was a mess."

"You're leaving part of the story out," Thistle said, smirking. "Landon refused to handcuff Bay, so Noah did it. Landon did handcuff Aunt Tillie, though."

"Well, she probably deserved it," Clove said. "What happened when you got to the station?"

"Chief Terry refused to bring charges, and Noah had a fit. Then Landon and I got in a big fight, and I worked from home all afternoon. I fell asleep, and when I got up to the inn everyone thought I was sick because I slept in my makeup."

"Did you cry?" Clove asked knowingly.

"No."

Thistle crossed her arms over her chest. "Not even a little?"

"Fine, I cried a little bit," I admitted. "It was, like, one tear."

"Which means it was about a hundred tears," Thistle said. "Continue. I'm listening."

"We had a big showdown at dinner, and Noah questioned our mothers about Sally's existence. Sally is the imaginary friend who was really supposed to be a dead girl from Aunt Tillie's childhood, mind you. In case he asks, that's the lie."

"Uh-oh," Clove said. "Did our moms rat you out?"

"No. They all lied. Twila even knew her name, which still has me confused."

"That's interesting," Thistle said. "What did Landon do?"

"He picked another fight on the way back to the guesthouse, and then gave up because I couldn't stop myself from crying," I replied. "We made up and went to bed because we were both exhausted. Aunt Tillie stayed up watching HBO."

"That doesn't sound so bad," Clove said.

"Wait for it," Thistle said.

"This morning we were talking in bed, and Aunt Tillie just wandered in and invited herself to breakfast with us," I said.

"And there it is," Thistle said, a devilish grin splitting her face. "How was your breakfast?"

"Well, Landon insists Aunt Tillie follow rules, and Aunt Tillie pretends she can't hear Landon when he says something she doesn't like, which is pretty much every word he utters," I answered. "It's going to blow up."

"That sounds absolutely delightful," Thistle said. "I'm so sorry I missed it."

"I'm going to throw you in a hole and shovel dirt on top of you if you do it again," I warned.

"Yeah, that's big talk for a pathetic crier," Thistle said, unmoved by the threat. "What else is going on?"

I told her about my conversation with Mrs. Little and Edith's tidbit about Victor Donahue. When I was done, my cousins were even more confused than when we started.

"I don't get it," Clove said. "I can see Mrs. Little convincing herself Aunt Tillie is a menace. Aunt Tillie is never anything but mean to her. But I don't understand why she would go after Chief Terry."

"I think his potential professional trouble is just a byproduct of Mrs. Little's hate for Aunt Tillie. She's willing to risk Chief Terry's future to win," I replied. "My bigger problem is the fact that she called the FBI's main office and told them Patty Grimes was murdered long before a cause of death – or a rumor of a murder – started circulating."

"Do you think it's her?" Thistle asked, intrigued. "Maybe she's trying to point the finger at Aunt Tillie to distract people from her own guilt."

I would've been lying if I said the thought never crossed my mind. Her husband was a murderer, after all. I wouldn't put it past her. "What would her motive be?"

"Maybe Patty and Mrs. Little have a past we don't know about," Thistle suggested. "You asked Edith about Aunt Tillie's history with Patty, not Mrs. Little's past with Patty. We might only be getting part of the story."

That was a good point. "I'll ask Edith about Mrs. Little when I see her again," I said. "I can't go back to the office now because Noah is there questioning Brian."

"About what?" Thistle asked.

"I'm sure it's about me ... and possibly Sally," I said. "There's nothing I can do about it so I'm ignoring it unless directly asked."

"That's probably wise, but Brian is a weasel," Thistle said. "I would be worried about him making stuff up."

"I can't stop him, so I'm choosing to ignore him," I said. "Things have been rough lately between us as it is."

"Was Landon with Noah?" Clove asked.

I shook my head. "I'm sure Landon didn't want to question Brian. They hate each other."

Clove inclined her head toward the front window, causing me to swivel. "Landon is coming this way. Hopefully we shouldn't have to worry about Noah following if they're not together right now."

I watched as Landon let himself in the store. He didn't look particularly upset or worried, but he didn't look happy either. "Is something wrong?"

"Nothing is wrong, Bay," Landon said, cupping the back of my head and giving me a quick kiss. "I only wanted to touch base and see what your plans were for the day. Noah is off talking to Brian, and I decided to take the opportunity to talk strategy with Chief Terry without prying ears horning in on the conversation. Then I had a few free moments and wanted to check in with you."

"How did you know I wasn't at the newspaper office?" I asked.

"Because I knew you would run the second you saw Noah, and I was right," Landon replied. "I saw you scurrying toward Hypnotic five minutes after Noah left. Did you speak to him at all?"

"He was in the hallway with Brian. I left right away without saying a thing," I said. "I did talk to Edith a little bit. She told me Aunt Tillie and Patty had a spat in high school over a boy named Victor Donahue. She seems to think it was a big deal."

"A high school crush?" Landon didn't look convinced. "I have trouble believing that would cause Aunt Tillie to murder someone."

"I also had words with Mrs. Little." I wasn't keen on admitting it, but I didn't want to keep anything from Landon given our argument the previous day.

"I figured you would," Landon said, not missing a beat. "Did she say anything?"

"Just that Aunt Tillie was evil and she was trying to protect the town," I said. "It wasn't pretty. She said I had to buy a porcelain unicorn for Clove as a housewarming gift or leave, so I left."

"Thank the Goddess for small favors," Clove said. "I would rather have nothing than a unicorn."

"That's good to know," Thistle said, smirking. "I shall therefore give you nothing."

"I'm going to help Bay feed you dirt," Clove said, scowling. "I hope you know that."

"I'm going to help, too," Landon said. "After what you pulled abandoning us with that woman last night, you deserve it."

"You obviously survived." Thistle is one of those people who will only apologize if her back is to the wall and someone has a knife at her throat. So, pretty much never.

"Yes, but we needed time together because we were dealing with some personal stuff," Landon argued. "You obviously don't care about that, but we do. Bay almost made herself sick she was so worked up."

"Don't tell people that," I said. "It makes me look weak."

"You weren't weak, sweetie," Landon countered. "You were upset. You were in cuffs. Your cousin didn't care enough about you to take that into consideration, though. She knew we were arguing, but helping you was out of her wheelhouse. I think there's a lesson in there."

Why do people keep trying to teach me lessons these days? "It's fine."

"It's not fine," Clove said. "Thistle was wrong. She should admit it."

"I definitely don't miss you now," Thistle said, crossing her arms over her chest. "For the record, I'm not sorry. I really did fall asleep by accident. If it helps, I promise to spend the night at the guesthouse this evening to … lighten your load."

It was as close to an apology as I would get. "That's great," I said. "I'm also going to need your help tracking down Victor Donahue. That can be your penance."

"You can't honestly believe this feud between Aunt Tillie and Patty has something to do with some random guy from sixty years ago"

Thistle scoffed. "Aunt Tillie is mean and diabolical, but she's not letting a high school fight fuel her rage."

"No, but anyone who has information on why they hated each other is someone I want to talk to if I can," I replied. "Edith said she lost track of him. I have to think that's because he moved. I can't be sure, though."

"He could be dead," Clove pointed out. "We might not be able to find him."

"I have to try."

"I'm going to pretend I didn't hear that name because I would have to share it with Noah," Landon said. "He's already gung-ho to prove Aunt Tillie is lying about Sally."

"That seems like a terrific waste of time," Thistle said. "She's lying but she'll never admit it. She's not the type to give in. She'll go to the grave pretending there's a Sally now rather than owning up to lying. In fact, her need to win is so great she'll start shopping for Sally and adopt a pet for her or something."

Clove shuddered. "Maybe it will be another scorpion."

That was a terrifying thought. "I think you inherited that need to be right from her, Thistle," I said.

"I'll spend the night at Marcus' place again," Thistle warned. "Don't push me."

"If you do that, I'll arrest Marcus," Landon threatened.

"For what?"

"I believe he helps with a certain pot field," Landon said, crossing his arms over his chest. "Noah would love that information. Do you want to risk that?"

Landon used his serious "cop" face, but Thistle didn't fall for it. "That's such a lame threat," she said. "You wouldn't squeal on Marcus or Aunt Tillie. Don't bother bluffing when we all know you're a good guy. Criminy. You were furious with Bay and you crumbled the second you realized she'd been crying."

Landon shifted his eyes to me. "I'll do it."

"It is a lame threat," I said. "It was a nice try, though."

Landon scowled. "I hate it when Thistle is right."

"We all do," I said, patting his arm. "I'll be available by phone if you need me this afternoon. We're going to track down this Victor guy if we can. I wish we could take you with us, but you're going to have to deal with the scourge that is Noah on your own and leave us to our own devices on this one."

"And I thought you loved me," Landon said, leaning over and pressing a quick kiss to my mouth. "Be good. Stay out of trouble. If something comes up and you're not sure what to do, call me first."

"I will."

"Be careful, Bay," Landon said. "We're all in a weird spot here. We have to be smart instead of lucky for a change."

"I'm both," Thistle said.

"I wasn't joking about helping them with the dirt, Thistle," Landon said. "You're on my list."

I pursed my lips to keep from laughing at the Aunt Tillie-inspired threat. "And just think, we've only spent one night with Aunt Tillie," I said. "What do you think we'll be like in a week?"

"I'm guessing circus folk," Landon said, giving me a brief hug. "Stay in touch. If I get anything, I'll call you. If you get anything, keep it to yourself until we're alone. I don't want to risk Noah overhearing a conversation he shouldn't."

I kicked my heels together and saluted. "Yes, sir!"

"Cute," Landon said. "Unfortunately, until we're out from under Aunt Tillie's watchful eye I can't act on the cuteness. It's a punishment for the ages. Apparently I've ticked off someone important in a previous life. Now I won't be able to touch you without worrying she's listening at the door."

Huh. I hadn't thought of that. Well, there went my week.

SEVENTEEN

Finding Victor Donahue was easier than we thought. I'd like to say we put our noses to the grindstone and came up with the answer, but Chief Terry showed up thirty minutes after Landon left to provide us with the information. Apparently my intrepid boyfriend knew we would meander on our own, so he offered us help on the sly.

Because I didn't have access to my car, Thistle served as chauffeur – and she didn't stop complaining for the entire drive to neighboring Bellaire. Because she didn't want to be left behind, Clove shut down Hypnotic and tagged along for the ride. We were a happy threesome again. Well, kind of.

"I think this is a complete and total waste of time," Thistle said, turning off the rural road and onto the main drag of the small hamlet. "There's no way Aunt Tillie and Patty are fighting about a guy neither one of them ended up with sixty years ago."

"I agree," I said, studying the street signs as we slowly passed. I wasn't familiar with the town, only visiting on several occasions throughout the years, and I didn't want to miss the turnoff to the retirement community where Victor now resided.

"If you agree, why are we taking the afternoon off work – on what should be a busy day, mind you – and chasing a ridiculous story?" Thistle pressed. "I've never met Edith, but I've heard her a few times while at your office. I don't think she's believable. She puts her own spin on things."

While Aunt Tillie and I were the only ones in the family who could see ghosts, Clove and Thistle could eventually hear them if they remained in my presence along with the ghost for long enough. After it occurred a few times with Edith, Thistle got annoyed and refused to visit the newspaper office again. She said it was bad enough to hear a living person whine. A dead person sent her over the edge.

"Edith isn't a bad person – er, ghost," I said. "She's just … stuck in a different time. She died when things were different, especially for women, and she can't seem to find a way to climb out of that mindset."

"She's a kvetch," Clove said, smiling. She rarely got to use the word and it was often applied to her when she complained, so she took advantage of the opportunity to bandy it about in conjunction with someone else.

"She's definitely a kvetch," Thistle agreed, leaning forward to study a street sign. "This is it, right?"

"Yeah," I said, gesturing toward the big building off to the right. "I think that's the retirement community."

"It looks like an old church," Clove said, wrinkling her nose. She seemed perfectly happy with the road trip. I think being away from us – and the excitement – was getting to her. "Why does look like a church?"

"I think it used to be part of an old church and they modified the building," I supplied. "I seem to remember talk about the building being donated to a charity group that could afford to renovate it because it didn't have to buy the property."

"It's neat," Clove said, unfastening her seatbelt and leaning forward. "This is fun. We should go on adventures more often now that I'm not living with you guys. That can be our new … thing."

I turned in my seat and fixed Clove with a serious look. It was time to nip this potential problem well before it budded. "Clove, you know we still love you and want to hang out, right?"

Clove balked. "Of course."

"Well, you don't act as if you know that," I said. "We're not going to forget you."

"No one called me yesterday," Clove said. "I don't think you missed me at all."

I wanted to shake her. "Clove, I spent my morning talking to senior citizens, my lunch hour fighting with Aunt Tillie and a ghost, my afternoon trying to stay out of jail and then worrying about Landon, and my evening having the worst dinner ever. I didn't have time to miss you."

"And we saw you in the morning," Thistle added. "I know you're worried we're going to cut you out of things, but come on! I'm going to see you practically every day. So is Bay, because she visits at lunchtime when her schedule allows. You'll still eat dinners at the inn a few times a week, too. When do you think we'll forget about you?"

"You don't understand," Clove said. "I was so excited to move in with Sam, and it's so peaceful out there, but … ." She broke off, frustrated as she searched for the right words.

"You're worried about missing out on the excitement," I finished for her. "I get it. The problem is, our brand of excitement is generally headache-inducing and heartburn-inciting. Do you wish you'd been taken into custody with Aunt Tillie and me?"

Clove chewed on her bottom lip. "No."

"Do you wish you'd watched me melt down on the couch while Landon stormed out?"

"No."

"I kind of wish you'd been there for that," Thistle interjected. "I'm not good when it comes to emotional stuff. Bay was crying like a baby, and Landon was pacing like a madman. All the while, Aunt Tillie kept demanding iced tea and ice cream. It was a nightmare."

I ignored her. "Things are changing in our world, Clove," I said. "You're the first one to move out, but do you really think Thistle and I will live together forever?"

"I don't know," Clove said, refusing to give up. "Maybe you'll find you enjoy living together more without me."

"Yeah, that's not going to happen," Thistle said. "Marcus is making noise about us moving in together, and I think it's only a matter of time before it becomes a reality. Once he has the stable finished and running how he wants it, I just know he's going to ask me to move in. He wants to turn that barn into a cool house. It's going to take a lot of work, but ... I think it's going to make a neat home and that's where I see myself landing eventually."

Wait a second ... . "So Clove is going to live in a lighthouse and you're going to live in a renovated barn? Where does that leave me?" I'm pretty sure I asked Landon the same question and he answered it for me, but I was still irked.

"You're going to find a place with Landon," Thistle answered. "He doesn't like being away from you three nights a week as it is. This isn't *Three's Company*. We can't live together forever."

"We kind of talked about that the other night," I admitted. "He says he doesn't want me moving to Traverse City because he would rather settle here, but he's not sure he can because of his job."

"Maybe he'll quit his job," Thistle suggested.

"And do what? Run the kissing booth at every festival the town holds?"

"I could actually see him running a restaurant that only serves bacon," Thistle said, grinning. "By the way, I made a gift for you to give him. Remind me when we get back to the store and I'll give it to you."

That was intriguing – and frightening. "What kind of gift? I'm not dressing up like a slice of bacon no matter what you've concocted."

"You'll like it," Thistle said, laughing as she shifted her eyes to Clove. "I think you're worried about things that don't technically exist. We're still family. We're just expanding that family and growing up. What is it exactly you're worried about?"

"I don't feel grown up," Clove said. "I feel ... left out."

"You're not left out," I argued, pushing open the door. I couldn't continue this conversation when I had bigger things to worry about.

"I'm sorry no one called you yesterday. It was an anomaly. Usually you would be in town and would've known about the arrest and my fight with Landon. You just happened to have the day off."

"She's right," Thistle said, exiting the vehicle. "You're making a big deal out of nothing. You're going to be involved in all of our adventures."

"Besides, you're usually the one who complains about going on adventures," I reminded her.

"Yes, but I enjoy complaining," Clove said, joining me on the sidewalk in front of the retirement home. "That's my thing."

"That is kind of your thing," I acknowledged.

"And it doesn't bother us in the slightest," Thistle lied.

"It will still be your thing, Clove," I said. "We're still going to go on adventures and get in trouble. That won't change because you've moved. It's in our genes."

Clove offered me a heartfelt smile. "Just … don't forget about me."

"That's not possible," Thistle said, flashing a cheeky smile before turning her attention to the sprawling retirement community. "Okay, how are we going to do this?"

"I think you should let me take the lead," I said. "We'll pretend we're old friends of the family and just want to catch up with Victor because we lost track of him."

"That sounds boring," Thistle countered. "Clove wants an adventure, so we should have fun. I think you should let me take the lead."

"Why?"

"I have an idea."

Oh, well, that had "disaster" written all over it. Still … why not? "Go for it."

"HI!"

Thistle's smile was so fake I cringed as the woman at the front desk lifted her eyes to study us.

"Hi."

"We're here to see Victor Donahue," Thistle said. "We're from the

Hemlock Cove Historical Commission, and because he's one of our oldest living representatives we have a fun stack of cash and prizes for him once he answers a few questions for our newsletter."

Newsletter? Cash and prizes? She never gets to come up with the plan again.

"He's in the solarium," the receptionist said, returning her attention to the computer on the desk. It looked as if she was playing Candy Crush.

"And where is the solarium?" I asked, exchanging a quick look with Thistle. I had expected more of a challenge ... or at least a few questions ... before being directed toward Victor.

"That way." The receptionist pointed toward a brightly lighted room to our left without raising her head.

"Don't we have to sign in or anything?" Clove asked. "You don't know anything about us. We could be kidnappers or something."

"Are you kidnappers?" The woman's tone was dull and lifeless.

"No."

"Then have a nice day," she said, frowning when she ran out of moves. "I hate you!" She was talking to the computer, but it was the most animated she'd been since our arrival.

I led Thistle and Clove to the solarium, keeping quiet until we were out of the receptionist's hearing range. "You're never allowed to make the plan again, Thistle. That was ridiculous."

"We got in, didn't we?"

"The only thing that would've kept us out is if we were carrying swords," I replied. "And I'm not even sure that's true because she would've had to look up to notice them."

"We could be kidnappers," Clove said. "I don't like this."

"Well, we're not kidnappers," Thistle said. "We have one senior citizen at home and she's more than enough. We don't want to add to the mayhem."

"Let's just find Victor and get out of here," I said, narrowing my eyes at the stained glass windows. They depicted various biblical scenes, some of them rather gruesome. "This place gives me the creeps."

"I think we have only one option," Clove said, pointing toward a table at the end of the room. She was right. There was only one person present, and he sat staring into nothingness.

"He looks out of it," I said, rolling my neck until it cracked. "Maybe he's ... you know."

"Cuckoo for Cocoa Puffs?" Thistle asked.

I pinched her wrist. "Be nice."

"Can I help you?" A male voice cut off Thistle's screech – and probably revenge – and when I turned to find a dark-haired man in a white uniform standing next to a rolling mop bucket. "Are you Victor's family?"

I licked my lips as I decided how to answer. "Um ... ."

"We're from Hemlock Cove, and Victor used to know our great-aunt," Clove lied smoothly, taking me by surprise. She was usually the worst of us when it came to thinking on her feet. "She mentioned him the other day, and we thought it might be nice to see how he was. We were hoping to see if he seemed up for a visit before we brought her to see him."

"We didn't want to risk the trip if seeing Victor would upset her," I added. "She's ... elderly."

"And feeble," Thistle interjected. "She can't take stress."

"Oh, that's too bad" the janitor said. "I'm not sure it's a good idea to bring your aunt here, but Victor loves visitors. He'll enjoy seeing you."

"Well, we'll make sure not to tire him too much," I said.

The janitor nodded and then turned his attention to the floor at the far side of the room as we turned back to Victor.

I approached the man with a wide smile. "Hi."

The man, his hair completely white and his expression blank, shifted his eyes to me. He didn't speak.

"I'm Bay Winchester," I said. "I'm from Hemlock Cove."

"He probably doesn't know where that is," Thistle said. "He left long before they changed the name."

"We're from Walkerville," I corrected. "Are you Victor?"

The man slowly nodded as he looked Thistle and me over. Finally

AMANDA M. LEE

he shifted his eyes to Clove, and his expression brightened as he offered her a warm smile.

"He seems to like Clove," Thistle said. "You try talking to him."

"What do I say?" Clove asked, nervously shuffling toward Victor. "Should I ask him about Patty?"

"I don't know," I replied. "Just ... talk to him. That seems like the best option."

"Hi, Victor," Clove said, sitting in the chair next to him. "How are you feeling today?"

Victor's smile never wavered. "Tillie."

I stilled, surprised. "Did he just ... ?"

"I'm not Tillie," Clove said, her smile faltering. "I don't look like Aunt Tillie, do I?"

"Yes," Thistle and I replied in unison.

"That's the meanest thing you've ever said to me," Clove groused.

"Tillie," Victor said, his hand shaking as he reached over and grabbed her wrist. "Tillie Winchester. You look exactly the same."

I bit my lip to keep from laughing at the murderous look on Clove's face.

"I'm not Tillie," Clove said. "I'm Clove. Tillie is my great-aunt."

"They look exactly alike, though," Thistle said, grinning mischievously. "In fact, they're practically the same person."

"Shut up, Thistle," Clove snapped, irritated. "We look nothing alike."

"How did you stay the same when I got so old?" Victor asked. "It's like ... magic."

"It is like magic," Thistle said, wriggling her eyebrows. "It's like witchcraft."

"Yes," Victor said, nodding. He was deathly serious. "Were all of those rumors about you true? Did you really have magic? I know the girls gossiped, but I always thought they were jealous."

I had an idea. "Was Patty one of the jealous girls, Victor?" I asked, sitting in the empty chair on his other side so he wouldn't have a problem hearing me. "Did she tell you things about Tillie?"

"She did," Victor said, licking his lips. "She said Tillie killed chickens and bathed in their blood because she wanted to be young forever."

"Well, that's just gross," Thistle muttered.

"What else did Patty say?" I asked.

"I'm not sure I'm supposed to talk about this," Victor said, confusion washing over him. It was clear he wasn't in control of all of his faculties. We might have only a small window to question him.

"Tillie wants you to talk about this, don't you?" I arched a challenging eyebrow in Clove's direction.

"I'm going to make you pay for this," Clove hissed, although she forced a smile for Victor's benefit. "It's fine to tell me, Victor. Patty isn't around, and she wouldn't mind anyway. We made up."

I sent Clove a thumbs-up. That was good.

"You made up with Patty after the big fight?" Victor asked, surprised. "But you said you would never talk to her again because of what she said to Ginger."

Ginger was our late grandmother. She died before we were born, but she and Aunt Tillie were extremely close. If Patty said anything to or did something to Ginger, that could explain the animosity between the two women. Aunt Tillie would hold a grudge forever where our grandmother was concerned.

"Ginger is ... gone, too," Clove said, her voice soft. "She didn't like it when I fought with people. She wanted me to make up with Patty. It's okay."

"Ginger always was the sweet one," Victor said, nodding. "You were the feisty one. That's why I liked you."

My mouth dropped open as Victor reached over and tickled Clove's ribs.

"Giggle for me like you did that time we were in the barn," Victor instructed. "Giggle and whisper my name."

"No, I don't think I'm in the mood to giggle," Clove said, shifting in her chair so it was harder for Victor to reach her. "In fact, I want you to stop doing that. Victor ... Victor ... I will break your fingers!"

Victor ignored Clove's outburst. "You're still pretty as a picture and feisty as a cat in heat."

Thistle snickered. "I'm starting to like this guy."

"You would," I said, scorching her with a look before trying to draw Victor's attention. "You were about to tell us about Patty, Victor," I prodded. "Remind us about the fight she had with Tillie. How do you remember it?"

Victor finally tore his gaze from Clove and focused on me. "Who are you?"

My heart sank as I registered the far-away look in his eyes. "I'm Bay."

"I don't know you," Victor said, leaning back in his chair as he scanned all three of us. "I don't know any of you."

"Yes, you do," Clove argued. "I'm Tillie. Remember?"

"I don't know any Tillie," Victor spat, pushing himself up on shaky legs as he took a step away from the table. "You're trying to trick me. Did the government send you? Did she send you? It was her, wasn't it?"

I had no idea who "she" was, but Victor wasn't happy with her. "No, that's not true," I said. "That's Tillie Winchester. You remember Tillie, right? You were just talking about her and Patty Grimes."

"I don't know any of those people, and I don't know you," Victor snapped. "Go away!. I … you people are trying to trick me. I'm old, but I'm not stupid!"

I watched shuffle away. There was no sense trying to stop him. Whatever magic allowed him to remember his past was gone now. There was nothing left for us to do except upset him, and I had no intention of doing that.

"Well, that was a bust," Thistle said.

"Kind of," I hedged. "Let's go to the car. We might not have gotten a lot of information out of Victor, but we got enough to give me an idea."

"Is it better than Thistle's idea?" Clove asked.

"Definitely."

EIGHTEEN

"What's this grand idea you have?" Thistle asked back in the car. "Do you want to strip Clove down and send her back inside to let Victor feel her up this time? He might crack if we give him a reward."

"I hate you," Clove muttered, crossing her arms over her chest. "And, by the way, I look nothing like Aunt Tillie."

I wasn't in the mood to argue, so I decided to play nice. "You don't look like Aunt Tillie."

"Thank you."

"You look like your mother, and she looks like Aunt Tillie," I said. What? Just because I'm not in the mood to argue doesn't mean I won't pull the pin and toss the grenade.

"That's it," Clove snapped. "I thought I missed you guys yesterday and was feeling low and sorry for myself. Now I realize I'm better off without you. I'm sick of adventures anyway. Next time you guys get a scheme, leave me out of it. I'd rather stay home and garden."

"I'm going to remember you said that when you start complaining again," Thistle warned, her eyes serious when she turned them on me. "What's your idea?"

AMANDA M. LEE

"Victor said he wasn't sure Patty wanted him to tell Tillie why she was angry," I said. "He acted as if it was a secret."

"So?"

"Mrs. Little acted as if there was a secret, too," I said. "She wanted to know why I didn't ask Aunt Tillie about her relationship with Patty."

Thistle snorted. "Did you tell her you didn't ask Aunt Tillie because you didn't want to be cursed or have to wade through a pack of lies to find the truth?"

"No. I didn't want to give her ammunition."

"Yeah, I probably would've done the same thing," Thistle said. "If there is a secret, more than one person is keeping it."

"And they're all old," I said.

"I don't think senior citizens appreciate being called 'old,'" Clove said. "That's insulting. That would be like everyone calling all witches crones or something ... or all women nags."

"What should we say?" Thistle challenged. "Long in the tooth?"

"Wrinkled and crinkled?" I asked, fighting the urge to laugh.

"Almost dead?" Thistle added.

"You guys are going to a bad place when you die," Clove said. "I hope you know that."

I sighed. I didn't have a problem with senior citizens. I wasn't particularly fond of Hemlock Cove's elderly population right now, but Clove had a point. "I'm sorry. We'll start speaking about them with more respect."

"Thank you," Clove said. "Call them ... seasoned."

"That sounds as if we're about to stick skewers through them and toss them on the grill," Thistle complained.

"I forgot how much I hate spending long stretches of time with the two of you," Clove muttered, shaking her head. "Let's go home. I need a breather from you guys."

"We're going home," I said, watching as Thistle stuck the key in the ignition and the car's engine roared to life. "We're not separating when we get there, though. I told you I had an idea."

"I can't wait to hear this," Thistle said, pulling out of the parking lot.

I gave the retirement community one last look, frowning when I saw Victor standing on the other side of one of the front windows watching us. The expression on his face was ... peculiar. "Do you see that?"

"What?" Thistle asked, fixated on the road.

"Victor is in the window watching us."

"He probably wants to give Aunt Tillie here another tickle," Thistle said.

"You're sick," Clove hissed.

"With his pickle," Thistle added.

"Now you're really sick!"

"No, that's not it," I said, straining for a last glimpse of the window before Thistle pulled onto the main road. "He didn't look confused. He looked ... angry."

"Now I think you're the one reading too much into things, Bay," Thistle chided. "That guy wasn't sure he had shoes on half the time we were there. He's old ... I mean seasoned ... and he's confused. That's what happens with age."

I wasn't so sure, but I decided to push the thought from my mind. Thistle was probably right. Even if Victor was angry, though, that didn't mean he was angry with us. He could've been angry with whoever "she" was. His mind was a jumble of past lives and partially forgotten hurts. He probably couldn't separate today from yesterday ... or ten years ago, for that matter.

"Right," I said, shaking my head. "What were we talking about again?"

"Your grand idea," Clove prodded. "I'm not participating in your grand idea no matter what it is, because I don't like how mean you guys are to me. I'm putting my foot down."

She always says that. "Duly noted," I said, refusing to catch Thistle's eye because I was afraid we would burst into laughter and make Clove even angrier. "Anyway, like I was saying, if there is a big secret, I think more people than Mrs. Little, Aunt Tillie and Patty know it."

"What about Kenneth?" Thistle suggested. "You said he was friendly and open to talking to you the other day."

"Kenneth hasn't always lived in Hemlock Cove," I reminded her. "He's only been in town for a few months. He lived a few towns over. Remember?"

"I forgot about that," Thistle said. "It seems like we've known him a long time, but we only met him during the greenhouse construction."

"I think Aunt Tillie still likes him, by the way, but we can't deal with that until we're sure she's not going to prison."

"Yes, because whatever you're thinking won't get us cursed or anything," Thistle grumbled. "Go back to your idea for discovering the secret. I'm mildly interested in that."

"I'm not," Clove said.

I ignored her. "I think we should go to the senior center when we get back to Hemlock Cove," I said. "They're holding a euchre tournament today. I saw it advertised on the board when I was there earlier this week."

"So what? Do you have a hankering to lose at cards to seasoned citizens?" Thistle asked, daring a glance at Clove, who declined to rise to the bait.

"No. I want to cast a truth spell and ask some of the people who have been around for a really long time if they know the secret."

"Oh," Thistle said, realization dawning.

"I'm also a great euchre player," I added.

"Yes, I'm sure you could play professionally," Thistle said. "I'm not sure the spell's a good idea. That could backfire on us."

"It could," I agreed. "I don't see where we have a lot of options, though."

"I think it's a terrible idea," Clove sniffed. "No one asked me."

"What happens if we lose control of the spell?" Thistle asked, her eyes flashing with mirth as Clove huffed about being ignored behind us.

"What always happens when we lose control of a spell?" I asked.

"We usually deny we did it and run to Aunt Tillie to cover our behinds. Then she blackmails us for a month and we swear we'll never cast another spell."

"Then we'll do that," I said.

"You know what? Why not?" Thistle smiled as she turned onto the rural highway that led back to Hemlock Cove. "What have we got to lose?"

"Well, I'm not doing it," Clove said. "It's a terrible plan and it's going to go badly for us. It always goes badly for us. I'm going to go home and garden. You two can go on this adventure yourselves. Frankly, I don't care what you do. This time I want to be forgotten."

"Oh, don't be like that, Clove," Thistle said. "We need you."

Despite her dour mood, Clove couldn't stop herself from brightening. "You do? You need me?"

"Of course we do," Thistle said. "Someone has to let the seasoned males tickle her while we're trying to get information out of them."

"I hate you!"

"Ah, this is the way all of our adventures should be," I said, eliciting a laugh from Thistle and a scowl from Clove. "It's just like old times."

"That's what I'm afraid of," Clove said. "This ... bites."

"I STILL THINK this is a terrible idea."

Two hours later we stood outside the senior center, the spell already cast. We hid in the bushes while we did it, which probably wasn't the smartest thing to do given Noah's presence in town, but we were too lazy to go someplace else.

I slid a dark look in Clove's direction. She'd done nothing but complain since leaving the retirement community in Bellaire. "For someone who spent half the afternoon complaining because she thought we didn't want to spend time with her, you have a lot of gripes."

"That's because I forgot how much I hate going on adventures with you guys."

"That's not what you said three hours ago," Thistle snapped.

"I believe that's exactly what I said three hours ago," Clove shot back. "You clearly weren't listening. You never listen when I talk. It's annoying."

"You're annoying!"

"You're both annoying," I said, stepping between them. "There's no reason to fight. Just ... knock it off."

"Fine," Clove said, rolling her eyes.

"If we were going to fight, though, I'd be on Thistle's side. She is totally right," I said. I have no idea why I felt the need to engage, but there was comfort to be found in the normalcy of arguing, and I gladly embraced it. "You whined like a baby about being ignored and wanting to go on adventures, and now you're being a ... ."

"Kvetch," Thistle supplied.

"I don't miss living with you guys at all," Clove groused. "I don't know why I thought I did. I must have been temporarily insane."

"Don't sell yourself short," Thistle said. "It's not temporary. It's permanent."

"Let's just get this over with," I said, my temper fraying as I tried to refrain from saying something ugly. "We'll go inside, track down Myrtle, Fay and Viola to ask our questions. Then we'll reverse the spell and be out of here."

"When you say it like that, it sounds easy," Thistle said.

"Good."

"You know that's not going to happen, right?" Thistle pressed. "This stuff always backfires on us."

"It worked the night we cast the spell on the guests at the Dragonfly," I reminded her. "They told the truth."

"And we missed the killer under the roof because we didn't think to look upstairs, your dad had a meltdown and Aunt Tillie cast the spell so it actually worked," Thistle said. "Our spells often backfire."

"It's because we're dabblers," Clove said. "Aunt Tillie says if we want our spells to go off as planned we have to work at it."

"That sounds really annoying and tiresome," Thistle said. "I prefer the way we do things."

"You just said it always backfires," Clove pointed out.

"Yes, but it's often fun when it happens," Thistle said, moving toward the door. "Now, come on. I want to see how many senior citizens pinch Clove's butt before the afternoon is over."

"You're dead to me," Clove muttered, following Thistle inside.

Because the afternoon was bright, it took a moment for our eyes to adjust to the dim lighting of the senior center. When things came into focus, I was stunned at the amount of people sitting at tables and playing cards. There had to be at least fifty people present.

"I didn't know Hemlock Cove had this many seasoned people in town," Thistle said, letting out a low whistle. "Holy crap!"

"It's all women," Clove said, knitting her eyebrows. "There's like ... two guys and forty-eight women. Why?"

"Kenneth told me that most men don't like coming here because they don't want to admit they're old," I said. "I thought he was exaggerating and that most women simply outlive men, but I'm not so sure now. This ratio can't be representative of the town."

"Well, this doesn't really change anything," Thistle said. "In fact ... yup ... here comes Fay. Let's ask her first. We might get lucky."

"When do we ever get lucky?" Clove asked.

"If you don't stop complaining, I'm going to give you something to complain about, Clove," Thistle snapped. "You're on my last nerve."

"You're always on my last nerve," Clove said.

"You're both on my last nerve," I said. "Just ... shut up." I pasted a bright smile on my face as Fay approached, hoping to come across as friendly and curious rather than deranged and dastardly. "Hi, Fay. How are you?"

"I'm doing well," Fay said, her expression reflecting confusion. "What are you doing here? You're not looking for Tillie, are you? If she's here, I need to warn everyone to stop drinking the coffee ... and the punch ... and probably the brandy."

"Aunt Tillie isn't here," I said. "We came to talk to you."

"Me?" Fay's expression was hard to read. She clearly liked being singled out, but she was understandably suspicious. "Why on earth would you want to talk to me?"

"Well ... ." I licked my lips.

"Oh, just do it," Thistle said. "She won't remember anyway."

"What am I not going to remember?" Fay asked, shifting from one foot to the other. She was antsy, not that I blamed her.

"We want to know the big secret everyone is keeping about Patty Grimes and her past with Aunt Tillie," Thistle volunteered. "You have to tell us the truth. Now, no one can overhear you, so it's the perfect time to lay it on me."

"You have such a way with people," I muttered, shaking my head as Fay frowned. "I can't believe you're not the most popular person in Hemlock Cove with conversational skills like that."

"I can believe it," Clove said.

"I'm not sure I understand what you're asking," Fay said finally.

Huh. That's not one of the reactions I expected. "We need to know the truth about Aunt Tillie's past with Patty Grimes," I prodded.

"I don't know anything about that." Fay's eyes darted to the left, a telltale sign she was lying.

"But ... you have to know about it," I said, refusing to give up. "You went to school with Aunt Tillie and you were around back then. You're friends with Mrs. Little. I know you're aware of the big secret."

"Well, Bay, I don't know what to tell you," Fay said. "If there is a big secret, I'm not privy to it." She did the eye thing again.

"You're lying," I challenged, my frustration getting the better of me.

Fay was offended. "I am not lying," she said. "I don't appreciate your attitude, young lady. I understand you're upset about Tillie, but that's no reason to take it out on me."

"We're sorry," Thistle said, grabbing my arm and wrestling me toward the door. "We didn't mean to upset you. Between the heat and the emotional upheaval, Bay just isn't herself."

Fay didn't look convinced. "Well ... take her home. Get her out of the sun. Don't let her come back here if she's going to spout off and call upstanding people liars."

"Of course," Thistle said, digging her fingernails into my skin when I tried to pull away from her. "Come on, Bay."

"I'm not done here," I argued.

"Yes, you are," Thistle said. "Clove, help me."

Clove was reluctant to join the fray but she eventually acquiesced. It took both of them to drag me outside.

"She was lying," I sputtered.

"That's because the spell didn't work," Thistle said, pinching my forearm for good measure before removing her hands from me.

"Ow! Why did you do that?"

"Because you're causing a scene," Thistle said. "We screwed up the spell. I think it's because I switched out mugwort in place of the graveyard dust."

"Why did you do that?" Clove asked, incensed. "There's no way that would work."

"Because we're out of graveyard dust and I don't want to collect any during the day when people will ask questions," Thistle replied. "We're already considered the weirdest people in town. How would it look if I'm digging in the cemetery in ninety-degree heat?"

"Well, crap," I muttered, tugging my hand through my hair. "That was for nothing."

"Oh, there was no harm done," Thistle said. "Fay already disliked us. Now, on top of being crazy, she thinks we're rude. It's no big deal."

"I still think the truth spell is the way to go," I argued.

"Well, then we have to wait until after dark," Thistle said. "They're having a dance after their tournament. They had a flyer on the table. We can sneak out of the inn after dinner, collect the graveyard dust and recast the spell."

I didn't see any other options. "I blame you for this," I said. "I hope you know that."

"I can live with that," Thistle said, unperturbed.

"Oh, now it feels like old times," Clove said, suddenly chipper. "I hope you know I'm not going with you tonight. This was fun, though."

"Oh, you're going with us," I countered. "If you don't, we'll curse you."

"And we won't be nearly as nice as Aunt Tillie would be," Thistle said.

"Fine," Clove muttered, resigned. "I really do hate you guys."

"And all is right with the world," Thistle said.

NINETEEN

I let myself into the inn through the front door shortly before seven, scanning the empty lobby before moving toward the library. Landon's Ford Explorer was in the parking lot, so I knew he was here, and I expected to find him in his favorite room. I heard voices as I approached and pulled up short. He wasn't alone.

"I'm not saying you're doing anything wrong," Noah said. "I'm simply saying that you're putting your career in jeopardy for this woman, and I want to know why."

I froze, worry and doubt colliding in my stomach and causing it to churn.

"It's none of your business," Landon said. I could see him through the corner of the window in the door. He had a glass in his hand, which meant he was drinking. "I don't need to justify my feelings or actions to you."

"That's not what I'm saying," Noah protested. I couldn't see him, but the sound of his voice made me think he was close to the drink cart. "When I first joined the Traverse City office, you were one of the guys I most looked up to."

"I'm thrilled," Landon deadpanned, leaning his head back to stare at the ceiling.

"I'm serious," Noah said. "Your reputation was amazing. The boss and other agents couldn't say enough good things about you. Now, though...."

My heart rolled. Now what?

"Are you saying Director Newton and my fellow agents are saying bad things about me?" Landon asked.

"Of course not," Noah said. "You're still the most respected man in the office."

"Then what are you saying?" Landon asked, snapping his head down and darting a dark look toward the far end of the library. "You obviously have something on your mind, Noah. You might as well spit it out."

"Listen, I don't want to tell you how to live your life...."

"But you're going to," Landon interjected.

"You could go far in the bureau," Noah said. "You could be a regional director one day, or even end up in D.C. if you set your sights that high. That won't happen if you get a reputation for covering for your girlfriend and her kooky family."

"I have no interest in being regional director or moving to Washington," Landon replied. "I'm happy here. Even if I wanted those things, though, Bay wouldn't stand in the way of me getting them. She would be my biggest booster."

Thistle and Clove walked into the hallway behind me and I lifted my finger to my lips to quiet them. Winchesters are perfectly happy eavesdropping on private conversations.

"Bay seems nice," Noah said. "She's very pretty. Heck, she's hot."

"Oh, you're hot," Thistle whispered, wrinkling her nose.

"Thank you for speaking about my girlfriend's hot factor," Landon said. "I can't tell you what a relief it is that you've been checking her out."

"I haven't been checking her out," Noah argued, his voice going squeaky. "I swear. She's not even my type. I prefer the little one with the big...."

"I wouldn't finish that sentence," Landon warned. "Bay is my girlfriend, but I'm fond of Clove and Thistle, too. I know exactly what you were going to say, and it's inappropriate – and hazardous to your health."

Clove glanced down at her impressive cleavage. "These are a powerful weapon," she whispered. "They bring men to their knees."

Thistle covered her mouth to choke her laughter.

"You're fond of Thistle?" Noah asked. "Are you sure? She seems mean."

"She is mean," Landon said. "She's also loyal and strong. She stands by Bay no matter what. Sure, she's a pain in the ass, but I'm still fond of her."

"That was both a compliment and an insult," Thistle said. "I'm impressed."

I patted my finger against my lips to remind my cousins to be quiet.

"All of that is well and good, Landon, but you're risking everything by covering for Bay and that crazy aunt of hers," Noah said. "We both know she's guilty. If she keeps covering for her aunt, Bay could go to jail. No one else would've let her slide on that Sally story. Why did you?"

Well, he wasn't wrong.

"First off, I don't believe Aunt Tillie is guilty," Landon said. "I still have to investigate the case. It's my job, and I'll follow the evidence. I've known that woman for more than a year now, though, and I don't believe for a second she killed Patty Grimes."

"How can you even say that? Look at the evidence. Are you blind?"

"I'm not done," Landon said, his tone getting chillier by the word. "Second, Bay will not go to jail, because she's a good woman. She's the best person I know. She has a wonderful heart. Sure, she's a little goofy sometimes, but I like that about her.

"As for the so-called evidence, we don't really have any," he continued. "You have one woman with a lifetime grudge claiming Aunt Tillie was at the senior center. We don't know where Patty Grimes ingested the poison. We don't know Aunt Tillie put anything in the coffee. There's no evidence pointing to anything.

"You want to believe Aunt Tillie is guilty," Landon said. "You don't know it, though."

"I think you're blinded by … sex … or something," Noah said. "I don't see how you can pretend Tillie Winchester isn't guilty."

"Because I believe in facts," Landon said. "And, while we're on the subject, don't ever say anything like that about Bay again. I'm not blinded by sex. I love her. There's a difference, and when you're older you'll understand that."

"You sound like you belong on a soap opera," Noah scoffed. "You love her? Are you willing to give up everything for love?"

"Bay has given me more than you can ever imagine," Landon said. "I'm not giving up anything for her because all I've done is gain since meeting her. If you say something negative about her again, by the way, we're going to have a real problem."

"We're on a case here, Landon," Noah said. "I have a right to express my opinion."

"Not about my relationship with Bay you don't," Landon argued, getting to his feet. For a moment I thought he was about to throw a punch at Noah. "You're new here, so you don't get how this family works. They're wonderful. You might want to pull your head out of your behind and take a look around before it's too late. You're missing the bigger picture – and it's extraordinary."

Noah wasn't ready to let it go. "And what if Tillie is guilty?"

"She's not," Landon said. "I'm not sure who is guilty, but we'll figure it out. Aunt Tillie would rather torture someone than kill them. Is that a defense? No. I believe it, though. At the end of the day, I can guarantee it's not Aunt Tillie."

Landon put his empty glass down on the coffee table. "If you'll excuse me … ."

"Wait, where are you going?"

"Bay and her cousins are eavesdropping in the hallway, and I want a kiss," Landon replied. "I haven't seen her in hours and I missed her."

My cheeks burned as Landon strode into the hallway and met my mortified gaze. He smirked as he pulled me in for a hug. "How did you know?"

AMANDA M. LEE

"I saw your reflection in the glass," Landon replied. "It took me a few minutes to realize what I was looking at, but you might want to tell your partners in crime to be quiet when spying. Also, Thistle's hair is a dead giveaway. There's nothing else that particular shade of purple in the house."

I pressed my lips together, flustered.

"That was the most romantic thing I've ever heard," Clove gushed, pressing her hand to the spot above her heart. "I want to kiss you."

"I'm taken," Landon said. "He might want to kiss you, though." He gestured toward Noah, who had the grace to look abashed as he stepped in the open doorway.

"Yeah, we heard the comment about Clove's boobs," Thistle said, narrowing her eyes. "I mean ... how rude."

"Very rude," I agreed, finding my voice. "It was almost perverted it was so rude."

"I agree," Thistle said. "I don't think our mothers and kooky great-aunt will like it."

"Ladies, I think there's been a misunderstanding," Noah said, hurrying toward us. "You weren't supposed to hear that conversation."

"Too late," I said, slipping my hand into Landon's and tugging him toward the dining room. "I might kiss you for what you said, too."

"That I'll take," Landon said, slinging an arm over my shoulders as he followed me. "Are you coming, Noah?"

"I'm not sure." Noah looked as if he was caught in a trap and the only way out was to gnaw through his own leg.

"Somebody's in trouble," Thistle sang as she passed him.

"And Aunt Tillie is going to be doling out punishments," Clove added, glaring at Landon's partner. "I would start begging sooner rather than later if I were you. Perverts make her crabby."

"DID YOU FIND IT?"

"No," Thistle said, shaking her head as she hit the bottom of the back staircase. "I searched all through Aunt Tillie's room and she doesn't have any graveyard dust. We have no choice but to collect it ourselves."

"Oh, I don't want to," Clove whined. "The cemetery is scary at night."

"We'll be with you," I said.

"Yes, and we won't let anyone hurt our poor Clove," Thistle said, grabbing Clove's cheek and giving it a good jiggle.

Clove jerked her face out of Thistle's grasp. "Stop doing that. You know I hate it when you do that."

"Well, I hate it when you complain, and you don't stop doing that," Thistle said. "Life is hard on everyone. Suck it up."

"Knock it off," I ordered, leaning around the couch in the family living quarters and studying the gap between the bottom of the kitchen door and the floor. If anyone was in the kitchen I would see shadows, but we appeared to be safe ... for now.

Dinner was uncomfortable – as it always seemed to be with Noah present – and Mom was pretty much at her limit when dealing with him. He had an oblivious nature that didn't let him know he'd crossed a line, or perhaps he didn't care, and his sense of humor was non-existent.

"Well, if we're going to collect graveyard dust, we have to leave now," Thistle said. "That dance only lasts until ten, and because they're old ... ."

Clove cleared her throat, causing Thistle to roll her eyes.

"Because they're seasoned they'll go to bed early," Thistle said, correcting her course. "We have a narrow window of opportunity here and we have to make it count."

"Okay," I said. "Let's go."

Clove furrowed her brow. "Don't you want to tell Landon where we're going? We excused ourselves when dessert was being served, but someone will notice when we don't come back to the table."

"I know, but I can't go back in there without drawing Noah's attention," I said. "I'll leave a note and apologize when I get back. I'm sure that apology will involve groveling, nudity and a massage before it's all said and done."

Thistle snorted. "Yeah. Marcus pretty much expects me to do underhanded things. He won't be angry. In fact, he'll probably be perfectly happy to go back to the guesthouse and watch whatever lame sports show is on tonight with Landon."

"What should I write in the note?" I asked, grabbing a notebook and pen from the table. "I don't want to go into too much detail in case Noah somehow stumbles across it."

"He wouldn't dare," Thistle said. "He's a nervous wreck after realizing we heard what he said. I thought he was going to pass out at least eight times during dinner."

"That's because every time he risked a look in Clove's direction she grabbed her boobs," I said, smirking at the memory.

"I have no idea what got into me," Clove admitted. "Landon just kind of … touched me … with what he said about Bay. Noah was a douche, so I touched myself to get to him. I'm just glad Sam wasn't here to see it. I'm not sure he would understand."

"Don't sell Sam short on this one," I said. "I think he would've approved of what you did. Why wasn't he at dinner, by the way?"

"He's meeting with some people in Traverse City about buying that tanker I told you about so we can build the haunted boat attraction," Clove replied. "He's excited about this one because it's a really good deal."

"I'm actually excited about that, too," Thistle said. "I want to help decorate."

"Me, too," I said, taking a moment to study the paper and then scrawling a haphazard note that would make Landon furious when he read it. I left the note on the coffee table and headed toward the door. "Come on. Landon is going to be ticked, but I don't know what else to do."

"It will be fine," Thistle said. "He's totally in love with you. He'll forgive you."

"Remind me to pick up some bacon on the way back."

"That will do it," Thistle said, following me outside. The sun had nearly set, but the air was still humid and oppressive. "Ugh. I love summer, but I could deal without the humidity."

"Ha!"

We jolted at the sound of Landon's voice, turning quickly to find him and Marcus watching us from the side of the house.

"You scared the crap out of me," I snapped.

"You deserve it for sneaking out," Landon said, strolling in my direction. "I knew you were up to something. I can't believe you were going to sneak out without telling me."

"So you enlisted Marcus to spy on us?"

"I didn't want to hang around with Noah," Marcus said. "I don't care why you guys are sneaking around. I'm used to it. Nothing you do surprises me."

"I do care," Landon said, his eyes flashing.

I told him about our day, and when I was done Landon's expression was unreadable.

"I think he's amazed by our ingenuity," Thistle offered.

"I think he's going to kill us," Clove supplied.

"I think that's a pretty good idea," Landon said finally. "I want to come with you."

"You can't," I argued. "There's no way for you to explain it to Noah. I'm sorry. You have to let us do this one on our own."

"We need to make sure Noah is here so he doesn't catch us there," Thistle said. "It's not like it's dangerous. We're going to a dance at the senior center."

Landon rubbed his chin. "I know in my head that you're right, but I really want to go with you."

"I want you to go with us, too, but you said we had to play this smart," I reminded him. "Is going with us the smart thing to do?"

"No." Landon exhaled heavily and ran a hand through his hair. "I just want our normal life back."

"Even though it's kooky?" I asked.

Landon grabbed the front of my T-shirt and hauled me up to the tips of my toes before planting a scorching kiss on me. "Even though," he said when we parted. "Do you promise to be careful?"

I nodded.

"Do you promise to call me if things get out of hand?"

I nodded again.

"Then go," Landon said, releasing my shirt. "Hurry back as soon as you can. Even if I only get a few minutes with you before we go to sleep, I'll take it. I feel like I'm going through Bay withdrawal we've had so little time to spend together."

"Oh, that's sweet," Thistle said. "Will you be excited to see me when I get back, Marcus?"

Marcus shrugged. "Don't wake me up when you come in. I have to be up early."

Thistle frowned. "Where's the love?"

Marcus leaned over and gave her a sweet kiss. "Hiding until you get Aunt Tillie out of the guesthouse," he replied. "Be good, and don't be mean to Clove."

"I'm never mean to Clove," Thistle countered.

"Oh, whatever," Clove said. "You've been mean to me all day."

"That's because you've been whining all day," Thistle shot back.

I shot Landon a rueful smile. "And Clove worried things would be different once she moved out of the guesthouse."

Landon planted his hands on the side of my face so he could kiss my forehead. "Some things will never change, and that is one of them. Hurry up and do this, and then get your butts back here. I don't want to give Noah a reason to be suspicious."

"What are you going to tell him we're doing?" I asked.

"Chick things."

"Do you want to be more specific?"

"I'm sure I'll figure something out," Landon said. "I am a professional, after all. It will be a breeze."

TWENTY

"I'm never doing that again," Clove announced, dumping the graveyard dust into a baggie and shaking the potion ingredients so they mixed completely. "You know how I feel about cemeteries. I can't believe you made me do that."

Thistle rolled her eyes. "We gave you the option of staying in the car while we collected it."

"You wanted me to stay in the car alone in a cemetery parking lot," Clove said. "How is that safe?"

"It's not even nine yet," Thistle snapped. "There are kids still playing in their front yards."

"And listening for the ice cream truck," I added.

Clove refused to let it go. "But they're not playing in the cemetery, are they?"

"I can't even talk to you when you get like this," Thistle said, shaking her head. "Next time I suggest we bring Annie. She's braver than Clove."

That was an interesting suggestion. "Did anyone else catch the way Annie's eyes lit up when Clove grabbed her boobs at the dinner table tonight?"

"Yeah, she liked it," Thistle said, smiling. "She's funny. Her crush on Marcus is adorable."

Thistle doesn't like most kids, but she has a soft spot for Annie. We all do. When Belinda finally got on her feet and moved, we would miss her. That didn't look to be happening any time soon, though.

"Aunt Tillie saw Clove messing with Noah, too," I said. "She thought it was funny. I guess that means she has the sense of humor of a child. I think we already knew that, though."

"She was drunk," Thistle said, turning so she could face Clove in the back seat. "Are you ready?"

Clove nodded. "I made it so we just have to toss it on the threshold," she said. "The spell will last only an hour. I didn't want to risk something happening and us not being able to remove it. I also tossed a piece of hair from all three of is in it so we'll be immune. We don't want to accidentally get stuck telling the truth."

"Yeah, that would suck," Thistle said. "That was a good idea. Let's do this."

We climbed out of the car and headed toward the senior center. The music pulsing from inside caused me to smirk. I recognized it, but sadly only from repeated viewings of *Dirty Dancing*. "You don't think they're putting Baby in a corner, do you?"

"Oh, man." Thistle made a disgusted face. "I can't believe you brought that up. Now I'm going to picture them doing dirty dancing moves. You don't think skirts are flying up in there or anything, do you?"

"They would throw a hip out," Clove said, widening her eyes when Thistle scorched her with an accusatory look. "What? That wasn't rude, just honest."

"I'm sensing a double standard here," Thistle said. "We're not allowed to say anything mean but you are? How does that work?"

"It's karma," Clove explained, tilting the baggie on its side and dumping the contents on the front walk. "I'm sweet and nice, so I get to say the occasional nasty thing. You're always mean, so you can't afford the bad karma." She pressed her eyes shut and whispered a short spell over the ingredients.

"That makes absolutely no sense."

"It does if you have good karma," Clove said, opening her eyes and dusting off her hands. "Are we ready?"

She wasn't thrilled with the cemetery portion of tonight's festivities, but she appeared excited for the dance. I couldn't help but be suspicious. "Why are you in such a good mood all of a sudden?"

"I think senior citizens are cute," Clove said, wrinkling her nose. "I'm excited to see them dance. We only get to see our senior citizen dance when she's naked, and that's terrifying. These senior citizens will be clothed ... er, well, hopefully."

"You're extremely odd sometimes," Thistle said. "You know that, right?"

"You have purple hair and you're calling me odd? That's rich."

This would get out of hand quickly if I didn't put a stop to it. "We're all odd," I said. "How about we take this show inside and be odd in there?"

"I'm only agreeing because I want to get home before Marcus goes to sleep," Thistle said. "Otherwise I would throw down and shove a mud pie in her face."

"Duly noted," I said.

"And that's why you have bad karma," Clove said, laughing as she scampered away from Thistle's slap and followed me into the senior center.

I don't know what I expected. I went to dances in high school, and unless they were for a special occasion they basically consisted of muted lights, Top 40 music and wandering hands. This was something entirely different.

"What the ... ?" Thistle's mouth dropped open as she took in the scene.

The center's main room served as a place to play cards and drink coffee during the day. Once a month, though, it apparently turned into a John Travolta movie from the seventies.

"I didn't know they still made strobe lights," Clove said, gaping at the twinkling orb turning in the middle of the ceiling as a group of women gyrated beneath it.

AMANDA M. LEE

"I didn't know they still made balloon arches for anything other than 'Under the Sea' proms," Thistle said, running her hands over the festive archway as we stood beneath it. "This is just ... so eighties."

"The music is from the seventies, though," Clove said.

"That music is from the fifties and sixties," I corrected. "The music from the seventies was much more ... ." I couldn't find the right word.

"Suckier?" Thistle suggested.

It wasn't the word I was looking for, but it wasn't incorrect. "Pretty much."

"Wow," Clove said, shaking her head. "Look how everyone is dressed. The women are in dresses and the men – both of them – are in suits."

"And they're real suits, not like those tracksuits I see all the old guys wearing at Wal-Mart," Thistle said, amused. "This is like traveling through time or something. It's ... far out."

I couldn't stop myself from laughing. "It's trippy."

"It's ... rad," Clove said. "Wait, that was an eighties thing, right?"

"Close enough," I said, scanning the crowd. Most of the women were split between the tables and the dance floor. Kenneth and Arthur sat at one of the tables regaling the women with stories. Because they were the only ones in the room boasting at least a hint of testosterone, they were the hit of the event.

"Look how popular they are," Clove mused. "I wonder if Aunt Tillie knows how many women fall over Kenneth on a daily basis. She might want him back if she sees something like this."

"We can't deal with Aunt Tillie's romantic life until after we clear her of murder," I said. "Speaking of that ... ." I pointed toward a woman standing alone next to the punch bowl. "There's Viola. Let's talk to her first."

"She was the one who told you about the hidden money in the first place, right?" Thistle asked, cringing as we walked past the speakers blaring music so loud it rocked our spines.

I nodded. "She has memory issues," I said. "Part of me thought she could've been faking that, though. Maybe she realized she said something she shouldn't have and covered with the memory lapse."

"I guess we're about to find out," Thistle said, her face splitting into an unnatural smile as she approached Viola. "Hi!"

Seriously, someone needs to talk to her about the way she approaches people. She thinks she's being pleasant and nice, but nothing could be further from the truth. She puts people off with her fake tone. That's what happens when you go through life being mean and stomp on the pedal pretending to be nice. It's ... unnatural. Wait, did I just sound like Clove?

"Your hair is purple," Viola said, focusing on Thistle.

"I guess we know the truth spell works," Clove muttered.

I wasn't so sure. "We need to ask her a pointed question she wouldn't generally answer to be sure."

Thistle held up her hand. "I've got this."

Should I be worried? I'm pretty sure I should be worried. Thistle is out of her comfort zone in this environment.

"What do you really think of Mrs. Little, Viola?" Thistle asked, going straight for the jugular. Apparently her nice and pleasant act was already discarded in favor of the hard questions. It was probably for the best.

"Well, she's my best friend," Viola said primly.

I waited. That couldn't be the end of it. If we screwed up the spell twice we were going to have to get help, and our best option for that wasn't likely to offer aid given what we were after.

"She's also a gossipy old biddy who is only happy when she's making others miserable," Viola added. "I'm pretty sure she has a stick up her butt because she sits like she does most of the time. Also, I think she's jealous of me because Kenneth clearly wants to get with me, and she doesn't understand it. I'm a freak in the bedroom, though. Everyone wants me."

"Uh-oh," Clove said, making a face. "I think I might have put too much graveyard dust in the spell. This is ... a little much."

"Do you think?" Thistle asked, widening her eyes to comical proportions.

I held up my hands to cut off an argument before they got up full

AMANDA M. LEE

heads of steam. "We'll fight about that later," I said. "We have to work with what we've got. At least we know the spell is working."

"And they'll forget in fifty-one minutes," Clove added.

"Spell?" Viola shuffled from one foot to the other as her gazed worriedly bounced between us. "Are you talking about a witch spell?"

"No," Thistle lied, shaking her head. "I was talking about a dizzy spell." Thankfully Clove's attempt at shielding us from the spell appeared to be working. We could lie to our hearts' content. We'd learned a hard lesson about casting the spell on ourselves when we did it at the Dragonfly a few months ago.

"Oh, that's a relief," Viola said, resting her hand on her stomach. "I thought you were going to cut my throat and bathe in my blood to keep yourselves young and fresh like Tillie."

Huh. There were so many ways to go with that statement I didn't even know where to start. "I thought the rumor was that Aunt Tillie had to kill virgins to bathe in their blood if she wants to stay young."

Viola nodded. "It is."

"Are you are a virgin? Because you just told us you were a freak in the bedroom."

"Well, no," Viola hedged. "I thought she might've eased up on her rules. She's no spring chicken."

"And yet you guys still think she's sacrificing virgins to stay young," Thistle said. "How does that even work?"

"I have no idea," Viola replied. "Why is your hair purple?"

"I like it that way."

"Why?"

"Because I do." Thistle's patience wouldn't hold much longer. I was sure of that.

"Why?"

"Because."

"Why?"

"Oh, someone end the pain," Clove moaned, rolling her eyes to the ceiling. "Oh, look, there are balloons up there, too."

"Yes, it's quite the shindig," I said, forcing Viola's eyes to me by snapping my fingers. "We don't have a lot of time here, Viola, so I have a few questions to ask. Do you think you can answer them for me?"

Viola shrugged. "I don't see why not."

"Great," I said, forcing a smile. "Mrs. Little, Patty Grimes and Aunt Tillie share a secret. Do you know what it is?"

"No," Viola said, widening her eyes. "Do you know what it is? I would love to spread that around."

"Do you spread gossip about Mrs. Little all the time?" Clove asked.

"Yes," Viola answered. "She thinks it's Fay, but it's really me. I don't correct her because I don't want to get on her bad side. I don't like her, but I don't want her disliking me. She's powerful – and vindictive – when she wants to be."

That was pathetic and sad. "Are you sure you've never heard about a shared secret between Aunt Tillie and any of those women?" I pressed, dragging Viola's attention back to me. "I know they're hiding something."

"I wish I could help," Viola said. "Honestly, Margaret would never confide in me. She doesn't trust me. In fact, I'm not sure she trusts anyone."

"She must talk to someone," Thistle prodded. "Everyone has to tell their deepest and darkest secrets to someone. No one can go through life without a confidant."

"That's true," Viola said. "Hey, speaking of that, did you know that you're supposed to sit on a hand mirror once a month to study your ... you know ... because it makes you more comfortable with your femininity? I saw it on television, so I know it's true."

"Holy crap," Clove said, dumbfounded. "I used way too much graveyard dust."

"Yes, and now I'm going to have nightmares forever," Thistle said, disgustedly cuffing Clove. "Way to go!"

I fought the urge to join in their disdain, silently reminding myself that Viola didn't have a choice in what she was volunteering. The spell made her do it. Er, well, at least I hoped that was true.

"Viola, that is a very important admission," I said. "I'm glad you told us, but you should probably keep it to yourself from here on out. Most people won't want to hear about that."

"Or be able to stop themselves from throwing up," Thistle added.

"That's because people aren't comfortable being in touch with their femininity," Viola replied, unruffled. "You guys should totally do it. You're all wound tighter than a virgin on prom night."

"I'm going to thank you for the offer, but decline," I said, pressing my lips together.

"It's your loss," Viola said. "I'm thinking about doing it right now. This dance is a major bust. Of course, they all are. We have only two men, and they're in their eighties. They only have so much energy to go around. Thank the maker for Viagra."

"Okay, now I'm definitely going to throw up," Thistle said. "You need to end this conversation now, Bay. If that woman pulls out a mirror, I'll take it from her and beat you with it."

I couldn't argue with the sentiment. "Viola, if Mrs. Little confided in anyone, who would it be? There has to be someone who listens to her."

"The only one is Fay," Viola said. "Margaret tells her some things, and what she doesn't tell her Fay finds out because she spies on Margaret when she thinks no one is looking. Margaret doesn't know that, though."

"Of course not," I said, shifting my eyes to the dance floor. Fay wasn't there, and after checking Kenneth's table and not finding her fawning over him, I turned back to Viola. "Where is she?"

"She's probably in the bathroom," Viola said. "We all had prunes at dinner, which was a terrible idea in hindsight. I can look if you want."

"We'll look ourselves," Thistle said, grabbing Viola's arm and directing her back toward the dance floor. "You should dance."

"And stay away from mirrors," Clove said.

"Okay," Viola said, happily hopping toward the dance floor and clapping her hands. "Who wants to limbo?"

"We have to get out of here," Thistle said. "This is just ... too much. The graveyard dust is working overtime, and now they're acting like crackheads instead of just telling us the truth. I can't take this."

I considered making fun of her, or challenging her bravery, but I couldn't take much more either. It was too ... frightening. Would we end up like this one day? "Let's look in the bathroom for Fay," I suggested. "If she's not there, let's go. We'll figure out something else. If she is there, let's question her. She might be our only shot."

"Okay," Thistle said, moving in the direction of the bathroom. "If she has a mirror and is looking at something in an attempt to get closer to her femininity, though, I'm out of here."

"You're not the only one," I said, watching as Thistle pushed open the bathroom door and disappeared inside.

"Oomph." It sounded as if someone stumbled, but I couldn't be sure because the music was so loud.

"Thistle?" Part of me feared pushing open the door. The other part knew it was necessary. Still, if Thistle was looking at something gross, I didn't want to be a part of it. "Say something if you're okay."

"Bay, get in here!"

Thistle's tone told me she wasn't messing around. I pushed open the door, frowning when I found Thistle sitting on the floor and rubbing her knee. "What happened?"

"I tripped." Thistle didn't move her eyes in my direction, instead focusing on something behind the door.

"What did you trip over?"

Thistle pointed, and when I turned my gaze from her face to the corner, my heart hopped.

"Fay," I said, swallowing hard.

"Is she ... dead?" Clove asked, fearful. "I mean ... she looks dead. Her eyes are open and she's staring at nothing."

"She's dead," Thistle said. "There's a knife sticking out of her chest."

"I ... um ... what should we do?" Clove asked. "Should we run?"

The question was so beyond the realm of possibility it snapped me back to reality, and I scorched her with a dark look as I reached for my phone. "We can't run. We have to call for help."

"Are you sure about this?" Clove asked. "I think running is a legitimate option."

I ignored her as I pulled my phone from my pocket. Landon answered after the first ring.

"What's wrong?"

"Things got out of hand," I said, briefly wondering how he knew I was in trouble. Then I realized I always ended up in trouble, so he probably expected it.

"How out of hand?"

"You need to get down here right now," I said. "Someone else is dead … and it's bad."

"I'm on my way, sweetie. Hang tight."

TWENTY-ONE

My second call was to Chief Terry, and he was extremely unhappy when he arrived. Because he lived in town, he beat Landon to the scene.

"This had better be good."

Thistle, her face paler than normal, wordlessly pointed toward the bathroom door. We had made a hasty exit from the restroom after calling Landon. Because the dance was filled with drunken elderly women, the fact that we refused to let them use the facilities didn't go over well.

Chief Terry poked his head inside, swearing when he caught sight of Fay. Instead of checking her body, though, he released the door and let it fall shut. "This is … bad."

"Oh, really?" Thistle deadpanned. "I thought you were going to take one look at Fay and then join everyone on the dance floor." It's not an excuse, but when Thistle is upset she lashes out with a snark-shaped whip.

Chief Terry had known us our entire lives, so he was used to it. He reached over and rested his hand on Thistle's shoulder, a move most people would avoid if they wanted to retain their hand. "Are you okay?"

"I tripped over her," Thistle admitted, her eyes filling with tears. It was only then I realized how truly upset she was. "I didn't see her at first and ... her shoe was kind of half off ... and I stumbled."

"It's okay, Thistle," Chief Terry soothed. "You couldn't have known."

Thistle offered him a watery smile. "Thanks."

"Do you want to tell me how this happened?" Chief Terry asked, shifting his gaze to me. "You'd better tell me the truth – and do it quick – because Landon and his new partner are on their way. He texted me when I pulled into the parking lot."

I related the events, leaving nothing out – including the truth spell. When I was done, he swore under his breath and shook his head. "You cannot tell Agent Glenn that. He'll lock all three of you in the loony bin. Although ... please go into excruciating detail when you explain the mirror story. I can't wait to see his face when he hears that."

"What should we tell him?" Clove asked, worried. "He's not going to arrest us, is he?"

"For discovering a body in a bathroom?" Chief Terry didn't look particularly perturbed. "No. That's not against the law."

"We'll just tell him we came to question the people at the senior center because we were curious about what they witnessed the day Aunt Tillie was supposedly here poisoning the coffee," I said. "He'll believe that because he thinks we're working overtime to clear her."

"Okay," Chief Terry said, nodding. "Keep it simple. That should work. The guy is an idiot, but there's no reason that story won't hold up."

"At least we're not telling him Sally did it," Thistle said, her hands shaking as she smoothed the front of her tank top. "I ... is it hot in here?"

"Go outside," Chief Terry ordered. "My officers are on their way. They'll question everyone here – and hopefully turn off that infernal racket – and then send everyone home so the coroner can do his thing. You girls need to wait outside for Landon and Agent Glenn."

"Okay," I said. "I ... she was stabbed."

"I saw the knife," Chief Terry said, placing his hand on top of my head. The weight was warm and familiar. He used to do it all the time when trying to center me as a teenager. "It looked quick, Bay. It was in the area of her heart."

I nodded, exhaling heavily. "We'll be right in front of the building."

"Okay," Chief Terry said. "Wait ... you didn't see anything else in there, did you? There wasn't a ghost or anything, right?"

I shook my head. "That doesn't necessarily mean there won't be one, though. Sometimes they don't show up right away. I don't think she's been dead long."

"No, the blood looks fresh," Chief Terry said, shaking his head as the senior center denizens continued dancing and laughing. They didn't even look in our direction. "Do they not realize what's going on?"

"We didn't tell anyone," I replied. "We didn't want to incite a panic."

"Or risk anyone taking off," Thistle added. "There were too many of them for us to watch."

"That was probably a good idea," Chief Terry said. "Go outside. Get some fresh air. This night is nowhere near over."

My heart sank. I didn't think this was what Landon had in mind when he said he wanted to spend time together. "What do you think it means?"

"I have absolutely no idea," Chief Terry answered. "We have to take it one step at a time, Bay. I don't know what else to tell you."

IT DIDN'T TAKE Landon and Noah long to arrive, and Landon hit the pavement at a dead run and swooped in for a hug the moment he saw me.

"Are you guys okay?"

I nodded as I returned the embrace, burying my face in his neck. "Thistle tripped over the body."

Landon brushed a kiss against my forehead, holding the hug until Noah cleared his throat before releasing me. He was all business when he pulled away.

"Tell me exactly what happened," Landon instructed.

AMANDA M. LEE

"I believe I should ask the questions," Noah said primly. "Your conflict of interest is even more pronounced in this situation."

Landon ran his tongue over his teeth, Noah's words obviously irking him even as he worked to tamp down his irritation. "Fine. You ask the questions."

"Okay, ladies," Noah said, puffing out his chest and pulling out his notebook. "Tell me exactly what happened here."

"Well, we were standing outside to get some air and then a really annoying douche showed up with Landon to bug us," Thistle barked, frowning. "Where's Marcus? I thought he would be with you."

"He's on his way," Landon said. "I wanted to bring him with us, but Agent Glenn didn't think it was a good idea because we're not allowed to transport civilians to crime scenes without approval from the higher ups."

"See ... he's a douche," Thistle said, sinking to the curb and resting her elbows on her knees. Clove wordlessly sat next to her and rubbed her back.

"What happened?" Landon asked, worry flitting across his features as he studied Thistle.

"I'm asking the questions," Noah reminded him. "Ms. Winchester ... er, any of the Ms. Winchesters ... what happened?"

I wanted to smack him. If I thought I could get away with it, or if it wouldn't cause more problems than we could handle, I totally would've done it. "We came to the senior center because we knew they were having a dance and we wanted to question everyone about what they saw the day Mrs. Little claims she saw Aunt Tillie here."

"We're trying to prove she's innocent," Clove said, pointedly glaring at Noah. "I guess we did, huh?"

"How do you figure that?" Noah asked.

"Because Aunt Tillie wasn't here tonight," I answered. "She couldn't have killed Fay."

"And who is Fay?" Noah asked, glancing at Chief Terry's police officers as they hurried past us. "Where was the body found?"

"We didn't get anywhere with our questions, so we decided to hit the bathroom before we left," I said. The story was mostly true, so I wasn't worried about Noah suspecting us of lying. "Thistle went in first and ... tripped ... over something. It turned out to be Fay's shoe. She was dead in the corner. She had a knife in her chest."

"Oh, man," Landon muttered, turning his compassionate gaze back to Thistle. "Are you okay?"

"I'm fine," Thistle said. "I just want Marcus ... and my bed."

"It shouldn't take long," Landon said, scanning the dark parking lot. "In fact ... here comes Marcus now."

Thistle hopped to her feet and hurried down the sidewalk, throwing herself in Marcus' arms as he approached. I wasn't used to her displaying vulnerability. Of course, she didn't often trip over a dead woman's shoe in a restroom.

"I'm not done asking questions," Noah said. "She can't leave."

Landon scowled. "Does it look like she's leaving?"

"How should I know?" Noah said. "She's very ... sneaky. I can tell just by looking at her. It's one of my super powers."

"Oh, that's funny," I said. "We have super powers, too. That's how we know you're a tool."

Landon shot me a warning look. "Bay ... don't."

I blew out a frustrated sigh. He was right. I knew it. I didn't want to deal with Agent Annoying, though. If Landon asked the questions we'd already be done. "We realized Fay was dead right away," I said. "I called Landon and then Chief Terry. Because he lives in town, Chief Terry got here first. He sent us outside while he handled the seniors and secured the scene."

"Thank you, Ms. Winchester," Noah said, writing something down in his little notebook. "Did you find answers to your questions regarding your aunt?"

"We had a chance to talk to only one woman," I answered. "She didn't have any helpful information."

"I see."

What did he mean by that? "You see what?" I challenged.

"Bay." Landon shook his head.

"It's just that this is mighty convenient is all," Noah said.

"How is this convenient?" Thistle asked, her fingers linked with

AMANDA M. LEE

Marcus' as she rejoined us. "We found a dead body. That's pretty much the least convenient thing to happen all day – and frankly, that's saying something because we've had a long day."

"It's convenient because everyone in your family – and other random people in the town – have been working overtime to convince me that your aunt is innocent," Noah supplied.

"Well, she is," I said. "Aunt Tillie wasn't here tonight. She didn't kill Fay."

"That doesn't mean she didn't kill Patty Grimes," Noah countered. "It simply means she's clear for this evening. I must say, sneaking out and leaving her with two FBI agents was a stroke of genius."

"What?"

I wasn't the only confused one, because the look Landon shot Noah matched mine. "What are you getting at?" he asked.

"When I asked you where your girlfriend and her cousins disappeared to, you said they had female things to do," Noah replied. "When I pressed you on the issue, you told me they had to pick up female hygiene products in town because their cycles linked up."

Well, that was the last time I left Landon in charge of thinking up a lie to cover our tracks. I shouldn't have been surprised by his lack of ingenuity – all men believe talk of tampons will freak out other men enough to make them skirt uncomfortable conversation – but even I was dumbfounded at this one. "Really?"

Landon shrugged. "You said you had female stuff to do. That's what I thought you were doing."

It took me a moment to realize he was covering. He didn't want Noah to know he was aware of our trip to the senior center before it happened. That would put him in an uncomfortable spot. "Female stuff doesn't always mean tampons," I said. "In this case it merely meant we wanted to spend time together … you know … bonding and stuff." That sounded feasible, right?

"And proving Aunt Tillie was innocent," Clove added, her chocolate eyes weary. "Can we go now?"

"Not yet," Noah replied. "I want to question everyone inside this facility. I want your locations at the time of death nailed down before you have a chance to go home and make up another story. I would hate to think Sally appeared to do the deed when no one was looking."

"I don't like your tone," Landon said, narrowing his eyes. "What is it you're accusing them of? You can't possibly believe they killed Fay."

"That's exactly what I believe," Noah said. "They were here. They're desperate to clear their aunt. What better way than to make sure she had an airtight alibi while they killed another senior citizen in an attempt to point investigative interest in another direction?"

"You're out of line," Landon snapped.

"And I think I'm on the right track," Noah said. "You clearly disagree, but since I'm in charge ...."

Landon growled, the sound low and unmistakable.

"What was that?" Chief Terry asked, joining the fray. "Did someone just growl?"

Clove helpfully pointed toward Landon. "He did."

"Why?"

"Because Agent Dumbass thinks we killed Fay to clear Aunt Tillie," Thistle answered.

Chief Terry's expression was incredulous as he turned toward Noah. "You've got to be kidding me."

Noah squared his shoulders. "I'm deadly serious. It's the only scenario that makes sense."

"Really? I have another one for you," Chief Terry said. "Whoever killed Patty did poison her at the senior center. The culprit clearly has ties to the center. They either liked doing it the first time and wanted to continue or have another motive, but they killed Fay tonight, too. The same person committed both crimes, and I can guarantee it was no one with the last name Winchester."

"I disagree."

Noah was stubborn. I had to give him that.

"Well, regardless, until the autopsy is complete and the evidence processed, you don't have the right to hold them," Chief Terry said. "Girls, go home. Get some sleep. I'll be in touch when I have more information."

"You can't do that," Noah protested. "I'm not done questioning them. I want to talk to the seniors at the dance and get a timeline. I have no intention of letting them go."

"Well, in that case, knock yourself out," Chief Terry said, inclining his chin toward the line of senior citizens exiting the building. Noah's eyes widened when he realized how many people were flooding the parking lot. "They're all right there ... and they're all yours."

"But ... fine." Noah tugged on his shirt to smooth it. "I will start the questions straightaway."

"Good luck with that." Chief Terry was blasé. "Until then, though, you can't keep these girls here. If you have questions for them tomorrow, you know where to find them."

"Yes, I do," Noah said, refusing to back down.

"Well, great," Chief Terry said, forcing a smile. "I guess we're in agreement then."

"Not really, but I recognize your right to clear the scene," Noah said. "I won't fight your jurisdiction. It's against the rules."

"Whoopee," Chief Terry said, his eyebrows flying up his forehead as he shifted his gaze to me. "What are you still doing here? Go home."

He meant business. He rarely raised his voice to me.

"We're going," I said, surprised when Landon grabbed my hand. "Wait ... are you coming, too?"

"Yeah," Landon said, smirking as Noah frowned. "As my partner has pointed out on numerous occasions, I have a conflict of interest. This is his case and he's in charge of the questioning. I could taint the witness pool, and that's against the rules. There's no reason for me to be here."

I bit my lip as I tried to keep from laughing. "I guess we're going to get to spend some time together after all, huh?"

"Absolutely," Landon said. "I think it's going to involve cookies and ice cream, too. I'll see you in the morning for your update, Agent Glenn."

"I'll be there," Noah said. "I'll definitely be there."

"We're all looking forward to it," Clove said, grabbing her boobs for good measure as she strode past him and causing Chief Terry's cheeks to color when he caught sight of the gesture.

"I'm not," Thistle said. "Just for the record, Agent Numb Nuts, I still think you're a douche."

TWENTY-TWO

Mom, Marnie and Twila were in the kitchen having tea when we arrived at the inn. Clove wasn't with us, of course. Her home was someplace else now. She wasn't even miffed a little when she realized she would miss out on the bashing session following our latest adventure.

Thistle and Marcus headed into the library for a drink first, promising to join us in the kitchen once Thistle's frazzled nerves settled. I figured they wanted a few minutes alone. I didn't blame them. Thistle was ... rattled. I wasn't used to seeing her that way.

"What happened?" Mom asked, shifting her weary eyes to me. "What did you do now?"

"I'm happy to see you, too, Mom," I said, shuffling to the teapot on the stove. "Do you want some tea, Landon?"

"I'm happy with the cookies," Landon replied, sitting on a stool and grabbing a chocolate chip cookie. "How much do you guys know?"

"So far we only know that Thistle, Clove and Bay snuck out of the house and went to the senior center," Mom said. "Then they called you because someone died, and you took off like a crazy person."

"I didn't take off like a crazy person," Landon argued, holding my

CHARMS & WITCHDEMEANORS

stool steady so I could sit next to him. He broke his cookie in half to offer me a treat. "You only get half because I need the sugar."

"Oh, so cute," Twila said, her eyes twinkling.

"Yes, it's adorable," Mom deadpanned.

"Oh, come on," Twila prodded. "There aren't a lot of men who would go after their girlfriend after she snuck out like Bay did. He's adorable."

"Hmph." Mom crossed her arms over her chest. She was in her pajamas, and I guessed she'd been spouting a litany of anger framed around my subterfuge during my absence.

"I am adorable," Landon agreed, briefly leaning forward and resting his forehead against mine before turning to everyone else in the room. "Do you want the long or short story?"

"Short," everyone said in unison.

"You're on, Bay," Landon said.

"We went to the senior center to cast a truth spell because we believe Patty and Aunt Tillie share some secret that might shed light on what's happening," I volunteered. "We also believe Mrs. Little knows about it, so we thought other people might be able to tell us the big secret.

"Clove used a bit too much graveyard dust in the spell and Viola Hendricks told us some freaky things, including how she's acrobatic in the bedroom and uses a mirror to stare at her ... um ... private parts when she wants to get in touch with her femininity," I continued.

Landon barked out a laugh. "You didn't tell me that part."

"That's because there was no way I could in front of Noah."

"Fair enough," Landon said, reaching for another cookie. "Continue."

"Viola said Mrs. Little doesn't confide in anyone because she's suspicious they're all working against her," I said. "That seems to be true because Viola admitted working against her.

"Anyway, she said that Fay was probably the only one who knew the secret," I continued. "I think Viola probably knows too, but her memory is shot and she most likely forgot it. That's not important to the story, though."

"This is the short version?" Marnie challenged. "I'd hate to hear the long version."

"You would," I agreed. "That involved Clove whining about having to collect the graveyard dust and Thistle melting down because Clove feels left out."

"Oh, good grief," Mom said, making a face. "Get to the important part, Bay. You get this dramatic storytelling thing you do from Aunt Tillie. It's not attractive."

"That's the meanest thing you've ever said to me," I groused.

"I can get meaner," Mom warned.

"Fine," I said, rolling my eyes so hard I worried I would topple off the stool. "We headed toward the bathroom and Thistle tripped going inside. She tripped over Fay's feet. She was dead in the corner. She'd been ... stabbed."

"That's awful," Twila said, horrified. "Where is Thistle now? She must be upset."

"She's drinking in the library with Marcus," Landon replied. "I would give them a few minutes alone. Thistle is on the edge."

"Well, that's not nearly as bad as I expected," Mom said. "It's not great, and I wish you would've asked me about this purported secret before you went on another of your little adventures, but it's not terrible."

"I don't think Fay feels the same way," I said.

Mom's expression softened. "You know what I mean," she said. "Aunt Tillie wasn't exactly tight with that crowd growing up, but they all knew each other. She and Margaret Little have hated each other for as long as I can remember. I can't recollect strife with Patty, though, and I've been racking my memory for hints of it. It's just ... not there."

"They called each other names at Patty's house the other day," I pointed out. "It was not pleasant. I've been considering going back out there to question Patty, but ... ." I cast a leery look in Landon's direction.

"Don't go back out there, Bay," Landon said. "Noah is threatening to set up cameras, and while he says he hasn't done it yet I'm not sure I believe him. He seems desperate to get dirt on Aunt Tillie, and I think he's willing to leave me out of the information loop to get it."

"We need information, though," I pressed.

"Well, we'll just ask Aunt Tillie about it tomorrow," Mom said. "She probably won't answer, but there's no harm in asking."

"Where is she?" Landon asked. "I'm stunned she's not here asking questions.

"She went back to the guesthouse to watch *The Walking Dead* marathon," Marnie answered. "She's agitated because of Noah's presence, but she doesn't want to admit it."

"She keeps saying she's having a grand time at the guesthouse, but I can tell she hates it," Twila added. "She wants to come home."

I glanced at Landon, conflicted. They needed to know about Noah's new suspicions, but I dreaded telling them.

"Go ahead," Landon said, squeezing my hand. "Don't put it off."

"Don't put what off?" Mom asked, narrowing her eyes suspiciously.

"They'll kick him out."

"I think that's the best option for us right now," Landon said. "I wanted him close because I thought I could control him. It's become obvious I can't. There's no reason to keep him here now. He needs some repercussions for his attitude."

"Oh, I'm already not liking this," Mom said. "Spill it, Bay."

"The good news is that Noah doesn't think Aunt Tillie was involved in Fay's death because she was out here at the inn with him at the time of the murder," I said, licking my lips.

"I hardly see that as good news. He would have to be a moron to think otherwise," Mom said.

"Wait for it," Landon interjected.

"The bad news is that now he thinks Thistle, Clove and I murdered Fay as a way to direct suspicion away from Aunt Tillie," I said. "He flat out told us that at the senior center."

Mom, Marnie and Twila remained silent for a moment, taking me by surprise. It was short lived, because utter pandemonium broke out not long after.

"What is wrong with him?" Twila exploded.

"He is the king of the idiots," Marnie said.

"That does it!" Mom slapped her hands down on the kitchen table. "He's out of here!"

"I told you," I said, shifting a sidelong look in Landon's direction. "We can't take it back now."

"I don't want to take it back," Landon said, brushing my hair out of my face. "Noah's presence here makes everyone tense. This place is tense enough without him. He can stay somewhere else."

"Where is he?" Mom asked, hopping to her feet. "I'm going to ... ." She broke off and mimed something that could either be an odd form of kickboxing or a really bad performance in the gymnastics floor routine at the Olympics.

"He's questioning everyone at the dance," Landon replied. "I left him there because I'm unhappy with him. He'll probably be at least another hour. He says he's going to get everyone on the record before letting them go, but there's no way it will really happen."

"Especially since it's ten at night and all of the seniors need to be in bed before the late news," I said.

"That's stereotyping," Mom said, cuffing the back of my head. "It's probably true, though." Her expression was thoughtful. "Okay. No one panic. This guy is an idiot. We know how to handle idiots."

"Are we going to bury him in the back yard?" Marnie asked, her expression hopeful. "We can plant rose bushes over him so no one will ever know."

"No," Mom said. "I have everything under control. Don't worry. This is going to be fun."

She stormed out of the kitchen in the direction of the main inn, Marnie and Twila close behind. I waited until they were gone to turn my gaze to Landon. "Tell me what you really think. Are you worried?"

"I'm actually looking forward to this, Bay," Landon said. "Noah isn't going to learn until he gets taken down a peg or two. I think your mother is exactly the person to do it."

I wasn't convinced. "You have to be worried."

"The only thing I'm worried about is getting five minutes alone with you," Landon said, grabbing another cookie. "Let's take advantage of the solitude and share some sugar."

The double meaning wasn't lost on me, so I cocked a challenging eyebrow. "What did you have in mind?"

Landon snapped the cookie in half and took a bite before swooping in and giving me a hot kiss. "Just wait and see, little missy," he said once we parted. "I think you'll enjoy it, too."

AN HOUR later Landon and I sat on the library couch while Thistle rested on Marcus' lap, trying to drink her weight in whiskey. She would have a raging hangover tomorrow, but Marcus didn't take the glass away – although I did notice him watering the whiskey before giving her another glass. Thistle didn't want to talk about discovering Fay's body. That meltdown was soon to come.

As much as I wanted to return to the guesthouse and sleep, Landon was insistent we wait for Noah's return. I thought it would be much later than it was when he poked his head into the room, but Landon's smirk told me Noah was right on schedule for what he expected.

"I'm surprised you're all up," Noah said. "I suppose you want to hear my findings."

"I'm here to drink," Thistle said, lifting her glass for emphasis. "We only have chocolate martinis at the guesthouse, but I wanted something harder."

"That's the last one," Marcus said, finally stepping in. "You'll be able to pass out now."

"Yes, but I'll still be able to dream," Thistle complained.

Marcus ran his hand down the back of her head, torn for a moment before making up his mind. "You'll thank me in the morning," he said. "This is the last one."

I thought Thistle would argue, but she merely nodded. "Fine."

"Well, I'm sure you waited up to hear my findings," Noah said, turning his attention to Landon. "Perhaps we should go to my room to discuss them so none of the ... ahem, suspects ... hear our plan of action."

By all outward appearances Landon was unruffled. Deep down I knew he was irritated, though.

"I'm here to spend time with Bay and eat cookies," Landon said. "In a few minutes we're going to bed. You can brief me on your findings – and I'm sure they'll be marvelous – when we meet at the police station tomorrow morning."

"Why can't I brief you now?" Noah pressed. "You're up."

"Because I'm busy with something more fun," Landon said, tickling my ribs and causing me to giggle. "I'm off the clock. In fact, I'm fraternizing with the enemy."

"I can see that," Noah said dryly, shaking his head. "Well, is there a reason we can't discuss things before breakfast tomorrow? I want to get an early start."

"There's only one reason I can think of why we can't do that," Landon replied.

Noah lifted an eyebrow. "Which is?"

"You won't be here," Landon said.

Noah's countenance shifted from irritation to confusion. "What does that mean?"

"Just that you're out of here," Mom said, appearing behind Noah and dropping his bag on his foot. I got the distinct impression she wanted to kick him for good measure, but she showed amazing restraint.

"I ... don't understand," Noah said, his gaze bouncing between Mom and Landon. "What's going on?"

"What's going on is that you're no longer welcome here," Mom said, not missing a beat. "We have the right to refuse service, and we're refusing it to you."

"That's right," Twila said, rubbing her hands together. "Shame! We never refuse service. Well ... maybe once. You're in terrible company."

"That's because he's an idiot," Marnie said, kicking his bag and causing it to hop off the ground. "We took a vote while you were gone. Because you believe our children are murderers, I'm sure you can guess how the vote went."

"It wasn't even close," Twila said.

"If it's any consolation, I abstained," Landon said, rubbing his thumb against my cheek. "I only did it because I didn't want to break any FBI rules I might not be aware of. Otherwise I would've voted with everyone else."

"And that's why you get as much bacon as you can eat tomorrow morning," Mom said, winking.

"Be still my heart," Landon said, grinning. "I might leave you for your mother, Bay. She keeps me in bacon."

"You can't be serious," Noah said, glancing around the room as if looking for hidden cameras. "It's the middle of the night. Where am I supposed to stay?"

"You have a car," Mom said. "If you keep it in our parking lot, though, we'll have it towed."

"I think you're being incredibly immature," Noah said, although he picked up his bag. "I can see reasoning with you when you're in this ... state ... is wasted effort, though."

"You haven't seen incredibly immature yet," Thistle offered. "That'll come when Aunt Tillie finds out."

"Yeah," I agreed. "She takes people going after us a lot worse than she does people going after her. She's going to turn into a demon."

"Maybe even a literal one," Thistle said, finishing her glass of whiskey and hopping off Marcus' lap. "Let's go to bed. I'm ready for sleep."

Marcus smiled as he scooped up her diminutive frame and carried her toward the door. "You're not going to puke, right?"

"I don't know," Thistle admitted. "If I do, it will be the second adventure of the day, and no matter how disgusting the outcome, it will still be better than the first."

"I can live with that," Marcus said, disappearing around the corner as Thistle nonsensically chattered away.

"I'm sure you'll feel differently in the morning," Noah said, moving toward the front door. "We'll talk then."

"You're not allowed on this property without a warrant," Mom said. "I'm not kidding. I will press charges. You've been duly warned in front of witnesses."

Noah's mouth fell open. "But ... ."

"Get out!" Mom pointed at the door, her face red. "Don't threaten my family and expect to stay under my roof. I don't want to see you again."

Noah glanced at Landon, desperate. "Don't you want to say something?"

"I'll see you at the police station after breakfast," Landon said, grabbing my hand as he pulled me to a standing position. "Let's go to bed, sweetie. I'm exhausted."

"Okay," I said, reaching for my purse. It was heavier than I expected, and that's when I remembered the gift Thistle gave me for Landon before we went into the senior center. "By the way, Thistle made this for you." I dug in the purse and returned with a hefty candle. It was shaped like a witch's conical hat.

Landon took it, his brow furrowed, and lifted it to his nose. "This smells like bacon."

"I know," I said. "Thistle found an oil and made the candle just for you. She's even going to put some in the shop if you like it because a lot of people love the scent of bacon."

Landon's face split with an impish grin. "I'm getting a second wind, sweetie," he said, grabbing my hand. "Let's put the candle to good use and then go to bed."

Noah was flummoxed as Landon led me past him. "What about me?"

Landon paused by the door. "Sweet dreams."

TWENTY-THREE

"What are you doing today?" I asked the next morning, shaking my head as Landon inhaled what had to be a pound of bacon. "You're killing yourself with all of that fat and salt, by the way."

Landon poked my side. "Shh. You're ruining my happy morning."

"What are you going to do today?" Mom asked, skirting her eyes to Aunt Tillie's empty seat before craning her neck to scan the hallway. Once Aunt Tillie found out Noah was out of the inn she couldn't wait to move back. She was at the guesthouse collecting her things. We all worried she would pop up and eavesdrop when we least expected it. "I asked Aunt Tillie about her past with Patty in the kitchen this morning, by the way, and she completely blew off the question."

"That can't surprise you," Landon said, licking his fingers and causing Mom to scowl. "She's hiding something. She always digs in her heels when she's hiding something."

"You know there are napkins, right?" Mom asked, making a face that caused me to stare at my coffee for fear I would burst into gales of hysterical laughter.

"You cooked the bacon for me," Landon said. "It's really your fault because you're the best cook in the world and I can't control myself."

Despite herself, Mom preened under the compliment. "Oh, well, thank you."

"Smooth," I said.

"And don't you forget it," Landon said, kissing my cheek. He was in a remarkably good mood for a man I knew would face a verbal onslaught once he met up with Noah at the police station in an hour.

"I'm going to talk to Edith," I said, leaning back in my chair. "She was around back then, too. I realized last night while Landon was making out with his candle that I only asked about Aunt Tillie and Patty specifically before Noah distracted Edith. She probably knows a lot more."

"That's not a bad idea," Mom said. "Edith is predisposed to dislike Aunt Tillie, though."

"Mom, don't kid yourself," I said. "Most of the town is predisposed to dislike Aunt Tillie. I can't let that stand in the way."

"I guess not," Mom said, exhaling heavily. "What about Thistle? I noticed she didn't make it down to breakfast this morning. Is she okay?"

"We ran into Marcus when we were leaving the guesthouse," Landon said, his good mood evaporating. "He said she had a headache, so he gave her some aspirin and sent her back to bed. She'll be okay."

"I understand her being upset, but it's not exactly as if this is the first body you guys have stumbled over," Twila interjected. "Why is she so worked up over this one? It's not like she was fond of Fay."

"No, but Fay's body was fresh," I said. "The other bodies we found together were … older. It's hard to explain. I think in Thistle's mind she's wondering if we could've done something. For all we know, Fay was killed in the bathroom while we were inside the center. Thistle probably thinks we could've saved her."

Landon's expression was thoughtful. "Why aren't you upset about that?" he asked. "Don't get me wrong, I'm thankful you're not morose and stuck in your head, but you're usually the first one to drive yourself crazy with what-if scenarios. Why aren't you worked up about this?"

That was a good question. Unfortunately, it was something I wasn't sure how to answer. "I don't know," I said finally. "I've become accustomed to death. It's awful to say, but I don't feel it as keenly as I used to."

Landon slipped his hand under my hair and rubbed the back of my neck. "Thistle is strong, but she hasn't seen the same things Bay has been forced to grapple with. Bay has seen bodies since she was a kid. She's been at crime scenes. You get numb to those things."

"Well, that makes me a little sad," Mom said.

"Thistle will be okay," I offered. "She'll be back to her sarcastic self in a few days."

"I'm not sad for Thistle," Mom clarified. "I'm sad for you."

Her admission caused my heart to roll. "Why? I'm fine."

"I don't think we protected you from this stuff enough when you were a child," Mom explained. "You could see ghosts, and we used you as a crutch sometimes because you were the only one capable of solving certain problems. That wasn't fair. I'm sorry about that."

"Mom, it's fine," I said, waving off her concerns. "I grew up to be a well-adjusted adult."

"With an attraction to men with poor table manners," Mom said, although she sent Landon a small wink to let him know she was joking. "We still should've done better by you. I'm sorry."

"Thank you, but it's completely unnecessary."

We lapsed into comfortable silence until Annie barreled into the room, her hair askew and her eyes bright. "Hi!"

"Hi," I said, smiling. "Where have you been?"

"Mom gave me doughnuts for breakfast in town because she had to pick up a few things at the store," Annie answered, climbing onto Landon's lap without invitation and grabbing a slice of bacon from his plate. "Mom said you guys had big things to talk about this morning and I wasn't to get in the way."

"That's my bacon," Landon said, feigning irritation. "Did I say you could eat my bacon?"

"I'm sure you've already had a whole pig," Annie said, unruffled. "Aunt Tillie says you're a ... glutton. I'm not sure what that is, though."

I snorted. "He is a glutton."

"Just for that, you can't have my bacon," Landon said, grabbing the plate and holding it away from Annie. Up until a few weeks ago Annie feared Landon because Aunt Tillie kept forgetting her little digs fell on impressionable ears. To my utter surprise and delight, when called on her behavior Aunt Tillie not only fixed the problem but also managed to put Annie at ease. I was thankful.

"Marcus would give me some bacon," Annie said, enjoying the game as she reached for the plate. Landon easily kept it out of her reach.

"Marcus is a softie," Landon said. "I'm not a softie."

"Aunt Tillie says you're a big marshmallow where Bay is concerned," Annie said. "She says Bay has you wrapped around her finger."

"Aunt Tillie needs to keep her mouth shut," Landon grumbled.

"Where is Aunt Tillie? She said we could work in her garden today." Annie scanned the room, disappointed when she came up Tillie-less. The inn was vacant after the guests checked out after the weekend and wouldn't be full again until later in the week.

"In the garden or greenhouse?" Landon asked, suspicious. Aunt Tillie had been known to let Annie into her pot field, although she tells her it's oregano. What? That's somewhat more responsible.

"Greenhouse," Annie said. "Aunt Tillie says it's too hot to be in the garden and she can make it cold with her fingers in the greenhouse."

I stilled. Was Aunt Tillie performing magic in front of Annie? Sure, the girl was young, so no one would believe her should she slip in front of the wrong person, but that was incredibly stupid if true. "How does she make it cool?" I asked.

"She has fans and stuff," Annie said, unbothered. She batted her big eyes at Landon. "Can I please have more bacon?"

Despite his comments to the contrary, Landon was a big softie, too. He handed the plate to Annie. "I wouldn't share bacon with anyone but you."

"What about me?" I asked, irked to be competition with a child.

"Okay, you, too," Landon said. "No one else, though. Everyone else is banned from my magical bacon land."

Annie giggled. "I want to be queen of bacon land."

"I'm queen," I said, poking her side. "You can be the princess."

"Screw being the princess," Annie said, grabbing two slices of bacon and hopping off Landon's lap. "I want to be the magical wizard who runs the land." She laughed maniacally as she took off in the direction of the kitchen, delighting in Landon's patented scowl.

"She's spent far too much time with Aunt Tillie," Landon said.

"Welcome to my world," Mom said. "You'll get used to it eventually. It will become … normal."

"And strangely enough, I'm fine with that," Landon said, shifting his eyes to me. "Do you want to have lunch with me if I can clear my schedule, bacon queen?"

I nodded. "Text me when you know what's going on."

"Speaking of that, I have to get going," Landon said, glancing at the wall clock. "I'm guessing Noah will be an angry mess, and I want to get the autopsy results from Chief Terry before he shows up."

"Good luck," I said. "I'll text you if I get anything from Edith."

"Text me regardless," Landon said, giving me a quick kiss. "In fact, if you want to throw in the occasional dirty text, I'll be more than happy to read it."

"Out!" Mom pointed at the door. "I'm on cuteness overload."

Landon saluted. "You can be the executioner in bacon land," he said. "I think you'd enjoy it. I hear the outfit is to die for."

Mom didn't want to smile, but couldn't help herself. "Don't make me behead you."

"Yes, ma'am."

I FOUND Edith watching morning talk shows on the television in the small cafeteria at The Whistler. Brian's car wasn't in the parking lot, which meant we had the building to ourselves. I was relieved and thankful.

"Have you seen this?" Edith asked. "They say that you can drink a

AMANDA M. LEE

glass of wine a day and not be considered an alcoholic. I never heard of such a thing."

"We drink a jug of wine a day at The Overlook and we don't care if anyone thinks we're alcoholics," I replied, sitting in one of the chairs at the design desk. I decided to get right to the point. "What do you know about Margaret Little's relationship with Aunt Tillie?"

Edith widened her eyes, surprised. "Um ... wow. I wasn't expecting that."

"We've had a lot going on and I don't have a lot of time to mess around," I said. "I need answers, and you always have good ones." It never hurts to praise the person you're trying to get information from, especially when it's a ghost who has limited contact with others.

"Thank you for that," Edith said, smiling. "I know you're just goosing my ego, though."

There was no point in denying it. "Something is going on and I want to know what," I said. "I tracked down Victor Donahue, by the way."

Edith brightened. "How is he? Is he still handsome?"

Because Edith's appearance hadn't changed since her death she often forgot how aging worked. "He's in a home in Bellaire," I said, choosing my words carefully. "He seemed ... confused. He briefly thought Clove was Aunt Tillie and mentioned Patty wouldn't want us to know her secrets, but then he kind of lost his train of thought."

"Huh," Edith mused, wrinkling her nose. "I never really thought about it, but Clove really does resemble Tillie. That poor girl."

I bit the inside of my cheek to keep from laughing. "Victor wasn't much help. That means I need your help." I told her about the previous day, including Fay's death. I left out Viola's colorful part in the story, because I knew it would offend Edith and I didn't want to risk her going off on a tangent. When I was done, Edith was dumbfounded.

"Fay is dead?"

"Someone stabbed her," I said, nodding. "I don't have all of the details yet. I'm supposed to have lunch with Landon and get them then. It had to be someone else at the senior center, though. Anyone else would've been noticed."

"Like you?" Edith challenged.

"We weren't there for more than a few minutes," I replied, tamping down my irritation. Blowing up at Edith would get me nowhere. "I know there's some ... hidden secret ... from Aunt Tillie's past that ties in with Patty and Mrs. Little. I have a feeling you know, too."

Edith blew out a frustrated sigh. For a second – and I have no idea why I thought so – I was sure she was giving herself time to organize her response. "I don't think it's a secret," she said. "At least not in the way you think it's a secret."

"Then what is it?"

"Walkerville has always been small," Edith said, her eyes distant as she glanced out the window that looked over the town square. "It was even smaller when we were younger. Most of the buildings you see today weren't here."

"Okay." I had no idea where she was going, but decided to let her reach the destination on her own, however meandering the trip.

"We had only thirty people in our graduating class. Did you know that?"

I shook my head.

"Small towns are great in some respects," Edith said. "They're bad in others. You never really get a chance to choose your friends in a small town. There aren't a lot of choices. You have to settle for what's available."

"I get that," I said. "It was kind of the same when we went to school, too."

"You had your cousins, though, and you genuinely liked them," Edith pointed out. "You didn't have to be friends with the other kids because you had options."

"And I'm guessing you didn't," I surmised. "Are you saying you were friends with Mrs. Little because you had no other choice?"

"Yes," Edith said, nodding. "I never liked Margaret. She was kind of the queen bee, though, so I had no other options when it came to choosing friends. Well, there was Tillie, but no one wanted to be friends with her."

I pressed my lips together to stave off a nasty retort. I was pretty sure Aunt Tillie didn't want to be friends with Edith either.

"There were always rumors about your family," Edith said. "People said you were really witches and there were a lot of whispers about Tillie being able to perform magic. I didn't believe them back then. After dying ... and meeting you ... I now understand.

"Margaret always hated Tillie because the boys seemed somehow drawn to her," she continued. "She was convinced she used magic to do it. She was also convinced Tillie and Ginger used magic to make the teachers like them and get good grades. She wouldn't shut up about it."

That sounded typical. "Love and emotional manipulation spells don't work," I said. "They always backfire. You can't change who a person is or what their heart desires."

"Well, like I said, I didn't believe any of it back then so I kind of listened to Margaret with half an ear and a lot of skepticism," Edith said. "At a certain point – I guess we were about sixteen or so – she decided to befriend Tillie because she wanted her to perform magic for us."

Uh-oh. "I'm sure that didn't go over well."

Edith shook her ghostly head. "Tillie was on to Margaret the second she approached her, and no matter how much Margaret threatened or begged, Tillie refused to cast spells," she said. "Margaret was convinced Tillie could keep us all young forever ... and get us any man we wanted. It was utterly ridiculous. We were naïve and stupid, and we went along with it.

"Things got out of hand at some point, and Tillie threatened to curse Margaret with eternal unhappiness if she didn't leave her alone," she continued. "Margaret wouldn't let it go, and started a campaign against Tillie. She tried to get her kicked out of school and shunned in social circles."

Huh. In a weird way that made sense. Aunt Tillie was never one to visit town unless she absolutely had to. It was as if she ceded the town to Mrs. Little and took the rest of the countryside as her domain. Still, I was missing something. "That sounds like normal stuff for teenagers," I pointed out. "How did Patty get involved? She was older than you guys."

"It was Victor," Edith said. "I wasn't privy to their actual conversation, but when a relationship didn't work out between Patty and Victor things kind of ... came to a head. Margaret got involved and claimed Tillie cast a spell. Patty went after Tillie, and they had a physical fight."

"This all sounds very high school."

"We were in high school," Edith reminded me. "Feelings got hurt. Horrible things were said. In the end, Victor didn't get anyone, and Tillie walked away with Calvin and was happy. No one appreciated that because they were convinced that meant Tillie really was a witch and was controlling people with her powers."

"That's still no reason to kill someone," I pointed out. "How did Fay play into this?"

"She was close with Margaret," Edith answered. "Everyone followed Margaret, and Tillie was left in the cold. She seemed fine with that, though. She didn't care what other people thought. I always admired that about her. That was the only thing I admired about her, mind you."

"So you're basically saying Mrs. Little has been bitter for years because of high school shenanigans?" There had to be more to the story.

"I'm saying that's where it started," Edith clarified. "Throughout the years, Margaret married a man she didn't love, lost a man she did love to Tillie's friend and blamed her for it, and has been generally unhappy. Things have continued to snowball, and Margaret thinks Tillie is to blame, or at least she used to. She never stopped complaining about Tillie."

That made more sense, but I still wasn't convinced. "I think we're missing something."

"I think we are, too," Edith said. "Unfortunately, that's the only insight I have to offer you."

TWENTY-FOUR

"You're here early." Landon shuffled through the front door of Hypnotic a half hour before I expected him, his arms laden with takeout bags. "I love you, too."

I rolled my eyes. "I just meant we weren't expecting you for another thirty minutes," I said, shaking my head. "I'm always happy to see you."

"I will puke if you two don't stop it with the cutesy banter," Thistle warned, leaning back in her chair and closing her eyes as she rested a cold compress on her forehead. "I have a headache, and I can't take cuteness."

"She means she has a hangover, and she's crabby," Clove corrected. "I like the cuteness."

"Thank you, Clove," Landon said, handing one of the bags to me and leaning over to drop a kiss on my lips. "Clove is nicer to me than you are, Bay. What do you think about that?"

"I think she didn't have to watch you romance a candle last night," I replied, digging into the bag. "Ooh. Thai! I love Thai food."

"That's why I got it," Landon said, settling next to me. "Thank you for the candle by the way, Thistle. I love it."

"I have more in the storeroom, so don't skimp on burning it," Thistle said, her energy level lagging. "I'm glad you're happy with it."

"I am happy with it," Landon confirmed. "I did not, however, romance it. Bay is exaggerating."

"You named it Lucille," I countered.

"It looks like a Lucille," Landon said, unperturbed. "She smells like a Lucille, too."

"You're sick. You know that, right?"

Landon shrugged. "You're stuck with me, so you'd better get used to it," he said, grabbing one of the entrees. "I got everyone's favorite, and extra spring rolls because they make Bay happy."

"You're such a good provider," I said, wrinkling my nose as I rested my cheek against his shoulder.

"Stop! No more cuteness!" Thistle's mood was dour. There was no way around it.

"Fine, we're done being cute," I said, grabbing my pad woon sen and happily flipping open the lid. "Do you want to hear about my conversation with Edith first, or relate your morning with Noah?"

"I'll go first," Landon replied. "Noah is in a mood. It kind of resembles Thistle's mood. I find that ironic."

"I don't need the sarcasm either," Thistle said. She didn't touch her lunch, continuing to rest with the damp face cloth on her forehead.

"Chief Terry got the autopsy results," Landon said. "Fay was stabbed once. It was quick and efficient. She died within seconds. Even if you'd been there when it happened you couldn't have saved her."

"That doesn't make me feel better," Thistle grumbled. "We might have been able to save her if we were in the bathroom when she was attacked."

"I don't think anyone would've attacked if you were there," Landon said. "The working theory is that our suspect is a woman."

"Because only two men were present or because a man would've been noticed going in the women's bathroom?" Clove asked.

"Well, kind of both," Landon said. "We believe Fay was attacked about twenty minutes before you found her."

"See, Thistle," I prodded. "We were outside then. There's nothing we could've done."

"Fine," Thistle said, whipping the cloth off her face and sitting straighter. "That does make me feel a little better. Where is my pad Thai?"

Clove wordlessly handed her a container, although I didn't miss the small smile playing at the corner of her lips. Thistle was a pain in the rear end, but no one enjoyed it when she was morose. For some reason, because it happened so rarely, it was harder to swallow.

"Noah is still convinced it's the three of you, but I pointed out your outfits were too skimpy to hide a knife, and I saw the inside of Bay's purse. The rest of you didn't have purses when questioned."

"How did he take that?" I asked, holding out my fork so Landon could have a bite of my lunch.

"Not well," Landon replied after swallowing. "He's convinced I'm making that up because it's a detail he would've noticed. He was a real ... pill ... this morning. To be fair, I don't think he found another place to sleep until it was really late. He had to Google local inns, and then he couldn't find the proper names of the roads on the signs in the dark. He was not happy."

"Where did he land?" Clove asked. "There are about ten inns in the general vicinity."

"I have no idea," Landon said. "Tell me about your chat with Edith."

I related the conversation, every surreal tidbit of it, and then sat back to study Landon's face as he considered the information.

"I don't buy it," Landon said finally. "What kind of person holds onto a grudge that long?"

"The kind who can't let things go and is bitter," I replied. "Mrs. Little is definitely bitter."

"Do you think she's also a murderer?" Landon asked. "I'm going to have to question her about all of this, and I'm not looking forward to it. In fact, I have no idea how to question her because I don't want to bring up the magic stuff in front of Noah."

"Maybe you should let Chief Terry question her," I suggested. "He's still involved in the investigation, and he understands all of the intricacies involving my family."

"Is that convenient way of saying you're all nuts?" Landon challenged.

"Dude, you canoodled a candle last night," I said. "You have no room to talk."

"I guess it's good I like my women crazy," Landon said, shaking his head. "Okay. I'll talk to Chief Terry and send him in Mrs. Little's direction this afternoon. I have no idea where to point Noah, though. He wanted to have lunch so we could strategize, but I couldn't take another second of his moaning.

"When I told him I was coming here for lunch he just about had a fit," he continued. "He reminded me of a kid melting down in the toy aisle because his mother won't buy him the spaceship he wants. His attitude is getting old."

"How angry was he that you stayed with me?" I asked.

"Very." Landon's eyes were warm as they locked with mine. "He knows where I stand with you, though, and he honestly wasn't surprised. He thinks you've cast a spell on me or something. That's what he said. He has no idea how close he is to the truth."

I balked. "You can't cast a love spell on someone," I argued. "They never work. People's hearts and minds can't be twisted that way. If you love me, it's because you really love me." I was being defensive, but couldn't seem to help myself.

"I know that, Bay," Landon said, his face incredulous. "I was teasing you. I didn't mean anything by it."

"Oh."

"Good grief, woman," Landon muttered, pointing to the tray for another mouthful of food. "Do you really think I believe you bewitched me?"

"I don't know," I hedged. "Sometimes you act confused about why you're still hanging around when we do something stupid."

"That's because I don't want anything happening to you," Landon said. "That's love. It's real love, in fact. I know how I feel, and I know the only thing you did to make it happen was be you. Just ... chill."

"Oh, so sweet," Clove said, sighing.

"Yes, it's delightful," Thistle deadpanned. She was still unhappy, but the color was returning to her cheeks. "Part of Edith's story makes sense. Mrs. Little has hated Aunt Tillie for as long as I can remember. I never gave much thought as to why."

"A high school grudge isn't something to kill over," Landon argued.

"It depends how deeply you feel things," Thistle said. "Besides, Edith said that's where it started. It obviously didn't end there. Mrs. Little has been building up resentment for decades. I'm guessing things really got out of hand when she fell in love with Floyd and had an affair with him.

"She was angry because she thought Aunt Tillie was helping to keep Floyd away from her when really the only thing Aunt Tillie wanted to do was kill Floyd because he was beating his wife," she continued. "Floyd was a nasty piece of work. That's why he turned into a poltergeist and tried to kill Bay."

"Don't remind me," Landon growled, squeezing my knee. He clearly wanted to anchor contact between us because he worried I was dwelling on the bewitching thing. I responded by resting my cheek against his shoulder, which caused him to kiss my forehead.

"Oh, I love you guys when you're cuddly," Clove said. "I miss seeing this at the guesthouse."

"Shut up, Clove," Thistle barked. "I'm talking."

"I don't miss that," Clove said, making a face. I couldn't help but smile. I did miss that. Our lives were in flux and nothing would be the same again. I realized things would eventually get better, though, and I wished that day would hurry.

"Mrs. Little is the type to let things boil her butt for decades and then snap," Thistle offered. "Maybe she finally snapped and this is the outcome."

"I think she's capable of murder," I admitted. "She has some sociopathic tendencies, even though I believe she truly loved Floyd. I'm not sure it's her, though. The only thing I'm sure about is that it isn't Aunt Tillie."

"We always knew that," Thistle said. "The old bat is crazy, but she's no murderer."

"No, she's not," Landon agreed. "Noah is convinced she is. As long as he's focused on Aunt Tillie, though, that allows Chief Terry and me to anticipate his moves. He's fairly predictable. Even though he's not staying at The Overlook, I'll still be able to keep an eye on him."

"We need to figure out where he's staying," I said, lifting my head as the wind chimes over the front door jangled to signify a customer's entry. To my surprise, I found my father standing in the doorway. "Hey, Dad."

"Hi, Bay," Dad said, offering me a wan smile as he stepped further into the store. "Am I interrupting anything?"

"We're just eating lunch," Landon said, gesturing toward the empty chair at the edge of the carpeted area. "Join us. I bought enough food to feed an army."

"I have to be back out at the Dragonfly because we're expecting a delivery, but I wanted to talk to you guys, and lucked out because you're all here," Dad said, sitting. His relationship with Landon wasn't exactly warm, but it was improving. He actually smiled when Landon nudged the container of spring rolls in his direction. "We had a surprise guest show up in the middle of the night, and given the rumors flying around town I figured you'd want to know."

"Well, that answers that question," Thistle intoned. "Agent Goober is staying at the Dragonfly. My only question is: Did he know our fathers owned the inn before he checked in?"

"He knew," Dad supplied. "He called in the middle of the night, and Teddy checked him in. We didn't think a lot about it at first. We were tired and distracted. He said he was an agent and he had a government credit card.

"This morning he took the opportunity to grill all three of us over breakfast," he continued. "He wanted to know what we thought about Tillie and the possibility of you guys covering for her."

"That jerkoff," Landon muttered, shaking his head. "I can't believe he did this."

I could believe it. I was more disappointed in the fact that we didn't anticipate it. "What did you tell him?"

Dad's eyes twinkled. "What do you think I said? I said that Tillie was a murderer and you guys would be more than willing to help her hide a body."

My mouth dropped open. "What?"

"He's joking, Bay," Landon admonished. "Your sarcasm detector must be on the fritz today."

"I told him the truth," Dad said. "I told him that our relationship with Tillie is tempestuous because she's a busybody. I also told him she's loyal to a fault and wouldn't murder anyone. Then I told him if he suggested the three of you were guilty of anything he would have to leave. He quieted down pretty quickly after that. He grumbled a little about crazy people not respecting his authority, but I have a feeling that has to do with how he got kicked out of The Overlook."

"Mom had a good time doing it," I said. "She was going to kick him in the face if she needed to."

Dad chuckled. "That sounds about right. I need to know what you guys want me to do. We'll kick him out, too. We're more than willing."

"Don't do that," Landon said, glancing at me. "It might be uncomfortable for you to have him there, but he also might tell you something he'd be less likely to share with me. He's not thrilled about my relationship with Bay, and I think he's withholding a few tidbits from me because of that."

"Do you want us to ferret out information?" Dad asked.

"If you can do it in an unobtrusive manner, go for it," Landon replied. "But if your unobtrusive manner resembles your daughter's, don't do it. He'll catch on to that pretty quickly."

I was pretty sure I should be insulted. "Hey!"

"You're beautiful, sassy and wise, sweetie," Landon said. "You're a terrible liar and your undercover skills are horrendous. We all have crosses to bear. Those are yours."

Dad chuckled. "We can feel him out," he said. "He's our only guest tonight. We have another couple checking in tomorrow. What's this all about?"

"It's a really long story," I said, pinching the bridge of my nose. "Suffice it to say this town's dark underbelly might be exposed before long."

"And Tillie?" Dad prodded. "How is she taking things?"

"Now that she's not rooming with Thistle and me, much better than before," I replied.

"It sounds as if I've missed a lot," Dad said. "We should have dinner and catch up." It was a pointed suggestion.

"We will," I promised. "We can't talk freely in front of Agent Glenn, though."

Dad pushed himself to his feet. "I understand that," he said. "As soon as he leaves, though, I expect a visit from you three. You can bring your boyfriends."

"We're looking forward to it," Landon said. "Thank you for telling us where Noah is staying. I think it might come in useful."

"Good luck," Dad said. "He's convinced Tillie is guilty because she's mean. I tried explaining that's her personality and that she'd rather torture someone than kill them, but he doesn't believe me."

"That's what I said," I chortled.

"Great minds think alike," Dad said, winking. "I'll be in touch if he lets anything slip. You guys take care of each other. If someone is killing people and they realize you're sticking your noses in it, you could become targets."

"That's exactly what I'm afraid of," Landon said, grim. "Don't worry. I'll protect them with my life."

"And that's the only reason I like you," Dad said. "Good luck. I think you're going to need it."

TWENTY-FIVE

I left Clove to deal with the remnants of Thistle's hangover after lunch, sharing a hug with Landon on the sidewalk in front of the store before he trudged off in the direction of the police station. Noah's suspicions were wearing on him, but there was nothing I could do to ease the pain except focus on the case. The sooner we solved it, the sooner Noah would hightail it out of Hemlock Cove.

I pointed myself in the direction of the bakery, breathing a sigh of relief when I found it empty except for the owner, Mrs. Gunderson. She lifted her eyebrows when she saw me, shooting me a warm smile.

"Hello, Bay."

"Hi, Mrs. Gunderson," I said, approaching the counter. My relationship with the woman wasn't one of ease and comfort. She'd always been pleasant and nice to me, but she knew I was aware of her husband's beatings. Her former friendship with Aunt Tillie eroded over the years, but at her core I knew Mrs. Gunderson was a good person. "How have you been?"

"I can't complain," Mrs. Gunderson replied. "We do better business in the winter because most people don't want coffee and doughnuts in the summer. I enjoy the down time, though."

I'd never considered that. "I need your help."

Mrs. Gunderson stilled, her face unreadable. "I see."

"I have a feeling you know what I'm here about," I said, pressing forward despite her obvious reticence. "I'm not trying to stir up trouble. I hope you know that. You've lived here all your life, though, and you're familiar with the players."

"And you're loyal to your aunt and desperate to protect her," Mrs. Gunderson said, filling in the blanks. "I understand why you're here, Bay. Take a seat and I'll get you something to drink. Do you want coffee or iced tea?"

"Iced tea, please."

I sat at the small table in the corner, watching Mrs. Gunderson prepare two glasses of iced tea before she joined me. She seemed resigned to my questions.

"Okay, let me have it," Mrs. Gunderson said once she was settled. "What do you want to know?"

"What do you know about Patty Grimes?" I asked, going for the easiest question first.

"Patty was a few years older than us," Mrs. Gunderson replied. "I wasn't particularly close with her. My family was very poor when I was younger and I had to work on the farm, so I didn't have time to play around like most of the other kids. I wasn't privy to a lot of the gossip, and the other girls looked down on me."

That made sense. "Still, I'm sure you were aware of her."

"I was," Mrs. Gunderson confirmed. "She always seemed ... lost. You know she never married, right?"

"I don't think there's anything wrong with that," I said. "Maybe she never found the right person."

"She was convinced a man named Victor Donahue was the right person. She was determined to nab him."

There was that name again. It seemed farfetched to believe Victor had a place in this tale sixty years after he had a leading role, but it appeared more and more likely. "I met Victor yesterday," I said. "He's in a home in Bellaire. Someone else brought up his name, so we checked him out."

Mrs. Gunderson's eyebrows shot up her forehead. "He's still in the area? I thought for sure he moved downstate or somewhere. That was the rumor I heard."

"He could've moved downstate," I clarified. "I only know he's in this area now. I have no idea where he's been. I also heard a rumor that he had some sort of weird triangle with Aunt Tillie and Patty."

Mrs. Gunderson chuckled. "When you say it like that it sounds like a small-town soap opera."

"I think it kind of is."

"You're probably right," Mrs. Gunderson said. "Victor Donahue was one of those kids who was a big shot in high school but you knew would amount to nothing in the real world. At least I knew that. What's funny is I could recognize it in him and not Floyd. But that's a whole other discussion."

Not for the first time my heart went out to the woman. She'd lived a rough life. "So what happened between Patty and Victor?"

"Victor was used to female attention, so when Tillie and Patty fought over him he enjoyed it," Mrs. Gunderson replied. "Patty really liked him and saw him as her future. Tillie was playing a game. She didn't really care either way."

"Victor chose Aunt Tillie and then realized too late she didn't want a relationship," I surmised. "Am I right?"

"Pretty close," Mrs. Gunderson said. "Tillie went out on exactly two dates with Victor before Calvin showed up on the scene. That was all she wrote for Victor and Tillie's romance. By that time he'd already hurt Patty's feelings, although I think she still would've taken him back. Victor was smart enough to know that she'd hold it over his head forever.

"Patty was convinced Victor would come running to her for reconciliation," she continued. "She told everyone who'd listen that it was about to happen. Margaret and her cronies fed into that. Viola and Fay told everyone it would happen, too."

"It didn't happen, though," I said. "Victor left town."

"He did," Mrs. Gunderson said, nodding. "He joined a logging crew. That was big business in this area back then. It seems strange to think about it now, but that was one of the primary ways for young men who weren't headed to college to make a living."

"What did Patty do?"

"She made excuses for a little bit, and then she fell apart," Mrs. Gunderson replied. "She let Margaret feed her rage, and picked a fight with Tillie. By that time Calvin and Tillie were engaged, so Tillie had moved past Victor and didn't care where he ended up. That made things worse for Patty, though.

"I married Floyd soon after, and my life was not what I dreamed, so I kind of fell out of touch with that crowd because I was embarrassed," she continued. "Margaret had a little club of gossipy nags, and she led full offensives against Tillie. Like I said, I was ... beneath ... them. That's what they thought, anyway. None of their efforts worked, though, and I often wondered what Margaret really wanted when she mounted an assault."

"Did she ever tell you?"

"No." Mrs. Gunderson shook her head. "In a place as small as Walkerville there's not enough population to have real problems. That allows the smaller problems to turn into real problems, and that's what happened here.

"Over the years everyone changed," she continued. "Floyd beat me. Margaret had an affair with Floyd. Margaret's husband killed Floyd. The body ended up on your property. You know all of this. Our lives overlapped, but they weren't interconnected."

"Why would someone kill Patty now?" I asked. "It sounds as if she led a solitary life. Fay is dead, too. The only connection I can find is old Walkerville ties."

"There's a lot of anger to go around, and everyone has secrets," Mrs. Gunderson said. "I'm sure Patty had her share of secrets. I don't know what they were, though. Have you asked Tillie about all of this?"

"Aunt Tillie won't talk to me," I admitted. "You know how she is. She's great at keeping secrets, even if we need the information to keep her safe."

"She's loyal," Mrs. Gunderson said. "The thing you have to remember, Bay, is that Tillie would tell her own secret to save herself and keep you guys out of trouble. If she's not telling the truth, it's because she's protecting someone else."

The thought hadn't occurred to me, but instinctively I knew Mrs. Gunderson was right. "Aunt Tillie isn't being a pain because she doesn't want us to know what she's hiding," I said. "She's being a pain because she knows Patty wouldn't want anyone to know her secrets."

"Exactly."

"Well ... crap."

Mrs. Gunderson chuckled. "You're a smart girl, Bay," she said. "I'm sure you'll figure it out. This tale is probably tangled, but when you unravel it, I know you'll find the common thread covers decades of lies and subterfuge."

"And it all leads back to Mrs. Little and her bitterness."

"I'm probably not the right person to ask about that subject," Mrs. Gunderson said. "Margaret betrayed me and I'll never forgive her. In the grand scheme of things, though, she did me a favor. Floyd would've killed me eventually. Because of what she did and the actions her affair set in motion, he never got the chance."

That was a nice way of looking at it. "I was talking to Viola Hendricks last night before we discovered Fay's body. She didn't have the answers we were looking for," I said. "I've tried talking to Mrs. Little, but she shut me down. Now that Patty and Fay are gone, that really leaves only Viola to provide answers. Do you think she's lying?" Given the truth spell, I had a hard time believing it. I didn't know who else to focus on, though.

"I think Viola is the smartest person in the room, yet no one notices," Mrs. Gunderson answered. "She might not remember things distinctly. Age does have disadvantages. She always kept a diary, though. If she does know something – or ever did – I can guarantee she wrote it down."

Wait a second .... "Are you suggesting I read Viola's diary?"

Mrs. Gunderson smirked. "I read one when I was a teenager," she said, her eyes twinkling. "It seems Viola is a lot more colorful than she lets on in polite circles."

That would probably explain the bedroom acrobatics – and the weird mirror fetish. "How am I supposed to read her diaries?"

Mrs. Gunderson shrugged. "I have no idea," she said. "I do know there's a euchre tournament at the senior center this afternoon. Viola loves euchre ... and she lives alone."

Was Mrs. Gunderson telling me to break into Viola's house? That was horrifying ... and kind of a fun idea. "Thank you for your help, Mrs. Gunderson," I said, digging in my purse for cash to pay for my iced tea. "You've given me a few ideas."

"I should hope so, dear," Mrs. Gunderson said, smiling. "I practically drew you a map."

Isn't that the truth?

BY THE TIME I returned to Hypnotic, Thistle was back to her snarky self. Clove pouted behind the counter, shooting occasional eye daggers in Thistle's direction as our cousin added new candles to the wall display.

"What's going on?" I asked.

"Thistle is being mean," Clove said, crossing her arms over her chest. "She won't let me arrange the candles."

"They're my candles," Thistle argued.

"Fine!"

"Good!"

"Whatever," Clove said, rolling her eyes.

Ah, all was right in the Winchester world. We were fighting over little things again rather than worrying about big things ... like murder. "I have news to share if anyone is interested."

"Just a second, Bay," Clove said, holding up a finger to stay me and narrowing her eyes. "Sam bought that tanker I was telling you about. It'll be here the day after tomorrow. I was going to invite you out to see it and start planning for the haunted attraction, but now I changed my mind."

Thistle scowled. She didn't want to admit it, but her imagination had been running wild since Clove mentioned the tanker. "Oh, come on."

"I'm going to decorate it myself. You're not going to be able to even visit it," Clove said. As far as threats go, it was fairly lame. Still, it was enough to shake Thistle. She was desperate to decorate the tanker.

"Fine," Thistle said, stepping away from the display. "You win."

"Good," Clove said, flouncing over to the shelf and shifting one of Thistle's candles so it faced outward instead of to the right. "Perfect."

Thistle's mouth dropped open. "That's it?"

"That's it."

"You're a piece of work," Thistle muttered, stomping toward the counter. "I just ... you drive me crazy!"

"I'm glad to see you're feeling better," Clove said, winking at me. "What about you, Bay? What's your big news?"

I related my conversation with Mrs. Gunderson, and when I was done my cousins' mouths were agape.

"That's all really interesting," Thistle said. "You got a lot more information out of Mrs. Gunderson than anyone else."

"It's because she hates Mrs. Little," I supplied. "Even though Floyd was a jackass, Mrs. Little still betrayed the friendship and slept with him. I don't blame Mrs. Gunderson for being bitter."

"It seems everyone is bitter," Clove said. "I never realized how ... petty ... things were. They're adults. I expected them to act like adults."

"I know," I said. "I'm glad we've never dated the same person. Can you imagine how bitter things would get if we overlapped men?"

"Yeah, we all have different taste in men," Thistle said. "I'm pretty sure that's divine intervention. What do you want to do about the diary?"

I smiled. "Well ... ."

"No way," Clove said, immediately shaking her head. "We cannot break into Viola's house and read her diaries. That's just ... no."

"Oh, come on," I whined. "This will be a fun adventure. I promise."

"We'll be breaking the law," Clove countered.

"When has that ever stopped us?" Thistle asked. "I'm totally in, by the way. I'm dying to read those diaries. After hearing about what a tiger Viola is in the sack, they're bound to be entertaining."

"And what if she writes about what she sees in the mirror when she plays that game she told us about?" Clove challenged.

"We'll skip that part," Thistle said. "This sounds fun!"

"Good," I said. "The euchre tournament starts in an hour. We'll watch the senior center and make sure she's inside before heading to her house. That should give us a few hours to break in and go through her stuff."

"How do you even know the tournament is still on?" Clove asked. "They found a body there last night. They probably shut the center down for the day."

"Mrs. Little would revolt," I said. "Those seniors are addicted to their euchre. Trust me. It's happening."

"Bay is right," Thistle said. "Chief Terry wouldn't risk the wrath of the senior population and shut down that tournament."

"But ... ." Clove wasn't ready to give in. "What if we get caught?"

"We'll lie," Thistle said. "We'll tell Noah that Sally made us do it. He already thinks we're crazy."

"Besides, we won't get caught," I added. "I got caught last time because Aunt Tillie distracted me. She won't be around this time."

"I don't know," Clove said, chewing her bottom lip. "I need to think about it."

"Go ahead and think about it," Thistle said. "Just remember, though, we're inviting you on our adventure and you're saying no. We won't forget it."

I caught on to Thistle's tactic. "That's right," I said. "Eventually we'll get tired of you turning our adventure suggestions down and stop asking you. It's inevitable."

Clove groaned and slumped her shoulders. I knew we'd won before she even opened her mouth. "Fine. I'm in. If we get caught, though, it's every witch for herself."

"That's the way it always is," I said, sharing a triumphant smile with Thistle.

"That's the way we like it," Thistle said.

Clove shook her head as she adjusted another candle on the shelf, practically daring Thistle to admonish her. "That Sally is turning into quite the troublemaker," she said. "I think our mothers are going to kick her out of the inn before it's all said and done."

"Oh, I'm looking forward to that," Thistle said.

"We all are." What? Clove isn't wrong. Sally is a pain. Oh, crap. Now I'm thinking of her as a real person, too.

I blame Aunt Tillie.

TWENTY-SIX

"This is the worst idea we've ever had."

After sitting in Thistle's car and watching the front door of the senior center until we saw Viola enter, we made our way to her house. Viola lived on a quiet street with only four other houses on the short drive, but we decided to play it safe and parked one street over to minimize our chances of getting caught.

To any outside observer we looked like three young women out for a walk. Of course, anyone who knew us would be immediately suspicious, but as long as we didn't draw unnecessary attention I figured we would be okay.

Instead of approaching Viola's house from the front, we cut through the back alley. Thistle used a little jolt of magic to unlock the back gate so we could gain entry into Viola's fenced-in back yard. Once inside and cut off from neighbors thanks to the privacy fence, we had another door to get through. That's when Clove decided to voice her dislike of the plan for what felt like the hundredth time.

"This isn't even close to the worst plan we've ever had," Thistle countered. "Do you remember when we were seventeen and we decided to glamour ourselves so we could get into that bar? We made ourselves look old enough to be mothers of teenagers?"

Clove frowned. "We ended up with eight different people asking us if we offered daycare services," she said. "We were teenagers then. We should be smarter now."

We should be smarter, but we weren't. "How about the time we decided to make ourselves invisible to sneak into Aunt Tillie's room and steal a bottle of wine?" I challenged.

"We couldn't see our own hands, so we couldn't cast the counter spell and we had to find our mothers and confess. We were grounded for a month."

"Ah, good times," Thistle said. "I can see why you were worried we would forget to bring you on adventures."

"I still hate you sometimes," Clove groused.

"You love us and you know it," Thistle said, reaching for the sliding glass door handle. "I'll spell the lock. I'm the best at it."

I made a face as I slapped her hand away and then tugged on the door. It easily slid open.

"How did you know it would be unlocked?" Clove asked, making a face.

"Because this is Hemlock Cove and the back gate was locked," I replied. "Most people don't lock their doors here. Given our murder rate these days, they should lock their doors, but they don't. Even our mothers don't lock their doors."

"Hey, when you live with Aunt Tillie, the bad element is already inside, so there's nothing to keep out," Thistle said, walking into the house. "Okay, where should we look?"

"I think we should start with the bedroom," I said, following Thistle. "I ... ." I lost my train of thought as I got a better look at Viola's house. There were blind circus folk with a penchant for plastic knickknacks with better decorating taste. "Oh ... my."

"Son of a freaking dingdong," Clove hissed, dumbfounded as she scanned the room. "Are those ... ?"

"Clowns," Thistle finished, nodding as a grimace washed over her features. "I just ... it's like fifty ceramic clowns."

"I don't like clowns," Clove whined. "They're freaky."

"No one likes clowns," I said, wrinkling my nose as I stepped closer to the curio cabinet in the corner. "What demented mind would even think of making something like this?"

"I think they're supposed to be cute," Thistle said, tipping her head to the side and studying one of the bigger figurines. It sported a red nose and large shoes, and held a bundle of balloons. He was supposed to be endearing, but he made my skin crawl. "These aren't cute."

"They're horrible," Clove said. "I'm going to have nightmares."

Thistle snorted. "Are you worried the figurines are going to come to life and find you out at the Dandridge? I can see it now. You'll wake up with little dents in your skin from their ceramic fingers."

Clove shuddered and made a disgusted sound in the back of her throat. "Oh, man. Now I'll have nightmares about that."

I fought the urge to chuckle, although the clown collection was discombobulating. "Let's find the bedroom," I suggested. "Hopefully the clowns are a kitchen thing."

"And a living room thing," Thistle said, pointing toward another cabinet in the next room.

"If they're a bathroom thing, I'm out of here," Clove warned.

"Yeah, because that will really scare the crap out of you," Thistle deadpanned.

Viola's ranch wasn't large, and offered only one floor to search. I initially suggested splitting up, but Clove balked so we remained together. The first room we found was the bathroom, which looked normal if you ignored the huge clown watercolor print on the wall above the toilet. The second room, a bedroom turned into a craft room, looked mostly unused. The next room was a small library or den, boasting floor-to-ceiling shelving units. One entire unit was filled with diaries.

"Jackpot," Thistle said, striding into the room and grabbing one of the diaries.

"Holy cannoli," Clove intoned. "Are all of these diaries full?"

"They look it," Thistle said, sitting on the small loveseat in the middle of the room. "Listen to this. It's from March 1985, which I think would've made Viola around fifty-two or so: 'Margaret insisted we get matching hats,' she read aloud. 'She got to pick everyone's hat

AMANDA M. LEE

color and I got stuck with orange. I hate orange. I look like a pumpkin. I want to douse the thing in gasoline and shove it up Margaret's you know what and light a match.'"

I snickered. "That sounds about right."

"I'm really starting to like Viola," Thistle said.

"Aren't you worried about stumbling across entries about her sex life?" Clove challenged.

"Not in the least," Thistle replied. "Maybe I'll get a few tips."

That was an interesting – and terrifying – thought. "Let's start reading," I instructed. "The faster we get through this, the faster we can get out of here."

"And away from the clowns," Clove said.

"Definitely away from the clowns."

"OKAY, HERE'S SOMETHING," Clove said an hour later, sitting cross-legged on the floor. "This is from when Viola was about seventeen."

"At least that's getting closer to the time period we're looking for," I said. "There doesn't seem to be any rhyme or reason to the order of the journals."

"Sure there is," Thistle argued. "She has them arranged by genre. Clove got the mystery section, you got the cooking section and I got the erotica section. I think I got the better part of the deal."

"Yes, and if you could stop reading the sex reenactments out loud that would be wonderful," I said.

"Do you want to hear what I found or not?" Clove asked, irritated.

"Yes, Clove. We're waiting with bated breath." Thistle's face was serious, but I could tell she would jump on the opportunity to annoy Clove as soon as it became available.

"Thank you," Clove said, her eyes flashing before shifting her attention to the diary. "'It's been two weeks since Margaret announced plans to make Tillie do her bidding. She's convinced Tillie is hiding something. I think Tillie is hiding something, too, but I'm not sure it's what Margaret is looking for.

"'Margaret wants Tillie to teach us to do what she does, but Tillie keeps saying she's imagining things,'" she continued reading. "'Tillie and Ginger are always whispering, and I know they did something that night at the dance to make the lights blow up at the same time Margaret was going after them.

"'Margaret is determined that Tillie has a big secret, and she thinks she knows what it is,'" Clove read. "'What if she's wrong and it's worse than we think?'"

I rubbed the back of my neck as I leaned forward, rolling the entry through my head. "It sounds as if everyone had suspicions about Aunt Tillie and Grandma, but no one could ever prove anything. That's not really a surprise."

"People think the same about us," Thistle said. "I don't understand how Mrs. Little thought she would force Aunt Tillie to do her bidding, though. That seems extremely odd."

"This whole thing seems odd," I said, stretching my legs out on the floor. "I think it's entirely possible that Mrs. Little flipped her lid after a lifetime of anger pointed in Aunt Tillie's direction. But why wouldn't she try to kill Aunt Tillie?"

"She's trying to frame her instead," Clove said.

"Maybe with Patty," I said. "The fact that Mrs. Little called the FBI before a cause of death was even released for Patty still doesn't sit right with me. She called Chief Terry the day before to report Aunt Tillie being at the senior center. That would fall in line with her laying the groundwork for an arrest if she intended to frame Aunt Tillie."

"So what's the problem?" Clove asked.

"Fay," Thistle supplied. "Why kill Fay?"

"Maybe Fay knew she killed Patty," Clove suggested. "Maybe they did it together to get Aunt Tillie out of the way or as some weird form of retribution we don't yet understand. Maybe Fay felt bad about it after the fact and decided to tell the truth, and Mrs. Little had to stop her."

"That's a decent theory," I said. "That means it would've been a 'heat of the moment' killing, though. Whoever stabbed Fay in the bathroom was carrying a knife. Does Mrs. Little strike you as the type of person who would carry a knife in her purse?"

Landon said it was one of those pocketknives you fold up. They're sold everywhere, so there's little chance of tracking the purchase."

"I forgot about that," Clove admitted. "Could they be wrong?"

"I don't think the coroner got his license from a cereal box, Clove," Thistle said, shaking the diary she held to get our attention. "Oh, hey, listen to this. This is when Viola is still in high school and right before graduation."

"Does it involve another sex fantasy?" Clove asked. "I cannot listen to another sex fantasy. That one about going to the carnival and seducing the clown with cotton candy and a squeaky horn almost made me throw up."

"I think that was supposed to be funny," Thistle said, giggling. "This one involves a relationship, but not sex. Well, kind of sex, but not creepy clown sex."

"What is it?" I prodded.

"'I saw Victor today,'" Thistle read. "'He was supposed to be working but he's been hanging around the school watching Tillie. Patty is still mad, and Margaret keeps trying to fire her up to go after Tillie. I think if she could convince Patty to kill Tillie she would do it. She denies it, of course.

"'Calvin is always waiting outside the school to walk Tillie home now, so we can't approach her when he's watching,'" she continued. "'Margaret swears she's going to get Tillie to fix things before we graduate, but I already think it's too late.

"'Victor keeps following Tillie around, and I'm beginning to wonder whether he's dangerous,'" Thistle read. "'He wants to hurt Calvin. He wants to hurt Tillie, too. Even worse, I think he might want to hurt me because of what I told him about Patty. I had suspicions and he brushed them off, but I didn't miss the look in his eye. He seems lost and confused. Trouble is coming. I can feel it.'"

"Wow," I said. "That's ... ominous."

"That's creepy," Clove said. "Do you really think Victor stalked Aunt Tillie?"

"It sounds like it," I replied. "They probably didn't call it stalking back then, though."

"It sounds to me like Victor was obsessed with Aunt Tillie and she abused his affection," Thistle said. "I know she's our aunt, but she's not perfect. In her mind she might not have realized what she was doing ... or maybe beating Patty and Mrs. Little took precedence over Victor's feelings. I can see that happening."

"Basically we're operating under the theory that Mrs. Little wanted Aunt Tillie to perform magic for her – whether to make them young forever or unnaturally get them ahead in life – and the longer Aunt Tillie worked against her the more bitter she became," I said. "I think the original problems stem from that, but I'm not sure I can picture Mrs. Little stabbing Fay."

"It's one thing to poison someone – that's killing from a distance," Thistle added. "Stabbing someone is entirely different. Even if it was in the heat of the moment, Mrs. Little would've acted surprised ... or upset ... or even appeared disheveled at the dance. Instead she held court at the table with Kenneth and Arthur. She didn't look upset, or even distracted."

"We need a list of people who attended the dance last night," I said. "We can't start ruling people out until we know how many people we have to sort through."

"What about the diaries?" Clove asked. "We can't sit here all day. Viola is bound to come home eventually."

As if on cue, the unmistakable sound of a door opening at the other end of the house froze us in place. I locked gazes with Thistle, my heart rate ratcheting up several notches. I was frozen in place for exactly five seconds before I shook off the terror.

"We have to get out of here," I mouthed.

Thistle sprang into action – she's always the best under pressure – and grabbed the diaries to shove them back on the shelves. They weren't in the right order, but we had no way of remembering their original locations. I moved to the window and quietly opened it, unlatching the screen and pushing it out. It hit the ground outside, and I poked my head through the opening to make sure no one could see our escape before climbing out.

Clove followed, Thistle giving her a good shove and causing her to

AMANDA M. LEE

land on top of me. I tried to catch her, but the force of Thistle's push toppled both of us to the ground. Thistle hopped out after us, gracefully landing and giving us a disgusted shake of the head before lifting the screen and settling it back inside its grooves.

This wasn't the first time we'd hopped out of a window and had to cover our tracks. Sure, most of the other times occurred when we were teenagers, but some skills never fade. The screen wasn't properly latched, but hopefully Viola wouldn't think anything of it, if she noticed at all.

I pushed Clove to a standing position before rolling to a crouch. Thistle pointed at the bushes to signify we should stick as close as possible before making a break toward the back gate. I nodded, lowering my head as I rounded a large shrub. We were only about twenty feet away from the gate when our plan imploded.

"Are you going somewhere, girls?"

I froze, the hair on the back of my neck standing on end. I recognized Viola's voice. Crap!

"We can explain," Clove said, jumping to her feet and holding up her hands in an effort to show she was unarmed.

"You can explain?" Viola challenged, her eyes dark as they briefly locked with mine. "How can you explain breaking into my house and pawing through my belongings? I saw my journals, by the way. You left them out of order."

"Just out of curiosity's sake, did you arrange them by genre?" Thistle asked.

I elbowed her in the stomach to quiet her. "I ... um ... ."

"We know you have memory problems, but we also think you probably knew the big secret between Aunt Tillie and Mrs. Little at some point," Clove blurted out. "We wanted to read about it in your journals because we're desperate to know what's going on. Please don't call the cops. I'm too small and cute for prison."

"Oh, smooth," Thistle said, rolling her eyes. "You're the worst spy ever!"

"You're all terrible spies," Viola said, crossing her arms over her chest. "You're the one I saw climbing out the library window, Thistle.

That purple hair is a dead giveaway. That's how I knew to come out here. How did you get in?"

"Your sliding glass door was unlocked," I said, opting for honesty.

"The gate wasn't, though," Viola pointed out.

"Yes, but the handle was rusty and it wasn't hard to jimmy," Thistle said. "We're sorry, but ... we need answers and we thought you were our best shot."

"I see," Viola said, shaking her head. "You girls remind me so much of Tillie it kills me."

"Hey, we said we were sorry," Clove said. "There's no reason to insult us."

Viola smirked. "That's something Tillie would say."

"We really are sorry." The apology sounded lame, but I didn't know what else to offer. "We know something happened back when you ladies were younger and we know Mrs. Little wanted something from Aunt Tillie."

"Something she couldn't give," Thistle added.

"Something she refused to give," Viola clarified. "I'm on to all of you. I know you're really witches. Heck, the whole town knows. Those who don't acknowledge it want to pretend it's not true, but I know better.

"Your family is surrounded by strange things," she continued. "Men have disappeared in your presence. Bay walks around talking to herself half the time. Storms spring out of nowhere and lightning strikes people on your property. I'm not an idiot."

"I don't talk to myself," I said. "I just ... ." Hmm. I couldn't admit talking to ghosts. That wouldn't go over well.

"She talks to herself," Thistle said, shooting me a warning look. "Fine. You've got us. We're witches. Abracadabra."

"That's magicians," Clove said.

"Alakazam?" Thistle asked, searching her memory.

"Also magicians," I said.

"And *Pokémon*," Clove added.

"Okay, I'm out of magic words," Thistle said. "We've admitted our dark secret. Now we want you to admit your dark secret."

"I don't have a dark secret," Viola said. "I can't remember anything these days. Why do you think I keep the diaries?"

"I think you have an erotica fetish," Thistle replied, not missing a beat. "That clown fascination of yours is creepy, by the way. We should talk. We could probably make a killing in fetish fiction on the web."

"Clowns are wonderful," Viola argued.

"They're creepy," Thistle said. "I don't care about the clowns, though. I care about the other stuff. I care about the dead people."

I decided to try a different tactic. "Someone killed Patty and Fay," I said. "It wasn't Aunt Tillie. I swear it. We need to figure out who it is."

"Of course it's not Tillie," Viola scoffed. "Margaret wants everyone to believe it's Tillie but no one does. My memory is shot, but I know who did it."

I was stunned. "You do? Who?"

Viola opened her mouth to answer, but her response died on her lips.

The deafening roar of a gunshot filled the air, causing me to cringe and duck my head. Something warm splashed across the side of my face. Even in my stunned state, I realized it was Viola's blood before her body hit the ground with a sickening thud.

Someone was shooting at us ... and Viola was already gone.

TWENTY-SEVEN

"Bay!" I was frozen, my muscles immovable. I could hear the blood pulsating through my body. It was as if a torrent of fluid rushed past my brain, choking the life out of me as the oxygen was stolen from my lungs. It was so loud it drowned out almost everything else. Thistle screamed my name, but it barely registered.

Thistle viciously grabbed my arm and yanked me into the bushes, shaking me as she tried to command my attention. I couldn't focus. My head was ... floating, as if detached from my body.

"Son of a ... ."

"Do something," Clove screamed, covering her head as another gunshot rang out. I jolted at the noise, but Thistle held me down as she rummaged through my pocket. I couldn't figure out what she was doing until she pulled out my phone.

Her hands shook as she pressed three numbers into the keypad and then lifted the phone to her ear.

"We need help!"

"**BAY?**"

Chief Terry's voice was gentle as he hunkered down in front of me. I recognized his face, but I remained quiet.

"Bay," Chief Terry said. "It's okay. You can stand up now."

I remained on the ground behind the bushes, my chin resting on my knees. After the second shot, things fell eerily silent. Chief Terry arrived minutes later, his officers scattering to search the area. He called for paramedics to help Viola. She was beyond help, but he made the call anyway.

"Leave her there," Thistle said, shaking her head. "She's in shock."

"I can see that," Chief Terry snapped. "What in the hell were you three doing here? What was going on when Viola was shot?"

"I ... ." Thistle held her hands palms up and shrugged. "It's a long story."

"Well, you'd better have your story together right quick," Chief Terry said, keeping his voice low. "Trouble just walked through the back gate."

I flicked my eyes in the direction Chief Terry indicated, my heart sinking when I saw Noah tread into the yard. I thought he was alone until Landon shoved him out of the way to give himself room to navigate. Landon blew past Chief Terry when he tried to intercept him, and raced to me.

"Bay!"

I forced myself to focus on him as he jerked me into his arms, pressing his hand to the back of my head. I could feel his heart racing against mine.

"Sweetie, what happened?" Landon asked, pulling away slightly so he could study me. "Whose blood is this?"

Chief Terry pointed at Viola's body. "Bay must've been ... splattered ... when Viola was shot."

My heart sank at the description. I could still see every gruesome moment of it as I relived it in slow motion.

"How close were you?" Landon's eyes glistened with unshed tears as his voice wavered.

I opened my mouth to answer, but no sound would come out.

"She was right next to her," Thistle answered for me. "We were all talking and ... then it happened. They were only a few inches apart."

"Oh, Bay, dammit!" Landon sat on the ground and pulled me onto his lap, resting my head against his shoulder and rocking me. It was surreal ... and comforting at the same time. "You're okay. You're okay." I didn't know whether he was trying to convince me or himself.

"Whoever it was had to be watching us," Thistle said. In the face of everything, she had it pulled together, and I envied her for it. "We were talking to Viola and ... she said she was about to tell us who the murderer was. The next thing we knew, a gun went off and there was blood all over Bay's face. It took me a second to realize what was happening. It didn't feel real."

"Then what happened?" Chief Terry asked gently, as he rested his hand on top of my head.

"Bay kind of froze," Thistle said. "I yelled at her, but she just stood there, so I yanked her into the bushes. I think she has some cuts."

"And you left me behind to fend for myself," Clove said, her lower lip jutting out. "I could've died, too."

"You weren't frozen," Thistle snapped. "You didn't have blood on your face."

Landon tightened his arm around my waist and – to my shock – began humming. The melody was familiar, yet I couldn't place it.

"Another gunshot went off after I got her in the bushes," Thistle said. "I knew her phone was in her pocket so I found it and called for help. We didn't hear anything after the second gunshot."

"Except Bay whimpering," Clove said. "She wouldn't talk to us, though. We thought maybe she was hit at first ... but it was all Viola's blood."

"And she was obviously dead," Thistle added. "If I thought she was alive I would've tried to help her, but ... ."

"I see her, Thistle," Chief Terry said, turning his kind eyes on my cousin. "You couldn't have done anything for Viola."

"What I want to know is what you ladies were doing here," Noah interjected. "Why were you at this woman's house?"

"She's part of the older crew that ran around with Aunt Tillie, and she was well acquainted with Patty and Fay," Thistle replied, her tone even. "We wanted to know whether she had any answers." She conveniently left out the part about us breaking into the house. Thistle was always cool under pressure.

"It's okay, sweetie," Landon whispered in my ear. "I'll take care of you." I thought he was almost more shocked than me.

"And what did Viola tell you?" Noah asked, pulling out his tiny notebook. He was all business.

"She didn't really get a chance to tell us anything," Thistle replied. "We talked to her for only a few seconds."

"And you expect me to believe that someone just happened to be watching at the precise moment when everything could've shifted in this investigation and shot her as she was about to reveal the big secret?" Noah challenged.

"I don't care what you believe," Thistle shot back. "She could've been about to tell us an evil clown did it. I have no idea what she was going to say. Someone wanted her silenced, though. Why don't you spend more time worrying about that?"

"Because I'm worried about you, Ms. Winchester," Noah replied. "This is the second murder you've been present for. I want to know why that is."

"What exactly are you saying?" Chief Terry asked, sliding a silencing look in Thistle's direction before focusing on the most annoying man in the yard.

"These three women have been present for two murders," Noah said. "That can't be a coincidence."

"They weren't present for Fay's murder," Chief Terry argued. "They found her in the bathroom after the fact. I've given you two sworn witness statements putting all three of them on the front sidewalk at the time Fay was murdered!"

"Those statements could've been coerced." Noah was stubborn. I had to give him that.

"And who do you think coerced them?" Chief Terry asked.

"I'm leaning toward you, but I haven't ruled out Agent Michaels,"

Noah said, refusing to back down. "He seems unnaturally attached to Ms. Winchester, and I believe he is capable of lying to protect her."

"Oh, that is just ... ridiculous," Landon hissed, pressing me tightly against him as he struggled to his feet. My dead weight proved to be too much, and Chief Terry had to help him, making sure Landon was steady with me in his arms before taking a step back. Landon shifted my body so he could keep me close as I rested my head against his shoulder. "They were just shot at, you moron!"

"Perhaps they did that themselves and then faked the call," Noah said. "Your girlfriend could be putting on an act for all we know."

"I will beat the snot out of you if you ever say that again," Landon spat, tightening his grip. "Bay's in shock. She has blood all over her face, you jackass! Thistle and Clove are white as sheets. The trajectory of the bullet that blew half of Viola's head off obviously came from a high angle.

"None of these girls have a gun, and they haven't had time to discard one," he continued, his chest heaving as he built up a full head of steam. "They have no motive for killing Viola. We have a serial killer on the loose. Whoever did this has access to multiple weapons and an agenda."

"It could be the mothers out at the inn," Noah argued.

"Shut up!" Landon bellowed, causing every head in the back yard to snap in his direction. "Stop acting like an idiot! Stop being so myopic you miss what's right in front of you. Whatever is going on has absolutely nothing to do with Bay, Clove and Thistle, and everything to do with something that happened in this town years ago.

"This is nothing more than history taking over the present," he continued, his nostrils flaring. "All of these older women are hiding a secret, or at the very least an ancient grudge. Bay, Clove and Thistle are trying to help their aunt. If you could pull your head out of your ass for five seconds you'd realize that!"

Noah was taken aback, his mouth dropping open under the full breadth of Landon's fury.

"Landon, maybe you should take Bay out of here," Chief Terry suggested, obviously worried things were about to escalate. "I'll take care of the investigation. You take care of Bay."

"Agent Michaels should stay at the scene," Noah said. "This is an ongoing investigation, and it does not revolve around his personal life."

"That did it," Landon snapped, taking an aggressive step in Noah's direction. Noah had the grace to look apologetic, but only briefly. "Everything in my life revolves around Bay right now. She's my priority. Chief Terry can handle this scene. There's absolutely nothing I can do here, so I'm taking Bay home."

"I have to question her first," Noah countered. "It's procedure."

"She's not ready for questions!" Landon was so angry his hand shook as he pointed his finger in Noah's face. "When she's ready, I'm sure she'll be thrilled to listen to your boneheaded theories. Until then, stay the hell away from my girlfriend!"

"Landon, take Bay home," Chief Terry instructed. "Take Clove and Thistle with you. I'll come out to the inn as soon as things are settled here and take statements. I'll take them so we won't risk an … incident."

"Whoopee," Landon said, gripping me tighter. "That's the best thing I've heard all day. Come on, Clove and Thistle. We're out of here."

My cousins dutifully fell into step behind Landon as he stalked toward the back gate. I was relieved to be going home. Noah wasn't quite done yet, though.

"Agent Michaels, if you leave this scene against protocol I will be forced to file a complaint with the home office," Noah said.

"Knock yourself out," Landon said. "Actually, if you could literally knock yourself out, that would be even better." His tone softened as he addressed Clove and Thistle. "Come on, guys. I'll get you home."

"I JUST WANT TO SEE HER."

I sat in the bathtub at the guesthouse an hour later, the steaming water washing over me as I tried to scrub my skin clean. I could still feel Viola's blood on my face, and I worried it would be a permanent stain.

Landon had dropped Clove and Thistle at the inn and told them to explain everything to our mothers before expressly forbidding anyone from bothering us at the guesthouse. Of course that was a challenge for my mother, and she arrived shortly after with a tray of food and a stubborn disposition. Landon met her at the door, and I could hear their discussion from the bathtub.

"Winnie, she's okay," Landon said, his tone weary. "She's in the tub. She needs to relax. Once she gets out, I'm putting her in pajamas and we'll eat the food you brought down. Then I'm forcing her into bed."

"What are you going to do?" Mom sounded worried.

"I'm going to be with her the entire time," Landon replied. "I won't let her out of my sight. I'll take care of her. I promise."

"Who's going to take care of you?" It was a sweet question. She was right, though. Landon needed someone to make him feel better, and I sure wasn't up to the task.

"I'll take care of myself," Landon said. "She's alive and safe. That's all I need. A good night's sleep will do a world of wonder for her. Make sure Thistle knows to be quiet when she comes home. Aunt Tillie is back at the inn, right?"

"She is, and she had an absolute fit when she heard what happened," Mom said. "She's been grilling Clove and Thistle. I told her to knock it off, but she doesn't listen to me."

"You make sure she knows I'll pitch an absolute fit if she comes down here and goes after Bay," Landon warned. "Bay has been through enough for one day. It's going to be quiet here for the foreseeable future, and Aunt Tillie doesn't do quiet."

"I'm leaving this to your discretion, but I still want to see her," Mom pressed. "She's my daughter."

"And she's my heart," Landon said, his voice cracking. "She's naked in the tub. I don't think she wants you in there. Quite frankly, I'm going to be naked in the tub with her in a few minutes. I know I don't want you in there when that happens. You'll be ruined for all other men after that."

Mom was silent for a beat. "You're a sick man."

"You can punish me tomorrow," Landon said. "We'll be at the inn for breakfast. Until then ... everyone should back off."

I didn't hear the rest of their conversation, but I knew Landon ushered Mom out the front door because the silence after her departure was disconcerting. He was quiet when he rejoined me in the bathroom, wordlessly shedding his clothes before climbing into the tub and settling behind me. He shifted my body so we both fit, and then rubbed my back as I rested my head against his chest.

"I suppose you want to know what we were really doing there," I said finally.

"Nope," Landon said, kissing my forehead. "I can figure that out on my own. It doesn't matter. Viola is dead and you're alive. I'm going to thank whatever goddess blesses your life and watch you sleep all night. We'll talk about the rest of it tomorrow morning."

"I ... ."

"Bay, I don't know what you're going to say, but I don't want you apologizing or feeling guilty," Landon said. "We'll deal with it tomorrow. For the rest of the day let's just ... let it go."

"Okay." I pressed my eyes shut and let his steady breathing lull me. "I love you, Landon."

"I love you, sweetie. I don't think you can possibly understand how much. Now ... rest. That's all that's going to help right now."

TWENTY-EIGHT

I woke to a heavy weight on my back, and it took me a few seconds to realize I'd shifted to sleep on my stomach during the night. Landon covered the bulk of my body with his, almost as if protecting me from something only he could see, and the fingers on our right hands were interwoven.

I pressed my eyes shut, savoring the moment and hoping sleep would reclaim me. The wish was fleeting, though.

"I know you're awake," Landon murmured, brushing a kiss against my cheek before rolling off me and settling back against the pillows. I shifted toward him, sighing as he slipped his arm under me and tugged me close.

"How did you know I was awake?"

"Because you make little sighing sounds in your sleep, and you stopped making them a few minutes ago," Landon replied, smoothing my hair down. "You always do that right before you wake up."

"You're pretty observant."

"I'm a professional."

I snickered and the act was enough to shake some of the emotional weight from my shoulders. "Do you know this much about everyone or just me?"

"Just you," Landon replied. "I've spent a lot of time studying you."

"Did you sleep at all?"

"I slept all night, Bay," Landon said. "I had every intention of watching you sleep for ten straight hours, but that lasted twenty minutes before I joined you. I guess I was exhausted, too."

"Because you were worried about me?"

"I'm always worried about you, little witch," Landon teased, tickling my ribs. He didn't expect me to laugh, but I flashed him a warm smile. His eyes sobered as he scanned me. "How do you feel?"

"I'm okay, Landon," I said, and I mostly meant it. "I'm sorry I fell apart yesterday. I'm not sure what happened."

"You could've been killed." His response was simple ... and brutal.

"I didn't register that at the time, though."

"You saw Viola's life snuffed out in a heartbeat and you retreated a bit to regroup," Landon said. "It's normal."

Now he was just making excuses for me. "I've seen death more times than almost anyone," I countered. "Only Aunt Tillie has seen more of it. I talk to ghosts, for crying out loud. I shouldn't have fallen apart like I did."

"Bay, there's a difference between talking to a spirit who refuses to let go and realizing you shared the last moment of someone's life with them," Landon said. "I love you dearly, but you have a tendency to act tough when it's not necessary.

"Yesterday you couldn't muster the energy to act tough," he continued. "It's okay. I'm glad you let me take care of you, because I needed to do that."

"Well, if you insist." I burrowed my face in the hollow of his neck as he chuckled and rubbed my back. I was happy to spend the entire day in bed just like this, but I knew it wouldn't happen. "So, what happens now?"

"We spend five more minutes here and then see what Thistle is doing in the other room."

That was an incredibly simplistic answer. "I mean about the case."

"I was talking about the case," Landon said. "I haven't gotten any new information. My phone is in the living room. I forgot it there when we went to bed."

I widened my eyes as I shifted my chin to lock gazes with him. "But ... won't you be in trouble if your boss called? Noah said he was going to tattle on you."

"I don't care."

"But you could be in big trouble."

"I don't care."

"Landon!"

"Bay!" Landon tugged on my waist to pull me higher so we could be eye to eye. He was serious when he started talking again. "You're all I care about right now. My boss will understand that. If he doesn't, well, I'll deal with it later."

"Landon." My heart rolled at the earnest expression on his face. "I don't know what to say."

"Don't say anything," Landon said, pressing my head back to his chest and hugging me close. "Do you have any idea how I felt when I heard you'd been involved in a shooting?"

"I wasn't shot, though."

"You could've been, Bay," Landon argued. "I've come to expect a lot where you're concerned, but I swear my heart stopped beating for a few seconds. Losing you would've broken me. You have to understand that."

"I'm sorry."

"Don't be sorry," Landon admonished. "You're alive. You'll be okay once we solve this thing. You dodged a literal bullet this time. I'll be happy with that and ignore the rest of it."

"For how long?"

"Five more minutes."

I snickered, warmth running through my chest as I realized exactly how much I loved him. "Fine," I said, giving in. "I guess you've earned your five minutes."

"Oh, sweetie, I've earned five days of whatever I want," Landon countered. "You can pay up when everything is settled."

"You drive a hard bargain, but I'll take it."

"**YOU** LOOK BETTER THAN YOU DID," Thistle said, her hair tousled from sleep as she eyed me from the couch.

Landon pressed his hand to the small of my back and urged me forward, keeping me close as he settled in his favorite armchair and tugged me on his lap. "How are you, Thistle?"

"I'm fine," Thistle said, her tough nature coming out to play. "I feel bad for Viola, don't get me wrong, but I'm okay."

Landon wasn't convinced. "How is she, Marcus?"

Marcus, his shoulder-length blond hair messy from a night of hard slumber, offered Landon a wan smile. "She's okay," he said. "She took Fay's death harder than Viola's. I woke up eight times to make sure she was okay, but she's good."

"I'm glad to hear that," Landon said, shifting his attention to the end table where his phone rested.

"It's been quiet," Thistle said, almost as if reading his mind. "We've been up for an hour and we haven't heard a peep."

"Maybe the battery died," I suggested.

Landon grabbed the phone and checked the screen, showing me the battery bar at half full. "I have zero messages or emails, sweetie," he said. "It looks like all that worrying you did about me losing my job via text message was for nothing."

"Do you really think you're going to lose your job because of Agent Maggot?" Thistle asked, her eyes widening. "You were mean to him and all, but he totally had it coming."

"I'm not worried about losing my job," Landon said. "Noah needed a hard dose of reality yesterday, and I'm not sorry for giving him one."

"I was kind of turned on," Thistle said, earning a dark look from Marcus. "I still love you best, Marcus, don't worry. Landon was just all ... growly. He carried Bay around like a superhero and threatened Noah with bodily harm at the same time. It was totally hot."

"I know you're saying that to irritate me, but I'm fine with that observation," Landon said.

"I'm serious," Thistle argued. "I almost fell in love with you myself yesterday."

I laughed as Landon uncomfortably shifted beneath me. "Now everyone in the family loves you," I said. "Well, maybe not Mom. I heard you two in the hallway last night. She wasn't thrilled with you, but she was worried about your emotional health."

"Your mother will be putty in my hands by the end of breakfast." Landon's confidence was often overwhelming. Today I welcomed it. "She understood why I wanted you left alone. She might not have agreed with it, but she understood it."

"Well, I'll tell you who didn't understand it: Aunt Tillie," Thistle said. "She was fighting mad last night. She wanted to come down here and check on Bay, but Winnie threatened to body slam her if she tried. I was actually rooting for them to wrestle."

"I wish I'd seen that," Landon said, grinning. "I think Winnie would've won."

"You were there in spirit," Thistle said. "Winnie completely unloaded on Aunt Tillie, too. She said if Aunt Tillie wasn't keeping secrets we wouldn't be putting ourselves in danger trying to clear her name. Then she said that she was sick of Aunt Tillie's secrets, and she had better spill them or shut her mouth. I choked on my wine when she said that because I couldn't stop laughing thanks to the look on Aunt Tillie's face."

"What did Aunt Tillie say?" I asked.

"You know her," Thistle said, waving off the question. "She said her private life wasn't for public consumption and she never asked for our help. She said we were busybodies and she couldn't understand where we got that from because she was a private person and didn't encourage that sort of behavior."

Landon and Marcus snorted in unison.

"Then she said that not everything in life could happen at the speed Winnie wanted, and she was sorry you were almost hurt but there was nothing she could do to fix things," Thistle added. "I think she thought that would shut your mom up, but Winnie exploded and told her she was full of herself and then sent her to bed without dessert."

Laughing felt somehow wrong given Viola's death, but I couldn't stop myself. "Did Aunt Tillie go to bed without dessert?"

"Yeah, but we caught her in the kitchen trying to steal a pie. Winnie slapped her hands with a wooden spoon," Thistle said. "It's midweek, so there's only one couple at the inn. They declared it the best dinner theater ever."

"This is a mess," I said, shaking my head. "If what happened yesterday isn't enough to loosen Aunt Tillie's lips, I have no idea what will."

"We'll handle that when we get up to the inn," Landon said. "I'm going to put my foot down and force her to tell me."

Thistle barked out a hoarse laugh. "You're going to force her? Did you sleep so long you forgot who you're dealing with?"

"I'm not messing around with her one second longer," Landon said, his tone grim. "We're missing part of the bigger picture it. It's extremely annoying because I know whatever Aunt Tillie is hiding could solve everything. She's just too stubborn to care."

"I think she's covering for Patty," I announced.

Landon shifted his eyes to me. "Why do you say that?"

"It's something Mrs. Gunderson said to me yesterday," I answered. "When she said it, I almost felt a light bulb switch on over my head."

"Well, don't keep us in suspense; out with it," Thistle prodded.

"Mrs. Gunderson said Aunt Tillie was a pain, but she was loyal," I explained. "She said Aunt Tillie valued her family more than anything else, but would never break her word. She also said Aunt Tillie would tell the truth about herself to save us, and the only time she would struggle in a situation like this is if she was keeping someone else's secret."

"Huh," Thistle mused, rolling the idea through her mind. "She has a point."

"Did you just explain something?" Landon asked, frustrated. "Patty is dead. Aunt Tillie doesn't need to protect her any longer."

"And that's probably why she went to Patty's house to talk to her," I said. "Think about it. They hadn't spoken in years, at least as far as we can tell. They had a falling out over a guy, this Victor dude. Aunt Tillie knows something about that situation. I think she went to see Patty because she wanted permission to let the cat out of the bag. She didn't get a chance to ask, though."

"Okay, let's say that's true," Landon said. "Why can't this Victor tell us the secret?"

"Because he's muddled and lost in his own mind," I answered. "He thought Clove was Aunt Tillie and was happy to see her, but then he got confused and claimed he didn't know a Patty or Tillie. If he ever knew the secret – and I'm not sure he did – he doesn't remember it."

"Well, I guess that brings us to the elephant in the room," Landon said. "I didn't want to bring this up, but I don't see a way around it. What were you doing at Viola's house yesterday?"

My cheeks burned as I felt his eyes land on me. "Oh. Well ... ."

"Oh, it's not like he's going to arrest you, Bay," Thistle grumbled. "We broke in because Mrs. Gunderson told Bay that Viola wrote everything in journals. When we cast the truth spell on Viola she couldn't remember. She wasn't lying. She simply forgot the information we needed.

"We broke into the house to read the diaries," she continued. "We knew Viola would be at the senior center for hours – and I'm still not sure why she came back early – and we thought we could find information in her diaries."

"I see." Landon's face was unreadable. "What did you find?"

"Well, for starters, we found Viola has a clown fetish that's utterly disturbing."

"Thistle." Landon's voice was full of warning. "Get to the point."

"Oh, trust me, the clown fetish is part of the point," Thistle said. "It's a really disturbing point, but it's still important. No one with a clown fetish can be trusted. Anyway, the diaries bounced all over the place."

"There were a lot of vague references to Mrs. Little wanting something from Aunt Tillie, and Victor possibly stalking Aunt Tillie after she broke his heart," I offered. "There was nothing concrete in them."

"We only made it through about a quarter of them before Viola came home and surprised us," Thistle said. "We hopped out the window, but she caught us. We were apologizing and asking her for the truth when ... well ... she was shot."

"Okay," Landon said, lightly pressing his lips to my cheek as he considered the new information. "You guys are jerks for breaking into an old woman's home. Given how things turned out, though, I'll let it go. You've been punished enough."

"Oh, thank you," Thistle said, making an outrageous face.

"Do you remember seeing anything when you walked up to the house?" Landon asked. "Did anyone seem out of place? Did anyone stare at you?"

"We entered from the back yard, but we didn't see anyone on the street," I said. "We didn't see – or sense – anyone. We thought we were safe."

"You're safe," Landon said, squeezing my waist. "I'll keep you safe."

"Everything we have leads us in the same circle," Thistle said. "The problem is the circle is shrinking. The only people left in it are Mrs. Little and Aunt Tillie."

"And Victor," I said. "He can't help us, though."

"Well, now Aunt Tillie is really going to spill her guts," Landon said. "We're out of options." He pushed me to a standing position and struggled to join me. "Everyone get cleaned up and dressed. We're going to the inn for breakfast ... and it's not going to be pretty."

"So, it's a normal day?" Thistle challenged.

"Not even close."

TWENTY-NINE

Landon kept me close during the walk to the inn, his fingers laced with mine and his eyes alert. It wasn't until we arrived that I realized why. "You're worried someone is following me, aren't you?"

Landon refused to make eye contact. "I think it's a beautiful morning and love the landscaping here."

"You're lying."

"Get inside, Bay," Landon ordered, giving me a small shove through the door. He double-checked the lock before glancing around the family's private living room. On a normal morning Aunt Tillie would be telling the news show personalities how much she hated them and to get a real job. She was conspicuously absent.

"She's hiding," Thistle said, shaking her head. "She knows she's in big trouble when Landon finds her."

"I can't tell whether you're being funny or obnoxious," Landon said. "Either way, you're right. Come on."

I expected to find my mother and aunts toiling over the stove in the kitchen. It was empty, though, the lingering scent of bacon remaining to tip us off that breakfast was cooked and maybe already served.

"Did she give my bacon to someone else?" Landon was outraged as he released my hand and strode toward the dining room door. "That is just ... rude!"

Thistle and I exchanged a look and somehow managed to keep from laughing as we followed Landon into the dining room. Because he came to an abrupt stop on the other side of the door I slammed into him, ruefully rubbing my chin as I stopped myself before tipping to the side. "Walk much?"

"Director Newton," Landon said, his voice low. "I ... what are you doing here?"

Uh-oh. I recognized the name. Steve Newton was Landon's boss at the Traverse City office. I peered around Landon's shoulder and locked gazes with the man sitting at the table. He had a full plate of food in front of him, and aunts on either side entertaining him.

Steve offered me a heartfelt smile before shifting his gaze back to Landon. "I'm eating breakfast, Michaels," he said. "You should recognize the action because I believe you do the same thing under this very roof five days a week."

"Four," Landon corrected, slipping his hand around my wrist as he led me toward our regular spot at the table. Despite his surprise – and the worry I knew he would later deny – he took the time to fix Aunt Tillie with a dark look as we passed. "Aunt Tillie."

"Landon," Aunt Tillie replied, her face unreadable.

Clove and Sam sat further down the table. The smile Clove shot me was nervous but encouraging. "You look much better today."

"Thanks," I said. "Hey, Sam. You haven't been around much."

"I've been busy buying that tanker I wanted," he said. "It arrives this afternoon. When you get a chance – um, all of you – we should have a party night and then Thistle can tell us her grand plans for decorating it."

Sam clearly had no idea the depths of what he'd unwittingly walked into, but he understood that a calm voice was probably warranted.

"That sounds good," I said, flashing him a thankful smile. "I'm glad to see you. I'm a little surprised, though. I thought you would keep Clove locked up at the Dandridge all day after what happened."

"She insisted on seeing you," Sam replied. "I feel the need to stick close to her so ... here we are."

"Yes, and we're all tickled to have you here," Aunt Tillie said, making a face.

"I'd keep my mouth shut if I were you," Landon warned, reaching for the juice carafe.

"Well, you're not me," Aunt Tillie shot back.

"What's your problem?" Thistle asked, settling next to Clove. "Are you still glum because Winnie spanked you with a wooden spoon? It's not as funny when you're on the receiving end, is it?"

Aunt Tillie scowled. "Listen, mouth, I know you're feeling full of yourself because you think I'm in trouble, but I'm still your elder," she said. "Besides, I never smacked you with wooden spoons."

"That's true," Clove said, digging into her eggs and hash browns. "She used a flyswatter."

"It still hurt," Thistle groused.

"It definitely hurt," I agreed, accepting my glass of tomato juice from Landon with a tight smile. "I ... um ... Mr. Newton, I've heard a lot about you. It's nice to finally meet you."

"I think you're supposed to call him Director Newton," Thistle offered. "Otherwise he'll probably throw you in jail."

Steve chuckled, taking everyone by surprise. "I see the stories about the Winchester bonding rituals weren't an exaggeration," he said. "That's nice. I'm happy to meet you, too, Bay. You're all Landon talks about."

"Really?" Is it wrong that makes me feel special? Okay, given the circumstances it's wrong. I know that. It still feels good.

"Don't let it go to your head," Landon said, reaching for the platter of toast. "I have a boring life otherwise."

"That's not true," Steve said. "He talks glowingly about everyone here. He thinks of you as family, and I understand why. This place has a warm quality about it."

"He talks glowingly about everyone?" Thistle challenged.

Steve chuckled. "You're Thistle, right?"

Thistle nodded, surprised to be singled out.

"Landon says you're very strong and witty," Steve said. "He also says you're a talented artist."

"Oh, well, now I'm hot for you again, Landon," Thistle teased, earning a rib poke from Marcus. He didn't look particularly perturbed, though. "What about Aunt Tillie? He can't possibly say nice things about her."

"I don't want him to say nice things about me," Aunt Tillie countered. "If the fuzz liked me I'd be doing something wrong."

I risked a glance at Landon's boss and found him beaming at Aunt Tillie. If I didn't know better I'd think someone slipped real hash into his morning potatoes.

"You're exactly how Landon described you," Steve said. "You're mouthy, funny and a terrific conversationalist."

I cast a sidelong look in Landon's direction. "Did you really say that?"

"Not even close."

Steve cleared his throat as he directed his attention to Landon. "I suppose you know why I'm here."

"I do," Landon acknowledged, his shoulders stiff. "If you would like a private area to talk we can go to the front library."

"I ... ."

My heart rolled and my mouth took advantage of Steve's pause to interject what I thought would be a glowing tribute. "You can't fire Landon," I said. "He was upset yesterday. He didn't mean to yell at Agent Goober. It's not Landon's fault that guy could start his own race of idiot tools. You can't punish him for something that was out of his control." That came out all wrong. Is it too late for a do-over?

"Wait ... what?" Steve looked legitimately confused.

"Bay, that's really not necessary," Landon said.

The damage was already done.

"Fire him?" Mom narrowed her eyes. "You can't seriously be considering firing him. That's outrageous!"

"And stupid," Marnie said. "He's a great FBI agent. He's saved

CHARMS & WITCHDEMEANORS

countless lives. Bay almost died yesterday. He acted as a loving human being. If he gets in trouble for that, well, then you're a butthead."

"Oh, no," Landon groaned, pinching the bridge of his nose as he stared at his plate.

"You're the king of buttheads if you fire him," Twila added, her face twisting into an unhappy grimace. "That's just ... terrible. Only a horrible person would do that. I can't believe I gave you seconds on the homemade toast."

Steve shifted his attention to Aunt Tillie. "Do you want to weigh in, too?"

"No," I said hurriedly, shaking my head. I truly feared she would tell Steve to fire Landon. If my family hadn't already ensured that, Aunt Tillie would drive home the final nail.

"Yes," Aunt Tillie said, flashing me a challenging look. "You may think Landon was wrong not to follow the rules. As a rule follower, I understand the inclination to want to beat into submission those who don't do as they're supposed to.

"Believe you me, I've wanted to do a lot of beating over the course of my life," she continued. "I helped raise six girls. Six! Every single one of them is mouthy, opinionated, far too involved in everyone else's business and altogether annoying when I'm trying to watch *Jeopardy*."

"I see." I didn't know Steve well – or at all – but for some reason I got the distinct impression he was fighting the urge to smile.

"They're also loyal," Aunt Tillie said. "They all have good hearts. I wasn't sure about Landon when he first showed up. I thought he was a braggart and possibly bad news for Bay. I thought she deserved better."

"Thanks," Landon said dryly.

"I'm not finished," Aunt Tillie said. "I was ... wrong."

All eyes zeroed in on Aunt Tillie, dumbfounded disbelief washing over the room.

"Can you repeat that?" Thistle asked. "Actually, can you wait until I get my phone out to record it and then repeat it?"

Aunt Tillie ignored her. "I'm very rarely wrong, Mr. Newton," she said. "I was wrong about Landon, though. He's gone out of his way to protect Bay every chance he gets. He loves her with his whole heart. If he said something bad to the other agent – who is a righteous moron, mind you – then the other agent had it coming.

"Bay could've easily died yesterday," she continued. "This family doesn't deal well with things like that. You can't expect Landon to simply pat Bay on the head after she was almost killed and then whistle a jaunty tune as he walks away."

"Just for the record, sir, I never whistle a jaunty tune," Landon offered.

Steve's laughter caught everyone off guard, his shoulders shaking as he bent over the table. "I can see why you love this family so much, Michaels," he said. "They're ... hilarious."

"I wasn't trying to be funny," Aunt Tillie sniffed.

"I know you weren't," Steve said. "None of you have to worry. Landon is not losing his job. He's not even in trouble."

"I'm not?" Landon raised an eyebrow, exhaling heavily. It was only then that I realized he had expected the worst. "Why are you here if I'm not in trouble?"

"Because someone has to rein in Agent Glenn," Steve said. "I knew he was headstrong when I hired him. His tests were off the charts, but he has poor personal skills. The higher ups thought a more rural area would do him good. I think they might've been wrong.

"I don't condone what Agent Glenn has done," he said. "I heard an earful from Chief Davenport when I got him on the phone. He can't stand him."

"That's because he's a douche," Thistle intoned, earning a delighted smile from Steve.

"I like you. You're feisty."

"We're all feisty," Mom said. "We're also exhausted and worried. This situation has taken a toll on all of us."

"I understand that," Steve said. "Bay was lucky yesterday, and you're all thankful because of it. You're also worried because people are dropping left and right around here, and this is a small town."

"We're hoping to narrow the possibilities today," Landon said, sliding a pointed look in Aunt Tillie's direction. "Agent Glenn has been gung-ho about collecting evidence, but he's fixated on certain people being guilty. I think he's wrong."

"You mean his theory that Tillie here killed the first woman, and Bay and her cousins killed the other two, right?"

Landon scowled. "I should've known he would float that theory to you," he said. "He's barking up the wrong tree. Bay, Clove and Thistle couldn't have been where the shooter was yesterday, and none of them were armed the night of Fay Reynolds' death. I swear to you that they're innocent."

"I don't believe they're guilty," Steve said. "You have terrific instincts, Michaels. I've only had one meal with the Winchesters, and I can say with absolute certainty that while I think they're quirky, I don't think they're murderers."

"Well, that's a relief," Clove said. "Worrying about going to prison for a crime I didn't commit was giving me heartburn."

"Yes, that's the true travesty in all of this," Thistle deadpanned.

Steve chuckled. "Seriously, I love this family." He glanced at Landon. "Do you want to stay on this case? You have accrued vacation time. If you would prefer spending time with Bay after what happened, I understand."

"I'm staying on the case," Landon said, moving his hand to the back of my neck. "I'm saving the vacation time for when Bay and I can go away together. We're getting close here. I can feel it. I don't want to be cut out now."

"Tell me what you have," Steve prodded. "I talked to Chief Davenport this morning. He believes the shooter made an easy shot, which would seem to denote that no special skills were needed other than a basic knowledge of hunting. We're not dealing with a professional."

"I originally thought it had to be a woman," Landon said. "Poisoning someone is typically a woman's way to murder, and Patty Grimes was poisoned."

"That makes sense," Steve said, grabbing another slice of toast. "Did you feel the same way after the second victim died?"

Landon nodded. "Fay was in the women's bathroom at the senior

AMANDA M. LEE

center," he said. "Only two men were present. They were the most popular people there. Someone would've noticed them going into the women's bathroom."

"Okay," Steve said. "I agree with your reasoning. Most women don't use a gun to shoot someone from a tree perch, though."

"They don't," Landon agreed. "And most senior citizens would be incapable of climbing a tree to shoot a gun."

"Hey!" Aunt Tillie pinched Landon's wrist to get his attention. "That's ageist!"

"Are you saying you could climb into a tree and shoot someone?" Steve asked, his eyes somber as they latched onto Aunt Tillie's.

"I could figure a way to do it if I really wanted," Aunt Tillie said. "I didn't do it, though, so don't look at me."

"I don't think you did it," Steve said. "From what Chief Davenport told me, you were furious when you found out your great-nieces were at Viola Hendricks' house. You didn't want them talking to her. Why?"

"Because Viola is a crazy person," Aunt Tillie replied. "She's nuts. Craziness rubs off on people. It's a proven fact."

"I can't argue with the 'being nuts' part," Thistle said. "That woman has, like, fifty ceramic clowns in her house. That doesn't denote sanity."

Landon shuddered. "I thought you were joking about the clowns."

"Oh, I never joke about clowns," Thistle said.

"You still haven't answered the question," Steve pressed, refusing to let Aunt Tillie off the hook. "Why don't you want your great-nieces investigating this? I greatly respect Chief Davenport, and he believes you know something that could help us. I want to know what that is."

Aunt Tillie blew out a frustrated sigh. "I don't know anything. How many times do I have to tell you people that?"

"Until we believe you," Mom replied. "Aunt Tillie, I don't know what's going on here, but enough is enough. Bay could've died yesterday."

"Me too," Clove said.

"And Clove, too," Mom added. "Just tell us what you know. We know you're hiding something."

"That's it!" Aunt Tillie slapped her hands against the table as she stood. "I'm the matriarch of this family. Me!" She thumped her chest. "I don't ask you people to do everything I say or to listen when I talk, but when I say I don't know something it's your job to believe me."

"That's crap," Landon said, slumping back in his chair. "I know you well enough to realize you're blowing smoke, because you're trying to cloud our vision. You don't want us figuring out what you're hiding. You'll eventually tell us, so it would be great if you would just get it over with and do it now."

"No!" Aunt Tillie extended a warning finger and wagged it in Landon's face. "You're not the boss of me, Fed. I like you almost eighty percent of the time. This is none of your business, though."

"Aunt Tillie, you're being unreasonable," Mom argued. "Do you want something bad to happen to Bay, Clove or Thistle? They're on a killer's radar now. You can stop this."

"I don't ever want anything bad to happen to any of them," Aunt Tillie said. "Well, that's not exactly true. I don't want anything bad to happen to them unless I do it. They've almost always earned it when that happens."

"Oh, the love here is almost overwhelming," Thistle deadpanned, pressing her hand to her heart.

"That's it, smart mouth! You're on my list."

Thistle groaned. "Again? Fine. Whatever. Stay away from my pants, though. I'm in no mood to wear tracksuits for a week."

"I'm not hiding anything," Aunt Tillie said, her gaze even as it landed on Steve. "Your answers are in this town, but they're not with me."

Those were her final words before flouncing out of the room. I expected Steve to complain or order Landon to go after her. Instead he chuckled.

"I'm really starting to like her," Steve said. "Are there more eggs?"

THIRTY

I watched the door Aunt Tillie disappeared through for a few moments before turning back to my breakfast. "She's definitely hiding something."

"Oh, what was your first clue?" Thistle asked.

"I'll talk to her," Landon said, digging his fork into his hash browns. "I'm going to eat breakfast first, though. Where is my bacon? I smelled it when we walked through the kitchen. I know it's here."

Twila handed him the plate hidden by her elbow. He almost looked relieved when he saw it.

"We wouldn't let Mr. Newton have it," Twila said, her eyes twinkling.

"Yes, they guarded the bacon with their lives," Steve said. "May I have some now?"

Landon shifted the plate closer to his chest. It was heaped with greased goodness, yet he didn't appear ready to share. "This is mine."

"There's like half a pig there," Steve argued. "I want some."

"You can't have it," Landon said. "I need it."

I rolled my eyes and snagged a piece, earning a murderous glance for my efforts. "You can't eat all of this bacon," I said. "You'll get sick."

"Fine. You can have some bacon," Landon said. "You almost died, and I feel like spoiling you. No one else, though."

"You cannot be serious," Steve pressed. "I'm your boss. You're supposed to be frightened of me. Give me some bacon."

"Give him some of that bacon or I'll never cook it for you again, Landon," Mom warned, her eyes flashing.

"Fine." Landon scooped a huge mound of the bacon onto his plate before handing it over. "I feel so unloved."

"I love you," I said, moving one of my slices to his plate. "You'll be okay."

Landon pushed the bacon slice back to my plate and added two of his own. "You need the protein," he explained. "You're still pale."

"That's because I scrubbed half of my skin off in the tub last night," I said, taking a sip of my juice before focusing on Steve. "What do you think is going on? You're an outsider, so you can't lean one way or the other. With only the evidence we have, where would you look?"

"Wherever your aunt went," Steve replied. "She knows something. I think she's covering for someone. Who could that be?"

"It has to be Patty," I said, rolling my neck. "No one else makes sense."

"What could Patty's secret be?" Twila asked. "What do we know about her?"

"She never married," Mom said. "She volunteered a lot of her time at the daycare center. She liked reading to the kids. She never had kids of her own, and I remember thinking it was such a shame because she enjoyed spending time with them so much."

"She thought Victor was the great love of her life," I offered. "He was more interested in Aunt Tillie, though, and when Aunt Tillie blew him off he opted to leave town instead of going back to Patty."

"Did Patty think he would return to her?" Steve asked.

"That's the rumor," I said. "Patty was a few years older than everyone else involved. It's not a big age difference now, but back then it would've been more pronounced."

"Women married younger back then," Marnie said. "Patty probably would've been considered an old maid by the time she hit twenty-five."

"And by that time Aunt Tillie was married to Uncle Calvin, Mrs. Little was married to her husband, Mrs. Gunderson was married ... what about Fay and Viola? I can't remember either of them ever marrying."

"Viola never married, but Fay was married for a short time," Mom said. "I don't know what happened to her husband, but my understanding is the divorce was acrimonious. Divorce was unheard of then, especially in a place as small as Walkerville. I think it was quite the scandal."

"Who else was part of that group?" Steve asked. "You have Fay, Patty, Mrs. Little and Viola. Did anyone else associate with them?"

I shrugged. "Just Edith."

"Who's Edith?"

Uh-oh. I took extra time chewing my bacon and made a big show of drinking my tomato juice to wash it down before speaking. "Oh, she was a woman who worked at the newspaper a long time ago," I replied. "She died at her desk in the late fifties or early sixties. I can't remember all of the details. She was young, though."

"Why did you bring her up now?"

Crap! I have such a big mouth. "I was looking into all of the relationships from that period. I recognized Edith's name, so I had to look it up. She's kind of a local legend – even a ghost, if you will – at the newspaper office."

"In a town this size, I guess that's to be expected," Steve said.

Landon gave my knee a reassuring squeeze under the table. "We're out of people to question. Mrs. Little will either lie or refuse to answer. That leaves Aunt Tillie."

"One of us has to go out there and question her," Mom said, her pointed gaze landing on me.

Double crap! "Why me?" That came out a lot whinier than I initially envisioned.

"Because you almost died yesterday and Aunt Tillie was really upset about it," Mom replied. "Besides that, for whatever reason – and

I don't truly understand it – she has a penchant for opening up to you."

"I think it's because she identifies with you," Thistle said. "You share certain ... things."

"Like what?" Steve asked.

"Loyalty," Landon answered. "Bay is extremely loyal, and Aunt Tillie respects that. I think you should question her, too. If you're not up for it, though, I'll handle it."

Well, wasn't this just a bite on the butt? "I'll do it," I said, blowing out a sigh. "Can I finish my breakfast first?"

Landon slid two more slices of bacon onto my plate and kissed my cheek. "Eat. You need your strength."

"Oh, you two are adorable," Steve gushed, utilizing a tone I knew would drive Landon batty. "You could be in a romance novel."

Landon cleared his throat and straightened in his chair. "This has not been my week."

I patted his hand. "It will get better."

"Oh, I know it will get better," Landon said, "once this case is solved. We have a bacon candle, and Aunt Tillie is out of the guesthouse. Things will be great then."

"You're a sick man," Mom said, shaking her head.

"You love me anyway," Landon said, popping a piece of bacon into his mouth. "Can someone pass the hash browns?"

AUNT TILLIE WAS PRUNING a plant when I found her in the greenhouse. She rolled her eyes as I entered.

"I should've known they'd send you," she said. "Do they think I'll go easy on you because you almost died yesterday?"

"They think you'll go easy on me because we share a gift," I replied. "They didn't come right out and say that in front of Director Newton, but that was the gist of it." I trailed my fingers along the metal bench as I moved closer. "What are you doing?"

"This is a greenhouse, Bay. What do you think I'm doing?"

I opted for honesty. "Hiding. I want to know why."

"I'm not hiding, Bay," Aunt Tillie said. "I'm just ... thinking."

I sat on a stool and rested my hand on one of the wire pieces Aunt Tillie used to shore up her tomato stalks. "Are you thinking about the secret you've been hiding for Patty?"

"What secret?"

"I'm not stupid, Aunt Tillie," I said. "Well, maybe I am. Mrs. Gunderson is the one who suggested you weren't lying to protect yourself. She said you would never put your family at risk for your own lie. Loyalty would force you to keep a secret for someone else, though. You've always been like that."

"Oh, good grief," Aunt Tillie muttered. "Fine. Do you want to hear a story?"

I nodded.

"I'll tell you a story then," Aunt Tillie said. "Patty was one of those people who never really fit in. She wanted the world and she thought a great boyfriend would give her that. She couldn't see beyond Walkerville or the people in it.

"Her life was exceedingly boring, normal even," she continued. "Then, one day people started dying. It was her best friend first. Patty was asleep in the next room and heard her screaming. There was blood everywhere when she got to the bedroom and the girl was already dead. There was no assailant in the room, though.

"After that Patty became obsessed with solving the murder. She did some stupid things along the way," she said. "She tracked down the murderer and realized he was a local child molester who had died years before. The people of the town killed him and he came back from the dead to murder their children for revenge."

I scowled. "That's the plot from *A Nightmare on Elm Street*."

Aunt Tillie stilled. "Oh, you've seen that, have you? It was on AMC the other night. That Johnny Depp is quite the looker. It's too bad his bed ate him."

"Okay, Aunt Tillie, enough is enough," I snapped. "What is really going on?"

"No matter what story I tell you, Bay, it won't live up to the hype in your mind," Aunt Tillie said. "You should let it go."

"I can't let it go," I argued. "It almost killed me yesterday. You need to let go of whatever is holding you back and tell me."

"Fine," Aunt Tillie muttered, shaking her head. "I think you know a lot of it. Patty was obsessed with Victor Donahue. I was never in with that crowd because Margaret was obsessed with my secrets. She was convinced I was hiding something."

"You were."

"That's not the point," Aunt Tillie said. "Margaret stalked me from one end of this town to the other for a full year. She was convinced I could magically make her happy. I told her that's not how the world worked, but she didn't believe me. She went out of her way to make me miserable, and I did what I always do."

"Declared war," I supplied.

"Exactly," Aunt Tillie said. "We went after each other every chance we got. We embarrassed each other. When she liked a boy I took him from her. When I liked a boy she tried to take him from me. It never worked, though, because people liked me better."

I refused to let her distract me. "How does Victor Donahue play into this?"

"Victor was handsome and sweet and going absolutely nowhere," Aunt Tillie replied. "We engaged in a game of sorts at his expense. It ended up being at Patty's expense, too. I'm not proud of what we did, but all I could think about was beating Margaret. I didn't think about what it would mean for others.

"We had a bet to see who could get Victor," she continued. "He was dating Patty, and she was in love with him. She thought they would marry. Margaret and I went after Victor with everything we had."

"And you won."

"I did," Aunt Tillie confirmed. "I didn't want him, though. I never did. I only wanted to win. There was a lot of fallout from that. Patty was broken-hearted because she thought Victor would return to her. Victor was bitter because I used him. Margaret was loathsome because ... well ... she's a horrible person.

"When Victor refused to go back to Patty she picked a fight with me," she continued. "It got physical. We had a showdown on Main

Street. Ginger made me realize after the fact that I was wrong and that I owed Patty an apology. I went to her house and offered her my sincere regrets, and she told me she was pregnant. Victor was the father, and now she was alone and knocked up at a time when that was not allowed."

"Holy crap," I said. "Why didn't Patty tell Victor about the baby?"

"She did. He didn't care," Aunt Tillie's pruning shears clipped a bit faster. "He was more interested in me. He was jealous of Calvin, and followed me for a time. There was an incident out at the old homestead. Victor tried to ... do something untoward ... when he caught me alone outside. He failed, and Calvin stepped in.

"In those times the police didn't follow every rule, so Victor was allowed to leave town for his job with the stipulation he didn't return," she explained. "Patty was beside herself. Her life was over. I decided to help her. She was already something of a recluse, so I supplied her with groceries and helped her with money when I could until she gave birth," she said. "Then we took the baby to Traverse City and placed it with an adoption agency."

"Oh, my ... Aunt Tillie."

"Times were different then, Bay. You have to understand that."

"What happened then?"

"Patty was full of guilt ... and hate. Even though I helped her, she cut me out of her life after that. We kept our distance. I respected her wishes and didn't press her."

"How does Mrs. Little play into this?" I asked.

"Somehow ... and I'm still not sure how ... she found out about the baby when he was about five," Aunt Tillie answered. "She tracked Victor down and told him she'd found the baby. I guess he always assumed Patty terminated the pregnancy. That's what he told Margaret, anyway. He was married at that point and he caused a big fuss and claimed the boy for his own.

"Patty tried to stop him, and Victor had harsh things to say to her ... I mean ugly things ... but he ripped the boy from his adopted home and raised him," she said. "Patty was devastated. Victor was raising her son with another woman. She never got over it."

"I can understand that," I said. "That still doesn't explain why someone would kill her now."

"I don't know why someone would kill her now," Aunt Tillie said, her tone earnest. "That makes no sense. It all stems from that time, though. Margaret, Fay, Edith and Viola all knew about the baby. They all ... attacked ... Patty – and even Victor a little by extension – when they found out. They told as many people as they could about the out-of-wedlock baby and went on and on about sins of the flesh."

"They were basically jerks," I supplied. "We're dealing with all of the players now. I asked Edith about this, and she didn't say a word. I'm so ticked off at her right now. She could've helped us."

"Edith was scandalized by what happened, and she was always an idiot," Aunt Tillie said. "She probably didn't want to admit what an idiot she was at the time. You have to understand ... those women were brutal. Did you know chickens peck a sick or wounded animal to death? That's what Margaret, Fay, Viola and Edith tried to do to Patty. I wasn't strong enough to stop them, and I had my own sins to deal with."

"But who would kill Patty?" I pressed. "Why kill her now? What good could possibly come of it?"

"I don't know, Bay," Aunt Tillie answered. "Whoever it is knows Patty's secret and the part everyone played in bringing about a terrible thing."

An idea occurred to me. "What happened to the baby? You said Victor raised him. Did he know about his mother? Could he be out for revenge?"

"I don't know, Bay," Aunt Tillie replied. "I've been trying to track him down, but so far I haven't had any luck."

"Well ... crap," I muttered, rubbing the back of my neck. "You answered a lot of questions but we still don't have all of the answers."

Aunt Tillie stretched and put her pruning shears in their leather sheath. "Welcome to the real world, kid."

THIRTY-ONE

"What do you think?"

I searched Landon's face for clues as we stood in the doorway between the library and foyer. Steve remained at the table, seemingly content to let my mother and aunts regale him with stories as they showered him with food and attention. He was a nice guy, and although I would've preferred meeting him under different circumstances I was glad he was here.

"It gives us more information, but it doesn't give us answers," Landon said, rubbing his thumb against my cheek as he thought. "It sounds like something horrible was done to Patty and Victor, but that was so long ago."

"Can you find the son?"

Landon nodded. "I think that's the best place to look. What are you going to do? And if the answer is anything other than get back in your pajamas and curl up with a good book while waiting for me we're going to have an argument."

I pressed my lips together, unsure how to answer. "Um ... ."

Landon blew out a frustrated sigh. "What are you going to do?"

"I don't want to fight," I said. "In fact, that's the last thing I want to do."

"I don't want to fight either," Landon said. "You have your 'investigative reporter' face on, though, and I know that means you're not going to sit still. You can lie to me and try to make me feel better and wait for it to blow up in your face or tell me the truth and risk the consequences."

"I don't ever want to lie to you," I said, inadvertently hurt by his words. "Why would you say that?"

Landon held up his hands in a placating manner. "Okay, 'lie' probably wasn't the best choice of words," he said. "You do have a tendency to think you're doing something simple and safe, and then keep doing it even as things fall apart. Don't even think about denying it."

He had a point. "I'm going to the newspaper office and demand answers from Edith," I said. "Aunt Tillie said she was a lot more entrenched in that group than she let on. She might know something."

"The problem is that we can't use the information she gives us," Landon said, "at least not right away. We have to be careful with this, Bay. Steve likes you – and he seems to love your mother and aunts – but he's not in on the big secret. How will you explain information you get from Edith?"

I shrugged. "I thought we'd cross that bridge when we come to it."

"Ugh." Landon made a low growling sound in his throat. "I'm not keen on the idea of you wandering around town. We don't know that you're a target, but we don't know you aren't."

"I'll be careful."

"Were you careful yesterday, Bay?" Landon challenged. "It seems you tried to be as careful as possible and only chance saved your life."

"I don't know what you want me to say," I said. "I can't change who I am. I can help this investigation. I promise to be careful. What more do you want?"

"I want you safe," Landon replied, not missing a beat. "I want to be able to separate from you today and know I'm going to crawl into bed with you tonight. I want to know that you're going to be around to sit on my lap ... and laugh ... and argue with your cousins."

"I will."

"You can't promise me that, Bay," Landon said, drawing me in for a hug. "I can't change you, though, and I don't want to. I need you to be really careful. Pay attention to your surroundings. It's important."

"I will."

"Okay." Landon pressed his lips to my forehead and continued to hug me, only shifting his body when Steve joined us in the hallway.

"What's going on?" Steve asked.

"Aunt Tillie gave us some information," Landon replied. "I'll fill you in on the way to the police station. We have to drop Bay off at the newspaper office first."

I balked. "I might need my car."

Landon stilled, a flash of irritation drifting across his face. "Bay ... ."

"Do you really want to leave me stranded without a vehicle?" I asked. "That doesn't seem like the safe way to go."

"She has a point," Steve said.

"Don't encourage her," Landon admonished, his eyes stormy as they latched onto mine. "You text me every twenty minutes. I don't care if it's only to say you're still alive and out of trouble. If you miss a text, I'm coming for you."

"I've got it," I said, smiling despite myself. "Do you still want me to text you dirty things when you're with your boss?"

Landon's face cracked into a genuine smile. "Always."

"You two are something else," Steve said, shaking his head. "By the way, did I mention I'm going to stay here tonight? I thought my presence would anchor Agent Glenn, so I figured staying in Hemlock Cove was the best option. I'm really looking forward to it."

"That's because you haven't seen the dinner theater yet," Landon said. "That sentiment won't last."

"Do you want to bet?"

Landon shrugged. "I'll bet a pound of pot roast these women drive you batty before you even realize what's happening."

"You're on."

I FOUND Edith staring out the window in my office. Her expression was forlorn, and I couldn't help but wonder what she was thinking about. I decided to get right to the point.

"I know."

Edith turned, her eyes somber. "What do you know?"

"Aunt Tillie told me all of it," I said. "She told me about her competition with Mrs. Little to see who could win Victor. She told me about Patty's pregnancy and how she had to give the baby up for adoption. She also told me you were part of the horrible little group that found out the truth and tortured Patty."

"I guess Tillie has been talking quite a bit," Edith said. "I didn't expect that of her. I thought she would keep Patty's secret forever."

"Keeping secrets is a funny business," I said, sitting in my desk chair. "It always seems there's a viable reason, but in the end love of family will always trump it. Aunt Tillie wanted to protect Patty because she knew she did wrong by her. She told the truth because she didn't want to do wrong by her family."

"Hmm."

"What's your excuse?" I challenged.

Edith jolted at my tone, frowning. "I don't think I deserve your attitude," she said. "What happened back then was a … lark. It was nothing more."

"A lark? I think it was a lot more than a lark," I argued. "You played games with people's lives and irrevocably changed them. Patty lost everything."

"And Tillie played a huge part in that," Edith spat.

"She did, and she knows she was wrong," I acknowledged. "She knows she did a horrible thing. She tried to help Patty the best way she knew after the fact. You couldn't let things be, though. You had to let Margaret Little bully you into going after Patty.

"Have you ever asked yourself why she did that?" I continued. "I think it was because she was so miserable she could only be content if she ensured other people were unhappier. She didn't go after Patty because it was the right thing to do. She did it to make Aunt Tillie pay."

Edith snorted. "How do you figure that?"

"Aunt Tillie felt guilty for ruining Patty's life," I answered. "Victor's attention turned ugly, and she was the reason he was forced to leave town. The times were different then, and Patty couldn't raise a child on her own, especially in a place as small as Walkerville. Patty made the best decision she could for her child and found him a good home until you all stepped in and told Victor where to find his son. Victor was so bitter he claimed the child for his own. Do you think that boy screamed when he was torn away from the only parents he'd ever known?"

"I ... don't know," Edith said. If ghosts could cry, I think she would've been shedding tears.

"Victor was bitter and violent," I said. "He attacked Aunt Tillie. Did you know that?"

"I ... there was a rumor," Edith sniffed. "It wasn't true."

"It was true," I snapped. "Uncle Calvin fought him off. Instead of pressing charges, they came to an agreement, forcing Victor out of town. Aunt Tillie felt guilty for using him, so she gave in and let Victor off the hook."

"Victor was a sad individual after what happened," Edith said. "Tillie was the one in the wrong, but she managed to move past things without repercussions. She never faces any repercussions!"

"I see through you now, Edith," I said, my heart rolling. "The stories about Uncle Calvin coming in and you hitting on him were true. It wasn't because you had a crush on him, though. It was because you let Mrs. Little twist your mind and build up this vendetta against Aunt Tillie. Even death couldn't make you let it go.

"Aunt Tillie knows what she did was wrong, but she tried to do right by Patty," I was now fuming. "Patty was never the same, and I don't blame her for hating Aunt Tillie and the rest of you. You earned it. Aunt Tillie respected her enough to leave her alone after she gave up the baby. Instead of letting it go, though, your bunch attacked when you found out about him.

"How did you find out?" I asked. "How did Mrs. Little find that information, and how did she convince you to wield it as a weapon against Patty?"

"She knew a man in the county's records bureau. He helped her look through old records," Edith replied, her head hanging. "She knew Willa wasn't really Tillie and Ginger's full sister decades ago. Because that information would've benefited Tillie, she chose to keep it to herself. She knew long before Ginger died, and hoped it would turn into something she could use."

"Well, great," I said. That didn't really surprise me. "So Mrs. Little stumbled over the information about the baby and realized Aunt Tillie helped Patty hide her pregnancy and give the baby up for adoption. Why give that information to Victor?"

"Because we thought Victor should know," Edith replied. "I still think he had a right to know. That was his son, too."

"Yes, but Patty told him she was pregnant and he walked away," I snapped.

Edith balked. "I ... no. He was surprised when we told him about the baby."

"That's probably because he figured Patty got rid of the baby after he refused to take responsibility for him," I said. "He didn't know she carried the baby to term. Abortion was one of those things nobody talked about, then. With years of bitterness fueling him, he took that kid. How do you think that kid was treated? Victor was violent and angry. Victor had a right to be angry, but that kid deserved the life Patty wanted him to have."

"I didn't know," Edith protested. "Margaret said that Victor had a right to raise his son. She said that Tillie made up the story about Victor attacking her. I ... Tillie deserved to lose at least once in her life!"

"Oh, she lost," I said, shaking my head. I used to feel sorry for Edith, but now all I felt was contempt. "She lost her sister ... and her husband. She did her best for Patty, but came up short. Aunt Tillie's life hasn't been perfect. You jerks were just so covetous you couldn't see past it."

"Tillie could've helped us with spells," Edith argued, refusing to back down. "She could've made our lives better. She refused because she's selfish."

"You can't make someone's life better with a spell," I countered. "You can't make someone love someone else. You can't make someone have a happy life. You can ask for good luck and fortune, but those often backfire because karma is a bitch and the world always finds a way to sort things out.

"Tell me about Victor's son," I continued. "He has to play into this mess. The people being killed are all tied to that secret, to that one spot in time. You're probably lucky you're already dead or you would've been on the list, too."

"The only people left to hurt are Mrs. Little and Aunt Tillie," I said. "I don't care about Mrs. Little. She's earned what's coming to her. I do care about Aunt Tillie, though. She's not perfect, but she tried to make things better."

"I don't know what happened to Victor," Edith said. "You saw him. You know where he is. You said he didn't remember anything."

"I don't believe Victor is the murderer," I said. "I think his son is."

Edith's mouth dropped open but no sound came out.

"Victor claimed a son he never wanted and raised him to hate the people who ruined his life," I said. "It makes sense. You know it does. I have no idea where Victor was for most of his life, but he's back in the area now. He's close. I think that means his son is, too.

"He went after the mother who gave him up first," I said. "That wasn't enough, though. He wants everyone to pay. I have to find him. So I need you to tell me what you know about Victor's whereabouts after he left Walkerville."

"I don't know a lot," Edith said, her eyes downcast. "He wasn't allowed back in town because of the thing with Tillie. That didn't stop him from sneaking back from time to time."

Well, that was interesting. "When?"

"I saw him probably five times or so after he was banished," Edith answered. "He usually came after dark. I talked to him a few times and he seemed ... odd. He always asked about Tillie and Calvin. He was obsessed with her."

"Because of the game," I said. "He thought she really cared even though she dumped him right away. He grew resentful. Patty giving up his child probably added to that. Mrs. Little was part of the game, so he hated her. Fay, Viola and you knew about everything but did nothing to stop it. You're all dead now."

"Victor always seemed agitated when I saw him," Edith said. "In fact ... yes ... I think the last time I saw him his hand was bleeding because he kept scratching at it whenever he was upset. He wanted to go after Tillie, but I told him it was a bad idea. He got angry and yelled at me. He called me a bitch and said I would get what was coming to me. Then he left. That was the last time I saw him."

"Do you remember when that was?"

"I ... ." Edith screwed up her face in concentration. "I can't really remember," she said finally. "I died relatively close to that time. All of my memories from that week are kind of jumbled."

"What about Victor's son?" I pressed. "He would've had him by that point. Did you ever see him?"

Edith shook her head. "Victor said the boy was a handful. That's all I know."

"I need you to be absolutely sure, Edith," I said. "Do you remember anything else that can help us?"

"Just that ... well ... Victor's daughter lives here in town."

I stilled. "Who?"

"Carolyn Manchester," Edith said. "She comes in to place ads occasionally. She married one of the Manchester boys, but her maiden name is Donahue. I know because I saw her placing an ad a couple of years ago and she laughed about it with the clerk who helped her.

"She said she never visited Walkerville as a child," she continued. "She knew her father was from here, but he never had anything nice to say about the town. She even said her father was angry when she moved here."

"I know Carolyn," I said. "She's a nice woman."

Edith shrugged and held up her hands. "I don't have anything else to tell you, Bay. That's all I know. I swear it."

"Well, I guess it's a start."

THIRTY-TWO

I knew where Carolyn lived. It was just around the corner and within easy walking distance. Landon's admonishment about playing it safe echoed in the back of my brain, though, so instead I headed for my car.

Because Brian was out of the office all day – he sent me an email claiming he had a great idea about boosting ad revenue and was following up on it – I was surprised to find a second car in the parking lot. I pulled up short, my heart hammering as I wondered whether I was about to find the trouble Landon was so worried about, but when I studied the occupant I realized I recognized the profile.

Agent Noah Glenn didn't look happy. I guessed Steve had reamed him out and he wanted to take his misery out on me. He didn't get out of his car, though, instead glaring at me as I shot him a challenging look and climbed in my car.

I called Landon right away.

"Hi, sweetie," Landon greeted me warmly. "Did you decide to do a dirty phone call instead of a text?"

"Maybe later," I said, frowning as Noah stared daggers in my direction. "Did you know Agent Glenn is in the parking lot of The Whistler?"

Landon chuckled. "I did."

"Do you want to fill me in?"

"Director Newton sat down and went through all of Noah's evidence with him when we first got to the police station this morning," Landon replied. "He then poked holes in each piece, and Noah ... did not take it well. He accused me of somehow poisoning Director Newton against him."

"How did that go over?"

"Not well," Landon said. "Chief Terry almost exploded when Noah accused you of faking your reaction to Viola's death. Director Newton essentially told Noah to shut up. He's been tasked with keeping you safe for me."

I groaned. "Landon!"

"That's the way of the world, Bay." Landon wasn't even remotely apologetic. "I want my woman kept safe." He adopted an alpha male voice. I could practically see him thumping his chest.

"You're very cute."

"Thank you."

"You're also ridiculously annoying," I said. "I'm perfectly fine. I'm sitting in my car right now and the only problem I have is the way Noah keeps staring at me."

"He's there to keep you safe, Bay, and he's not going anywhere," Landon said. "I don't care how much you plead or pout, your safety is more important to me than your happiness right now. As long as he's around, our killer is less likely to approach you."

"That sounds very pragmatic," I said. "I don't think our killer is going to approach me, though."

"Why?"

"I talked with Edith."

"Hold on, sweetie, my signal isn't good in this room," Landon said. "I need to go outside to hear you better. I'll be right back."

I could hear Steve and Chief Terry mocking him, calling out various versions of "sweetie" as he retreated. I waited for Landon to return to the call, and when he did he was all business. "What did she say?"

"Are you away from prying ears?"

"I am," Landon confirmed. "Noah can't hear you, right?"

"No. He's just glaring at me."

"He'll live," Landon said. "Tell me what Edith said."

I related the full conversation and then waited for Landon to respond.

"I've never met Edith, but I can't stand her," Landon muttered. "So Victor came back to town when he wasn't supposed to, and I'm guessing he spent a lot of time watching Aunt Tillie."

"That would be my guess."

"I think you're probably right about it being the kid," Landon said. "Kid is a relative term now, because this man would be older than me ... by a long shot. I don't like it, but it seems to make the most sense."

"Have you had any luck tracking him down?"

"We just started, but when I get information I'll text you," Landon said. "When that happens, I expect you to move your behind to Hypnotic and stay there until we have this guy in custody. Do you understand?"

"Yes, sir. I live to do your bidding, sir!"

"Very cute," Landon said. "What are you going to do until then?"

"I'm going to see Carolyn."

Landon was quiet.

"Are you still there?"

"I'm here," Landon said, exhaling heavily. "Maybe you should let me talk to Carolyn, Bay. I would feel better if you removed yourself from this situation."

"I want to know," I said. "Carolyn is a nice woman. I've known her for years. She's not a threat. If she has information on her brother ... or her father and this situation ... she'd probably be more likely to share it with me than law enforcement."

"I know you're right, but ... ."

I cut him off before he could wear me down. "You assigned me a bodyguard," I reminded him. "I'm sure he'll follow me to the house and pout in the driveway. I'll be perfectly safe."

CHARMS & WITCHDEMEANORS

"Okay, Bay," Landon said. "Keep alert, though. Noah isn't infallible. Call me if you get anything."

"You do the same."

"Hey, Bay?"

"Hmm."

"I love you," Landon said. "When this is all over, you're going to be all mine for an entire weekend. I'm talking no mothers, aunts or cousins."

"That sounds like a plan. And, Landon, I love you, too."

CAROLYN MANCHESTER GREETED me with a bright smile when she opened the front door. Her strawberry blond hair was cut into an attractive pageboy, and her round cheeks gave her face a wholesome appeal that I always admired.

"Hi, Bay," Carolyn said. "Is something wrong?"

I suppose I should've expected the question. I knew where she lived, but I'd never been inside her house. We weren't exactly coffee buddies. "Well, maybe," I hedged. "Can we talk? I have some questions and I need a little information."

"Is this for a story? I would've thought you'd be knee deep in everything associated with Fay and Viola's deaths."

"I am."

It took a moment for my words to sink in, but Carolyn pushed open the door and gestured for me to enter. I cast a backward glance at the street, where Noah sat in his car watching the house and then walked inside.

"Can I get you some coffee?" Carolyn asked.

"I don't want to be any bother," I said, following her into the living room. The house was small, but cozy. It had that quaint appeal that's only welcome in small towns. "I don't want to take up much of your time, but I have a few questions about your father."

"My father?" Carolyn knit her eyebrows as she sat next to me on the couch. "What do you want to know about my father?"

"He went to high school with my Aunt Tillie," I said. I'd worked

AMANDA M. LEE

out part of my approach during the drive over and figured I would wing the rest. "In fact, they kind of dated at one time. Did you know that?"

"No," Carolyn replied, her eyebrows disappearing under her bangs. "I had no idea they were acquainted. That's ... odd."

I fought the urge to smile. "Aunt Tillie has quirks," I said. "It's okay if you don't like her."

"I don't know her well enough not to like her," Carolyn said. "I've never really talked to her. I've seen her at various events, but I'm much more familiar with your mother and aunts."

"Yes, well, Aunt Tillie isn't much of a joiner," I said. "She's not a big fan of the town."

"So this is about my father dating your great-aunt?" Carolyn asked. I couldn't blame her for appearing confused. "I'm not sure why that matters. I didn't even know about it."

I wet my lips and decided to go for broke. "I'm worried these recent murders play into something that happened between your father, Aunt Tillie, Margaret Little and their old friends."

"That was more than sixty years ago."

"I know, but ... it was bad," I said.

"Well, you've piqued my interest, so go on," Carolyn said, resting her hands on her knees.

"I guess I should start with my biggest question," I said. "Do you have a brother?"

Carolyn bobbed her head, causing a momentary surge of triumph to course through me. "Clay Donahue. Well, I should say he was my brother. He died ten years ago."

Wait ... what? "He died?"

"Yes. He was in a car accident on M-88 at the time," Carolyn replied. "You know that big hill that's kind of close to the resort sign? There were whiteout conditions and someone crossed the median. He was hit head-on and died almost instantly."

Well, that put a crimp in my theory. Maybe there was more than one brother. "Was he your full brother? I mean, did you both have the same mother and father?"

Carolyn stilled, her eyes shifting from open and friendly to something I couldn't quite identify. "What are you getting at?"

"I'm just going to come out with it because I don't know an easy way to say any of this," I said. "There was some strife a long time ago between your father and a few of the women in town, including Aunt Tillie. He got a woman pregnant. Her name was Patty Grimes."

"The woman who died?" Carolyn asked, surprised.

"The first woman who died," I clarified. "My understanding is that he was under the impression she terminated the pregnancy. Five years later, Mrs. Little notified him of the location of your brother, and your father took custody of him. Does that sound familiar?"

"I knew that Clay and I didn't have the same mother, but I was under the impression Clay's mother died in childbirth," Carolyn explained. "He was older than me, and we were never really allowed to talk about it. My mother treated Clay as if he was her own flesh and blood."

"And what about your father?"

"My father ... ." Carolyn looked lost, unable to answer.

I decided to help her out. "Your father was angry?"

"He had anger issues," Carolyn said, bobbing her head. "We weren't allowed to be loud or noisy, and if we were there were ... stern repercussions. Mom tried to protect us the best she could, but Dad would fly off the handle and yell over absolutely nothing. As I'm sure you can imagine, I moved out of the house the second I turned eighteen. It was a relief."

"And Clay?"

"He left right away, too," Carolyn replied. "He did a stint with the military and then married a really nice woman when he came back. They were happy for a long time, but she was in the car with him when he died. We lost them both that day."

"That's awful."

"It was awful," Carolyn said. "My father didn't take things well. By then my mother was dead. He got drunk and fell down the stairs and broke his hip. He wanted to move in here with me to convalesce so I could take care of him, but I didn't want that. I knew it would be a disaster. Moving to an assisted-living facility was his only option."

"Is that how he ended up in the home in Bellaire?"

Carolyn snorted, stunned. "How did you know that?"

"Because I visited him the other day when I was trying to track down the truth about this secret," I explained. "I thought he might be able to help. I knew that whatever was happening was tied to that period, but no one was talking ... especially Aunt Tillie. She finally told me the story today, and it was ugly. I believe your father's anger and bitterness sprang from the things that Mrs. Little and Aunt Tillie did to him. He never recovered from it."

"Do you think my father killed Patty, Viola and Fay?" Carolyn asked.

"I ... no," I said, hurriedly shaking my head. "I saw him in the retirement center. I don't believe he's physically capable of murdering someone. I mean, sure, he might've been able to poison Patty. There's no way he could stab Fay or shoot Viola, though."

"You're probably expecting me to say I'm relieved, but I've always feared what my father is capable of doing," Carolyn said. "My husband wanted to put him in a home in a different city – one that was farther away – but my father freaked out and demanded to remain close to Hemlock Cove. Well, he keeps calling it Walkerville, but you know what I mean."

I nodded. "Since you're being honest, I feel I owe you the same thing," I said. "I came here because I thought your brother had to be the one killing people. I couldn't come up with another suspect. If your brother is dead, though ... ."

"I don't know what to tell you," Carolyn said. "Part of me is curious and wants to hear the entire story behind all of this, but I'm guessing you're on a timetable so that will have to wait. My brother was a good man who never understood why my father was so abusive and angry. He cut all ties with my father after leaving the house. My father was resentful. He felt Clay owed him something.

"I continued to see my father, but I never went out of my way to do it," she said. "We saw each other about twice a year. Even now I only visit him once every few months. He's still too ... angry."

"Does the dementia confuse him and make things worse?" I asked, sympathetic. All of this must be so hard on her.

"Dementia? He doesn't have dementia. He has a heart problem and is on medication, but other than that he's pretty healthy. I talk to his doctors once a month."

That made absolutely no sense. "I spoke with him," I said. "He mistook my cousin Clove for Aunt Tillie. Then he got confused and angry, and said he didn't know a Tillie or Patty. I was sure he had some form of dementia."

Carolyn shook her head. "No. He doesn't remember everything, but for a man his age he's remarkably sharp. That doesn't sound like him at all. In fact, I saw him six weeks ago and he reminded me of things I'd forgotten."

"Like what?"

"The time I stole money from the cookie jar when I was a kid," Carolyn replied. "I paid it back, but he still brings it up. He's kind of a jerk."

"Do you think your father could be slipping out of the retirement center without anyone noticing? When we were there they paid no attention to us."

"I'm not thrilled with the staff. I'm sure he wanders off whenever he feels like it," Carolyn said. "He doesn't have a car, though, and he doesn't have the money for cab fare. I think he just walks around when he takes off."

I was frustrated. My best lead was gone and I had nowhere else to look.

"Well, unless Shane gives him rides," Carolyn said. She almost looked as if she was talking to herself.

"Who's Shane?"

"My nephew," Carolyn answered. "He was seventeen when his parents died. He lived with us for two months until he turned eighteen, and then took off. I don't see much of him now, but he's still in the area."

"How do you know that?"

"Because he got in trouble for stealing and his lawyer asked me to write a recommendation to the court," Carolyn replied. "I declined because I thought some punishment might help him straighten up. He was lost after his parents died – and I get that, don't get me wrong – but he needed discipline."

"When was the last time you saw Shane?"

"Six weeks ago when I visited Dad," Carolyn said. "He's the janitor at the retirement center. Well, technically they don't pay him. That's where he does his community service. He's performed community service here in Hemlock Cove a few times, too. I saw him cleaning the senior center about two months ago."

Holy ... bingo! "What can you tell me about your nephew?"

Carolyn shrugged. "Not much. He was a bright kid, but fell behind in school at some point. Instead of doing the work to catch up, he gave up. After his father died he hated the rules here. He's always gravitated toward my father, and that's always worried me."

Son of a ... . "Do you think your father could convince your nephew to take him out of the retirement home?"

"I think my father could convince Shane to do almost anything," Carolyn said.

"I need to make a phone call."

THIRTY-THREE

"Well, that answers that question," Landon said when I finished reciting my conversation with Carolyn to him. I practically raced to my car so I could call him upon leaving the house. "Clay is dead, and this Shane kid is angry and looking for a role model."

"He's not a kid," I said. "He's my age."

"Yes, but he was a kid when his father died, and the only male he had in life was apparently a demented one," Landon said. "He's probably stunted emotionally."

"You're so wise."

"I'm going to paddle your bottom blue for not respecting me when I see you next," Landon said. "You've been warned."

"Yes, I'm quaking in my boots," I shot back, sighing. "When will I see you again?"

"As soon as we find Shane," Landon answered. "I don't think it will take long. You said he performed community service at the retirement center. They should know how to get in touch with him. Did you see him when you were there?"

I racked my brain. "Yes. We talked to him really briefly. He didn't say much."

"So he saw you and knew you were asking his grandfather questions," Landon mused. "That was before Fay and Viola died."

"But after we talked with both of them," I said, realization dawning.

"What do you mean?"

"I think Shane followed us back to Hemlock Cove because he was worried what we would find and that we were suspicious about Victor," I explained. "We talked to Fay at the senior center when we tried to cast that first truth spell. It didn't work, but he didn't know that."

"And Fay was killed that night," Landon said.

"If Shane was dressed as a janitor, he wouldn't have been out of place," I supplied. "Carolyn said Shane has done community service at the senior center before. If he was familiar, people would've thought he belonged there. He would've gone unnoticed."

"That's pretty good, sweetie," Landon said. "He also probably watched you go into Viola's house and waited for you to leave. I don't know why he killed Viola instead of you, but … ."

"But what?"

"I was going to say I would be forever thankful, but that sounds really obnoxious," Landon said. "I will be forever happy you're alive. Viola's death was unnecessary, though."

"Shane is probably taking direction from Victor," I said. "Victor remembers these people as they were sixty years ago. He has no idea how things have changed. If he did, he'd know Viola wasn't a threat."

"That still doesn't explain the changes in killing methods, but we'll get our answers when we arrest Shane," Landon said. "I need you to go to Hypnotic now. I know you don't want to, but I'll feel better knowing you're with Thistle and Clove."

"That's the first time you've ever said that."

Landon chuckled. "That's the first time I've ever meant it," he said. "You stay at that store. Have your food delivered, and work there for the afternoon. I'll call you as soon as it's safe to leave."

"Okay," I said. I had no reason to argue. My part in this story was over. There was nothing more I could do. "I'll text you when I get there."

"Make it a dirty one," Landon said. "I'll see you as soon as I can."

"I'm looking forward to it."

After disconnecting with Landon I backed my car out of Carolyn's driveway and rolled the window down as I pulled parallel with Noah's car. I expected some sass and snark when he rolled down his window, but he wasn't in the driver's seat.

Curious, I parked in front of his vehicle and exited my car. I scanned the tree line and sidewalk, just to be safe, but I appeared to be alone. I tugged on the car door handle and it opened easily. I couldn't help but frown as I leaned forward.

This wasn't right. Noah's cell phone and notebook sat open on the passenger seat. There was a bottle of water in the cup holder and an iPod plugged into the console. Wherever he wandered off to, he was coming right back.

"What are you doing?"

I jumped at the voice, scowling as I turned to find Aunt Tillie standing behind me. "What are you doing?"

"I'm pretty sure I'm doing the same thing you are," Aunt Tillie replied. "Carolyn Manchester is Victor's daughter. I just figured it out, and came to talk to her. I guess you beat me to it."

I narrowed my eyes. "You figured it out? How?"

"I ... have keen deductive skills, and it just occurred to me."

She was lying. I could always tell. "You went to the newspaper building looking for me and stumbled across Edith, didn't you?" I challenged. "She's feeling pretty low and was easy pickings."

"You're smarter than you look sometimes," Aunt Tillie said, glancing in the car. "Are you going to steal this thing? If so, I think it's a waste. Your car is nicer."

"This is Noah's car," I snapped. "He got in trouble this morning, and as punishment Landon sent him to follow me."

"That sounds like punishment," Aunt Tillie said. "You live a pretty boring life, unless you're into watching people grope each other, that is."

"Ha, ha," I said. "I can't figure out where he went. I talked to Carolyn, and when I came out Noah was gone."

"What did Carolyn say?" Aunt Tillie asked, unconcerned about Noah's apparent disappearance. "Did she tell you where her brother is?"

"Clay."

"What?"

"His name was Clay."

Aunt Tillie stilled, her excitement diminishing. "Was?"

"He died ten years ago," I said, cringing at the momentary flash of pain that crossed Aunt Tillie's face. "He was killed in a car accident with his wife."

"So it's not him," Aunt Tillie said, disappointed. "That takes us back to square one."

"Not quite," I said, opting to put her out of her misery. I wasn't particularly thrilled with the idea of emotionally bolstering her after she lied to us for days, but I didn't want her upset either. "Clay Donahue had a son named Shane. He would be about my age now. He was obsessed with his grandfather, and has been performing community service at Victor's retirement center."

"Holy blue balls," Aunt Tillie exclaimed, causing me to roll my eyes. "Victor probably complained to Shane about what we did to him, and Shane decided to get revenge for his grandfather."

"I think that's close to the truth," I confirmed. "Carolyn told me her father doesn't have dementia, which means he was putting on an act for us. He's probably been slipping out of the retirement center with Shane. They had very lax security the day we were there."

"Well, that's just a bite on the butt," Aunt Tillie said, shaking her head. "Victor was behind it after all."

"Kind of," I said. "Landon is out looking for Shane right now. He wants me to go to Hypnotic and lay low. I think you need to go with me."

"No way," Aunt Tillie said, her hands landing on her hips. "Landon isn't the boss of me. I want to find Shane on my own ... and Victor if he's with him."

"Well, you can't," I said. "That's Landon's job and you need to let him do it. The only reason I'm still here is because I can't figure out where Noah went. I thought he should know what's going on."

Aunt Tillie made a noise in the back of her throat that suspiciously sounded like a chicken. "You just have to be the good girl, don't you? After all this flaming asshat has done, you still want to be nice to him. You need to learn to kick your enemies in the butt and move on, Bay. Your life will be more enjoyable that way."

"That's pretty funny coming from a woman who spent a year desperately trying to help a woman she wronged and then kept her secret for sixty years despite the fact that she hated you."

"You bug me sometimes, Bay," Aunt Tillie grumbled, glancing around. "Where do you think Agent Gasbag went?"

"I don't know," I said, scanning the sidewalk. "Unless ... maybe he had to go to the bathroom."

"He's probably watering a tree like a typical man," Aunt Tillie said, her eyes landing on a small stand of trees across the road. "Let's go bust him."

"Eww! I don't want to see that."

"Then shut your eyes," Aunt Tillie said, grabbing my arm as she dragged me across the street. "I can't wait to catch him breaking one of his beloved rules. I'm going to do a little dance when I make fun of him. You can join in if you promise to kick him in the butt when you're done."

"I'll pass," I said dryly, ducking my head beneath a tree limb as I followed Aunt Tillie. "Make sure you give him fair warning we're coming. The last thing I want to see is Little Agent Glenn."

I slammed into Aunt Tillie's back when she ceased moving forward. Because she's shorter than, me my chin clipped the top of her head. "What the ... ?"

"Crud on toast," Aunt Tillie whined.

"Well, thank you so much for joining us, ladies," said a man who gestured to a small clearing in front us with the gun clenched in his hand. "Why don't you have a seat next to our FBI friend? I think we need to have a talk."

Son of a .... "I blame this on you, Aunt Tillie."
"Yeah, I'm going to blame Margaret. That sounds more fun."

"YOU MUST BE SHANE," I said, dusting my dirty hands on my jeans as I sat on the ground next to Noah. He had an angry red mark on his cheek and looked furious.

"And you must be Bay Winchester," Shane said, flashing an evil smile as he held the gun flat against his chest. "I didn't get a chance to properly introduce myself when you came to see Gramps at the retirement center, but I've been watching you."

"I know," I said, working overtime to tamp down my fear. "That's why you killed Fay after she talked to us at the senior center and Viola after she talked to us in her yard."

"Actually, Viola was already on my radar because you talked to her at the senior dance," Shane said. "It was a coincidence you were in her yard when I did the deed. I had already planned on killing her."

"Well, bully for you," I said, helping Aunt Tillie get comfortable next to me. "What's your plan?"

"I'm going to kill you." Shane's response was perfunctory. "I'm going to kill all of you, for that matter. Everyone here ... everyone out at that inn ... and everyone in that unicorn store."

I exchanged a quick look with Aunt Tillie. We were in a vulnerable position. Shane was armed – and apparently crazy – and Landon thought I was on my way to Hypnotic. It would be at least ten minutes before he realized I wasn't where I was supposed to be. If he was busy looking for Shane, it would be a lot longer.

I decided to distract Shane with questions. If he was unbalanced, he might be happy to boast about his exploits. "Why did you kill Fay?"

"I saw her talking to you at the senior center," Shane replied. "I knew that I was safe as long as everyone kept my secret. That was unlikely given the participants, though. When I saw her talking to you I knew I had to act."

"She didn't tell us anything," I pointed out. "You killed her for nothing."

"She was going to die anyway," Shane said. "Everyone involved in ruining my grandfather's life has a date with death. Granted, you changed my list and when and how it was all going to unfold because you stuck your nose where it didn't belong, but I was still going to kill her."

"You look like Victor," Aunt Tillie said, looking Shane up and down. He was thin, very little muscle definition, and his nose was long and sharp. "That's not a compliment."

"Aunt Tillie," I hissed, shaking my head.

She ignored me. "Did your grandfather put you up to this, or did you come up with it together?"

"My grandfather has been planning his retribution against you old biddies since you ruined his life," Shane replied. "He even enacted his own plan fifty years ago, but he lost his nerve. He didn't get it back until we started chatting more regularly."

Fifty years ago? Wait a second .... "Edith," I said, exhaling heavily.

"Why are you bringing up that nag now?" Aunt Tillie asked. "She's already dead. She can't die twice. Worry about us."

"That's what I'm saying," I said. "Victor killed Edith."

"Oh," Aunt Tillie said, her eyes flashing. "I guess that makes sense."

"Is Edith the busybody who worked at the newspaper?" Shane asked, intrigued. "If so, yeah. My grandfather poisoned her food. He couldn't stand her. He said she was a judgmental harpy. I find a knife or gun more fun, but Gramps wanted to do it quietly."

"And he got away with it because they didn't have sophisticated forensic tools back then," I surmised. "Edith's death was originally ruled a heart attack. We only knew about the poisoning because she told us."

"How did she tell you?" Noah asked, speaking for the first time. "You just said she was dead."

"Oh, er, well ... ."

"That doesn't matter," Aunt Tillie interrupted. "Focus on the big picture, Fed. How did he get you over here?"

Noah's cheeks colored. "I had to ... relieve myself."

"I told you," Aunt Tillie said, slapping my arm for emphasis. "He was peeing in the bushes. That's against the law. You know that, right?"

"I didn't have a lot of options since I was put on babysitting duty," Noah spat.

"Yes, and you're doing a marvelous job," Aunt Tillie deadpanned. She didn't look worried. I expected to find an underlying current of tension wafting off of her when I leaned closer, but it wasn't there. In fact, she was perfectly calm. "So Victor killed Edith and lost his nerve. Then he spent fifty years hating everyone else for his own shortcomings, and when he got you under his thumb he realized you could do the dirty work while he sat back and enjoyed your handiwork."

"Not quite," Shane said. "Grandpa lost his nerve after Edith, but he's older now. He doesn't have anything to lose. Everyone knows he won't end up in prison because of his age. That knowledge gave him a little ... courage ... so to speak."

Things were finally slipping into place. "Victor killed Patty, and you killed Viola and Fay."

"Ding, ding, ding! We have a winner!" Shane crowed. He was clearly deranged.

"How did you know that?" Noah asked.

"Because Victor doesn't have the stomach for a messy murder," I replied. "He poisoned Edith fifty years ago and then got frightened. When he came back to finish what he started he used the same method. He got away with it then and probably figured he could get away with it now."

"Yeah, he's not the sharpest tack in the wall these days," Shane said, scratching the side of his head with the barrel of the gun. "When he realized the cops knew within hours that it was a poisoning he panicked. He wanted to frame someone else. I suggested that unicorn lady, but he was more interested in framing the witch."

Noah's eyes widened. "Witch?"

"The whole town is full of witches, Noah," I said. "Don't worry about it."

"Nice deflection, blondie," Shane said, shooting me an incredulous look. "Doesn't your friend realize you guys are magic?"

Crap on toast! "Did your grandfather tell you that?" I challenged. "He's off his rocker. Where is he, by the way? If you're doing this together, why isn't he here to finish the job?"

"He's collecting the last member of our happy group," Shane answered, grinning.

"Margaret," Aunt Tillie said grimly. "Criminy! I don't want to see her before I die."

"We're not going to die," I argued.

"I know," Aunt Tillie said, patting my knee. "I'm just being ornery. You'll be fine. Just ... relax."

"Oh, no, you're all going to die," Shane said. "We're just going to have a little talk before it happens. And look, here come our final guest of honor now."

I heard the sound of shuffling feet before I saw Mrs. Little. She was disheveled, her eyes swollen and hair standing on end. When she saw Aunt Tillie and me she burst into tears.

"I can't believe they got you, too," Mrs. Little sobbed. "It's the end times!"

"Oh, shut up, Margaret," Aunt Tillie snapped. "You're being a baby."

"They're going to kill us!" Mrs. Little wailed.

"I hope they start with you," Aunt Tillie said, infuriating me enough to pinch her wrist. "Ouch!"

"Shut up, hags," Shane ordered, rolling his eyes until they landed on Victor. "Hey, Gramps. I'm glad to see you got her out here on your own. Good job."

Victor looked markedly different from the day we met him at the retirement center. His white hair was smooth and in place, and his eyes keen. I had to give him credit. He was a master manipulator.

"Well, I see the gang is all here," Victor said, moving into the clearing with a bright smile. "I wasn't sure it would work out – especially when I went out to the inn and found Tillie gone. I guess she came to us, though."

"Hello, Victor," Aunt Tillie said, her tone icy. "The years have been ...."

"Kind?" Victor prodded.

AMANDA M. LEE

"I was going to say beat-you-with-a-stick ugly, but I think you've already figured that out on your own," Aunt Tillie said. "You're a jerk, by the way. I haven't seen you in almost sixty years to tell you, but I didn't want to forget."

"You're still a pip, Tillie," Victor said. "For the record, the years haven't been kind to you either." He shifted his malevolent eyes to me. "Hello, Bay. It's so good to see you again. You look just like your mother."

"This is no time for insults," I said. "Why don't you tell us what you want so we can get this show on the road."

"Wait a second," Aunt Tillie said, her mind clearly busy. "How do you know Bay looks like her mother?"

"Lucky guess?" Victor held up his hands, as if playing a part as a soap opera villain.

"He slipped back into town multiple times after he was banished," I supplied. "He spent most of that time spying on you. He took a brief detour to kill Edith and get married at some point, but he's been obsessed with you ever since you broke up with him."

"You mean used me, right?" Victor challenged. "She was never interested in me. I was nothing but a game to them."

"It's not like you're a prize," I said. "You're a murdering psychopath who abandoned his own kid."

Shane furrowed his brow. "What?"

"Ignore her," Victor instructed. "She's full of it."

I saw an opportunity to drive a wedge between the two of them and I took it. "Didn't you know that, Shane?" I asked. "Your grandfather knew Patty was pregnant with his child but told her he didn't care. Because an unmarried woman couldn't raise a child on her own without a certain stigma attached, Aunt Tillie helped her until she gave birth, and then they gave your father up for adoption."

"That's not true," Shane protested. "My grandfather raised my father."

"That's right," Victor said.

"Only after Mrs. Little found out about Clay and told Victor," I said. "She thought Victor didn't know about his son. He might not have known Patty gave birth, but he certainly knew she was pregnant, and he turned his back on her."

"That's a lie," Victor hissed, extending a gnarled finger. "You shut your mouth!"

"You shut your mouth," Aunt Tillie shot back. "You abandoned Patty and your son. Then, when you found out things didn't go as you thought, you ripped that child out of the only decent home he'd ever known."

"And then you emotionally and physically abused him and his sister throughout their childhoods," I added, internally crowing as Victor's face turned a mottled shade of red. "Your children knew you were a monster, and they ran as soon as they could. Their one mistake was not telling Shane what you were and leaving him to be manipulated by you."

"No, that's not true," Shane said, shaking his head. "I ... I would know if that was true."

"Your father was a good man," I said. "That must've been Patty's genes and Victor's wife's influence. He probably didn't want to poison you against your grandfather, even though that's exactly what he should've done.

"Your aunt says you're very intelligent but fell behind in school and gave up," I continued. "Then things got worse when your parents died. I don't think you had a chance. Unfortunately, though, you get off on killing. This isn't about revenge for you. You enjoy hurting people – just like your grandfather."

"Shut up!" Victor screeched, spittle appearing at the corners of his mouth. Man, he was really red. "That's not what happened. I was used and abused by these ... whores."

"Mrs. Little and Aunt Tillie treated you badly," I said. "They know it. Aunt Tillie admits it. Mrs. Little will never admit it because she's sad and pathetic. She's only happy when others are miserable. I think she's going to be the miserable one going forward because she's out of friends."

"Hey!" Mrs. Little scorched me with a murderous look. "How did this become my fault?"

"Shut up, Margaret," Aunt Tillie ordered. "Let Bay talk." She was focused on Victor. I was convinced she sensed the same thing I did. Instead of thinking of a magical way out of this situation, nature – and karma – would do the heavy lifting for us.

"Victor, what you did was worse," I said. "Patty really loved you. You used and abused her just like Mrs. Little and Aunt Tillie used and abused you. You abandoned a child in the process, though. Then you stalked someone who didn't care about you. You're pathetic."

"Stop it!" Victor howled, his right hand crossing his chest as he rubbed his left arm.

I knew it!

"What's going on?" Noah asked, finally sensing a shift as Shane focused on his grandfather.

"Get ready," Aunt Tillie ordered. "Hey, Victor!"

Victor shifted his eyes to Aunt Tillie, sweat beading on his forehead. "What?"

"No one really wanted to win you," Aunt Tillie said. "We only wanted to beat each other. That's why we picked a loser like you. We figured you would be grateful we let you play at all. I guess we were wrong."

"That's it!" Victor reached for Shane's gun, gasping as he missed and pitching forward. "Oh, god!" He grabbed his chest as he writhed on the ground.

"Grandpa?" Shane leaned over Victor, confused. "What's going on?"

I jumped to my feet, ready to fight Shane if I had to. I didn't, though, because Landon appeared in the clearing behind him. Landon hit Shane at a dead run, slamming him into a nearby tree.

The gun discharged as Shane fired wildly into the air. Steve and Chief Terry were right behind Landon, their faces reflecting bewildered relief.

"Is everyone okay?" Chief Terry asked.

"Victor is having a heart attack," Aunt Tillie offered. "Also, Margaret should be locked up for being the worst person ever."

"I'll consider it," Chief Terry snapped, turning his attention to Landon as my boyfriend slammed his fist into Shane's face.

The gun hit the ground as Shane groaned. Steve collected it quickly, making sure Shane couldn't grab it again as he attempted to fight off Landon. Landon hit Shane a second time, the sickening sound of crunching bone filling the air as Shane's nose broke.

"Don't ever go near her again!" Landon roared, rearing back to hit Shane a third time.

"I think he's got it, son," Chief Terry said, grabbing Landon's arm. "Go to Bay. We'll handle Shane."

Landon didn't have to be told twice. His chest heaved as he turned, his eyes wild when they locked with mine. I launched myself at him, relieved when he caught me and pulled me in for a tight hug.

"I knew you would come."

Landon cupped the back of my head for a moment, taking the opportunity to suck in three deep breaths before leaning back to study my face. "I love you, but I'm going to have to kill you for this."

"It wasn't my fault!"

THIRTY-FOUR

"Are you going to yell at me now?"

Landon joined me in Chief Terry's office an hour later, slipping his arms under my legs as he lifted me before settling in the chair and resting me on his lap. "I'm saving it for later."

I sighed. "I'd rather get it out of the way so I won't have to dread it all night."

"Fine," Landon said. "Brace yourself, because here it comes."

I sucked in a breath as I waited for the verbal onslaught.

"I'm furious at myself for not realizing this would happen."

His admission startled me. "What?"

"Bay, I've known you long enough to realize that you're a trouble magnet," Landon replied. "I should've recognized the very real possibility that Shane would go after you. You shouldn't have gone into the trees, but it's over."

It couldn't be over. That was far too easy. "I can take it if you want to yell."

"I don't want to yell," Landon said, burying his face in my hair. "I'm too tired to yell."

"That's good," Aunt Tillie said, sliding into Chief Terry's chair behind his desk and resting her feet on his computer keyboard. He would kill her if he saw what she did. "I don't think anyone needs to be yelled at."

"Oh, I'm going to yell at you," Landon said, shifting his eyes to Aunt Tillie. "It was your bright idea to go into the woods."

"It all worked out," Aunt Tillie protested.

"Only because Victor had a heart attack and distracted Shane," Landon said. "You're in big trouble once I've had time to rest and gear up for your dressing down."

Aunt Tillie didn't look worried. "Whatever. Can I go?"

"Not yet," Chief Terry said, strolling into the room and pulling up short when he got a gander at Aunt Tillie. "Get your feet off my desk!"

"I'm comfortable, so I'm going to decline," Aunt Tillie said. "You're holding me against my will. It's cruel and unusual punishment to refrain from letting an old lady get comfortable." Aunt Tillie only referred to herself as "old" when she wanted to manipulate someone.

To my utter surprise, Chief Terry didn't press her, and instead sat in the chair closest to Landon and me. "You make me tired."

"I hear Marnie is making a blackberry pie at the inn," Aunt Tillie offered. "That should perk you right up."

"I do love blackberry pie."

"I thought so," Aunt Tillie said. "What happened to Agent Goober?"

"He's on his way back to Traverse City," Landon replied. "He said he couldn't wait to get out of here and never wants to visit again. He said the women are crazy, and he's convinced there's something in the water making the men who love them crazy."

I tapped his cheek. "Cute."

"I try."

"He's only saying that because he was wrong and didn't want to apologize," Aunt Tillie said. "That's fine. I'm sure I can track him down the next time I'm over there."

"Leave him alone," Landon instructed. "The last thing we need is him poking his nose into our business. Just ... let it go."

Speaking of that .... "Where is Director Newton?"

"He went to the hospital to check on Victor," Chief Terry replied. "If anyone's interested, Victor died while in transit. It looks like a massive coronary. Carolyn said he had heart issues, so that's the doctor's best guess until the autopsy."

"That's good," Aunt Tillie said. "Justice is served."

"Not for everyone," I countered. "Patty didn't get justice."

"She will," Aunt Tillie said. "I'm stopping out there on the way home. I'll take care of that situation, Bay. It's my responsibility. You don't have to worry yourself with it. I'll send her on her way, and hopefully she'll be reunited with her son. That's her happy ending."

That was actually a relief. "What about Shane?"

"He's in a holding cell and will be charged tomorrow," Chief Terry replied. "The prosecutor will decide charges, and there will be a lot of them. Fay and Viola are both being laid to rest in a joint ceremony tomorrow, by the way. I'm sure you'll want to go."

"I do," I said.

"We're both going," Landon said, kissing my cheek. "After that, we're locking ourselves in the guesthouse for days, and no one is allowed to visit."

"We are? Don't you have work?"

"I have the rest of the week off," Landon replied. "Well, technically I'll be wrapping up stuff here, but I can do it all by phone. You're to be ready to do my bidding as soon as the funeral is done."

"We'll talk about that later."

"No, it's going to happen," Landon said, tickling my ribs. "I'm the boss. I've earned it."

"Oh, give him what he wants," Aunt Tillie said. "The sooner you do it the faster I won't have to listen to him complain about it."

"Amen," Chief Terry said, although he offered me a small wink.

"There is one thing I need for my report," Landon said, sobering as he turned his eyes from me to Aunt Tillie. "Why were you at the senior center the day before Patty's body was found?"

It takes a lot to catch Aunt Tillie off guard, and his question clearly accomplished that. "I wasn't there," she lied.

"I know why she was there," I said, smirking.

"You do?" Landon was intrigued. "Would you care to share with the class?"

"No, she wouldn't," Aunt Tillie replied. "She doesn't know anyway, so there's no sense asking her."

That was a challenge if I ever heard one. "She was there to see Kenneth."

"Oh, really?" Chief Terry asked, arching an eyebrow. "Are you going to put a claim in on your man after all?"

"That is just ... preposterous," Aunt Tillie sputtered, her cheeks flooding with color. "I ... how did you know that?" She glared at me, suspicious.

"It's the only thing that makes sense," I replied. "You said he didn't fight long enough for you. That made me realize you wanted him to fight. You were there to see whether the rumors you heard about the other women in town – like Mrs. Little – throwing themselves at him were true. You had bad timing."

"Oh, Aunt Tillie and Kenneth sitting in a tree," Landon sang out, his chest rumbling with laughter. "Are we going to see him at dinner again?"

"I'm done talking about this," Aunt Tillie said, crossing her arms over her chest. "You're all ... idiots."

That wasn't a denial.

"And, just for the record, Margaret Little is beneath Kenneth," Aunt Tillie added. "I just thought he should know that."

I couldn't help but picture Kenneth's imminent return, and it made me happy. It wasn't a great love, but it was still a lot of fun ... for both of them.

"What happened to Mrs. Little?" I asked. I hadn't seen her since we separated on the street near the clearing in the trees. Carolyn raced outside when she realized there was a ruckus. She was given the option of riding to the hospital with her father, but declined. I had a feeling she also was happy things were over.

"I dropped her off at her store after taking her statement," Chief Terry answered. "She's an emotional mess. She's blaming everything on Tillie."

"That rat," Aunt Tillie muttered. "I'll deal with her, too."

"Leave it alone," I said, shaking my head. "You two are done now.

Just ... go your separate ways. Steal Kenneth back and call it a day."

"I would but ... that really sounds nothing like me," Aunt Tillie said. "I'll give her a few days to regroup and then lower the boom."

"Aunt Tillie!"

"Stay out of it, Bay," Chief Terry said, his admonishment taking me by surprise. "This war has been going on for longer than you've been alive. Let Tillie handle her own affairs."

"You just want to see what she comes up with," Landon said, laughing.

"I could use some entertainment," Chief Terry agreed, nodding. "What happens next for you, Bay? Are you ready to go home and tell your mother everything that happened? She's going to be ticked."

"She is."

"Don't let her ruin my pie," Chief Terry said. "I might be a few minutes late for dinner due to wrapping up things here. I'll be ticked if that pie is gone."

"I'll protect your pie with my life," I said. "I have one stop to make before going home."

"What? Why?" Landon whined. "I'm too tired for a stop."

"You don't have to go with me."

Landon was suspicious. "What are you doing? If you end up in trouble again I'll add five days to your slave sentence."

"I won't end up in trouble," I said, my stomach clenching as resignation washed over me. "Aunt Tillie is going to deal with Patty, but I have a ghost of my own to deal with."

Aunt Tillie's eyes flooded with sympathy. "Are you going to tell Edith how she died?"

I nodded. "She needs to know. She's blamed you for more than fifty years."

"What will happen then?" Landon asked. "Will she move on?"

I shrugged. I had no idea. "Most ghosts move on when they know what happened to them or they've been avenged. Edith has been around a long time, though. She might not want to go."

Landon brushed my hair from my face. "Do you want her to go?"

"I ... ." Did I? I let my gut answer. "Yes."

"Bay, you shouldn't hold everything against Edith," Aunt Tillie said. "She wasn't alone in doing wrong. We all were a part of it."

"Yes, but what Edith, Fay, Viola and Mrs. Little did to Patty after she'd already lost so much was despicable," I said. "I've made excuses for Edith for as long as I can remember. I don't want to deal with her any longer."

"Well, I don't blame you," Aunt Tillie said. "She always was an idiot."

I snickered, leaning my head against Landon's shoulder a moment before pushing myself to my feet. "I need to get it done. I don't want it hanging over my head."

"Let's go then," Landon said, following me toward the door. "After that I'll buy you an ice cream cone if you promise not to let it spoil your appetite."

I cocked an eyebrow. "You're coming with me?"

"Where you go, I go."

"But ... I'm safe now," I reminded him. "You don't have to shadow me."

"Yes, but I like doing it," Landon said, his impish grin lighting up his handsome face. "I don't want to be separated from you, and I don't want you doing this alone. We're a team, missy. You need to get used to it."

"Oh, I might gag," Aunt Tillie said, shaking her head.

I slipped my hand into Landon's and smiled. Having someone to lean on was something I was still adjusting to, but I never wanted to give it up. "Let's go."

"After that you still owe me a dirty text," Landon said. "I feel neglected."

"So I have to give you dirty texts and be your slave? That doesn't seem fair."

"Life isn't fair, sweetie," Landon said. "For now, though, I'm king of the world."

"And I'm queen of the barf bag," Aunt Tillie intoned. "Seriously, I can only take so much."

"You'll live," Landon said. "And for that ... I'm mostly thankful."